WAYS

the

WORLD

COULD

END

WAYS

the

WORLD

COULD

END

A Novel

KIM HOOPER

KEYLIGHT BOOKS
an imprint of Turner Publishing Company
Nashville, Tennessee

www.turnerpublishing.com

Ways the World Could End

Jacket design by Lauren Peters-Collaer
Book design: Erin Seaward-Hiatt

Library of Congress Cataloging-in-Publication Data

Names: Hooper, Kim, author.
Title: Ways the world could end : a novel / by Kim Hooper.
Description: First edition. | Nashville, Tennessee : Turner Publishing
    Company, [2022] |
Identifiers: LCCN 2021030554 (print) | LCCN 2021030555 (ebook) | ISBN
    9781684428007 (Hardcover) | ISBN 9781684427994 (Paperback) | ISBN
    9781684428014 (Ebook)
Classification: LCC PS3608.O59495 W39 2022 (print) | LCC PS3608.O59495
    (ebook) | DDC 813/.6—dc23
LC record available at https://lccn.loc.gov/2021030554
LC ebook record available at https://lccn.loc.gov/2021030555

Printed in the United States of America

For Chris.
Consider this the longest love letter I've ever written to you.

And for my dad.
You would have loved this one.

April 2019

CHAPTER 1

Dave

There are several ways the world could end. And it *will* end. It's not something that depresses me, which Cleo thinks is weird. I can hear her voice in my head now: *Dad, you're such a weirdo.* She says it lovingly—with a laugh instead of an eye roll. I've decided this means I'm doing okay as a father.

We've had a good run, as a species. Half a million years. We've built cities from nothing, created complex languages, visited outer space. We've invented and engineered and made the impossible possible. But, as I said, it will end.

Cleo says I'm a pessimist, but I do not agree with this assessment. I am a realist. The fact is that ninety-nine percent of all species that have ever lived have gone extinct, including every one of our hominid ancestors. Our turn will come—sooner rather than later, by my estimation.

The question, of course, is: How?

I believe an asteroid is the most likely culprit of our extinction.

When I was in college, I started reading Neil deGrasse Tyson's monthly essays in the "Universe" column in *Natural History* magazine. I've been following him ever since—more than twenty years now. He is one of the world's most renowned astrophysicists, and he's concerned about asteroids too. He once called them "harbingers of doom." Theoretical physicist Michio Kaku expressed a similar sentiment: "Sooner or later, we will face a catastrophic threat from space. Of all the possible threats, only a gigantic asteroid hit can destroy the entire planet."

We've come close to catastrophe before. In 1908, a 200-foot-wide comet fragment exploded over the Tunguska region in Siberia, Russia. It had nearly a thousand times the energy of the atomic bomb dropped on Hiroshima. Astronomers say similar-sized events occur every one to three centuries.

Asteroid impacts are more likely to occur over the ocean, and small ones that happen over land are most likely to affect unpopulated areas (because much of the Earth is water, and much of the land is unpopulated, with humans clustering in relatively few locations). The thing is, with a big asteroid, it doesn't matter much where it lands. If it's big enough, it will trigger a devastating chain of events. Asteroids more than a half mile wide strike Earth every 250,000 years or so, and these would cause firestorms followed by global cooling from dust kicked up by the asteroid's impact. Some humans would survive—and I hope Cleo and I are among them—but the world as we know it would effectively end.

If the asteroid is *really* big, like five miles wide, there would be no hope for Cleo and me. Humans would be extinct. It would be just like what happened to the dinosaurs.

The greatest asteroid threat seems to be 99942 Apophis. It's about a quarter-mile wide. This asteroid was formed in the asteroid belt in the earliest days of our solar system more than four billion years ago, meaning it has been orbiting the sun all that time. It gradually moved, as many asteroids have, to near the Earth's orbit millions of years ago. Back in 2004, when it was discovered, early observations suggested a three-percent probability that it could hit Earth on April 13, 2029. Scientists have since ruled out the 2029 possibility, but some are still concerned about 2036 or 2068.

Neil deGrasse Tyson has said that if 99942 Apophis does hit Earth, it will trigger tsunamis and submerge parts of North America. NASA says there is no longer anything to worry about. But I don't know; I have my doubts. I don't trust the government to have an adequate asteroid defense plan in place. And I certainly don't trust them to tell us if we're really in danger. They don't want mass hysteria. I have to assume the worst. I have to be prepared—for Cleo's sake.

"Can you add shampoo to the Costco list?" Cleo says, walking into the kitchen, her hair wet from the shower. The cat follows on her heels, like he does every morning. She is the one who feeds him. Cats are very uncomplicated in their love and loyalty. You would think this would mean I like them, but I cannot forgive them their need of a litter box.

"Sure. Are you completely out, or can you wait until my next trip?"

Cleo knows I only go to Costco one Tuesday a month. I do not enjoy venturing out into the world, so I keep a set schedule of necessary errands. I am a fan of schedules, in general. They give me a sense of control, an "illusion of control," as Jana used to say. Jana—Cleo's mother, my wife. She was always encouraging me to step outside my comfort zone, to deviate from my routines, so I tried as much as I could. It was important to her, and she was important to me. But now she's gone, and it's just me and my schedules against the world.

Cleo does not share my fears of the outside world, much to my chagrin. If it were up to me, I would home school her and we would remain confined to a safe and comfortable bubble, just the two of us. But she is fifteen now and reminds me on a daily basis that not everything is up to me anymore.

"Dad, I would die if I had to be with you twenty-four seven." She said that recently. It didn't hurt my feelings. Like Ewan McGregor's character says in that one movie, "The great thing about people with Asperger's is that it's very difficult to hurt their feelings." What was the name of that movie? Jana made me watch it with her. She was always looking for information on my *disorder*. When I was first diagnosed, years ago now, I'd find stacks of books on her nightstand with titles like *22 Things a Woman Must Know If She Loves a Man with Asperger Syndrome* and *Marriage and Lasting Relationships with Asperger Syndrome*. I never had any interest in flipping through those books. I didn't want to know what kinds of things she was finding out about me, what kinds of flaws she was identifying. I hated The Label. I still hate it. *Asperger's. Autism Spectrum Disorder. ASD.* When you hear that, you think of an awkward guy who shuffles his feet, stutters, and can't look you in the eye. That's not me. I don't shuffle or stutter. I look people in the eye. "You are high-functioning," The Therapist told us. She is the one who diagnosed me, the one responsible for The Label. She tried to sell me on it by naming famous people who likely had it—John McCarthy (renowned mathematician and engineer), Henry Cavendish (discoverer of hydrogen), Albert Einstein, Sir Isaac Newton, Bobby Fischer.

"But they were never given The Label," I told The Therapist.

"Well, autism wasn't a diagnosis when—"

"So they didn't know they had anything wrong with them."

Both she and Jana nodded their concession.

"It's the knowing that's the problem," I said.

Salmon Fishing in the Yemen.
That's the name of the movie with Ewan McGregor.

"Daaaad. Dad. Earth to Dad."

Cleo is staring at me with wide eyes that express disbelief at my ability to completely zone out. I get this look a lot.

"What? Sorry."

She puts dry food in the cat's dish. The cat is named Apophis, after the asteroid. This was Cleo's choice (she calls him "Poppy" for short). At first I thought she was showing respect for my interests. She had to explain that it was sarcastic. I'm not great with sarcasm. I've been told that this is part of having The Label.

"I said I probably have, like, a week of shampoo left. When is your Costco voyage?"

I look at the calendar I have tacked to the wall next to the fridge. It is where I keep my schedule of all required outings.

"I'm going next week."

"Well, doesn't that just work out swimmingly."

I can't tell if that's sarcasm.

She goes to the cabinet for two boxes of cereal—frosted flakes and granola. She likes to mix them, which I find odd, but I don't comment on it. I know she finds many of my behaviors odd, and she doesn't comment on them. We have a truce. She pours what I consider to be way too much milk on the cereal, then proceeds to pack her lunch, letting the cereal get soggy because that's how she likes it, which I also find odd.

She's made me start buying non-dairy milk—milk made from almonds and oats and coconuts and soybeans. I told her, "It's not milk then; it's more like juice. Almond juice. Oat juice. You are basically 'juicing' these things to create a liquid." She rolled her eyes and said she didn't care what I called it, as long as it's not from udders meant for a baby cow. I fear she will declare herself vegan soon.

"Looks like your worst nightmare is coming true," Cleo says, standing over the sink, looking out the window. She juts her chin in the direction of something outside.

I go over to her, look over her shoulder.

We live in the hills of San Juan Capistrano, what Cleo describes as "the middle of nowhere." But that's just her being a dramatic teenager. It's not the middle of nowhere. It's less than fifteen minutes from her high school. It's just not close to other houses. It's not in a traditional neighborhood. The land used to belong to a cattle rancher, but he died, and his family sold off his cows and put the property up for sale. So it's a large, empty pasture with a 1200-square-foot house on it. I don't have any aspirations of being a rancher. I moved Cleo and me here nine months ago, in summer. I wanted to get away from Before. This is the most away I could get, without Cleo needing to leave her friends and all that. Unlike me, she has those. Friends. I figured she's been through a lot; as her father, it's my responsibility to help ensure that she doesn't have to go through more. The Therapist told Jana and me that people with The Label have trouble with empathy; but I think I've cracked that particular nut, at least when it comes to Cleo.

"There's a moving truck," Cleo says.

She is pointing to the house two football fields away, a house my Realtor told me had been abandoned long ago. Of course, I did my research: I went to the county office and looked up the deed. The land was owned by a man named Diego de Silva who, as the Realtor said, hadn't lived on the land since 1995—a failed cattle-ranching endeavor, apparently.

"It just looks like a truck. How do you know it's a moving truck?" I say.

"I guess I don't know for sure, but there appear to be people transporting things out of that truck and into the house. I believe this is what some people call 'moving.'"

Sarcasm.

"There's no way that house is livable."

Cleo and I had gone over to investigate the house when we first moved in. It was locked up, but we peered through windows. It's a suitable house, structurally. It's bigger than ours—two stories. But it's in complete disrepair—paint peeling off in strips, wood rotted, likely infested with rodents.

"Maybe they're going to fix it up first," she says, with a pep to her voice that tells me she's excited about this development.

"Or maybe they're coming to tear it down."

She turns from the sink, her wet hair whipping around and depositing droplets of water on my face.

"Oh, Dad," she says, with a pat on my back, "always the optimist."

CHAPTER 2

Cleo

I cannot wait for my sixteenth birthday. Well, I say that with the assumption that Dad will allow me to drive myself to school when I turn sixteen, which may be unlikely. He did let me get my learner's permit, so there is hope. I'm rather proud of myself for accomplishing that feat. I told him that in the event of the coming apocalypse, it would be important that I be able to drive. I did my best to look earnest, even though I was giggling on the inside. He responded with "Good point," and has been taking me out to drive the back roads where we live every weekend. Next, I'll have to persuade him to get me my own car—you know, in case something happens to his during the apocalypse.

Even if he does get me a car, though, I can't see him allowing me to drive myself to school. I know he takes comfort in dropping me off and seeing me walk into the building. If I didn't show up to a class, he would be notified immediately—the school has a text alert system for parents. Every day when I walk out of my last class, he's the first in line, waiting to pick me up. As it is, he knows my whereabouts at all times. If I drove myself, there would be small windows of time when my whereabouts would be unknown to him, when he would have to trust me on my own out here in the world. I keep telling him that he's going to have to do that eventually. A couple weeks ago, I said to him: "Dad, I can't just go between our house and Via Sierra High School forever. I'm going to graduate. I'm going to go to college. I'm going to have my own life. You know that, right?" He looked dumbstruck, like he'd never considered the inevitability of this future.

"Do you want to drive today?" Dad asks, dangling the keys in front of me.

It's like he can read my mind, which I know he cannot. Not that anyone can read minds, but Dad is like the least intuitive human being on the planet.

"Seriously?"

He never lets me drive to school. I think it makes the whole thing too real for him.

"I know your birthday is next month," he says. "I know you're going to want to drive."

I cannot wait to tell Carter about this conversation. I can already hear his voice: *Holy shit, are you cold? Because I think hell just froze over.*

"Does that mean you're going to let me drive? Like, by myself?"

"I didn't say that," he says. "We only have one vehicle, at present. I think it's best if I keep it at the house in case of any emergency."

Dad's entire existence is predicated on the possibility of an emergency. Carter said he should write a book and title it *Playing with Dire.* Then we decided that that should be the name of our future band. Neither of us plays an instrument or sings, but the name alone gives us reason to learn.

"Well, if there's an emergency, I can always come to you," I say, though I know this is a losing battle.

"That doesn't make logical sense. I'm your father. I'll have the car. We will transition to your driving more often with me in the passenger seat, then see about your having your own vehicle."

Yes, this is how my dad talks.

"I told you I can get a job to pay for my own car."

This is another losing battle. Dad doesn't think I'm old enough to work. Or, that's what he says. Really, I just think that my having any independence scares him. I understand why, but it's still annoying.

"You know I don't think it's appropriate for you to have a job. You're a student."

I put the key in the ignition and start the car. Out of the corner of my eye, I can see Dad clutching the door handle, holding on for dear life.

"Dad, you are so extra," I say with a laugh. Because if I didn't laugh about him, I would cry.

"Extra what?"

I make sure to drive perfectly to school—slightly under the speed limit, coming to full stops at all stop signs, even when there are no cars in sight (a common occurrence where we live). I made the mistake of doing a rolling stop recently, and Dad acted as if I'd just run a red light in downtown Los Angeles: "Cleo, a car can come out of nowhere!" I've never heard him sound so afraid.

When we get to school, I put the car in Park and hop out. Dad comes around to the driver's side and says his good-bye, which is the same every day: "Be safe. I'll see you after school." I wish he'd just drive off at that point, but he watches me walk across the quad, as if I'm a child on her first day of kindergarten. It's incredibly embarrassing, but I know it makes him feel better, so I try to just pretend like it isn't happening and make a beeline for homeroom.

Via Sierra High School was built ten years ago, but people still call it "the new high school." It's in the hills of San Juan Capistrano, near a landfill and not much else. Carter says it seems like a more suitable location for a prison, and I can't disagree. The school itself is nice, though—modern, clean.

I'm not popular; but I'm not unpopular. I'm in the "sort-of-smart-but-not-in-an-annoying-way" social group. If you hadn't noticed, Carter is my best friend. He became my best friend last year, when we were both having the worst year of our lives. Nothing bonds people like misery.

Homeroom is abuzz with chatter, like it is every morning. It's five minutes until the bell—which isn't a "bell"; there's just this tone that plays over the loudspeaker. It doesn't even sound like a bell. Carter is sitting on top of his desk, his feet in the seat, talking to Nicole Ethers, who I'm friendly with but wouldn't call a friend. I've gotten even more shy since last year, like I'm afraid to get close to people now. The school guidance counselor, Ms. Murray, says that's normal, considering everything.

"Hey, guys," I say to Carter and Nicole.

Carter's eyes go big. They are his I-have-some-juicy-gossip eyes.

"There's a new kid," Nicole says. "Carter is all excited about it."

"I'm excited on Nic's behalf," he says. "Looks like Nic's type."

"Where?" I ask.

Carter cocks his head. "In the front row, talking to Mr. Johnston."

I let my backpack slide off my shoulders, then turn around, pretending to find something inside it while sneaking a glance at this new kid. She's tall, with short dark hair that makes her neck look giraffe-like. She has a sharp nose, stupid-long lashes, skin the color of butterscotch.

"She's pretty," I say.

"Or *he* or *they*," Nicole says.

Nicole identifies as non-binary—not male or female—and is committed to educating the entire school about how "gender is a construct." I'm supposed to refer to Nic as "they"—not "her" or "she"—but I always screw up.

"She or he or they is pretty," I say.

"Can we just say 'she'? I am way too lazy to be politically correct," Carter protests.

Nicole ignores him, says "Not really my type," then walks away to talk to Brad Whitley, who Carter and I both know is Nicole's type.

"Maybe she's *your* type," Carter whispers to me, giving me a nudge with his elbow.

Carter is the only person who knows I like girls. Not girls exclusively: I like boys too. I like to think I'm an equal-opportunity crush-haver. I didn't know this about myself until last year. Or I guess I *knew*, but I didn't realize it was a *thing* until last year. Mom was the first person I told. It wasn't this big dramatic I-have-to-tell-you-something conversation. It just came up one day when we were at the mall, sharing a pretzel in the food court.

"I haven't heard you mention Justin lately," she'd said.

Justin was a kid I'd had a crush on for a few months. He lived down the street from us at our old house.

"I'm sort of over him," I'd told her.

"Impressive."

"I have a problem, though."

She'd looked at me expectantly, not worried, just curious.

"I think I have a crush on Brooklyn," I'd told her.

Brooklyn was one of my best girlfriends back then, before everything went to shit.

Mom had raised her eyebrows. But, still, she hadn't looked anything but curious. Not disgusted or concerned or any of the other things kids worry about when confessing something like this to a parent.

"Oh," she'd said.

She'd taken a bite of pretzel, which assured me that my confession had not turned her stomach, and then passed the pretzel to me.

"Is this a new thing?" she'd asked.

"The crush on Brooklyn? Or girls in general?"

"Girls."

I shrug. "I guess I've always liked girls. And boys. I thought everyone felt that way until recently. I was reading this girl's blog and she sounded like me and she's bi. I guess I'm bi."

"Well, I don't care what you are, as long as you're happy."

"Thanks."

I took a bite of pretzel and passed it back to her.

"I always kind of wished I liked women. A relationship with women would be so much easier," she'd said.

I'd laughed.

"And this way you have so many options," she'd said.

"There are bright sides."

"But what are you going to do about Brooklyn?"

I shrugged. "I mean, she's straight as can be. So it'll just live in my imagination."

"She's a pretty girl."

I'd nodded. "She knows it, too."

And that was it. We finished our pretzel and went to check out the sale at the Gap.

Mom didn't ask me if she could tell Dad, and I didn't tell her she *couldn't* tell Dad. Now she's gone, and I have no idea if Dad knows. He hasn't alluded to it; not that he would. He tends to avoid all potentially awkward conversations.

Carter and I became friends after Mom was gone. I probably chose him as a friend because he's gay, because I knew he'd accept me. I need at least one person to know who I really am. I don't really talk to my old friends anymore, the ones who knew me before the worst year of my life, when I was a totally different person. Even if I did, they wouldn't accept me if I told them. They would think I'm weird. Maybe I *am* weird. Maybe the weirdness is genetic.

"You're staring, so I'm guessing you're interested," Carter says, nudging me again.

I refuse to comment on that and say, "Kind of strange to have a new kid now, isn't it?"

It's April. The school year ends in a couple months.

"Maybe she got kicked out of her old school," he says. "A bad girl!" He makes his hand into a cat claw and meows.

"You are too much."

The non-bell rings, and we take our seats. There's been an empty seat next to mine ever since Brenna Alvarez moved out of state over the holiday break, so it shouldn't surprise me when New Kid sits next to me, but it does.

"All right, ladies and gentlemen," Mr. Johnston announces with his booming, take-control-of-the-room voice.

Someone behind me clears their throat. Probably Nicole.

"And people who do not identify as a lady or a gentleman," Mr. Johnston corrects himself with obvious exasperation.

"Love you, Mr. Johnston," Nicole says, and a few people giggle. Mr. Johnston has rosacea, so he looks extra-embarrassed when he blushes.

"We have a new student joining us today. Eden, do you want to introduce yourself to the class?"

Eden is her name.

I watch her face as Mr. Johnston motions for her to stand. She looks mildly horrified, understandably, but then she stands. She turns to face the class, and I can't help but cringe. Mom used to say I'm an empath, like her. It's like I can feel people's distress and then it makes *me* distressed. I want to hide under the table right now. The ants I imagine under Eden's skin are migrating to my own.

"Uh, hi, everyone," she says.

More giggles.

"I'm Eden Walker, but you can call me Edie. Only my mom calls me Eden, and only when she's mad at me."

There are a few quiet courtesy laughs.

"Uh, I just moved to San Juan Capistrano."

She starts to lower back into her seat when Mr. Johnston says, "Why don't you tell us about yourself? Interests? Hobbies?"

Edie remains half-standing, awkwardly. "Yes, I have some," she says.

More giggles.

"I like to surf."

Mr. Johnston looks satisfied. "Well, then you've moved to a good place. We're just a few miles from some of the best surf spots in California."

Mr. Johnston claps his hands together, which is what he does as a transition between topics. I watch Edie sit and exhale. I let my gaze linger too long, because she turns and looks at me, her lips curving into a small smile. I smile back so quickly, it probably looks like a strange facial twitch, then turn forward, heart slamming in my chest.

If I'm honest, Edie is exactly my type. I mean, she's beautiful. She must be everyone's type. Except Nicole's.

On Mondays, I don't have lunch period with Carter, which means I sit alone. I used to make fun of kids who sat alone at lunch. I never thought I'd become one of them. I used to sit with Brooklyn, Amy, and Julia. We were a foursome. After what happened, I shed them like a snake sheds its skin—naturally, necessarily. I couldn't stand their pity, the look on their faces whenever they were near me—jutted-out bottom lip, furrowed brows. Sometimes I pass them in the halls and they still give me that look. It's like they think I have no hope of ever being fun again. Maybe I don't. In any case, I don't miss them.

So I usually sit alone. There's a lawn on the outskirts of the lunch area, usually reserved for couples wanting a quiet place to make out. I have a favorite tree trunk there. It's just wide enough for me to hide behind it and not have to explain to anyone why I'm eating alone.

"Hey," I hear a female voice, just as I'm unwrapping my peanut-butter-and-banana sandwich.

I look up to see Edie and feel like I'm suddenly in a John Green novel.

"Uh, hi," I say. I'm already thinking about how I'm going to tell Carter about this, about how his jaw is going to drop.

"I see you got the best tree trunk," she says.

"You're observant."

She stands there for a second and I fiddle with the plastic wrapping of my sandwich.

"You mind if I sit?"

"It's a free lawn."

I don't know why I'm trying to act all blasé, like her presence is nothing to me. I guess it's a defense against the possibility that her presence might mean *some*thing.

She sits, extending her long, lanky legs out in front of her, backpack at her side. She unzips it and withdraws her own sandwich. In the John Green book, it would also be a peanut-butter-and-banana one, but in reality it's some kind of gross deli meat. I don't eat meat.

"I figured I should probably try to sit with someone on my first day," she says. She takes a bite of her sandwich.

"Probably a good idea. The kids here are ruthless."

"The kids *everywhere* are ruthless."

"Where did you move from?" I look at my sandwich as I say it, perpetuating the idea that I couldn't care less.

"San Diego. My parents split up. My dad's staying there, my mom and I came up here."

"That sucks," I say. "The splitting up, I mean. Not you coming here."

My face tingles with heat.

"Yeah, my dad's a dick, so it's for the best, but moving in the middle of junior year is less than ideal."

When Dad wanted to move out of our old house, he kept saying he would choose a new house in the same school district. I wanted to tell him it didn't matter, that my friends weren't my friends anymore. But I thought that would worry him, so I didn't say anything. It's probably a good thing I didn't change schools. My social life has changed, but there's something comforting about the consistency of the buildings, the teachers, the cafeteria menu.

"You'll do just fine here," I say. Because she's pretty, and obviously friendly. She looks at me like she's confused, though, as if she's not aware of her own positive attributes.

"Mr. Johnston kind of killed my mojo already."

"Mr. Johnston kills everyone's mojo."

She laughs, and I can't help but smile at my ability to make her laugh.

"Uh, what's your name?" she asks, and I feel stupid for not giving it to her already.

"Oh, god. Sorry. Cleo."

"Cleo," she echoes.

"As in Cleopatra."

"You're not serious."

"I'm not."

She laughs again. I remember asking Mom and Dad why they named me Cleo, hoping for an interesting answer. I didn't get one, though. Mom just said, with a shrug, "I don't know. Always liked it. It was that or Lily, and you seemed like more of a Cleo." Whatever that means.

"And you're Eden? As in 'Garden of . . . '?"

"Yeah. Edie, though, please."

"Okay. Garden of Edie."

She laughs again.

"You've been in this district since you were a kid?" she asks. "Like, you know all these kids?"

I nod. "And yet I eat lunch alone."

"They're that bad?"

"No, it's fine. I've just become a bit of a loner."

"I've always been a loner, so welcome to the dark side."

The face-tingling returns.

We resume eating our respective sandwiches in silence. I search my brain for an appropriate topic of conversation.

"Where are you and your mom living?"

I figure that's better than asking her if she's straight or gay or what, which is what my ridiculous brain wants to ask.

"We're in one of those extended-stay hotels right now," she says. "So, I get terrible coffee and a stale muffin every morning, and a chocolate on my pillow at night."

"Perks!"

"My mom inherited this property from my grandpa a while back. That's the whole reason we moved here. She has big plans to fix it up. It's a dump right now, so I'm pretty sure we'll be in this hotel for months."

"Property?"

I don't know why I'm asking. Of course this would be the case. Edie Walker is my future neighbor. I'm imagining my email to John Green now:

Dear John Green,

I believe I am living the plot of your next novel. Please respond and let me know if this is possible. If you have superpowers that are affecting my life, I believe I have a right to know about it.

Most sincerely,
Cleo Garrison

"Yeah, it's this old cattle ranch, been abandoned for years. Up in the hills."

I must be nodding without realizing it, because she says, "You know it?"

I ball up the plastic wrap from my sandwich in my palm and squeeze it. "Oh, yes," I say. "I know it."

CHAPTER 3

Dave

It stands to reason that one of the biggest threats to human existence is . . . human beings. The United States and Russia still have a few thousand active nuclear warheads. Even if there is not an outright war, there is the possibility of an accidental nuclear exchange, or something made to look accidental. The ballistic missile defense system, as I understand it, would catch only a handful of stray missiles at best.

There are also other weapons systems that could have global effects. Every now and then, the topic of chemical and biological warfare will come up on the news, and they talk about it as if it's this novel concept, as if it hasn't happened before. But it has.

During World War II, the Imperial Japanese Army utilized a covert biological and chemical warfare research and development unit called Unit 731. Unit 731 and other units acted as biological-weapons production, testing, deployment, and storage facilities. They routinely tested biological weapons on human beings at the facilities, and also deployed them in cities and towns in China. It's estimated that Unit 731 and related programs killed up to half a million people. *Half a million.* That was in the late 1930s and the first half of the 1940s. With the technological advancements we have now, imagine the catastrophe.

I, and others, suspect that the United States is still engaging in biological-weapons research that is outlawed by the United Nations. We had a biological-weapons program for twenty-seven years, ending in 1969. In those twenty-seven years, the program weaponized and stockpiled seven bio-agents—*Bacillus anthracis* (anthrax), *Francisella tularensis* (tularemia),

Brucella spp. (brucellosis), *Coxiella burnetii* (Q-fever), Venezuelan equine encephalitis virus (VEE), Botulinum toxin (botulism), and Staphylococcal enterotoxin B. Even if the United States has abandoned biological weapons, I'm quite certain other countries, namely Russia, have not.

The former Soviet Union has a long history of biowarfare programs. At one time, these programs employed more than 50,000 people and produced tons of weaponized viruses—for example, 90 to 100 tons of weaponized smallpox annually. In the 1980s and 1990s, many of their biological weapons were genetically altered to resist heat, cold, and antibiotics. Russia signed an agreement to end bioweapons programs, but there does not seem to be any evidence that they have destroyed their bio-agents or repurposed the facilities used to create them. The internet has led me to believe that Putin has an active biological warfare program in place. And why wouldn't he? Compared to atomic bombs, bioweapons are relatively cheap, simple to produce, and easy to hide. I believe he's lying in wait. In the United States, we are close to a second Civil War. We are vulnerable, distracted. We are perfect targets.

Worrying on its own is a pointless waste of time. So I have aimed to make my worry productive. One of the selling points of our property was the large basement, described as a wine cellar by the Realtor, but appearing to me as an optimal bunker. Homes in California never have basements, so this is quite the find. I have removed the wine racks and begun stock-piling supplies for Cleo and me. So far, I have three Tyvek suits (an extra, just in case) to protect us against hazardous materials, three self-contained breathing apparatuses, a nine-month supply of food (mostly ready-to-eat meals—MREs), and two 100-gallon water tanks. I would like to invest in a 500-gallon water tank. I would also like to construct a greenhouse on the property so that we can grow our own vegetables and fruits, with the long-term goal of being completely self-sustaining. Some preppers (that's what they're called: doomsday preppers) recommend breeding rabbits for an endless supply of meat. Cleo would be horrified, though.

I know it's essential that I acquire guns and ammunition too, for defense purposes. I've read that a 40-caliber is the most effective handgun to stop a threat with a single shot, so that will be a good place to start. I've never liked guns; Jana hated them. Sometimes, if I close my eyes, I can see her shaking her head at me, arms crossed over her chest. *Dave, you're a crazy person.* Whenever I used to talk to her about things like asteroids slamming into Earth, she'd call me Doomsday Dave. It was a joke at the time, because I was more of a science nerd than an actual doomsday prepper then. I can hear her: *Oh, Dave, look at you now.* She would hate to see me this way. *You're all spun up*—she used to say that when I would get, well, spun up. I can't help myself, though. Given what's happened, given the responsibility I have now as Cleo's only parent, it's impossible not to be spun up.

––––––––––––––

My computer dings with a fifteen-minute reminder of a work meeting that is beginning at 2 p.m. I work for a major pharmaceutical company, which I prefer not to name, preparing submissions to the Food and Drug Administration. I have worked for this company for twenty years, starting as an intern at the age of twenty-four and, well, never leaving. Apparently, people with The Label have difficulty with change. Apparently, we prefer our routines. Some call us rigid; I call us reliable.

I have been working from home for the past year, since Jana left us. It was supposed to be a temporary arrangement, my boss wanting to be understanding and whatnot. I have been taking advantage of the fact that he clearly does not want to ask me when I'm returning to the office.

I don't want to return to the office. I am happiest working alone, undisturbed by the noise and distraction of others. At home, I do not have to worry about someone infringing on my personal space or, god forbid, assaulting me with physical contact (Greg used to do this back-clap thing anytime he saw me in the company kitchen). I have never understood the benefit of congregating in an office with others, especially as the day-to-day requirements of my job are not dependent on social interaction. I prepare documents. The only interaction I require is with my trusty loyal computer. It is a solitary endeavor. When I do need to solicit information from others, email serves just fine. Sometimes a phone call is required if said emails are unreturned. I detest phone calls, but I see them as the price I have to pay for working at home.

The office is in Irvine, which is where the majority of commercial businesses in Orange County are located. San Juan Capistrano is approximately twenty miles from Irvine, but that twenty miles can take up to an hour in traffic. It's a waste of time that people have succumbed to for years, and I am thankful to not have to endure this inefficiency at present. It may be the only silver lining in losing Jana.

At 2 p.m., I dial in to the team meeting. What's ridiculous is that even the people in the office often call in to meetings from their desks in lieu of convening in a conference room. So the screen looks like the opening of *The Brady Bunch*, nine of us talking heads. I'm in the middle, in the Alice spot.

"How's everyone doing today?" Greg says.

Greg manages my group, which they have started referring to as a "pod." I don't know the reason for this change in terminology. I can only presume that they think "pod" is more appealing to the millennials our department is hiring with reckless abandon.

"All good in this hood," one of the millennials says.

"Same," another says.

I have always felt old, even when I was a child. I've always sensed that I was too serious, too high-strung to ever do youthful things like say "All good in this hood." But, lately, I feel especially old. Jana kept me feeling young— or, at least, she kept me from feeling like an eighty-year-old curmudgeon. Paul Dirac, the famous theoretical physicist who was never bestowed The Label but most definitely was on the spectrum, wrote to his wife, "You have made me human." And that's what Jana did for me.

Perhaps I chose Jana because I knew she would compensate for my personality deficits. Certainly this was not a conscious choice. On the spreadsheet I kept during my dating years, "compensate for my personality deficits" was not one of the traits in the "desired" column. I was not aware I *had* personality deficits for which compensation would be required. Jana possessed traits that I would have put in the "avoid" column of my spreadsheet. She did things like dance in the rain, which is something I would never do because I am not a spur-of-the-moment type of person and I detest getting wet. There were so many things about Jana that baffled me when she was here—her emotionality, her dramatic flair, her spontaneity, her sensitivity. And yet, without those things, I feel lost.

Cleo helps, of course. She's so much like Jana. If it weren't for her, I probably would have packed it in months ago, walked into the Angeles National Forest to lie down and die. I feel like my mind operates much like a computer processing unit. If it instructed my body to die, I believe my body would die. *You're like a robot.* Jana used to say that—sometimes with a laugh, other times with an eye roll.

By the time I start paying attention to the conference call, seven minutes have passed and it is woefully apparent that nothing of import has been discussed. This is why I hate meetings. Nobody seems to value efficiency. At least I am at home, where I can work on my survival-preparation spreadsheet or peruse the internet while everyone else wastes time. When I had to be in the office, I would literally resort to just staring at walls, timing how long I could go without blinking. My record is four minutes and thirty-three seconds.

You're like a robot.

There is a blog I like to visit called Spaced Out, written by a seventeen-year-old science nerd named Nathan. He, like me, is very concerned about asteroids. Recently, he published some interesting information I'd never read before about the Kuiper Belt. NASA is only beginning to explore KB (Nathan's abbreviation; I am not one to abbreviate when left to my own devices), so there is not a ton of information publicly available. In basic terms, KB is a donut-shaped zone of icy bodies beyond the orbit of Neptune. There may be millions of these icy objects, collectively referred to as Kuiper Belt Objects (KBOs) or trans-Neptunian objects (TNOs). Some of these iceballs are more than fifty miles in diameter, according to Nathan. If one of those comes earthward, we're all done for.

"Dave, how's the Glovista submission coming?" Greg asks.

Whenever he addresses me on a call, he says my name very loudly because I think he knows I'm not paying attention. I'm grateful for this act of kindness.

"I should have it finished by Thursday."

He really doesn't need to ask. The agreed-upon deadline has always been Thursday, and I have never missed an agreed-upon deadline.

"Good man," he says.

He always says that.

Glovista is an oral medication to treat adults with Fabry disease, a rare and serious genetic disease that results from buildup of a type of fat called globotriaosylceramide in blood vessels, the kidneys, the heart, the nerves, and other organs. One benefit of my job—which Jana used to say is not a benefit at all—is that I am well aware of many strange disorders that can befall humans. When Jana was pregnant with Cleo, I insisted that she do as much genetic testing as possible. It was a bone of contention, but she agreed. When the doctor said Cleo was "perfectly healthy," I was skeptical. It just seemed so unlikely for anyone to be perfectly healthy in a world with so much tragedy. So far, though, Cleo does appear to be perfectly healthy. At this juncture, some would knock on wood, but I do not believe in these types of superstitious behaviors.

Greg continues with asking different members of our "pod" about the status of their projects. I don't know why we all have to listen to these updates. An email between relevant parties would suffice. A few years back, Jana got me a mug that says "I survived another meeting that should have been an email." My coworkers commented on the humor of it, but then did nothing to reduce the number of meetings, so they missed the point entirely.

The call finally ends at 2:48 p.m., which I consider the unofficial end of my workday because I need to pick Cleo up from school. I check work emails on my phone during the rest of the day and reply as needed. Sometimes I reply even when not explicitly needed, to create the illusion of productivity. It is the closest I will ever come to "sticking it to the man."

Cleo is waiting on the corner, at the very end of the pickup area, like always.

"Hey, Dad," she says when she sits in the passenger seat.

She closes the door and the car fills with the smell of her vanilla body spray, something she uses so often that I have to order new bottles of it from Amazon on a monthly basis.

"How was your day?"

"Good," she says, with more enthusiasm than usual. I find enthusiasm unsettling, categorically.

"There's a new kid. She's moving into the house by us. With her mom."

She is definitely *chipper*.

"So they aren't tearing it down?"

I had kept an eye on the activity at the house throughout the day. The people coming and going appeared to be laborers, bringing supplies, removing bags of whatever has been decaying in that house for twenty years.

"No, Dad, sorry to disappoint you."

Sarcasm.

"Well, I hope they are good neighbors," I say.

I would rather not have neighbors at all. They are a threat to our isolation and, ultimately, safety. They could, for instance, come over at any time, without warning, to request a cup of sugar. Supposedly, that is the type of thing neighbors do, though I have never requested anything of a neighbor. Even when we lived at our old house, the only contact I had with the neighbors was to exchange improperly delivered mail. Jana and Cleo were friendly with the neighbors, and I was fine with that. I figured it was essential for our household to be in good standing with the community, in the event of an emergency that would require us to need our neighbors for something. Now that Jana is gone, I have done my best to ensure that we never need anything from anyone, no matter the emergency.

"I'm sure they'll be fine, Dad," Cleo says. "It might be nice to have people, you know, *around*."

Sometimes it's like my daughter does not know me at all.

"They are at least two football fields away," I say, "so I don't expect them to be *around* frequently."

I am staring at the road in front of me, but I can feel Cleo's eyes rolling as she looks at me.

"Edie said it would be a while before the house is ready for them to actually live in, so that should put you at ease."

"Edie?"

"The new kid."

Cleo knows her name. There may be a risk of them being *friends*.

"Did this Edie say how long?" I ask.

"A few months, but she didn't really know for sure. They're staying at an extended-stay hotel right now."

"Oh," is all I say, my grip on the steering wheel getting tighter.

"Dad, don't worry," Cleo says.

She is just like her mother—somehow always aware of my feelings before I am.

"Do I seem worried?" I ask.

In the past, I would have said, "I'm not worried." This used to drive Jana crazy. *Dave, denying your feelings is not going to get us anywhere.* The Therapist helped us see that I wasn't denying my feelings; I truly am not aware of them. The Therapist told Jana, "When you sense he's upset and you ask him what's wrong and he says 'nothing,' he's not trying to shut you out. He just doesn't have the ability to access and explain the emotions that you think are so obvious." On the way home from that particular session, Jana said her mind was blown. "You don't have the *ability*," she said, as if this were a revolutionary concept. I let her be awestruck because it seemed to please her. Honestly, the whole therapy session went over my head. But what I did learn is that instead of saying "Nothing's wrong," I should ask "What makes you think something's wrong?" The Therapist gave me two words of advice that I have carried with me to this day: "Be curious, Dave."

"You do seem worried," Cleo says. "And I get it, Dad. You're worried about them infringing on our lives, messing up your routines and all that."

Jana and I told Cleo about The Label when she was twelve. I didn't want to tell Cleo at all, but Jana thought it was important. "I don't want her to think that some of your behavior is typical. Girls grow up pursuing men similar to their fathers. I don't want her to chase after emotionally unavailable men." This went over my head too, but I agreed we'd tell her.

We had the talk at the dinner table, which is where we always had our important conversations. My favorite dinner-table "meetings" were about our summer-trip plans—we always did one trip a year, each of us bringing an idea to the table and then arguing our case. Our last trip, the three of us, was to Utah—Cleo's idea. We visited the National Parks—Bryce, Zion, Arches. And, per Cleo's request, we spent a day volunteering at the Best Friends Animal Sanctuary in Kanab. If I'd known it would be the last trip, I would have extended it a week so we could also go to Colorado and camp at Mt. Elbert. That was Jana's idea. We should have done it. It was only a two-and-a-half-hour drive.

Before Cleo came into our lives, Jana and I used to eat dinner in front of the television, enjoying a show while satisfying our nutritional needs. I appreciated this two-birds-one-stone efficiency. When Cleo exited the baby phase and began to communicate like a human being, Jana expressed a desire for "family dinners." This was a new concept to me. I did not have such dinners growing up. My father was an aerospace engineer for Lockheed Martin. He worked late—I was usually in bed when he came home. In his absence, I took it upon myself to make my own TV dinners while my mother talked on the phone with her excessively chatty friends.

Despite my lack of experience with "family dinners," I told Jana that I was fine with our instituting them. At our first one, Jana brought the plates to the table and Cleo pounded her tiny fists on her high-chair tray in excitement. I ate my food quickly, as I do not see the point in belaboring anything, including meals. Then I took my plate to the sink, cleaned it, and went to the living room to watch TV, thinking I had succeeded at this family-dinner endeavor. Later that night, after putting Cleo to bed, Jana informed me that this was not the case.

"You just ate and *left us* there," she said.

She said it as if I'd abandoned them on the side of the road in the middle of the Mojave Desert. If I wasn't mistaken, there were tears in her eyes.

"What was I supposed to do?"

She looked exasperated.

"Family dinners are for *talking*," she said. "About our days, our thoughts, our feelings."

She spoke slowly. Ever since Cleo had been born, I'd gotten the distinct feeling that Jana thought I was an idiot.

"I thought dinner was for eating," I said.

She sighed heavily.

"You don't want to be part of a family," she said. "You just want to do whatever you want to do."

That wasn't it at all, but I didn't know what "it" was.

"We need to see a therapist," she said.

And that's what led us to The Label.

When we told Cleo about The Label, we were eating spaghetti and garlic bread. Jana did most of the talking. I just sort of stared at my plate, twirling the same spaghetti noodles around my fork, doing nothing to help my cause.

Honey, your father is a little different from other people.

You know Bryan down the street? Remember how his mom was telling us about his autism? Well, there is a whole spectrum of autism disorders, and your father is on that spectrum. Your father is high-functioning, which is why many people aren't aware that he has this.

It's helpful for Dad if you reflect feelings back to him if he appears to be struggling with recognizing them.

Cleo nodded along like all this made sense, like puzzle pieces were coming together. She had that same mind-blown look that Jana did when Jana first found out about The Label.

From that point on, I'd catch the two of them staring at me as if assessing a monkey in a zoo, then whispering and conferring. It didn't bother me *per se*. I just wasn't sure what they found so fascinating.

I pull the car onto the long dirt driveway leading up to our house.

"It's just Edie and her mom?" I ask Cleo.

"Just Edie and her mom," she says. "No other invaders."

I wonder about the absent father, if he is absent in the way Jana is absent, or if he's absent in the way many modern fathers are absent. As challenging as I have found fatherhood, I cannot imagine abandoning this particular post. I do not know how other fathers are capable of doing this. Jana always said this was one of my greatest qualities—my sense of duty, my commitment. *Give him a task and it gets done. You should see him put up the Christmas lights.* That's what she told The Therapist when asked to list the reasons she loved me. I wish I had a transcription of that session. I can't remember anything else she said.

"I told Edie we'd come to their housewarming party," Cleo says.

I put the car in Park. I can feel her looking at me, can see a smile spreading across her face.

"Dad, you should see how panicked you look."

She hops out, a literal skip in her step. I follow behind her.

"When is the party?" I ask, trying to sound composed, though I'm already strategizing ways to avoid attending.

"I'm joking, Dad. I would never subject you to a *party*."

She runs ahead to the house, and I'm left with this feeling of immense relief, coupled with something else that's hard to name.

Jana liked parties, something that surprised me about her, given her self-professed introversion. She didn't like big groups of people, but she liked sidling up next to one lucky person and talking to them in-depth about something that mattered, something besides the weather or the latest reality TV show. And she liked wine. She never would have let me convert a wine cellar into a survival bunker.

I miss her—for my own sake, but more for Cleo's. Cleo does not have a parent who can enjoy a party. Cleo does not have a parent with an infectious laugh. Cleo does not have a parent who "gets it." Cleo does not have a parent who is willing to dance in the rain.

Cleo has me. Cleo doesn't have Jana. These are two separate things, two separate sadnesses. I guess that's what the hard-to-name feeling is: sadness. Sometimes I think I should go back to The Therapist who gave me The Label and show her how good I've become at identifying emotion.

The thing is, I had considered the possibility of Jana leaving me in the more usual way—filing papers, moving into her own condo somewhere, sharing custody of Cleo with an 80/20 split that highlighted my ineptitude at parenthood. I never considered the possibility of Jana leaving me in the way she did. As adept as I am at imagining worst-case scenarios, I never imagined the one that became my life.

CHAPTER 4

Cleo

On the way to school, my phone buzzes with a text, which I assume is Carter because he texts incessantly; but it's not. It's Edie.

Do we think Mr. Johnston is going to embarrass me again today?

I feel my cheeks redden. We had exchanged numbers at the end of lunch yesterday. She said it would be nice to have a "school contact," in case she had a question about the block schedule "or something." I wanted to think that was just an excuse to get my number, but I played along and said, "Oh, sure, yeah. The schedule can be confusing, so text me whenever." I didn't think she would, especially not the next day.

I text back:

I sure hope so.

I must be smiling like an idiot, because Dad says, "What is it?"
I try to rein in my smile, but it's like my cheeks won't cooperate.
"Nothing," I say.
He glances at my phone, looking suspicious. He didn't want me to get a phone, but I used the same logic with him that I did to get my learner's permit: in the event of the apocalypse, I'm going to need a way to call him.
"Are you texting with the new neighbor?" he asks, as we pull up to the drop-off area.

I have to say, I'm impressed he's guessed this. He's not usually so perceptive, something Mom always found annoying and I always thought could work to my benefit.

"Edie, Dad. Her name is Edie."

I hop out of the car before he can respond.

Carter is waiting outside the door to homeroom, looking at something on his phone. He's wearing his usual black skinny jeans, one Converse-sneakered foot crossed over the other. It's like he can feel my presence approaching, because he looks up when I'm about ten feet away, his eyes saying, with urgency, "We need to talk."

"What?" I ask him.

"Clee," he says. My body tenses. I've become someone who is always on high alert for bad news.

"What?"

"You need to tell me more about this meal you shared with the adorable Eden," he says.

My muscles relax and I roll my eyes. "You scared me, you asshole," I say, hitting him in the arm.

"I scared *you*? You scared *me*. You can't just text me and say you had lunch with this beautiful new girl and not give me any details. It's frightening, truly."

"There are no details," I say. "She saw me eating lunch alone and came over. We didn't *share a meal*. Oh, and her sandwich had deli meat, in case you're looking to dock some points."

Carter is a staunch vegan. He cringes.

"Gross."

"She's nice. She's actually going to be my neighbor."

Carter looks confused. "You do not have neighbors, my dear. You live where serial killers take their dead bodies."

Carter has been to my house a handful of times. Visitors cause Dad all kinds of anxiety, but sometimes I like to subject him to some exposure therapy. Carter and I hang out in the backyard—we sit on the rickety wood bench left behind by the previous owner, staring out at the empty pasture, eating microwave popcorn with chocolate chips melted in it (Carter's favorite). Dad leaves us be, much to Carter's disappointment. Carter thinks Dad is fascinating. He thinks anyone who doesn't fit the conventional mold is fascinating.

"There's another house out there," I tell him. "Another old rancher's house. We always thought it was abandoned for good, but it turns out Edie's mom inherited it and they want to fix it up."

"Look at all the intel you have. I'm proud," he says, hand to chest.

"It's not *intel*. I was just *talking* with her."

Now it's Carter's turn to roll his eyes.

"Anything juicy?"

We really hadn't talked that much. In retrospect, there'd been many awkward silences. "Her parents are recently divorced. That's why she moved here."

Carter sighs. "That's not juicy. Everyone's parents are recently divorced."

That was a big part of last year for Carter—his parents' divorce. The worst part is that they got divorced because of him. It's not that he assumes that, like every child of divorce seems to; no, they basically *told* him that. His mom was fully accepting of him being gay, while his dad was (and still is) very much not accepting. His dad is one of those who believes that "kids go through phases." It was enough to end their marriage. It's hard for me to understand how people with such different beliefs ever came together in the first place. But then, what do I know about love?

"Anyway, I don't think she's into girls, so you're getting all worked up for nothing," I tell him.

"Eh, you never know. I get a vibe. She might be one of us."

I appreciate the "us," the acknowledgment that I belong somewhere.

Then his eyes fix on something over my shoulder and he clutches my hand.

"Speak of the devil," he says.

I turn around to see Edie coming toward us from some distance, her eyes on the ground in front of her. I'm embarrassed at how quickly I start finger-combing my hair. I spend a few seconds contemplating whether I should remain standing outside to greet her, or if I should go inside and take my seat, pretending I didn't see her. I decide to stand and wait, though the deliberateness of that action makes me feel stupid.

"Oh, hi," she says when she finally looks up and sees me.

"Hi," I say. "I was just out here talking to Carter."

I glance around for Carter—but, of course, he's nowhere to be seen. Edie smiles with one half of her mouth. It's at times like this that I wish I was more like Dad—emotionless, stoic.

"I was hoping you were waiting to give me moral support for my second day."

"That too," I say.

There are some eyes on us as we walk into homeroom together. Carter stands and approaches us, initiating the introduction.

"I hear you're Cleo's new friend," he says. "I'm Carter."

"The infamous Carter," Edie says.

Carter fans himself with his hand. "Infamous?"

"I'm new, so if I hear your name more than once, you're infamous."

"I'm gonna go ahead and be flattered."

The not-bell rings and we all sit. Mr. Johnston conducts homeroom like he usually does, not calling any special attention to Edie. If I'm not mistaken, I can see her exhale.

"Are you doing loner lunch today?" Edie asks as we file out of homeroom.

"Not today. I actually have a thing at lunch today."

She raises her eyebrows. "A *thing*?"

"A thing."

I tense at the anticipation of her request for details, but she lets it go.

"Then I guess I'll see you tomorrow?" she says.

Tomorrow seems so far away.

"Unless you're good at math," she adds.

"Why? You need a tutor already?"

"I was born needing a math tutor," she says.

I've always been good at math. It's my favorite subject, though science is a close second (I'm taking Advanced Placement Physics this year, and it's fascinating). Carter says I'm like the poster child for Girls in STEM. Mom was more of a literature-and-humanities type person, so it's safe to say I get my math-and-science proficiency from Dad. It's good we have this in common, because we might not converse otherwise. Just the other night, we spent two hours talking about thermodynamics. According to the second law of thermodynamics, the universe inevitably becomes more disordered over time. Any order we impose requires a lot of energy and, no matter how carefully we plan, that order will be reversed over time. As my teacher said, "It's much easier to shatter a glass into a thousand pieces than it is to put it back together." I tried to use this to persuade Dad to chill out on all the disaster preparedness.

"Order is fundamentally unnatural," I told him.

He nodded along, but his brows were furrowed.

"All these things you do to try to create order oppose the universe's impulse for chaos."

I could tell he was impressed with me, but also disturbed.

"Well, I don't have anything better to do with my time than oppose the universe's impulse for chaos."

And that was that.

Edie looks at me expectantly.

"Math is my jam," I tell her. "I'm in pre-calc. You?"

"Like I said, math is definitively *not* my jam. I'm in algebra 2, which I'm sure was so last-year for you."

"It was."

I will always associate algebra 2 with the worst year of my life. And yet I still got an A.

"My mom would pay you," she says.

I must look disgusted, because she adds, "Or not."

"Um, yeah, don't pay me. That feels weird."

"Like you're a math prostitute?"

"Okay, that feels weirder."

We stand across from each other in the hallway as the other kids begin to disappear into classrooms. Next period is going to start any minute. My internal clock knows the school schedule.

"I'd invite you over, but my dad . . . he's different," I say. I don't want to get into it, and there's not time right now anyway.

"You could come by the hotel I'm staying at," she says. "There's a pool."

"I feel like if I'm coming to your hotel, I really am a math prostitute."

She laughs.

Are we flirting?

I can't tell if we're flirting.

"I have to ask my dad," I tell her, the wind already leaving my sails. I know Dad will say no. I can't even imagine asking him—*Hey, Dad, can I go to a hotel with a person I barely know?* His eyes would pop out of their sockets. I could lie. I could say there's a study club after school and tell him to pick me up late. Then I'd just have to find a way to get back to school from the hotel.

The hallway is now completely empty except for the two of us. We are going to be late.

"Well, ask him. Text me. No worries either way," Edie says.

The tone sounds and we drift away from each other. I'm going to Spanish class and Edie probably has no idea where she's going.

———————

The *thing* I have at lunchtime is my weekly meeting with Ms. Murray, the school guidance counselor. She calls it "Tuesdays with Tina," but I can't get comfortable with calling it that because I can't get comfortable calling her Tina, even though she said I could, even though she's in her late twenties and feels more like a friend than a counselor.

The door is open just a crack, so I knock lightly.

"I bet I know who that is," Ms. Murray says. "Come in, Miss Cleo."

I do, closing the door behind me. Ms. Murray is sitting behind her desk, a half-eaten apple in front of her.

"My favorite time of the week," she says as I sit in the bucket seat across from her. I take out my brown-bag lunch and bite into my own apple.

I didn't even know who Ms. Murray was until she reached out to me the day after Mom died. There was the barrage of pity texts from the friends I no longer consider friends: **omg i just heard** and **Cleeee, im SO sorry** and **call me** and **thinking of u**. They all had way too many heart emojis—some broken, some intact. I especially hated the "call me" texts. Like, what? My mom had just died. Why was I being given this obnoxious to-do item?

There were lasagnas and casseroles and huge bowls of chili, all covered in plastic wrap, left on our front doorstep. It was way too much food for two people. Dad and I made a project of divvying it up into several plastic containers, labeling them, and then stacking them in the freezer. I suppose it was good for us to have that project. I'm more thankful for that than the food itself.

The weird thing is that nobody ever knocked on the door or rang the doorbell. Dad and I found sick pleasure in watching the footage from our outdoor camera of people showing up with their flowers and covered trays of food, setting their offerings on our doormat, and then scurrying off. It was like they were afraid of us, like they thought our tragedy was contagious. They didn't want to actually support us; they just wanted to do something that seemed supportive, to check a box in their own minds, so they could go to bed at night thinking of themselves as kind and generous.

I've made a mental note that when someone I know experiences a tragedy, I will show up with food only after the initial wave of sympathy-givers return to their merry lives, awash with gratitude for their good fortune, posting on Facebook about how life is fragile and we all have to hug our loved ones tight. And I will text before I come to say that I will knock on the door, in case they want a visitor. Honestly, I didn't want visitors when Mom died. I didn't want someone else's sadness to compound my own. But, still, the offer would have been nice.

Ms. Murray was the one pleasant surprise, a phone call I didn't expect. She left a message the first time she called: "Hi, Cleo, this is Tina . . . Ms. Murray . . . the counselor at Via Sierra. I wanted to talk with you. You don't have to call me back. I'll try you later." And she did try me later. I still didn't pick up. When she called a third time, I couldn't help but admire her persistence, so I picked up. She said exactly the right thing, the only person to do so: "I'm sure you don't want to talk to anyone right now. I totally get it. I just want to be here for you however I can. I am assuming you will be out of school for a little while, so I will plan to call you every couple of days, if that's okay. You don't have to pick up if you don't want to talk. But if you do want to talk, I'm here."

I was out of school for two weeks. And in that time, I talked to Ms. Murray five times. At first, I didn't know what to say, so she'd just ask me questions. Then I stopped needing the questions—I just talked. I didn't realize how much I needed to talk until I started. I talked about Dad and how he was basically mute. I talked about how he thought we should move to a new house. I talked about my friends, who suddenly seemed so shallow. I talked about Mom and how I still expected her to be in the kitchen, making breakfast, when I woke up in the morning. I talked about how I was dreading the funeral. (I was right to dread the funeral. It was awful. There were so many people we didn't even know there, people drawn to the service because they'd heard about what had happened on the news. It felt like an event for them, not for Mom.) Ms. Murray just listened to me. When she did talk, she said things like, "It totally makes sense that you feel that way." To which I'd say, "It does?" And she'd say, "Tooootally."

I was nervous about my first day back at school, so Ms. Murray told me to come to her office at lunchtime to check in. I did, and then I spent the rest of the day there. I cried and she rubbed my back just like Mom used to do. That first day sucked. It was weird to see school going on as if nothing had changed. Teachers were teaching like normal, kids were gossiping and laughing like normal, homework was assigned like normal. I felt everyone's eyes on me, staring. I heard them whispering. It wasn't hard to imagine what they were saying: *That's her.* I was a spectacle, a circus marvel: *Behold the teenager who has lost her mother!* I was every kid's worst fear, personified. It was like they were waiting for me to break down in the hallway, collapse in tears. Most of them wouldn't meet my eyes. When they did, all I saw was pity. No genuine concern or care; just pity. I hate pity. Pity makes me feel small and weak. *You poor thing. How will you ever go on?* That's what they must think. Sometimes, on the days I don't want to get out of bed, it's imagining their stupid pity faces that motivates me. I won't let them be right. I will go on. Mom would want me to go on.

I visited Ms. Murray at lunchtime every day of that first week, and the week after that. Then I visited every other day. Then I befriended Carter, who has never given me The Pity Face, and ate lunch with him whenever we had the same lunch period. By the time school let out for the summer, I was seeing Ms. Murray on Tuesdays and Thursdays. I prepared myself to not hear from her over the summer, but then she kept calling. She didn't ask me if it was okay, she just called. When fall came around, she suggested that we set up one day a week to meet. That's how "Tuesdays with Tina" began.

"How's your week so far?" Ms. Murray asks.

One of her braids falls across her face. She puts it back behind her ear.

"Good, actually."

She feigns a look of utter shock. "I'm sorry, give me a second. I don't think I have heard an answer besides 'nothing new' in response to that question for the last several months."

She's probably right.

"Oh, god help us, is this about a boy?" she says.

"Nope."

She leans forward, elbows on her desk, chin in her hands, looking at me skeptically.

"I thought you said all the boys in this school were idiots, a conclusion that I could not dispute in good conscience."

I don't know if school counselors are supposed to talk to students like this, but I love it. I wouldn't tell anyone this is how we talk anyway, because I want it to be ours. If other kids find out how cool Ms. Murray is, they'll want a piece of her too.

"It's not about a boy," I say.

She doesn't break eye contact, just stares into my eyes as if she can uncover the truth that way.

Carter is the only one who knows my truth. Before him, Mom was the only one. I decide it's time to include Ms. Murray in this inner circle of knowing.

"It's about a girl."

She sits back in her chair. She doesn't look surprised; she looks satisfied. Maybe she already knew somehow. I swear she has superpowers.

"The plot thickens," she says, crossing her arms over her middle.

"I've wanted to tell you for a while. It just never came up and I haven't really been interested in anyone. . . ."

"But now you are?"

"Well, there's a new girl. I'm sure you're aware."

She types something into her computer and nods.

"Oh, yes, right. Eden Walker."

"Edie," I say.

"We're on a nickname basis? I see."

I wonder what her computer screen is telling her about Edie—academic history, personal baggage. Her face betrays nothing.

"She just happens to sit next to me in homeroom," I say. "And I found out she's going to live next to me too."

"Say what?"

"I know, right? It feels like. . . ."

"Fate?" she asks, with a skeptical raise of one eyebrow.

"It sounds stupid. I know."

"It sounds age-appropriate," she says.

"In other words, stupid."

"No, it's sweet."

"She's probably straight," I say. "So, moot point or whatever."

I wonder if whatever is on her computer screen says something about Edie's sexual orientation. Do schools make note of that?

"I'm sure you'll find out in time," she says. "I just like seeing you excited."

I look away in embarrassment. Is my excitement that obvious?

She takes a bite of her apple and then says, while still chewing, "What is your dad going to think about having a neighbor?"

"Oh, he hates them already."

She nods. "New people. . . . He's going to have a hard time with that."

Ms. Murray gets Dad, which is a colossal relief because I'm not even sure I get Dad sometimes. She says her brother is autistic, that he inspired her to become a counselor. Nothing I tell her about Dad makes her flinch. She just nods, as if Dad is any other dad, which is all I've ever wanted him to be.

"How's *your* anxiety been?" she asks.

I didn't even know what anxiety was until I started talking to Ms. Murray. I mean, I'd heard the term, obviously, but I didn't know that all the stuff I was feeling could be described as anxiety. Ever since Mom died, I've had trouble sleeping. I find myself worrying about something bad happening to Dad. I'd be an orphan then. Where would I go? Like me, Mom and Dad were both only children, but Mom had a half-sister, my aunt Susan. She lives in Riverside, which is what Carter calls "the armpit of Southern California." I don't want to go there. I've only been in the same room as her, like, three times in my life. Mom didn't even like her, but there's literally no other family nearby. Sometimes I get so caught up in the worrying that I can't catch my breath. Or I get these bubbles in my chest and I start rapid-fire burping. Attractive, I know.

"It's been okay," I say.

The truth is that I haven't noticed it since I've been distracted by Edie. I don't want to tell Ms. Murray this, though, because she'll be worried that I'm putting all my mental-health eggs in this Garden of Edie basket.

"Did you check out those YouTube yoga videos I told you about?" She thinks I should do yoga before bed.

"Not yet," I say. Yoga reminds me of Mom. I think if I did yoga, I'd just sob.

"What about your dad? Anything new?"

I shake my head. "Still obsessed with his underground bunker."

When I first told Ms. Murray about Dad's obsessions, she nodded and said, "It's his way of grieving. We all do it differently." The way she said that made me wonder what *she* was grieving, or had grieved, in her own life. I didn't have the nerve to ask.

"How is his anxiety affecting you this week?" she asks.

"It's not getting to me as much this week," I say. *Because of Edie*, I don't say.

This is Ms. Murray's main concern—that I'm absorbing Dad's anxieties. I can't help but do that. I live with him. I can't turn off my awareness of his feelings. I've tried to suggest to him that he should get help for himself. When several boxes of those meal packets meant for astronauts arrived at the house, I told him he needed a therapist. I want him to have his own Ms. Murray. He doesn't know that Ms. Murray is basically my therapist; he doesn't even know who Ms. Murray is. I know he and Mom used to go to therapy sometimes. Mom used to tell me about it—not the specifics, but that they went. At first I thought it meant they were going to get a divorce, but then I realized it was keeping them *from* getting a divorce. Dad says there's no point to therapy, because Mom isn't here. "We used to do it together," he said. As if it's something that one cannot do alone, as if it requires a partner, like salsa dancing. I haven't pressed the issue because, as Ms. Murray says, I'm the kid and it's not my job to take care of him.

"What's your opinion on white lies?" I ask her.

She squints at me. I'm convinced that the squinting is tied to her psychic abilities.

"Who is the recipient of this white lie? Your dad?"

I nod.

"A white lie is, by definition, harmless. Is your lie truly harmless?"

"I think so," I say. I can't see any harm in hanging out with Edie at an extended stay hotel for a couple hours.

"Well, in general, I am a big fan of the truth."

"Me too," I say. "Big fan."

She squints again. "That said, I trust your judgment."

"My dad would say that's a mistake."

"Your dad lives with a lot of fear," she says, tone turning serious again.

"He does."

"I don't want you to live with a lot of fear, Cleo." There's an earnestness in her eyes that makes me want to cry. I look away, feigning interest in Ms. Murray's bookcase.

"So, what I'm saying is, if the white lie helps you be fearless, you have my blessing."

She stands from her chair. "I have to go talk to Principal Potts. You mind if we cut this short today?"

I stand too. I figure I can use the remainder of lunch period to find a quiet place to send Dad my white-lie text.

"Okay," I say.

She comes around the desk and gives me a hug, which she does every week. It's not a light hug, either. It's one of those tight hugs that lasts a beat longer than what most people consider normal. It's a hug that quiets the voices in my head that say *She doesn't really are about you. She's the school counselor. She's just doing her job.*

When she pulls away, she says, "Are you going to tell me what the white lie is?"

I take a bite of my apple and say, "Maybe next week."

CHAPTER 5

Dave

I do not think a single earthquake could end the world, but it could do damage that would dramatically impact life as we know it. I've been interested in earthquakes since I was a child. It's hard not to be interested in earthquakes when you grow up in Southern California.

I lived with my parents in the San Fernando Valley until I graduated from high school and went off to college. When I was in elementary school, I have a distinct memory of a morning earthquake rattling the sliding glass door in our kitchen before my mother came running, wearing only her bra and underwear, hair wet from her shower. She and my father hurried me to the backyard, and the three of us stood there, my mom's hands shaking as they held mine. I can still remember the look of terror in her eyes as she stared up at the sky, as if she was expecting it to fall right on us.

I was in high school when the Northridge Earthquake hit. We lived just a few miles from the epicenter. I was dead asleep when it started. In my memory, I was bouncing in bed so much that I had to hold on to the bedpost. It's hard for me to believe that that was the reality, but that's how I remember it. Then I ran to my parents' bedroom, and the three of us fled to the backyard again. There were aftershocks for days after. We didn't have power. It was January, cold. I walked around the house with a blanket wrapped around me. School was canceled. Houses in our neighborhoods were red-tagged, marked as uninhabitable. My mother cried a lot, said she couldn't stop thinking about the people who had lost their lives. I didn't feel a need to cry, which is probably because of The Label. Instead, I took to educating myself about earthquakes.

The San Andreas fault line is to blame for the earthquakes in California. Most people know it by name. It's the one they fear. But scientists say the most powerful earthquake it could produce would be magnitude 8.2. While that's strong, it's only 6 percent as strong as the 2011 earthquake that hit Japan.

The truly worrisome fault line is the Cascadia subduction zone, which hardly anyone knew about before the *New Yorker* ran a story about it a few years back. I was aware of it, given my proclivity for studying earthquakes. I had been living in fear of it for years before that article. In a way, it was nice to have my fears validated. I printed it out for Jana, said, "See? This is what I was telling you about." I don't think she read it.

The Cascadia subduction zone runs for seven hundred miles off the coast of the Pacific Northwest, beginning in northern California, continuing along Oregon and Washington, and ending around Vancouver Island in Canada. Scientists say this zone is capable of a 9.2 magnitude earthquake. The director of FEMA for the region was quoted as saying, "Our operating assumption is that everything west of Interstate 5 will be toast." Thousands will die; up to a million people will be displaced. When it happens, it will be the worst natural disaster in the history of North America.

And it is a *when*, not an *if*. In the past ten thousand years, the Pacific Northwest has experienced forty-one subduction-zone earthquakes—that's a recurrence interval of one every 243 years. The last one was in 1700, so we are overdue.

The scientists know exactly what will happen. The shaking will begin, and the electrical grid west of the Cascades (and possibly beyond) will fail. The entire Northwest will jolt westward. An estimated one million buildings will collapse, along with half of all highway bridges and the majority of railways, airports, and hospitals. That's not even the worst of it. A colossal tsunami will follow close behind the earthquake. People will have between ten and thirty minutes to get out.

A grown man is knocked over by ankle-deep water moving at 6.7 miles an hour. The tsunami will be moving at more than 13 miles an hour when it arrives. It will not look like a traditional wave. It will look like the entire ocean is elevated, overtaking the land. It will bring remnants of coastal towns with it—cars, boats, utility poles, pieces of buildings.

They expect that the tsunami inundation zone will be uninhabitable for years. Even outside of that immediate zone, people in the I-5 corridor will be without electricity, drinking water, sewer service, major highways, and healthcare facilities for months.

A few years back, Cleo proposed the San Juan Islands as her summer-trip idea. She wanted to hike and bike and kayak. She wanted to see the orcas. She still does. I've told her that it's just not possible. It's too dangerous. She said to Jana, "Mom, come on, is he serious?" Jana said, "I ask myself this question almost every day, sweetie." I offered to take the two of them to Sea World to see Shamu and got an earful from Cleo about how the whales are depressed in captivity. I can't keep up with her causes.

———————

There was a small earthquake the morning I met Jana. I was up early, 4 a.m., as is my preference. I enjoy the quiet before the rest of the world awakens and annoys me with its demands. This is why the infant phase with Cleo was so challenging. The early mornings were suddenly marked by piercing cries and I was, frankly, beside myself.

Due to my personal earthquake history, I dove under the table immediately when the shaking began, not knowing if it would escalate. In this particular instance, it did not. Despite the insignificance of the event, I thought it prudent to open the door of my apartment and peer into the hallway to ensure that there was no structural damage in my vicinity. When I opened the door, there was a woman standing there in boxer shorts and a long-sleeved baseball t-shirt that read INTROVERT where the team name would usually go. Her legs were long and blindingly white. Her overall paleness suggested a life spent mostly indoors. I was, as they say, smitten.

"That was an earthquake, right?" she said, looking far too flustered given the unimpressive magnitude.

"A small one, yes. I assume you're not from California?"

She shook her head. "Arizona. Just moved here a few months ago."

I hadn't noticed that someone new had moved into the apartment next to me. The previous tenant had been a middle-aged man with whom I'd never had a conversation (though I did communicate with him via knocking on his walls when I did not appreciate the sounds generated on particularly raucous nights with his lady friend). It occurred to me that I had not heard such sounds recently, and now I knew why.

"I would estimate that one to be a 4.1," I said.

"A 4.1?"

"On the Richter scale."

"Right."

(I would like to point out that it *was* a 4.1, which led me to briefly consider a career with the U.S. Geological Survey.)

"There's no need to worry . . . unless it's a foreshock," I told her.

"A foreshock?"

"Meaning there would be a much bigger earthquake coming."

Her eyes grew larger, and I realized I'd scared her.

"It's unlikely," I said. "Most earthquakes lack obvious foreshock patterns."

She looked confused.

"Meaning most small earthquakes are not precursors to a bigger quake."

She nodded slowly. "Ooookay."

We both stood there, saying nothing, for at least thirty seconds.

"Well, there's no way I'm going to be able to get back to sleep," she said. "How about you?"

"Oh, I was already awake."

I could tell that she thought I was strange, but I am used to people having this first impression of me. Truthfully, it's probably their lasting impression of me.

"Do you want coffee or . . . ?" she said, cocking her head back toward her apartment door.

I was perplexed by the invitation. The male boxer shorts implied to me that she had a boyfriend or husband, and I thought he would be rather perturbed about a stranger having coffee with his girlfriend or wife at four o'clock in the morning.

"Oh. Would that be okay with your . . . roommate?" I asked.

For the second time in our brief interaction, she looked confused.

"It's just me," she said. "These studios are like 400 square feet."

"Oh," I said. "Okay, then."

I followed her into her apartment, fixated on the boxers she was wearing. Had she visited the men's section of a store to buy them? Why didn't she purchase female shorts?

Her apartment was so messy that I second-guessed my estimation of a 4.1-magnitude quake. There were just so many books on the floor. She must have seen me staring at the disarray, because she said, "I haven't had time to organize yet. I need a bookshelf, I know."

I knew better than to comment. I just nodded.

The layout of her apartment was the same as mine, but hers appeared so much smaller because of all the clutter. I would have understood if she'd just moved in, but she'd said she'd been there a few months. It was unclear to me how a person could withstand such living conditions for a few months. One of the things in the "desired" column of my dating spreadsheet was "orderliness." I made a mental note of this, but could not help but be interested in her anyway. She was attractive, which ranked higher in priority than "orderliness" on the spreadsheet. Admittedly, I was overtaken by the baser instincts that overtake every man.

Like me, she had a queen-size bed pushed up against one wall, facing a couch and a small coffee table. If she had visitors, they would essentially sit and stare at the place where she slept. I'd never felt comfortable with this awkward arrangement and, therefore, never had visitors. A half-wall separated the bed space from the tiny kitchen. And off the kitchen were the bathroom and closet.

"I'm guessing it looks familiar," she said.

"It does."

She cleared a stack of manila filing folders off a couch cushion and invited me to sit. Then she went to her kitchen and went about programming her coffee machine to fulfill its one purpose in life.

"Do you take cream? Sugar?"

"I don't really drink coffee," I said.

Because it was true. I didn't, and still don't. It makes me jittery.

She looked confused yet again, but she recovered nicely and said, "Tea?"

"Yes, I drink tea."

She did not appear to own a kettle. She filled a mug with water from the sink, then put it in the microwave. This wasn't—and still isn't—how I prefer to make tea, but, as I said, I was attracted to her in that most basic way and didn't want to be difficult. Previous women had used that word with me—*difficult*.

"I only have green tea," she said. "Is that okay?"

I nodded, pleased with the selection. Green tea has always been my tea of choice because it contains polyphenols and antioxidants that help prevent cancer.

"That's perfect. Thank you."

Once her coffee was done percolating and my tea was prepared, she brought the two mugs to the little table. I thanked her again, because I'm nothing if not polite.

"So," she said. "You're my neighbor."

"It appears that I am."

"Well, neighbor, I'm Jana."

"I'm Dave."

"Nice to meet you, Dave. I suppose things have escalated quickly because you've already seen me in my pajamas."

She laughed, and I did the same. I've learned that, over the years: laugh when others laugh. Most people want validation of their own sense of humor.

"How long have you lived here?" she asked.

"In this building? Or in Orange County?"

"Both," she said with a shrug.

"I've lived in Orange County since attending UC Irvine. I graduated two years ago. That's when I moved into this apartment building."

"Oh, okay. What did you study? Earthquakes?"

She laughed again, so I did too.

"No. I got my degree in Biological Sciences."

"Close enough," she said, though it wasn't close at all. "And you work in that field now?"

"I work for a pharmaceutical company. I help prepare submissions for the FDA."

She looked impressed, which made me like her more.

"Wow, that sounds . . . important." She laughed again. There was so much laughing.

"What brought you to California?" I asked.

She took a big gulp of coffee. When she tipped the mug toward her mouth, it covered almost her entire face.

"Oh, well, I just needed a change, you know?"

I didn't know, though. I have always hated change: have never wanted it, let alone needed it. In time, I would find out that she'd been engaged to another man in Arizona. He was in medical school there and had cheated on her with a classmate. If I'd been her, I would have been grateful for this insight into his true character; but, as Jana would often tell me, I "lack emotional depth." In retrospect, perhaps the boxer shorts had belonged to her ex. If this was the case, it was disturbing.

"That's brave," I said, because I thought it was. It wasn't something I'd ever be capable of doing. I chose UC Irvine because it was less than a two-hour drive from where I'd grown up in the San Fernando Valley. I have never been interested in relocating out of state. I will never be someone who decides to live abroad for a year to "expand my horizons." I am very pleased with my current horizons. Cleo says I live in a bubble, and I take this as a compliment. I enjoy the bubble.

"Thank you," she said, "for saying that. It felt brave. Necessary, but brave."

"Do you have a job here?"

She sighed. "Well, that's been a bit of a thing. See, I'm a kindergarten teacher. Or I was. In Arizona. So now I have to apply for a certification here, through what they call a reciprocity agreement."

She waved a hand. "It's boring and complicated."

I wasn't bored, though, and I was following along easily.

"I'll get it. It's just a hoop to jump through, and I've been too tired for hoops. So right now I'm working at a Montessori school. I'm the teacher in the toddler room."

I have never been a kid person, mostly because kids seem to be the epitome of chaos and I have a strong disdain of chaos. I couldn't imagine being surrounded by a group of them on a daily basis.

"That's brave too," I said.

More laughing. "I love it. I love kids," she said. "They're just so . . . open, you know?"

Again, I didn't know.

She turned toward the oven. The clock on it said 4:48 a.m.

"Actually," she said, "maybe I should make the most of this earthquake situation and get to work early. I've been meaning to set up this painting activity for them all week."

She stood from her seat, seemingly confirming this impulsive plan.

"Sorry," she said. She looked genuinely regretful. "Do you mind if we chat another time?"

I understood that I was supposed to stand. I drank the remainder of my tea much too quickly, scalding my throat. I must have winced, because she winced.

"Maybe we could do this properly, like wearing real clothes at an actual coffee shop?" she said.

I realized then that "this" had been a date. She wanted to pursue getting to know me. Whenever this happened to me with a woman, I was utterly shocked. And, unbeknownst to me, the obvious shock came across as endearing (as Jana told me later).

"Oh. Yes," I said. "That would be great. Should I call you, or. . . ."

". . . or knock on the door?" she said. "Let's do it the old-fashioned way, no technology."

I much preferred technology, but she was pretty and kind, so I acquiesced.

"I'll knock on your door this evening," I said. "And we can set up a time to go to a coffee shop."

She looked amused.

"I'll be awaiting your knock."

I've been told I'm attractive, by conventional standards. Jana used to say I look like Jim from *The Office,* but I think she was just saying that because she knows how much I enjoy that show. (My insistence on watching reruns I have seen multiple times was actually a topic in one of our therapy sessions. She used my regimented watching of this show as an example of my "rigidity" and "lack of openness to new experiences." *Hearing that theme song every day is taking years off my life.* Jana said that to The Therapist, and now I have to think of that every time the theme song comes on.)

I do have Jim-like features—I am tall, and I have brown hair that could be described as "floppy." Cleo says I have "caterpillar eyebrows," and it appears that Jim has those as well. I have assumed that my supposed attractiveness is why I have managed to accumulate a fair number of relationships, though "relationships" may be an overstatement. I have kept the company of a fair number of women. My *modus operandi,* before Jana, was to dismiss that company after approximately two months, a pattern Jana made me aware of when I attempted to break up with her at that time point.

I delivered the same words to her that I'd delivered to others before her: "I think we shouldn't see each other anymore."

I admit it was rather out of the blue. We were in the car, driving back to our apartment building after dinner at a pizza place in Newport Beach. The dinner had been fine, the conversation pleasant. We had been seeing each other regularly for exactly two months. It was hard not to see each other regularly because of our living arrangements, but we had "dates" twice a week. We had slept together starting in week 3, though we had yet to spend an entire night at each other's apartments. The first time we had sex was at her place, and it seemed to make perfect sense to me to then return to my own home to sleep. I've never enjoyed sharing a bed with another person for sleeping purposes. It doesn't make logical sense. The sounds, the body heat—I'm not sure how most people find it appealing. When we had sex at my place, she asked, "Do you want me to stay, or . . . ?" And I must have hesitated, because she said, "I'll go."

I was somewhat unnerved by her messiness, her impulsivity, her outbursts of laughter. But she did check off many items in the "desired" column of my spreadsheet. She had been generally understanding of me, accommodating, which is what any woman who made it to two months had to be. She thought my hobbies were charming. The first time she came to my place, she was enthralled by my model cars. Or at least she acted like she was enthralled. "It has a working steering wheel and suspension, and a detailed 289 engine," I told her when she placed my 1:18 scale 1965 Mustang GT 2+2 Fastback in her palm. "You're kidding," she said, eyes aglow. I reviewed the features with her—the detailed interior, the carpet fabric seatbelts, the rear fold-down seat. I believe her exact words were, "These cars are the coolest thing ever."

She was patient, as I imagine is a personality requirement for people who work with small children: *Education degree and endless supply of patience required.* She seemed to find me humorous, entertaining. On more than one occasion she referred to me as "quirky." These were all pros, but I began to feel suffocated. Her presence began to bother me in the same way tags in the necks of shirts bother me. To this day, I always cut out the tags.

"You think we shouldn't see each other anymore?" she said, repeating my statement as a question.

I came up to a red light and glanced over at her. Her eyebrows were raised halfway to her forehead. She didn't look angry, which was how most women looked upon my making this statement. Instead, she looked surprised, like she'd just walked into a room of people wishing her a happy birthday.

The light turned green, giving me reason to turn my eyes back to the road. It was not by accident that I routinely chose to have break-up conversations in the car.

"Right, I think it's best if we, you know, go our separate ways."

She startled me with a sudden and robust "Ha!"

"Dave, you are ridiculous," she said. Out of the corner of my eye, I could see her shaking her head, a bemused smile on her face.

"What?" I asked.

"That makes no sense. Why would we break up?"

"Because that's what I think is best."

"That's what *you* think is best?" she said. "So, this is just a unilateral decision?"

I have to say I appreciated her use of the word "unilateral."

"I just—"

"Why?" she asked.

Others had asked this question, and I had given pat responses: *I don't think we are a good fit. The chemistry isn't right. I'm not looking for a relationship right now.*

With Jana, all I could manage was "I don't know."

"Yeah, you don't know."

We pulled up to our apartment building and I parked in my assigned carport.

"Why don't you think about it and we'll talk in a couple days?" she said.

Others before her had cried, had imposed demands upon me that cemented my faith in the hollow reasons I'd given for the breakup. With those others, I had walked away relieved, thinking I had narrowly escaped losing control of my entire life at the hands of a love-obsessed woman. With Jana, as she closed the car door and walked to the building without looking back, I felt like the only thing I was losing was her.

A couple days later, I knocked on her door.

"I may have been rash," I said.

"Rash," she repeated.

"Rash."

"Who says that?"

"Me, I guess."

She laughed and, just like that, we were together. And I knew that we would stay together. She had managed to challenge my rules and win. Nobody had accomplished this feat before her. We had a talk about the "before her" era, and that's when she pointed out the two-month pattern.

"I think two months is probably when you become aware that a woman wants more from you than you're capable of giving. Or that's what you think. I actually think you're capable of giving a lot."

I wasn't following her psychoanalysis, but it seemed to make her feel more affection for me, so I smiled and said, "Maybe."

Once I was in, I was all in. I became someone I had never been before. I was, dare I say, *attentive*. I listened to her with more interest than I'd ever listened to anyone. As I fell more in love with her, I fell in love with this version of myself too. With the benefit of hindsight and a robust understanding of the human brain, I have come to see that this new version of myself was the result of neurons awakening in me that had never been awakened before. I was both a victim and a beneficiary of the chemicals that make all fortunate humans unrecognizable to themselves. The grievous error I made back then—perhaps a grievous error all humans make—was to think I'd remain this new person forever, or at least as long as we were together (which I'd come to hope would be forever).

I asked Jana to marry me on the one-year anniversary of the morning we met in the hallway after the 4.1 earthquake. I was nervous because I wasn't sure she would say yes. We hadn't discussed marriage in any direct way. We had alluded to wanting to spend the future together, but these allusions were vague. What I did know is that Jana wanted to get married at some point, to someone, and it seemed reasonable that I be that person. Despite enjoying time to myself, I had always assumed I would get married. I appreciate the structure of a good institution. It makes rational sense to have a partner in life, someone to wash the dishes while you dry. It's more efficient, and I believe I've established my affinity for efficiency. Given my idiosyncrasies, I couldn't conceive of a better partner for myself than Jana.

Within six months of our marriage, we entered a "settling down" phase when we both returned to our more comfortable forms. I became re-enamored with my model cars and took less interest in hearing Jana's daily thoughts. For her, the luster of my "quirkiness" began to wear off and she expressed something she had not expressed during our courtship—annoyance. She started saying things like, "Sometimes I feel like you don't appreciate me at all." But that was never it. I always appreciated her. I was just terrible at showing it.

It's just before 1 p.m., and I am about to log in to another meeting that should be an email when my phone lights up with a text from Cleo.

> Hey dad. There's a study club after school today. Forgot to tell u. Ok if I go? It's 2 hours, so pick me up at 5?

I don't know why Cleo would need a study club. She excels in all her studies without the need of a club. I take great pride in this, though I really cannot take credit for her intelligence. She's always been a kid who does her homework without prodding. I suspect this "club" is more of a social gathering and, while I do not see the value of such a thing, Jana was adamant that I not "project" myself onto our daughter. That's a therapy word—*project*. I understand it to mean that I should not impose my eccentricities upon

Cleo. While it is often difficult for me to imagine that others see the world differently than I do and do not share my same preferences, I have learned to accept that this is the case. Jana used to say that was Step 1—accepting that others see the world differently than me. Step 2 is accepting that my way is not the best way. I assume I will spend the remainder of my life working on Step 2.

I text back:

If you would like to attend the club, I can pick you up at 5.

My computer dings with a reminder that the online meeting is beginning. I see faces start to populate the screen, the Brady Bunch configuration taking shape.

Thanks dad. Ur the best.

Teenagers are known for dramatic overstatement but, still, I cannot help but smile at this declaration of my superiority.

I text:

Love you.

I never used to text such things. I never used to say those words out loud, or even think them in my head. It took me seven months to say them to Jana and, even then, I only said them because she had said them to me first—slurred, after a day of wine-tasting. It was clear she did not remember saying them, which was in my favor. I was both gifted with the knowledge that she loved me and alerted to the fact that we were at a stage in our relationship when I would be expected to express reciprocation of that love. So I did. And she said, "I've loved you for a while, goofball."

When she took me to see The Therapist for the first time, one of her grievances was that I wasn't expressive of my love for her. "He used to be," she told The Therapist. Used to be, back when the neurons were firing. It's not that I was trying to fool her during our courtship; I really did find emotional expression easier then. She'd thought I'd "gotten lazy" after we got married. It wasn't that: I'd just returned to being who I always was.

"He needs to try harder," she told The Therapist, talking about me as if I weren't sitting right next to her on that uncomfortable couch indented with the memory of other troubled marriages. "Not just for me, but for Cleo. I don't want Cleo growing up in a house without any affection."

I made a mental note in that moment to say "I love you" to Jana and Cleo once a day. When I got home, I set a reminder in my Outlook calendar. I still have the reminder, though I find I have already met the "I love you" quota by the time the reminder dings at 2 p.m. I have, essentially, trained myself.

Cleo responds to my "Love you" text with a series of rainbow hearts, an immediate reward. Positive reinforcement, as they say. I am a fan of emojis. When I struggle to decipher the tone of a text, emojis clarify.

"Dave, we still looking good to have that Glovista submission ready for Thursday?" Greg says, interrupting my thoughts.

I channel Jana every time I restrain myself from calling someone a moron. I'd just told Greg yesterday that I would have the submission ready, so I do think he is a moron, but I know it is not my responsibility to break this news to him.

Be nice, Dave.

That's what Jana would say. That's what Jana did say, many times, usually whispered in my ear, her breath hot on my face, while at some social function that required me to do my best not to embarrass her (and/or Cleo).

For the record, I don't believe in an afterlife. I don't think there is a heaven full of loved ones sitting on clouds playing harps. Jana is gone. Cleo likes to remind me that she's not really gone, based on the first law of thermodynamics, which states that energy cannot be created nor destroyed. She interprets this to mean that Jana's soul will persist until the end of time. *I* interpret this to mean that the collection of atoms that were Jana have been repurposed, in the same way the atoms of any living being are repurposed once it decomposes and becomes part of the Earth again. I trust what I see, what scientists know. For all intents and purposes, Jana is gone.

Sometimes, though, I can't help but entertain the idea of her sitting atop a cloud, smiling down at my ability to carry on without her, watching me as I cling to the words of wisdom she imparted to me in the years she was with me. If I follow those words, it's like part of her goes on living.

Be nice, Dave.

"Yes, Greg," I say. "It'll be ready on Thursday."

CHAPTER 6

Cleo

My dad's gonna pick me up at school at 5... so we can hang at ur hotel until then if u or ur mom can drive me back to school

My heart pounds as I await Edie's reply. I reread my text three times, berating myself. She's going to think it's weird that Dad can't pick me up at the hotel. I watch the three dots on screen appear, expecting a reply that confirms the weirdness, something like "Uhhh, ok? Complicated much?"

Sure thing. I have my car

I exhale a breath I didn't even realize I was holding.

Cool cool. Meet u in the lot then?

My heart is literally pounding so hard I can hear my pulse in my ears.

Yep. I'm in the last row. Maroon Jeep Cherokee

My insides feel all tingly as I walk toward the student parking lot after school lets out. The last row is the one that butts up against the baseball field. I walk slowly because I don't want Edie to think I raced out of class to meet her, though that's exactly what I did.

I see her before she sees me. She's standing against her car, a maroon Jeep

Cherokee, as described. It's an older one, old enough to have a dent in the back bumper that must have been deemed unworthy of fixing.

Her head is craned down, looking at something on her phone. Dad says Australian researchers found that young people are growing horns on the back of their skulls from all the phone time. Doctors call it "tech neck." I didn't believe him, thought it was one of his crazier scare tactics. But no. I googled it and it's true, though "horns" is a slight overstatement. They're bone spurs. Apparently.

"Hi," I say.

When she looks up, she's already smiling.

"You found me," she says, seemingly impressed.

"It's not that big of a parking lot. And I'm also not an idiot."

"That's a relief," she says. "Ready?"

The inside of her car smells musty, like a locker room. The pointy end of a surfboard sits on the center console, the rest of it occupying the back of the car. She has the back seat folded down to accommodate it. A wetsuit is draped over the board. There's sand everywhere. And a few crumpled Del Taco bags. Dad would literally have a panic attack at the sight of this.

"I'm more of a Taco Bell girl," I say.

She scrunches her nose in a look of disgust. "I'm going to have to reconsider our friendship."

"It's a budding friendship, so nip now or forever hold your peace."

She laughs. "I'll take some time to consider."

"It's awesome you have a car," I say. "I turn sixteen next month. Hoping to get my license and, eventually, a car."

She turns the key in the ignition, and the car comes to life. "You're not sixteen yet?"

"Oh, yeah, no. I started Kindergarten a year early, so I'm younger than everyone else."

"Okay, smarty-pants."

"It was my dad's doing. He wanted to accelerate my learning or something."

"When you were *five*?"

"I told you he was weird."

We drive through the parking lot to the exit, and I look out the window, hoping someone will see me in the passenger seat with the pretty new girl. Then I feel silly for hoping this, for giving a shit what people think of me.

I didn't think to ask where the hotel is. As we drive on Ortega Highway, farther and farther away from school, I start to think of all the true-crime shows I watch after Dad goes to bed—because he goes to bed at 7 p.m., no joke. I look at Edie's face, analyzing her profile. Is it the profile of a sadistic killer? Strangely, I'm less worried about my safety than I am about how disappointed Dad would be if I met my end this way. *But you're such a smart girl, Cleo.* I can hear him saying that.

"Where's the hotel?"

"It's over by Costco," she says. "We wanted to stay at the one by the Mission, but they don't allow dogs."

"You have a dog? What kind?"

Dad is opposed to dogs. They're messy, and dad is opposed to messy. It took me weeks of consistent pestering to persuade him to get Poppy (our cat), and I still think he only agreed because he felt he had to give me something after losing Mom. I also promised to take full responsibility for the litter box, assuring him that pieces of litter would not end up all over the house, sticking to our bare feet. This was Dad's big fear.

"I don't know. Some kind of mutt. We got him at a shelter. His name is Doug. My mom's divorce dog."

"Divorce dog?"

"She got him right before filing for divorce from my dad. I swear he's a therapy animal."

"You should get him one of those little vests."

"Oh, you'll see. My mom's one step ahead of you."

The Residence Inn is about five miles from where Mom, Dad, and I used to live. It's strange to be back here, in what used to be our neighborhood. It feels like I lived here decades ago, though I'm not even decades old.

Edie pulls into a parking spot and says, "Temporary home sweet temporary home."

I get out of the car when she does and follow her toward the front of the building.

"You mind if I check in with my mom? Then we can go study out by the pool."

I can't help but feel disappointed at her mention of the word "study." I had hoped the math tutoring was a guise.

We take the elevator to the second floor, and I follow at her heels to the end of the hallway. She swipes her keycard in the door and pushes it open. I'm immediately overcome with the smell of cooking.

"*Mija*?" a voice calls.

The entry hallway leads us directly into the small kitchen, where her mom is standing at the stove, wearing a flowery boho dress, her black hair in a bun on top of her head. A little dog, small enough to fit in a purse, sits at her feet. Doug, I assume. He is, in fact, wearing a vest. It's argyle and makes him look like a fan of croquet, cigars, and eighteenth-century British literature.

"Hey, mom," Edie says.

Her mom turns around, clearly startled at the appearance of me. The little dog starts barking.

"*Dios mío*," she says. She slaps Edie on the forearm. "You could have warned me you were bringing a guest. I haven't even showered today."

Just as quickly as she scolds Edie, she pulls her into the side of her body, arms wrapped around her middle.

"That's gross, Mom. You only shower when people come over?"

She pushes Edie away and slaps her forearm again. Then she picks up the still-barking dog, kissing his nose. The barking stops.

"*Qué molestia*," she says to Edie. Then she turns to me: "My daughter is rude. You must be Cleopatra." She extends a hand while Edie giggles behind me. I give her a look and take her mother's hand. It's the smoothest hand I've ever touched in my life.

"You can just call me Cleo," I say, my mind stuck on the fact that Edie has already mentioned me to her mother.

"I hear you made my girl's first day a little better," she says. She puts the dog down and he curls into a ball at her feet again.

"Did I?" I say.

"Mom, don't be weird," Edie says, peeking over her mom's shoulder at what's on the stove. "Burgers?"

"*Sí*. Turkey burgers, *mija*. Cleo, would you like to stay?"

"Oh, thank you. But my dad is picking me up back at school at five."

"You should tell him to come here. Your mom too. Burgers for all!"

She appears genuinely enthusiastic about this idea. I've already pegged her as the entertaining type, someone who loves to walk around a room and offer people glasses of wine. I don't have it in me to tell her that my mom is dead and my dad would rather submerge himself in a vat of live rattlesnakes than socialize over turkey burgers in a stranger's extended-stay hotel room.

"Cleo doesn't eat meat," Edie says.

I feel simultaneously pleased that she's protective of this part of my identity, and guilty for rejecting the meal offering.

Her mom doesn't skip a beat: "Burger buns with cheese? Cheese sandwiches for all!"

I smile. "Thanks, but my dad probably has dinner going already."

"A man who cooks. I appreciate that," she says with a wink.

She turns around and tends to the patties on the stove. I also don't have it in me to tell her that Dad doesn't really cook. Most nights, our meals come from plastic trays that we place in the microwave. We've actually talked about getting a second microwave so we don't have to wait for each other. Sometimes I flip my tray onto a plate to fool myself into thinking we are enjoying a homecooked meal. Dad doesn't understand when I do this. He laments the "needless dirtying" of the plate.

"Well, you will have to come for dinner next time. Edie said we will be neighbors?" She turns around again, eyebrows raised.

"Sounds like it. That's great that you're renovating that house," I say.

"It's quite the project," she says. "I'm probably a bit *loca*."

She makes a circle with her finger around her temple, indicating her alleged craziness.

"'Probably'? You're definitely *loca*," Edie says.

"I just hope it doesn't take half a century, because this place is. . . ."

She sticks out her tongue and gives two thumbs down. I look around the suite and see what she means. The furniture, the décor, is all so . . . business-y. It reminds me of going to visit Dad at his work (when he still went in to the office). Once a month, Mom would play hooky from work and let me skip school for what we called Random Fun Days. Dad never joined us, because he wasn't willing to end his "consecutive days of work" streak. I asked him if he was trying to set a record or get some kind of attendance award, like I got once in elementary school, and he said, "No. The attendance is the reward," which made Mom and me crack up for, like, twenty minutes straight. We usually took lunch to his office—sandwiches from Spunky's Deli or burritos from Lupe's. He'd always save his food for later, saying that eating midday ruined his concentration; but Mom and I would eat. Then we'd go to the mall or a movie. We always stuffed ourselves on snacks—ice cream dots, popcorn, licorice ropes—and came home not hungry for dinner. It worked out fine for Dad, because he had his lunch leftovers.

I feel the tears coming, as they sometimes do, always at the worst times. I shake my head, willing them away.

"Mom, we're going to study by the pool, 'kay?" Edie says. "What time's dinner?"

Her mom glances over her shoulder at the clock on the oven. "Burgers are almost done. Going to let them rest. Just need to make pasta salad . . . and take a shower since you think I'm such a disgusting human being. Five thirty?"

"Okay, I'll be back," Edie says. She brushes by me, her fingers grazing my arm. I wonder if she can feel the instant goosebumps all over my skin. "You ready?"

I nod.

"It was nice to meet you, Ms. Walker," I say.

"*Ay, dios mío.* Call me Camila."

I nod, though I doubt I'll be able to do that.

Once we are back in the hallway, walking to the elevator, Edie says, "My mom's a bit much."

I laugh.

"She's like an excited puppy," she says.

"You say that like it's a bad thing."

Coming from Dad, possibly the least excitable person in the world, Camila Walker is a welcome shot of adrenaline.

"She can be intense. She kisses my cheek like thirty times every day, like she has a quota to meet or something."

I consider commenting on how her cheeks are extremely kissable, but think better of it. I mean, who do I think I am?

"Also, *Cleopatra*?" I say. "Seriously?"

She turns around, gives a shrug. "It suits you."

There's not a single person in the pool area, just a bunch of lonely-looking lounge chairs with towels rolled up at the end of them.

"I wonder if some poor person has to roll up new towels every day for the chairs that nobody is using," I say.

"Probably," Edie says. "Or that's what they're *supposed* to do. I'd just reuse the same ones."

She leads us to a table with an umbrella, and we both sit. We paw through our backpacks—I pull out a notebook and a pencil and she takes out her algebra 2 textbook.

"Do we have to do this?" she asks, dread all over her face.

"Uh, it was *your* idea."

"What if today is just a 'get to know you' day?" she says. "Then we can start fresh next time."

I feel my face flush at the mention of a next time.

"Whatever you want. It's your study session."

Let's just study each other. That's what I want her to say. That's what John Green would have her say.

She puts her textbook back in her bag and taps the screen on her phone. The time flashes—3:43 p.m.

"We only have an hour, anyway. How about you just tell me your favorite thing about math, and we'll consider that our lesson for today? Then on to more interesting things."

"My favorite thing about math?" I say with a little laugh, feeling self-conscious of my obvious nerdiness. "I guess I just love that it's so . . . *clear*. There is a right answer and a wrong answer. My dad has this quote: 'Life is like geometry: you can never assume that anything is true unless you have proved it.' I like that. It's very black-and-white, you know?"

She nods, squinting her eyes as if contemplating my thought process. It's the same unnerving look that Ms. Murray gives me on a weekly basis.

"So, you don't like gray areas?"

"I don't know. . . . I guess it feels like my whole life has become a gray area, so I like things that are black-and-white."

She sits back in her chair, arms crossed over her chest.

"I get that," she says, seemingly satisfied. "My life's a gray area too. Like, I'm living at a hotel; I just started at this new school where I know exactly nobody."

"Hey, you know me now," I say, wondering how much of a consolation I am.

"I kind of forced myself to know you, huh?" she says. "Nothing says 'I'm desperate' like invading your lunch spot and basically demanding friendship . . . *and* tutoring."

Her self-consciousness alleviates my own.

"Seriously, you really homed right in on the class loner. Impressive skill."

"It's your fault. You made the mistake of smiling at me after that lame introduction Mr. Johnston made me do. I took that smile and ran with it."

"I didn't smile at you," I say.

"You did."

"Are you sure it wasn't just a facial twitch?"

She considers this. "Possibly. But I chose to interpret it as a smile. My bad."

"And here we are. A budding friendship that started with a misinter-preted facial twitch."

She leans forward, elbows on the table.

"Tell me about your gray area," she says.

I can't help but giggle. "I don't think I know you well enough to tell you about my *gray area*."

She laughs, a surprised bark of a laugh. "Mind in the gutter, Cleopatra. I like it."

Our mutual laughter subsides, and I realize she's still waiting for me to explain my "gray area." I stare at my bitten nails, the mess of my cuticles.

"It's been just my dad and me since last year," I say, vaguely. "And he's . . . different. And it's just . . . hard. Some days, I feel like shit and some days I feel okay, and I guess that's the gray area of it. Like, I was a happy person before and the future seemed all good, and now the future just seems like this big question mark."

I figure that's enough. I don't want to scare the poor girl with the complete details of my life. Yet. I look up and she's staring at me, brows furrowed like she's really concentrating on what I've said.

"I can relate to that," she says.

But I think she can't, not really.

"Do you still see your dad?" I ask her, shifting the focus away from myself.

She leans back in her chair again.

"I'm supposed to, I guess. But I don't want to. I don't even think my dad wants to. He just didn't want to 'lose' the custody game," she says, putting air quotes around "lose."

I must be making one of my faces that cause Dad to say "Careful, you'll get stuck like that," because Edie says, "Yeah, I know, it sucks. But I'm sure you can relate."

She must think Mom and Dad are divorced. She must think I stay with Dad because Mom left us—one of those mothers who just up and leaves to find herself in Bali or something. The absurdity of that makes me want to tell her the whole story, but the whole story is depressing as hell and I can barely stand to tell it to myself.

Thankfully, she doesn't ask about Mom. She must sense that she shouldn't go there, which makes me like her even more. *You're a sweet, sensitive soul, my girl. You're going to find yourself a sweet, sensitive mate someday.* Mom said that to me when I was, like, thirteen and heartbroken because Jason Parks wanted nothing to do with me. She hugged me and held me close, as if my heartbreak mattered when I know now that it didn't matter at all.

"My dad's an alcoholic," Edie says. "But not like a falling-down-drunk alcoholic. He's a covert alcoholic, the kind of alcoholic who's everyone's best friend and buys the drinks at the bar. And nobody thinks he has a problem, because he has a big fancy job and a nice car and expensive clothes and blah blah blah."

"So, like, the worst kind of alcoholic."

She touches her index finger to her nose. "Ding, ding, ding."

"My mom and I are the only ones who know the truth. Because we saw him when he drank too much or not enough and then he was a total dick. Like, verbally abusive."

I scrunch my nose. "And you still have to see him?"

"Two weekends a month. Technically. So far, it's been one weekend a month. And not even a full weekend. I drive down Saturday afternoon and drive back Sunday morning. He sneaks drinks when I'm there and I don't even care, because that means at least he's in a good mood."

"God, Edie, that sucks."

"I know. At least my mom finally left him, though," she says. "Much better this way, even staying in this lame hotel."

"Your mom is so nice. I cannot imagine her married to an asshole."

I've often wondered how Mom and Dad ended up together. Sometimes the ASD makes Dad seem like an asshole. He gets all up in his head and seems totally self-absorbed. And Mom was, like, the nicest person. She died because she was too nice, basically. Ms. Murray said something once that stuck with me—*We're drawn to people who fill in our gaps.* It's like in chemistry—very few atoms have the right number of electrons to achieve peak stability, so they have to bond with others. Relationships, for most, are inevitable. *We're drawn to people who fill in our gaps.* I'd looked at Ms. Murray's wedding finger when she'd said that, saw it was bare. She's never mentioned a significant other. Not that she talks much about her own life, but you would think it would come up in passing. Maybe Ms. Murray has no gaps. Or maybe they are complex gaps, hard to fill. Maybe everyone's are.

"I think the assholes pick the nice ones because they know the nice ones are forgiving," Edie says. "My mom is like the queen of second chances."

Edie's parents had an ionic bond too.

"You think she's happier now?"

She shrugs. "Yeah, most days. I think she misses him sometimes. He could be, like, really fun. When he drank the right amount. He'd twirl her around the kitchen and they'd laugh. I think she misses that."

"Does he miss her?"

She shrugs again. "I wouldn't know. His enormous ego won't even let him discuss her. It's like she's—*poof*—gone from his life."

"Adults are weird," I say.

"Quote of the day."

Over the next half hour, I give Edie a breakdown of the social hierarchy at school, she tells me about her love of surfing and explains why I shouldn't be afraid of sharks, and we agree that we should start a communal garden between our properties when she officially becomes my neighbor. We have plans for tomatoes, zucchini, spinach, and strawberries, to start.

"Just curious," she says, as we walk to her car to drive back to school, "does your dad even know you came over here?"

I consider whether I should lie, whether I should make Dad seem laid-back and cool, or if I should help Edie begin to understand that Dad will never be laid-back and cool.

"Um, no," I say.

We get in the car, buckle our seat belts. I can tell she's waiting for me to elaborate on "Um, no."

"My dad's kind of—"

"Different," she says. "You've said it a few times."

"Yeah, sorry. I don't know how else to describe it."

This is a lie, though. I know exactly how to describe it: *My Dad has autism spectrum disorder, ASD. It used to be called Asperger's. He has trouble with empathy, and understanding emotions, and relating to people. It makes him come across as odd, but he has a good heart.*

"Well, he has a pretty cool daughter, so he can't be all that bad."

I smile. "He's not bad."

"Just different," she says.

"Right."

She pulls up to the curb in front of school and puts the car in Park.

"Drop you here?" she asks.

"Yeah, perfect, thanks."

My hand is on the door handle, but I don't want to leave. I know Dad will be here any minute, though. I told him five o'clock, so he will be here right at five o'clock, maybe a minute or two early, never a minute or two late.

"When's our next tutoring session?" she asks.

Next. My heart picks up its pace.

"Whenever you want," I say, trying to sound like I'm very go-with-the-flow, though I'm not. I'm not as anti-flow as Dad, but I still have a hard time *going* with it. If the tutoring sessions, or whatever they are, continue, Edie will realize this about me. I wonder what parts of herself Edie's trying to hide. Maybe none. Maybe she's not trying to impress me. Maybe the attraction is one-way.

But, then again, maybe it's not.

"I'll text you," she says.

I open the car door.

"Okay, but we have to try to actually learn something next time."

I swing my legs out, put my feet to the ground.

"You didn't learn anything?" she says. "I learned a ton."

May 2019

CHAPTER 7

Dave

Underneath Yellowstone National Park is a reservoir of hot magma five miles deep, fed by a gigantic plume of molten rock welling up from hundreds of miles below. This heat is responsible for many of the park's famous geysers and hot springs. But what many people don't know is that the supervolcano underneath Yellowstone has the potential to be thousands of times more powerful than a regular volcano. A supereruption is anything that measures magnitude 8 or more on the Volcano Explosivity Index. If a supereruption were to occur, the amount of material ejected would be enough to bury Texas five feet deep.

If this were to happen, the states closest to Yellowstone would experience pyroclastic flows of hot lava, pumice, ash, and volcanic gas, with the potential of destroying everything in their path. A paper published in *Geochemistry, Geophysics, and Geosystems* a few years ago stated that the volcano would be capable of burying Wyoming, Montana, Idaho, and Colorado in three feet of volcanic ash, in addition to blanketing the entire Midwest. People would die, buildings would be damaged, crops would be smothered, electrical equipment would short-circuit, power plants would shut down. Volcanoes can emit sulfur aerosols that reflect sunlight back into the atmosphere, so it's possible the entire world would experience a cool climate for years to come.

A supereruption would be, in a word, disastrous.

There have only been three truly enormous eruptions in history—one occurred 2.1 million years ago, one 1.3 million years ago, and one 664,000 years ago. The last eruption ejected so much material from below that it left a 34-mile-by-50-mile depression in the ground—the Yellowstone Caldera.

They say there is no indication that we are due for a supereruption any time soon, and some think Yellowstone might never have an eruption again, but I still have concerns. There were 636,000 years between the second and third supereruptions in Yellowstone, so, just looking at the numbers, it's time.

Yellowstone is not the only supervolcano to worry about, either. Geologists have found evidence of at least 47 supereruptions in Earth's history. The most recent occurred in New Zealand's Lake Taupo some 26,000 years ago. Fifty thousand years before that, the Toba eruption triggered a dramatic six-to-ten-year global winter and, according to some, may have nearly decimated the human race.

Given the above facts, I will not entertain the idea of visiting Yellowstone. In retrospect, our last family trip to Utah was unwise, as Utah is in the supereruption danger zone. At the time, I was aware of the risks but had yet to become consumed by the possibilities of the worst happening. At the time, I was a person who said things like, "The odds are in our favor." Now I no longer believe that the odds—or anything, for that matter—are in my favor.

―――――――――

It's been three weeks since construction began on the house that's two football fields away. Cleo has made me aware of the fact that I've adopted a morning habit of staring out the kitchen window for at least ten minutes. She says if she attempts to converse with me during this time, I show no signs of hearing her. She says I'm *obsessed*. I think *obsessed* is a strong word. I am appropriately interested, as anyone would (or should) be when presented with the possibility of living in close proximity to other human beings.

"Has your friend given any updates on their progress?" I ask, proving to Cleo that I can converse during my daily ten-minute observation time at the kitchen window.

"Dad, you know her name," she says.

I do. Edie. But somehow using it makes it seem like she will be around a while, in our lives. I am not prepared for someone to be around and in our lives.

"I do know her name. Did she say when they would be moving in?"

Cleo bumps my shoulder as she puts her cereal bowl in the sink.

"No, Dad, *Edie* has not said anything besides 'summer.'"

Summer. As if that's specific enough.

"I know you'd prefer an exact date," Cleo says, proving she knows me alarmingly well, likely much better than I know her, "but I don't have one. Neither does Edie."

I don't like how she groups them together, herself and Edie.

"Hey, your birthday is this weekend," I say. It's an abrupt change of subject, which is my conversational specialty.

Cleo dries her hands on a dish towel after washing her bowl and says, "Hey, you're right" with her usual generous dose of sarcasm.

"That may have sounded like I just realized it was your birthday, but I have been aware for months."

She looks like she's going to laugh, like she's straining to keep her face straight. "I know, Dad. You're the master of dates."

I remember that was one of the statements on the autism spectrum questionnaire that Jana gave me: *I am fascinated by dates.* I indicated "definitely agree," proud of my fascination, not realizing that I was filling out a form that would indicate a *disorder*.

"Did you have something in mind?" I ask her.

"The usual."

The usual is pizza from Surfside Pizza and an ice cream cake from Baskin-Robbins. That has been the usual since she was old enough to declare that she wanted pizza and ice cream cake. I suspect it will be the usual forever now, because neither of us wants to deviate from traditions that used to involve Jana. It feels sacrilegious.

"Okay. Saturday. Pizza. Ice cream cake. It's a plan."

"Maybe Edie can come," she says.

I've been waiting for—and dreading—this request. Carter is the only friend of hers who has come over since we moved into this house. I don't know why she hasn't invited her girlfriends—Amy, Julia, and . . . I can't remember the third girl's name. It's the name of a city. Paris? Sydney? Savannah? Madison? In any case, I haven't missed them.

We have never had an outsider at the traditional birthday celebration; it's always been just Jana, Cleo, and me. In past years, there has been a separate celebration with friends—the dreaded sleepover or the even-more-dreaded trip to Disneyland. But I do not want to deny Cleo's wishes. It's her birthday, after all. Jana and The Therapist coaxed me to realize that I can be somewhat closed-minded, fixated on my own per-spective. "It's not your fault. It's just how you're wired," Jana had said. I accepted that because it was better than her thinking I'm a jerk for no reason. As a point of fact, the word *autism* comes from the Greek word *autos*, meaning self. Apparently, those of us with this affliction have a hard time thinking beyond ourselves. So, I try to defy The Label and think of others. Specifically, Cleo.

"If you would like her to come, that would be fine with me," I lie.

Cleo makes robot arms, which is what she does to indicate that I sound . . . robotic.

"Thank you, father," she says, in her robot voice.

"Brooklyn!"

I blurt it out by accident, the city name of her friend.

"What?" she says.

"What?" I say back.

She eyes me askance. "Dad, if you tell me you have Tourette's too, I'm literally going to die."

"Hey, I want you to take this test," Jana said.

She'd presented a couple pieces of paper to me, folded in half. I'd just gotten home from work and she had just put Cleo in her booster seat at the table for dinner. Cleo was two years old, developing a personality that frightened me on a daily basis. It wasn't that her personality itself was frightening; it was, and still is, objectively delightful. But as she entered toddlerhood, I became increasingly aware of how little control I had over her, which made me increasingly aware of how little control I had over anything at all. She was becoming this human being with her own thoughts and feelings that appeared to be quite different from my own. The feelings and inexplicable mood swings—crying and carrying on one minute, giggling psychotically the next—made no sense, and the lack of sense unnerved me in a way I'd never been unnerved before. Previously, when I'd felt off-kilter, I was able to amend the situation by retreating to my bubble and adhering to the routines and rituals that make me feel whole. But as a parent, there is no retreat. "It's relentless," I'd told Jana. She'd looked at me like she thought I was a complete imbecile: "What did you think parenthood was going to be?" I suppose

I hadn't thought about it much, or at all. She must have been able to tell that I was taking the inquiry seriously, searching my mind for what my expectations of fatherhood had been, because she snapped, "It was a rhetorical question, Dave."

I unfolded the papers she'd presented me and asked, "What is this?"

As I looked closer, I saw rows of statements like "I prefer to do things on my own rather than with others" and "I do not enjoy social chit-chat," with blank spaces next to them where I was supposed to enter a number from 1 (definitely agree) to 4 (definitely disagree).

"It's just one of those personality-test things," she said before continuing her usual manic busyness in the kitchen, preparing Cleo's daycare lunchbox for the next day, cleaning up dinner pans, sipping from her glass of wine.

It wasn't unusual for Jana to give me one of these personality tests. She was into that kind of thing. Because of her, I know that my dosha, according to Ayurveda, is Vata. And my astrological sign is Aquarius (which I believe has no significance whatsoever).

This test was different from the others; in that I felt like many of the prompts were representative of me, which is not how I felt on most tests.

I find it hard to know what to do in a social situation.

I am at my best first thing in the morning.

Friendships and relationships are very difficult for me.

In a conversation, I tend to focus on my own thoughts rather than on what my listener might be thinking.

It is hard for me to see why some things upset people so much.

I am very blunt, which some people take to be rudeness, even though this is unintentional.

I can't relax until I have done everything I had planned to do that day.

I usually stay emotionally detached when watching a film.

New situations make me anxious.

I find it difficult to imagine what it would be like to be someone else.

"What is this?" I asked, as I filled out my answers. "Did you make this up just for me?"

I thought maybe it was a joke, that she was going to reveal the quiz to be titled "How Dave Are You?"

"Just finish it," she said, sitting at the table and coaxing Cleo to eat her food, a task I never had the patience for.

I finished and then folded the paper and gave it back to her, satisfied with the familiar rush of completing a task. She put it on the kitchen table and said nothing about it until after she had put Cleo to bed (another task I never had the patience for).

"So," she said, joining me on the couch once Cleo was in her crib. "The test."

She unfolded the papers and set them on the coffee table in front of us. She exhaled loudly, which I had learned was a precursor to an uncomfortable conversation.

I kept my eyes on the episode of *The Office* I was watching. It was the "Christmas Party" episode from Season 2—a classic.

"I was talking to a new friend at work," she began, "and I've started to suspect something."

I had no idea where this was going. Jana had started a new job at an education nonprofit called Brighten, a deviation from her original teacher career path, and she had been mentioning these "friends" she was acquiring. It didn't surprise me—Jana was a very likeable person, a self-described "sociable introvert." But I'd be lying if I said these new "friends" did not feel like a threat to what had become a very predictable life. Was she going to propose dinners with other couples? *Outings?*

"My friend—her name is Vicky—said that her son was just diagnosed with Autism Spectrum Disorder. And as she was talking about it, I thought it sounded a lot like . . . you."

At this point, I turned my attention away from the episode to look at her. "What?"

My brain was slow to process what she was saying.

"That's what the test was—an autism spectrum test," she said. "Not that it's, like, an official diagnosis. It's just something I found online. But it might be on to something."

"You think I have autism?"

I sounded defensive, because I was.

"Well, your score indicates you might have Autism Spectrum Disorder. Have you heard of Asperger's Syndrome?"

She asked the question with the tone I'd heard her use with preschoolers.

"Yes, I've heard of Asperger's Syndrome," I said, making no attempt to hide my annoyance.

"I can already tell this isn't going well." She looked more flustered than I'd ever seen her. "I feel like you're taking this as a bad thing, when I think it could be very helpful."

"How is it helpful if I have Asperger's?"

She sighed heavily, defeated. "It's not helpful . . . or unhelpful . . . if you have certain traits. It's just helpful to have a name for it, so I can understand."

"Understand what?"

"Why you do certain things. And say certain things. And act certain ways."

"So, I'm doing things wrong, and you think that's because I have a disorder."

"I didn't say you were doing things *wrong*. You're—"

"But I have a *disorder*."

She put up her hands like a crossing guard telling cars to stop. "Dave, I get it that you're not stoked about this, but can you just try to understand what I'm saying."

"I think I understand what you're saying perfectly well."

She stood up from the couch. "Okay, well, this isn't going anywhere."

She went to the kitchen, and I could tell from the clinking that she was making herself a cup of tea. She probably wanted me to come in and apologize, to insist on talking it out. But I didn't do that. Because I have a *disorder*.

A few days after that, she told me she'd scheduled an appointment with a couples therapist who had experience with adult ASD. She didn't ask if I wanted to go; she just said, "It's at 12:30, so you'll have to take a lunch break." I went because I am very good at following clear instructions. As much as I've struggled with certain aspects of marriage and parenthood, I've always succeeded with specific to-do items, like purchasing items at the store or vacuuming. Jana pointed out that I'd become rather obsessive with cleaning during Cleo's infant and toddler years. "I think it's one place you feel competent, and it gives you very clear results, which you like. So you stick with that. Which is great. My girlfriends are jealous, honestly. But it would be nice if you could, like, *connect* with Cleo and me too." That's what she didn't understand—doing the dishes *was* my way of connecting. It was my way of showing that I cared.

"Daaad."

Cleo's voice interrupts my thoughts. I turn around. She is standing there, looking slightly irritated, holding my keys in the air. She jingles them.

"Can I drive today?" she asks. I get the sense she is repeating the question. I do not know how many previous attempts she has made to get my attention.

"Yes, that's fine."

She is taking her driver's test next week. As much as I want her to succeed in life, I do not want her to succeed at passing this driver's test. More teens die in car crashes than from any other cause. In half of the crashes, the teen is not wearing a seat belt. I am reasonably confident that Cleo will never forget her seat belt. She's always been cautious, a rule-follower. My biggest concern is the influence of others. Like Edie. I know nothing about Edie's seat-belt-wearing habits.

I follow her to the car and get in the passenger seat. Before she starts the car, she turns to me:

"I'm kind of proud of you, Dad," she says.

I must appear confused, because she goes on: "I made two requests that I know make you uncomfortable, and you said 'yes' to both."

"Uncomfortable?"

Jana had said I do this thing of repeating words back to people when my brain is still processing what they've said. When she was still here, it used to annoy me that she knew me so well. I could get nothing past her. She saw things in me that I was blind to myself until she revealed them. It was like I had to rely on her to pull back the veil of my own identity. Now that she's gone, I regret the annoyance. I regret not thanking her for the effort it must have taken to pull back that veil, especially in the face of my stubborn resistance.

"I mean, I know you don't *want* Edie to come to the birthday thing. And I know you don't *want* me to drive the car right now."

Jana taught Cleo to pull back the veil too. It is her legacy.

"Well, I want you to be happy." Because this, of course, is true.

Cleo smiles. "Thanks, Dad. Seriously."

The way she says it makes me think that it hasn't always been clear to her that her happiness is my utmost priority. Maybe it *hasn't* always been my utmost priority. Maybe this is what Jana meant when she said I seemed selfish at times. I am predispositioned to being a neglectful husband and father. Well, I am no longer a husband, I guess, but I am still a father. And though I can blame The Label for certain things, I still have to do what I can to improve, and sooner rather than later. Because there are so many ways the world could end.

CHAPTER 8

Cleo

"I'm offended," Carter says.

We are sitting on the lawn at lunchtime, just the two of us. It's Thursday, so Edie doesn't have lunch period with us. I've just told Carter that I'm going to invite Edie over on Saturday for birthday pizza and ice cream cake with Dad.

"Don't give me that," I say. "You're going to Santa Barbara with your mom this weekend."

"Well, yes, but I'm offended that you did not extend a courtesy invite to me."

I roll my eyes.

"It's okay," he says. "I know you wouldn't have invited me anyway."

This is probably true.

I say, "I seriously don't know if my dad could handle two houseguests at one time."

"And Edie is the priority houseguest," he says. "After all we've been through."

He drops his head, his chin hitting his chest, his shoulders heaving with fake sobs.

"You are something else."

He looks up, completely dry-eyed. "I am, aren't I?"

"How should I warn Edie about my dad?" I ask.

Carter winces. "You haven't told her anything?"

"I've just told her my dad is 'different.'"

"That's what you told me too, and that was incredibly vague and not helpful at all. I thought I was going to show up and meet someone with three eyes or something."

I nearly spit out my Snapple.

"It would have been much better if you'd just told me he was on the spectrum. This isn't 1950. Everyone knows what that means. Everyone is basically *on* the spectrum."

"Now I'm afraid Edie thinks my dad has three eyes."

"Seriously, Cleo, I was prepared for some real weirdness. And then I met him and was like, 'Oh.'"

"You didn't think he was bizarre?"

He does a quick glance at himself—in his purple skinny jeans and his T-shirt with Mickey Mouse on it. "I'm pretty sure I am not one to judge someone's bizarreness."

"I guess you have to spend some time with him to really get it," I say.

"I mean, yeah, if he had started talking to me about the apocalypse, I might have given you some major side-eye."

I laugh. Thankfully, Dad seems to know not to bombard people with tales of his doomsday-prepping endeavors.

"He's just quirky," Carter says with a shrug.

"And you don't think Edie will break up with me because my dad is quirky?"

He leans forward and takes me by the shoulders. "*Break up?*" he says. "Who the hell said you two were dating? What are you keeping from me, you sly minx?"

"I don't know why I said that. We're not *dating.*"

"In your mind, you are," he says, tapping his temple.

He's right. In my mind, the study sessions—a total of six so far—are dates. We certainly don't do much studying. We talk. We never run out of topics. In my mind, we are growing closer. But the facts do not indicate anything beyond friendship. She hasn't mentioned an interest in boys—or girls. She hasn't hugged me or held my hand or anything. Yet I can't help but hope. I'm going to get myself hurt with all this hope.

"I figure this birthday thing may tell me more about what's going on in *her* mind," I say. "Because I have no idea."

"Is this the first time you're doing something together outside of your study sessions?" He puts "study sessions" in air quotes, as he should.

I nod. "I haven't even asked her if she can come yet. We're getting ahead of ourselves."

He sits back and smiles. "That's where the fun is—ahead."

After school lets out, I meet Edie in the parking lot, as has become our Tuesday/Thursday routine. I still get heart flutters when I see her. She always smiles in the same relaxed way, suggesting that she is experiencing zero flutters.

"Hey, you," she says.

I love when she says this. *Hey, you.* It feels so intimate. It's something Mom used to say. I can picture it now—me sitting at the kitchen table in our old house, doing my homework, her pulling up a chair next to me, annoyingly close (on purpose), and saying it: *Hey, you.*

"Did you bring your swimsuit?" she asks.

After all our "study sessions" by the pool, we finally determined that we should actually *use* the pool. We haven't seen anyone else use it. It seems a shame that they keep it heated and cleaned for nobody.

And I'd like to think Edie wants to see me in a bikini.

I reach over my shoulder and pat my backpack. "Got it," I say.

She winks—*winks!* And then we're on our way.

After that first time I came to Edie's hotel, when I met her mom, Edie and I have gone straight to the pool area to hang out. I imagine Edie told her mom our routine, so there was no need to check in. I've been wanting to check in with her, though. I liked her. I liked being around a mom for a few minutes. Not that she's much like my mom. Mom was not that gregarious and loud. With me, she was; but not with strangers. I got to see parts of her that nobody else did, and now she's gone and I'm the only one who knows the funny faces she made and the ridiculous way she danced around the house. Dad saw those things too, but I don't know if they registered as being special. He's not a noticer of details; he's not good at registering "special."

But, anyway, I liked Edie's mom. All moms have a certain energy, I guess. I miss mom energy. So when Edie asks if I want to change into my suit upstairs, I say, "Oh, yeah, sure."

We go up to her suite and her mom calls, "*Mija?*" the moment we walk in the door.

"*Sí*, Mom. It's me," Edie says. "And Cleopatra."

I slap her arm.

"Hi, Ms. Walker," I say.

She's sitting on a couch in the living area, a book folded open in her lap, Doug the dog curled at her feet. She's still wearing pink scrubs. Edie told me she's a home health nurse. She works 6 a.m. to 3 p.m. so that she can be home after school.

"Oh, my favorite friend of Edie's," she says.

I wonder if this is true, or if she's just saying that because she can sense that I want her to like me. Because I like Edie. Moms always sense these things. Or that's my experience. I suppose my mom had to sense everything because Dad senses nothing.

"And it's de Silva," she says to me.

"De Silva?"

"Mom and I are going to change our last name," Edie says. "Her maiden name."

Her mom beams. "Edie printed out all the forms for me, gave them to me as a birthday gift."

"It was your birthday?" I ask.

She nods, and Edie says, "Last weekend."

"Happy birthday!" I say.

She stands and gives me a hug, which simultaneously makes me feel uncomfortable and loved. As she squeezes me tighter, I'm overcome with the too-familiar sudden urge to cry. Ms. Murray keeps saying these urges are normal. No matter what I tell her, she says it's normal. "But I started to cry in the cereal aisle at Ralph's," I told her. That happened over the summer, when I saw someone who looked like Mom and thought, for the splittest of split-seconds, that it *was* Mom. We used to do the grocery shopping together, so my subconscious was programmed to look for her in Ralph's. When the look-alike turned around and I realized she wasn't Mom, I fell to my knees. I thought only actors in movies did something so dramatic, but it happens in real life too, apparently. Then I cried while holding a box of Raisin Bran. I thought for sure Ms. Murray would recommend some kind of psychological evaluation, but she didn't. "It's all normal, Cleo," she said. But, no matter how many message boards I visited online, I couldn't find anyone who had fallen to their knees in a cereal aisle.

"Mom, we're just changing into our suits for the pool," Edie says. "Don't get too attached."

Edie's mom releases me from her hug. "Oh, fine."

Edie shows me to the bathroom adjoined to her bedroom so I can change. It smells like perfume. My bikini is old and scratchy, the red polka dots on it faded. I haven't worn it since before Mom died. I haven't been up for a pool party or a fun beach day since she died. I'm still not. This is neither of those things. This is swimming in a hotel pool with a girl I like. Mom would approve.

I stop and assess myself in the mirror before I return to the common area. I'm not as scrawny as I remember being the last time I wore this suit. I'm "filling out," as they say. I got my period for the first time a few months before Mom died, and I'd just started a cycle the day she died. So that time of the month continues to be especially torturous. My boobs are definitely bigger now. They fill out the top of the swimsuit. I dare to say I have *cleavage*.

I wrap my towel around myself and come out to the living room where Edie is already waiting in a vintage-looking one-piece suit that hugs her hips just so. She is not hiding her body with a towel. It is there for me to see—*in all its magnificent glory*, I can hear Carter say. I try not to stare, because I can feel Edie's mom watching me.

"You two have fun," her mom says to me. If I'm not mistaken, there is a mischievous smile on her face, as if she's on to me. Edie just nods, seemingly clueless as to what either of us is thinking.

When we get to the pool, Edie dives right into the deep end while I go to the steps and hold on to the railing. I take off my towel and throw it on a nearby lounge chair, then lower myself into the water. When I look up, Edie's treading water, smiling at me. I blush.

"This pool is a rectangle," she says. "Today's math lesson is done."

"So, we're regressing to preschool-level math?"

"May as well just start over. From the beginning."

"That will require years of tutoring," I say.

"Sign me up."

She submerges herself in the water and swims halfway across the pool, coming up right in front of me.

"Hi," she says, our faces closer together than they've ever been before.

She goes back under and swims to the steps. I turn around just as she's coming up again.

"I like your swimsuit, Cleopatra," she says.

"I like yours, Garden of Edie."

She sits on the step and runs a hand through her wet hair. When it's wet, it looks jet-black.

"What are you doing this weekend?" I ask. I do a strange pirouette-y thing in the water so that I don't have to look at her reaction.

"That question makes me think I'm doing something with you," she says.

I smile. I cannot help it. "Maybe you are."

"What do you have in mind?"

I do another strange pirouette-y thing. "Well, it happens to be my birthday on Saturday."

"*This* Saturday?" she asks.

I nod, looking at her now, the eye contact making me all kinds of nervous.

"No wonder my mom likes you so much—a fellow Taurus. You guys can bond over being incredibly stubborn."

"You sound like a jealous Scorpio," I say.

She looks at me, shocked. "I know you're smart, but are you also psychic?"

I laugh. "Just a guess."

"Well, anyway. I'm glad you said something. About your birthday. I'd feel like a real asshole if it passed and I had no idea."

"It's really no big deal," I say. Though it is, or could be.

"It's your sixteenth," she says. "That's always a big deal."

"I have a sneaking suspicion that sixteen won't feel that much different from fifteen."

"I beg to differ. As your elder, I can say that I felt a dramatic difference."

I shake my head at her, then duck under the water where I can smile hugely without her seeing.

"So, you're having a party or something?" she asks after I resurface.

I laugh. "Do I seem like a party-having kind of person? I thought you knew me pretty well."

"Well, you're doing *something* to celebrate, right?"

"A small something," I say. "Every year on my birthday, my family does pizza and ice cream cake. Just at the house. It's nothing, really. I just thought you might want to come."

She doesn't jump in with a response, so I keep rambling: "Carter is out of town and I didn't want it to be just my dad and me, because that seems depressing. And—"

She interrupts me: "I'm in."

"Okay. Cool. Yeah."

"I'll bring party hats."

"Please don't."

"And balloons."

I roll my eyes.

"I wanted to warn you that my dad is—"

"Different," she says. "You've established this."

Here it goes.

I say, "I guess what I mean by that is, he's on the autism spectrum. So, he can come across sort of odd sometimes."

Her eyes go big with . . . surprise? Shock? Concern?

"Oh," she says. "Wow. Yeah. I've heard of that."

"It's very mild. He's considered high-functioning. You might not even notice. But if you do notice, that's what it is."

"That's cool," she says, though her tone communicates that she's still considering the coolness of it.

"It's not, really, but I can't do anything about it."

"Like, what will I notice?"

I look up at the sky. It's one of those cloudless days, the sky a crisp blue you only see in paintings.

"He doesn't show a lot of emotion, like, on his face. He speaks very robotically. Sometimes he sounds like he's mad when he's not. It's just the way he talks. It's confusing. I still have to ask him if he's upset about something and he usually doesn't know what I'm talking about."

I dare to meet Edie's eyes.

"He gets fixated on certain things. He likes the dish towels folded a certain way, stuff like that."

"Like OCD?"

"Kind of."

"Has he always been like this?" she asks. She seems truly interested, which is better than truly weirded out.

"Yeah. I mean, I guess. People are born with it. It's not, like, uncommon. I read that there are about as many people on the spectrum as there are Jews in the world."

"Wow, I had no idea."

"Anyway, I've always just known him as Dad, so he's never seemed strange to me. They told me he had it when I was twelve."

Edie nods. "That must have been a trip."

I shrug. "It explained a lot. I'm glad they told me."

"Still, must be hard sometimes."

I shrug again. "Yeah. Isn't everything hard sometimes?"

"Truth," she says.

She launches herself off the step and swims over to me, not as close as the first time, but close enough for me to see the droplets of water migrating down the slope of her nose.

"Was it hard for your mom?" She asks the question tentatively, the appre-hension obvious in her voice.

"My mom?" I ask, buying time.

I haven't told Edie anything about Mom yet, and she has passively allowed the avoidance of the subject. Of course, we can't avoid it forever.

"Yeah, is that why she left . . . or . . . ?"

I submerge myself in the water again, the only avoidance tactic I have. When I come up, she's still there, looking at me expectantly.

"Can we not talk about it right now?"

She nods, once, definitively. "Got it."

I look up at the clock on the wall. It's 4:30 p.m.

"We better get out. I need to dry my hair."

Because Dad doesn't know I'm here, in a hotel pool with a girl I like.

The drive back to school is the most awkwardly silent one yet. It's the Mom Topic, hanging over us, a dark and ominous cloud. When we pull up to the usual dropoff spot, Edie puts the car in Park and says "So, Saturday. We're on?"

It relieves me to know that she's still coming, despite my weird evasive-ness and despite what I told her about Dad.

"Yeah," I say. "No party hats."

She smiles slyly. "I make no promises."

CHAPTER 9

Dave

Most people have heard of black holes and thrown the term around without any real understanding of its scientific meaning. Greg at work once said "Sorry, I fell into a black hole" when someone made him aware that he'd missed a meeting. Interestingly, "spacing out" has the same meaning.

A black hole is a place in space that is so massive that its gravity is so strong that even light cannot get out. Because no light can get out, black holes are invisible. Special telescopes are used to find them. Researchers guesstimate that there could be about 10 million black holes in the Milky Way, or even more. Some are very small—scientists think the smallest black holes are in the range of a millionth of a gram. Some are called "stellar" and can be many times more massive than the sun. There are many of those. The largest black holes are called "supermassive." These black holes are millions or even billions of times as massive as the sun. Scientists have found proof that every large galaxy contains a supermassive black hole at its center. The supermassive black hole at the center of the Milky Way is called Sagittarius. It has a mass equal to about 4 million suns and would fit inside a very large ball that could hold a few million Earths.

Black holes orbit the center of their galaxy, just like stars, so it's not likely that one is headed our way. But if a normal star were headed for us, we'd know it, because we'd see it. With a black hole, we would have little warning.

With their strong gravitational attraction, a black hole wouldn't have to come all that close to Earth to wreak havoc. Just passing through the solar system would distort all of the planets' orbits. Earth could get drawn into an elliptical path that would cause extreme climate swings, or it could be completely ejected from the solar system and go hurtling into deep space.

Like I said, it's unlikely. But aren't all horrific things unlikely? And yet they still happen.

Cleo is pacing the living room, something I have done enough times myself to know that it takes twelve steps to cross the room. I also know that it takes twenty-three steps to get from the kitchen to my home office.

Cleo is also picking at her cuticles, which even I know means she is nervous. She is sixteen years old today. When Jana was alive, Cleo used to ask her to recount the story of her birth. She persisted in this request until the last birthday she had with Jana—her fourteenth. Jana told the same story every year, but Cleo wanted to hear it anyway. I'm not great at visualizing things, seeing scenes in my head, but I can see the scene from that birthday. The two of them were sitting on the couch, Cleo curled into Jana's side in a way that made her look far younger than fourteen. Jana was holding Cleo's hand, her thumb stroking the inside of Cleo's palm. I don't know why I remember this detail. Usually, I cannot remember any details. And I can almost hear Jana telling the story she told every year:

"We were watching *Survivor*. The show was in the Amazon that year. I felt a tightening in my belly and I said to Dad, 'I think that was a contraction.' And he just kind of sat there and nodded like 'Roger that.' When I had a second one, then a third, he went to the kitchen and got a spiral notebook from the junk drawer and sat down next to me, writing down the time and duration of each contraction. By midnight, he'd fallen asleep with the pen in his hand. I didn't understand how he could possibly sleep while knowing we were about to meet you, but your dad's sleep needs have always trumped everything else."

This is true. When I get tired, I power down like a cell phone drained of battery.

"I had contractions all through the night, and by the next morning I was in a lot of pain, so we decided to go to the hospital. When we got there, they said I wasn't far enough along to be admitted, so we walked up and down the hallways, stopping every few minutes so I could grip a railing during a contraction. Finally they admitted me. My contractions started coming closer and closer together and I couldn't take it anymore. My plan had been no epidural, but I was in so much pain. I had instructed Dad beforehand to talk me out of the epidural, so he kept saying, 'Jana, you can do this. No epidural.'"

Whenever she got to this part of the story, she used the robot voice to impersonate me, the robot voice that Cleo has now adopted.

"I started cursing at him and he just stood there, blank-faced. No expression."

At this point, the two of them started laughing until there were tears in their eyes. The blankness of my face during times of crises is—was—a favorite family joke.

"Finally, I think he was so scared of me that he stopped saying 'Jana, no epidural,' and I got my epidural. And for the first time in hours, I opened my eyes—I'd been shutting them tight through all the pain. The nurse said 'Oh, you have blue eyes' and we all started laughing. I was giddy with relief. A couple hours after that, they said I was ready to push. I pushed for just ten minutes and then you came into the world. They took you right to the warming table to check on you, and Dad followed them. He looked so worried."

I *was* worried. I had never experienced childbirth before and it was truly horrifying. Jana had told me not to watch when the baby emerged—not because she was coy, but because she feared I would pass out. I did watch, because I couldn't help myself, and I did almost pass out. I did not expect all the liquid and whatever else that came with the baby. And I did not expect the baby to be covered in so much gunk and to have such a purplish tint to her skin. She looked more alien than human. I would never tell Cleo this, but my first reaction to her was not love but fear. Sometimes, still, that's my reaction to her.

"It took you a few minutes before you started crying. They laid you on my chest and Dad leaned over next to us and the nurse took a photo—the first family photo. Then you latched on to breastfeed for the first time and cut my nipple."

The story always ended with that—the cut nipple.

"I'm sorry I cut your nipple," Cleo said on that last birthday Jana celebrated with her.

And then they laughed again.

Future neighbor Edie is supposed to arrive at five o'clock. It is 4:58 p.m. Cleo is wearing a dress I haven't seen her wear before. It might be something she took from Jana's closet. She insisted on keeping most of Jana's clothes, was downright offended when I initially planned to donate them to Goodwill. I told her it was fine, that I would keep them in my closet, but she took them to her own closet, which is not at all big enough for all of them. She has them sorted in piles on the floor, or crammed into drawers that no longer close properly. Cleo is stubborn, like me. I suppose this is something I can try to find endearing.

"I like the dress," I say.

It's a forced compliment, something The Therapist used to refer to as "a script." I know the right things to say. Sometimes I am just too lazy to say them. My natural inclination would be to not comment on someone's clothing at all, because I do not see the significance in that. But there was significance for Jana. There is probably significance for Cleo.

"Wow, thanks, Dad," Cleo says, clearly surprised by my comment.

She is also wearing makeup. Something on her eyes, something on her lips. In one of our first sessions, The Therapist had Jana and me sit across from each other and asked me, "What do you see when you look at your wife?" I said, "I see that she is wearing makeup." Jana looked at The Therapist and said, "Do you see what I mean?" The Therapist gave her a small nod and said to me, "I mean, what do you see in her *as a person*? In her heart and soul?" I had no idea how to answer that. I mumbled something that clearly did not satisfy the request. Then The Therapist asked Jana to say what she saw in me. She said, "I see a man with a good heart, someone who is very loyal and dependable, a rock." I don't know how she saw all that just looking at me.

"Oh, I think that's her," Cleo says, going to the window and peering behind the curtain. She is right—there is a car coming up the dirt road to our house.

She backs away from the window as if she doesn't want to be seen, and resumes picking at her cuticles. This level of nervousness makes me worry that she has inherited my social anxiety.

"Dad, can you go . . . organize the pizza or something?"

I do not know what this means—organize the pizza?

"Just put some slices on a few plates or something," she says, shooing me away.

I go to the kitchen, as instructed, and stare at the two large boxes—a pepperoni for me (and possibly Edie, depending on her affinity for meat), and cheese for Cleo. It is already sufficiently organized. I take three plates out of the cupboard and set them next to the boxes and then await further instruction.

This is what I overhear in the other room:

"Hey, you're actually here," Cleo says. Her voice sounds different, higher-pitched.

"Of course I'm here, weirdo."

Cleo laughs, not taking any offense to the "weirdo" comment, apparently.

"And, as promised, I brought party hats."

There is more laughter.

"These are ridiculous," Cleo says, still in that different-sounding voice.

There are footsteps across the wood floor, on their way to the kitchen. I stand straighter, then hear Jana's words: *Babe, you're all bug-eyed. Relax.*

When they come into the kitchen, they are walking closely next to each other, their arms bumping into each other. Cleo has a pointy party hat that says IT'S MY FREAKING BIRTHDAY, and Edie has one that says IT'S NOT MY FREAKING BIRTHDAY. There are llamas on the hats, for some reason.

"You must be Mr. Garrison," Edie says, approaching me with hand extended. I try my best not to look bug-eyed.

"I am."

I stick out my hand to meet hers, though I'd really rather not because of the potential germ transfer. I figure I can wash my hands shortly.

"I brought a hat for you too," she says, taking the hat that's in her other hand and offering it to me.

When I look at Cleo, she's scrunching her nose. She knows I do not want to wear this hat.

"Dad, you don't have to—"

"I can wear it."

Her attempt to spare me from discomfort is appreciated, but I know a daughter should not have to make these kinds of attempts on behalf of her father. Her father is supposed to be able to handle himself.

When I put the stupid thing on my head, I immediately hate the way the elastic band cuts into the underside of my chin.

"Oh my god, I have to get a picture of this for Carter," Cleo says, coming next to me and motioning for Edie to do the same. She does, so that I am standing with Cleo on one side of me and Edie on the other, feeling extremely absurd and sweaty.

Cleo reaches into a pocket on the side of her dress and produces her phone, like a magician producing a rabbit from up his sleeve, and says "Okay, on three."

She holds the phone out in front of us and counts: "One, two, three."

Then she presses the button and captures a handful of photos. She steps away from me to analyze them and Edie does the same. I go to the sink to wash my hands.

"You guys hungry?" Cleo asks, looking from Edie to me.

"If the birthday girl wants to eat, let's eat," Edie says.

With that, the three of us take our respective plates and retrieve the slices we desire from the boxes. I see that Edie is not a vegetarian, which makes me like her a bit more, though I am still not pleased that she has intruded on our family birthday celebration. Yes, I allowed her presence, but it still bothers me. The fact that she will soon live so close bothers me more.

I know Edie and Cleo are done eating when they each crumple up their paper napkins and place them on their plates. I take this as my cue to clear their plates, and my own, and then tend to the pizza, which now requires organizing. Half of the slices from the cheese pizza remain in the box; there are only two pepperoni pieces remaining. I place the cheese slices in one Ziploc bag, the pepperoni in another. I know Cleo will not appreciate the pepperoni commingling with the cheese, and I'm not a fan of commingling food myself. I rinse the three plates and put them in the dishwasher, then go to the freezer to take out the ice cream cake. It needs approximately ten minutes to soften to the desired consistency.

"Can I give you your gift now?" Edie says to Cleo.

This is not the time we do gifts. Gifts come after cake, never before.

Cleo deviates from the agreed-upon order of things and say, "Sure!" Her enthusiasm indicates that her allegiance to tradition is not as strong as I had previously thought.

Edie gets up from her chair and goes back into the living room. She must have placed her gift there. When she returns, she has a very small gift bag hanging from her index finger. She places it in front of Cleo, who sits straighter at the table, a smile spreading across her face. Generally, I am not that affected by others' emotions, but I am affected by Cleo's happiness. And her sadness. It is hard to remain perturbed when I see how happy she seems in this moment.

"Wow, thanks," she says.

This gratitude seems premature. She doesn't even know what's in the bag. Judging by the way Edie held the bag with one finger, it could be a paper airplane for all Cleo knows.

She paws at the tissue paper, removing it from the top of the bag. I hate when people take their time opening gifts, making a show of the reveal. She removes a piece of paper, folded in half, and continues to paw through the tiny bag.

"That's all there is," Edie says. She's smiling, seemingly not embarrassed by her folded-paper gift.

Cleo opens the paper. I watch her eyes scan it. Then she looks up, that smile still on her face.

"How cool," she says.

She turns to me, waving the paper in the air. "Dad, she got me tickets to the Ghost Walk in San Juan Capistrano."

Cleo has mentioned this Ghost Walk before. It's a nighttime tour of historic sights, paired with ghost stories. It's something Jana would have taken her to. Jana didn't *believe* in ghosts, but she was always game for suspending disbelief. I, on the other hand, do not believe in ghosts and, as a general rule of life, am *unwilling* to suspend disbelief. In my opinion, a "Ghost Walk" is a shameless attempt to take money from gullible people.

"That's very nice," I say. A script.

She gives me a nod that confirms I've said the right thing, then turns back to Edie. "So, two tickets," she says. "Did you want to come with me or . . . ?"

Edie laughs. "Well, yeah, I kind of hoped the second ticket would be for me. But they're your tickets; so if you want to take Carter or—"

"I want to go with you," Cleo says, a bold assertion.

"Cool, yeah, let's pick a date. Maybe next weekend?" Edie says. Then Edie turns to me. "I can drive us if that's okay with you, Mr. Garrison."

It's not okay with me.

"Cleo and I can talk about it later," I say.

Cleo rolls her eyes.

There is a prolonged silence. I know, from lifelong analysis of human behavior to better understand how not to seem strange, that this silence is not socially acceptable. The Therapist told me once that I had "obviously learned how to be in the world" and that I must have "cultivated adaptive strategies." I must break the silence.

"Are you ready for cake?" I ask Cleo.

She goes from looking glum to smiling. I cannot decipher whether the smile is genuine or fake.

"Sure, Dad."

I'm relieved to have the task of tending to the cake, putting the "1" and "6" candles in it, lighting them. I carry it to the table and commence singing "Happy birthday." Edie joins in wholeheartedly, and I have to admit that it's nice to have another contributory voice. Last year, it was just my voice, and the song couldn't help but be sad, despite my attempts to infuse the verse with compensatory joy.

Cleo closes her eyes and blows out the candles, and we all clap, even Cleo. Jana used to clap for her own birthday songs too. She said her culmination of another trip around the sun deserved hearty applause. *I made it another year*, she used to say. Sometimes I wonder if she knew her life would be cut short. She had the gratitude of someone who knew her days were numbered. But, of course, there is no way she could have known. She never professed to have any psychic abilities. And I do not believe in such abilities either. Psychics fall into the same category as ghosts and astrology. And therapy.

I cut the cake because I am always the one who cuts the cake. I enjoy the precision of it—creating eight equal-sized triangular pieces. It always unnerves me to go to a party and see someone cutting a sheet cake willy-nilly—a huge square here, a rectangle sliver there. They pass the pieces around on small plates and the recipients must settle for a size they do not desire, or trade with someone else. It would be much simpler and less mentally taxing if there was a standard size we could all expect. I told Jana that I wanted to go on that TV show *Shark Tank* with a metal device that one could press down into a sheet cake to extract a perfect square. Jana said, "Like a cookie cutter but for cake," and I said, "Yes!" She was not as enthusiastic about the idea as I was.

I give a slice to Cleo and a slice to Edie. I take one for myself too, then stand against the kitchen counter to eat.

"You can sit with us," Cleo says.

I prefer to eat standing, on the outskirts of social situations. Whenever I tried to eat standing up during family dinner time, Jana got mad. "It's weird," she said. "You're like a horse." So I forced myself to sit most of the time, at least for the duration of the actual eating.

"That's okay," I say, remaining where I am. Like a horse.

I finish my cake in six succinct bites. Edie and Cleo appear to be in a contest to see who can take the longest amount of time to consume cake. I decide to go to the living room to watch *The Office* while they finish.

The moment I turn on the show, I can hear their voices in the kitchen picking up volume—talking, laughing. My exit seems to have intensified their dialogue. I try to pay attention to the episode—the one with the luau-themed warehouse party—but it's difficult with their chatter. The cat comes to sit next to me, purring in anticipation of my petting him. He knows I always pet him. *I prefer animals to humans.* That was on the autism assessment. It was—still is—difficult for me to understand how someone could prefer humans to animals. Animals are very simple and largely predictable. It is not difficult to gain their affection. They do not have complicated emotional needs.

I watch another episode—the traveling salesman one—before Edie and Cleo come into the living room, heading for the door. I stand from the couch.

"You heading out?" I say to Edie.

"I am," she says. She sticks out her hand again, and I have no choice but to shake it. "Thank you for having me over so I could share Cleo's birthday with you."

Her persistent eye contact is unsettling. Many people with The Label struggle with eye contact, but I have not had this particular difficulty, generally. "It's a *spectrum*," The Therapist told us. "No two people on it are exactly the same. In fact, they say, 'If you've met one person with autism, you've met one person with autism.'" Now, though, I am having a noticeable difficulty with eye contact.

"Right, yes, thank you for coming," I say.

I drop her hand and instruct myself to smile.

"I'll text you later," Cleo says as she opens the door for Edie. I don't know why she would text her later. What more could they possibly have to say to each other?

Edie stands on the welcome mat, as if waiting for something. Cleo gives her a wave and says, "Okay, then, see you soon."

She watches Edie go to her car. If I'm not mistaken, she appears . . . what's the word? *Enamored?* It's quite possible I'm misreading this. I have never seen Cleo enamored with her friends before—and for good reason: most of them have been dreadfully annoying. She was enamored with Jana. She looked at Jana in a way she'll never look at me. I was always fine with that, just grateful that Cleo had someone to look at that way. And I guess that someone is now Edie.

It's better that she's enamored with this new friend than with a boy. I'm not mentally prepared for Cleo to have anything resembling a love life. If she's had crushes already, I have not been privy to the existence of them. Jana was probably privy to them. She dealt with that aspect of parenting. And, frankly, with most aspects of parenting.

The engine of Edie's car starts and Cleo closes the door. She has the soft smile of a drunk on her face when she goes to the couch and sits on the cushion that has long been designated her cushion. I sit on my designated cushion.

"Come here, Poppy," Cleo says to the cat, and he goes to her, curling up in her lap and purring so loud I can hear it from my cushion.

Cleo juts her chin toward the TV, says, "This is a funny one."

She has seen it, more than once. I have subjected her to *The Office* since it first aired when she was two years old. I was an early adopter of the series because I'd been a fan of the original BBC show.

"Did you have fun?" I ask.

"I did, Dad. Thanks," she says. "I know you don't like visitors. You were cool."

Nobody has ever described me as "cool" before.

"Well, I'm glad you had a happy birthday," I say. "I do have a gift for you."

She looks surprised, but I know it's not genuine. She cannot be surprised. I get her a gift every year. Jana always insisted that I get my own gift. We would give her gifts from the two of us too (always procured by Jana), but Jana thought it was important that Cleo have a unique relationship with me alone. Like I said, it's as if she knew she would not always be around.

I reach behind the couch where I have hidden Cleo's gift. It is a box wrapped in red paper that I found in Jana's Gift Cabinet above the washer and dryer. Where most people would keep sensible things like detergent, she stored rolls of wrapping paper and gift bags and ribbon. "It's the only cabinet wide enough to fit the rolls," she told me, by means of explanation. To accommodate this, she put the detergent in the hallway closet, with the towels and sheets. It always bothered me and, yet, I have not deviated from this organizational system. She has been gone more than a year and the detergent is still in the wrong cabinet.

Cleo unwraps the box carefully, not tearing the paper but removing the tape and pulling back the paper to reveal the box. It is a repurposed cardboard Amazon box that arrived the other day with Cleo's monthly supply of vanilla body spray.

She removes the tape holding the box closed and peers into the box. I have not wrapped the gift inside the box because that seems like entirely too much wrapping.

She removes it and holds it up, as if inspecting it in better light. She looks both perplexed and hopeful.

"Is this a car key?" she says, still holding the key up in the air.

It is a car key, but not for a new car. I see now how I may have created confusion.

"It is. For the Escape," I say. That's my car—a Ford Escape.

Her shoulders slump.

"Oh," she says. Even I can tell she's disappointed.

"I thought it was important for you to have your own key, in case you need to drive yourself somewhere and I'm not available . . . or able."

"Able?"

"If something happens to me. . . ."

"During the apocalypse?"

"Just in general," I say. "I think it's good for you to have access to the car."

She twists her mouth to one side. "Okay," she says. "Thanks, Dad."

She stands from the couch, holding the cat in her arms.

"Wait," I say.

She turns.

I pat the cushion next to me, the cushion that used to be designated as Jana's.

Cleo sits. The cat jumps out of her arms, having had his fill of human interaction.

"I wanted to tell you about the day you were born," I say.

I didn't do this last year. I wasn't thinking straight last year. It was too soon.

Cleo lets herself recline into the back of the couch, her back slouched, her arms at her side. She uses her index fingers to pick at the cuticles of her thumbs.

"We were watching *Survivor*. The show was in the Amazon that year," I say.

Cleo is already starting to cry. I hate seeing people cry. I cannot relate to their emotion, and I'm aware I must seem cold and unfeeling in comparison. I never know the right way to respond. It is not in my nature to hug, and while I am adept at writing words, saying the appropriate ones on the spot is not a strong suit.

"Your mom told me she had a contraction, and I said, 'Roger that.'"

Cleo puts her hand on my forearm. I think she is going to tell me to stop. I am not doing it right. I am not Jana. I'll never be Jana.

She leans her body against mine, rests her head on my shoulder. Then she says, "Keep going."

CHAPTER 10

Cleo

Monday after school, Dad takes me to the San Clemente DMV for my driving test. I wasn't worried until Edie told me that she had failed her test the first time because she'd looked down at her lap when her phone (which was in her pocket) made a strange noise. It turned out to be an Amber Alert notification.

"I'm sure you'll pass," Edie told me at lunch. "Just make sure to turn off your phone."

Dad is quiet the entire drive to San Clemente, which is not out of the ordinary. If he doesn't have anything of practical importance to say, he doesn't say anything. It's like he's immune to the social pressures the rest of us feel to fill silences.

"Do you want me to come inside with you?" he asks when we get there.

"No, I'm good."

He says he'll wait on the bench in front of the building. When I go inside, I can see him there through the window. He looks like Forrest Gump. That movie came out before I was born, but it was one of Mom's favorites, so I've seen it a few times. Forrest reminds me of Dad in some ways. They are both . . . different.

The guy in charge of my driving test is a middle-aged man who is completely bald. He has a DMV identification badge attached to the chest pocket of his shirt, and it says his name is Larry, which seems somehow perfect for a middle-aged bald guy who works at the DMV.

"Okay," he says, looking at his clipboard. He has a clipboard! "Cleo?"

He looks up.

"That's me," I say.

I want to text Edie so bad about Larry and his clipboard, which reminds me to give my phone to Dad.

He's looking at something on his phone when I approach. "Here, hold this," I tell him, setting my phone on his lap. I can see he's playing Words with Friends, which breaks my heart every time I see it because that's what he used to play with Mom all the time. To her, it was just a fun way to pass time. He was serious about it, though, hemming and hawing for hours over which letters to play. He used to spend money—*actual* money, not game money—for the ability to play without ads popping up. He was *that* serious. He usually won. I don't know who he plays now. Strangers, maybe. Or bots. All those app games have bots made to look like real players to occupy people like Dad. If I think about it too hard, I could cry.

"Wish me luck," I tell him.

"Good luck."

Twenty minutes later, I sit in the driver's seat while Larry the DMV guy makes notes on his clipboard. I can't think of anything I messed up during the test, but still I'm nervous. Maybe he's docking points for how tightly I gripped the steering wheel.

"Well, Cleo Garrison, I am happy to report that you passed," he says.

He smiles a no-teeth smile, opens the passenger-side door, and lets himself out. I follow him back toward the DMV building. Dad looks up from his phone when we approach, and I give him two thumbs up. He does the same back, though his face remains unexpressive. People on the spectrum are incredibly confusing. It's not their fault, but still.

A few minutes later, I am in possession of my California provisional driver's license. I wave the paper in front of Dad's face and say, "I guess I'm driving us home."

"I guess you are," he says. His tone says he is not pleased with this circumstance, but his face displays a smile (forced, no doubt). Like I said, confusing.

We get in the car, and I start the engine with the key Dad gifted me for my birthday. It was an odd birthday gift, but definitely not the oddest birthday gift I've ever received from him. Some memorable ones: a mug with a drawing of a dinosaur and the words TEA REX; a multiuse pen that includes a ruler and a screwdriver; a purse made of recycled tire rubber that Mom says he saw at the farmer's market and thought was so cool (it actually was, or is; I still have it). My favorite odd gift was a framed picture of stars in outer space with my name at the top of it. "I named a star after you, and that's the star," he says. "Well, it's supposed to be. It could all be a scam." It was the sweetest thing. I still have the framed picture on my nightstand.

My phone buzzes with a text—likely Edie or Carter. I don't look at it because I know that would be enough for Dad to revoke my driving privileges for life.

I pull out of the DMV parking lot and onto the road.

"Dad, can we talk about me going to this Ghost Walk thing with Edie?"

It was a strategic decision to have this conversation now, while I'm driving. Driving means I can avoid having to look Dad in the face when talking about Edie. It's like I can't control my facial muscles when I talk about her. I just smile like an idiot.

"What do you want to talk about?" he says.

I can almost hear his teeth grinding.

"I mean, I'd like to . . . *go*. With her. In her car, preferably."

"I know nothing of her driving proficiency."

I roll my eyes, even though I know he can't see them. "Well, you know *my* driving proficiency. What if I drive?"

"I've told you I don't feel comfortable with you driving the car while I'm back home without access to a vehicle. If something were to happen—"

I grip the steering wheel as tightly as I did during my driving test.

"If what were to happen, Dad? There is Uber or Lyft or whatever. You could ride your bike if things were truly dire," I say. "It seems very unlikely that the apocalypse would happen in the two-hour window of this Ghost Walk."

He is quiet, and I fear I have really pissed him off.

Finally, he speaks: "It's only two hours?"

"Yes, Dad. Two hours. Four episodes of *The Office*."

"Let me think about it."

I feel a rush of anticipatory giddiness. I know he'll say yes.

When we get home, Dad turns on the TV to do what he does every night, and I go straight to my room so I can text Edie in peace.

Two things. One, I can drive a car legally in the state of CA. Two, I think my dad is going to say OK to the Ghost Walk this weekend.

She texts back right away with two celebratory party-hat emojis, then:

I don't know which is more exciting, TBH.

Me: I do. The Ghost Walk. Duh.

Her: OK, that's what I think too, but I didn't want to say that and sound weird.

Me: So you let me take the risk of sounding weird?

Her: Duh.

Me: I mean, don't get too excited until he tells me for sure, but he seemed to be leaning toward yes.

Her: OK. Fingers crossed for continued leaning.

I text the crossed-fingers emoji and then go to the kitchen to heat up a frozen burrito.

The next day at school, I go to Ms. Murray's office at lunchtime for our weekly chat, and before I even sit down she asks, "What's with this glow of yours?"

I sit. "Glow?"

She eyes me very suspiciously, brows furrowed. "Don't be coy."

I have told her that Edie and I "study together" a couple times a week, but I have tried to be, as she says, coy. I believe in the concept of jinx, and I'm quite certain that the moment I speak of Edie as if she is more than just an acquaintance-friend who needs help with math, she will become even less than that. *You live with a lot of fear*, Ms. Murray told me once, months ago. She didn't say it like there was something wrong with me, just as a fact, like *You have brown hair*.

"Maybe it's my just-got-my-driver's-license glow," I say.

She smiles and pulls out the top drawer of her desk. Then she takes out a small gift-wrapped box and hands it to me.

"Sixteen," she says. "It's a big birthday."

I can feel myself blushing, so I look away. I don't want her to know how much it means to me that she remembered my birthday.

"What is it?" I say, stupidly.

"I'm pretty sure you are capable of discovering the answer to that question."

The box is wrapped in a thick, expensive kind of paper, not the cheap stuff Mom used to get from the Dollar Store. She loved the Dollar Store, said she couldn't rationalize spending anything more than a dollar on items that would get one use. She got all our party supplies and most of our holiday decorations there—flimsy plastic Jack-o-lanterns, Christmas tree ornaments made of Styrofoam.

I unwrap the box carefully, thinking I'll save the paper for something, though I know it will sit in the drawer of my desk at home and serve no purpose but to remind me of Ms. Murray's thoughtfulness.

Inside the box is a little ceramic succulent pot with a girl painted on it, her hands holding up her chin as if she is in deep thought. She kind of looks like me—something about her long nose, her small lips.

"It reminded me of you," she says. "And I suppose I should have put a plant inside, but I cannot be trusted with plants."

I look up, despite the fact that I'm still blushing. "Thank you."

"You are welcome." She sits back in her chair. "So, is your glow really about the driver's license?"

Nothing gets by her.

I cave and tell her about Edie coming to my house on Saturday for my birthday.

"That's huge," she says.

I shrug. "Yeah, I don't know, I guess."

"It is. I remember the first time a date came to my house. When the poor kid came inside, my dad was sitting on the couch with his shotgun, which I'd never even known he owned until that day."

I laugh. "Well, my dad's greatest weapon is his weirdness."

"But he let you have a guest," she says.

I nod. "He's let Carter come over a couple times, so it's not totally unprecedented."

"Still, I'm sure it's disconcerting for him."

Disconcerting. I like when Ms. Murray uses big words with me, fully expecting that I will understand, as if I'm one of her friends, an equal.

"Probably," I say. "He did seem, like, super nervous."

"I'm sure it's hard for him to have guests come to the house, outsiders attempting to be close to people he loves," she says.

I crack a smile remembering Dad referring to our soon-to-be-neighbors as *interlopers*.

"Yeah, I know."

Because I do know. I realize what she's getting at. Mom brought her friend, Mirai, into our lives, and then Mom died. The two things aren't really related—what happened was a freak thing—but to Dad they are. *People on the spectrum gravitate toward patterns. They look for control in their lives.* I read that online somewhere.

"But you had a good birthday?" Ms. Murray asks.

When she smiles, lines gather around her eyes, and I know women aren't supposed to like lines like that, but I do. They make her look warm and friendly, and I can't imagine her without them.

"I did," I say. "I really did."

"You seem happy."

The way she says it makes me think this is a first for her, that she hasn't seen me happy since she's known me. Maybe she hasn't. Have I been happy for even one moment since Mom died? I have laughed with Carter. I have felt the rush of getting an A on a math test. I have had flickers of happy, like the little sparks emitted from a lighter before it finally achieves a flame. Maybe now there is a flame.

"I am," I say. Then quickly add: "For now."

Because even though I'm just a kid, I've already learned how quickly flames can go out.

CHAPTER 11

Dave

Some say it's already too late to reverse climate change: It's happening, and ultimately it will be the death of us.

I admit that, like most people, I didn't give much attention to climate change when I first heard of it. I watched Al Gore's documentary and it disturbed me, but I was consumed by other more-pressing concerns then—a wife who seemed endlessly irritated with me, a toddler who seemed endlessly irritated with everything, to name a couple. I figured that "they" (the government, scientists, people more powerful than me) would make decisions in the face of this dooming data and right the ship, so to speak. But, of course, "they" are never as competent as I like to think they are, and the ship is always more unwieldy and massive than I realize. I have often said that high-functioning people with ASD should run the world. We are good with tasks. We are not distracted by emotion. We make decisions with our heads. We get things done. It does not surprise me that one of the most influential climate activists, teenager Greta Thunberg, has Asperger's. It also does not surprise me that some people write her off as hysterical.

The Earth has experienced five mass extinctions before the one we are living through now (yes, I believe we are going extinct). About 450 million years ago, 86 percent of all species died. Seventy million years later, 75 percent. one hundred twenty-five million years later, 96 percent. fifty million years later, 80 percent. And 135 million years after that, 75 percent. Most of us think that asteroids are the cause of mass extinctions because that's what happened to the dinosaurs. But the truth is that the mass extinction that killed the dinosaurs was *the only one* that did not involve climate change due to greenhouse gases.

The fact is this: for the last 200,000 years or so that we have existed, it took until the mid-1800s for us to reach our first one billion humans. Since then, we have added nearly seven billion more humans, and we are expanding at the rate of 80 million additional humans per year. A safe population to sustain the Earth's resources is between one and two billion. So we are already way past sustainable levels.

An increase in the number of humans means more greenhouse gas emissions, which means more global warming. Scientists predict that we are on track to see the planet warm by 3 to 4 degrees Celsius (5 to 7 degrees Fahrenheit). That might not sound like much, but the difference in global average surface temperatures between the depths of the last ice age and today is only around 4 to 7 degrees. And in the depths of that ice age, Chicago was under about a half mile of ice.

Even if the Earth warms by "only" 2 degrees, there will be catastrophic effects. At that temperature, the ice sheets would begin to collapse. Cities along the equator would become unlivable.

Over the next few decades, several hundred million people will be exposed to dangerous climate-related risks—droughts, flooding, famine. Some will have to migrate to other areas, leading to increased problems with overpopulation, competition for resources, and even wars. There have been more than 20 million climate refugees since 2008, and the United Nations projects 200 million by 2050. For context, that was the entire world population at the peak of the Roman Empire.

A warmer planet could also assist the spread of infectious diseases by providing a more suitable climate for parasites and by spreading the range of pathogens that were previously confined to the tropics. There could be crop diseases that would further exacerbate famine.

Again, this is all based on a temperature increase of 1.5 to 2 degrees Celsius. To stay on the 1.5-degree path, we need to decrease global emissions of greenhouse gases by around 60 percent by 2030. So far, we haven't been able to decrease global emissions by even one percent.

The thing is that scientists don't know where exactly the tipping point lies. If the global temperature increases slightly, that leads to ice melting faster. People don't realize what melting Arctic ice means. It's not just dying polar bears. Less ice means less sunlight reflected back to the sun and more absorbed by the planet, which gets even warmer as a result. The Arctic permafrost contains nearly two trillion tons of carbon, and when that ice thaws and the carbon is released, it may evaporate as methane, which is thirty-four times more powerful than carbon dioxide when it comes to warming the planet. A hotter planet is bad for plant life. Plants serve to absorb carbon and turn it into oxygen; not having them means even hotter temperatures, fewer plants, and on and on.

A warmer planet means more water vapor in the atmosphere, and water vapor is a greenhouse gas, so that means more warming still. Warmer oceans can absorb less heat, which means more stays in the air. The warmer oceans are not good for phytoplankton, which do for the ocean what plants do on land—consume carbon and produce oxygen. That leads to more carbon, and more warming.

If it sounds like I'm going in circles, it's because I am. The point is that things can get out of hand very quickly. According to the World Wildlife Fund, more than half of all the world's vertebrate animals have gone extinct in just the last forty years. This does not bode well for humans.

Is it possible that Earth will end up like Venus, where the high on a typical day is 900 degrees Fahrenheit? Could this happen in my lifetime? In Cleo's lifetime? Nobody knows for sure.

Climate change is one of the only interests of mine that Cleo does not find absurd or boring. She says that the solution is for all of us to go vegetarian, with a vegan diet being the ideal. I know there is science to support this theory. We kill and eat nearly 50 billion animals every year just to feed ourselves. These animals, in turn, need to be fed, housed, transported, and processed. They require vast amounts of land to feed them and an enormous quantity of water (which is mostly nonrenewable and will eventually run out). Eating animals is tied very closely to destroying the planet. I know this, and yet I still enjoy a good hamburger, which makes me question if I really do make all decisions with my head after all.

———————

Last night, I had a dream, which is strange because I do not dream. Jana didn't believe me when I first told her this. *Everyone has dreams. You just don't remember them.* But I was very sure that I did not dream. *Well, then, maybe you're a psychopath.*

When we saw The Therapist and I acquired The Label (which, I'm aware, is a better label than *psychopath*), I learned it's common for people with ASD not to dream.

"Dreaming is an act of the imagination, and many people with ASD struggle with imagination," she said.

In retrospect, I feel that this assessment was unfair—or, at least, incomplete. While I cannot imagine another person's feelings and thoughts, I can imagine the intricacies of a 1:18 scale 1970 Plymouth GTX.

"Struggle with imagination?" Jana parroted back. I could tell she was doubtful. She was probably thinking about my intimate knowledge of model cars too.

"Meaning they can be very much in the world of facts, very literal."

Jana nodded, and The Therapist looked at me.

"Like, Dave, have you ever imagined what Jana is doing during her workday?"

"What do you mean?" I asked.

"Do you ever, say, look at the clock at noon and think 'she must be having lunch'? Or text her after a work meeting that you know she was nervous about?"

I shrugged. "Not really."

The lack of "check-in" texts had been a grievance Jana had expressed soon after going back to work after having Cleo. When I asked her to specify how many texts she wanted to receive, and at which time points, she exhaled so heavily that her bangs fluttered. She replied, "If you have to make it a *thing*, don't do it at all." I came to assume that things like this were why men found women confusing, in general. It's like Greg at work said once when complaining about his on-again-off-again girlfriend: "Bitches be cray." (To be clear, I understood the sentiment but would never use such crass language.)

"Not only does he not text, he doesn't even like to *ask* me about my day when I get home from work," Jana interjected.

They both looked at me, these intimidating women.

"I guess," I replied, "I figure that our day together starts when we are both in the same physical location. I do not think about what goes on at her workplace, because I do not work there."

Jana sighed. The Therapist remained stoic.

"But it would be less about the actual work and more about who she is as a person, going through her day," The Therapist said after a minute.

Jana nodded emphatically.

Honestly, this concept had never occurred to me. Jana often said some variation of "I feel like you don't *see* me." And this therapy session explained more what she meant. I did not *see* her. I did not imagine her. I did not envision her day or her thoughts or her feelings. It had simply never occurred to me to do so.

"Do you think about Cleo during the day?" Jana asked me. "Like, do you think, 'oh, she's taking a nap at daycare now'?"

I looked at her: "No. *You* do that?"

"Yes, Dave, I do," she said.

I glanced at The Therapist for quick confirmation that my wife was, in fact, "cray," but she did not nod or smile or display any other sign of allegiance with me.

"What I'd like to do is model a conversation between two neurotypicals," The Therapist said, talking to me but maintaining eye contact with Jana. I still hate that term—*neurotypical*. With The Label, I am considered *atypical*, which the thesaurus says is synonymous with *odd, peculiar, strange*. All those things I've felt about myself since childhood, confirmed.

"Jana, how has your day gone so far?" The Therapist asked Jana.

Jana uncrossed and re-crossed her legs, sitting up straighter on the couch. "Oh, well, Cleo was a handful this morning, so I've been frazzled. It took a while to persuade her to put on her shoes and then I had to bribe her with a gummy bear to get in the car. I ended up getting to work late and having to run in to a meeting. And then I had to leave early from another meeting to get here on time. So, frazzled. That's how my day has been."

The Therapist looked at me and said, "Now I'll act as if I'm her partner, okay?"

I thought she was going to deepen her voice in an attempt to sound male, but she did not.

"I'm sorry you've been frazzled. Sounds like you've had a busy day, ping-ponging all over the place. How's the rest of your workday look?"

Jana said, "Do you really want me to answer, or . . . ?"

The Therapist did that strange thing of answering Jana while looking at me: "I think that's good for a start. Dave, what are your thoughts on that interaction?"

"I don't think anybody actually talks like that," I said. "Except on television shows."

"No, Dave, that's how most people talk," Jana said.

Even I could tell she was upset.

The Therapist put her hands up, as if to show she was not carrying a weapon.

"Dave, for neurotypicals, such dialogue is considered a part of intimacy. They share and process feelings."

My first thought: *What a waste of time.*

Wisely, I did not say this.

In retrospect, I suppose I thought that Jana was like me in thinking that this type of "intimacy" was unnecessary. And I suppose this assumption is another example of my self-centeredness.

"Are you even *interested* in my feelings?" Jana asked.

I could see her looking at me out of the corner of my eye, but I kept my gaze fixed on The Therapist. The quaver of Jana's voice suggested that there might be tears coming; I did not want to see those.

Was I interested in her feelings?

The truth: Not really.

The truth: I'm not interested in feelings, categorically. It was never personal to Jana.

"I'm interested in what's important to you," I said.

The Therapist nodded.

"That's where we need to start," she said. "With that sentiment."

She began to stand from her chair, signaling the end of the session.

"People with autism spectrum disorder can learn," she said, looking back and forth from Jana to me. "What Jana needs may not always come naturally for you, but as long as you are interested in trying to meet her needs, progress is possible."

Jana stood, and I followed suit.

The Therapist led us to her door.

"The goal is to right the ship one degree every day, so it's back on course in the direction you two both want to go," she said.

Right the ship.

"Speaking of which, I want you both to think about that direction. Make a list of what's important to you in an ideal marriage. We'll discuss next time."

I did not realize how unhappy Jana was in our marriage until her friend Mirai started coming over and I overheard them talking. Which brings me back to the dream I had last night. I feel I must state that I do not support people sharing their dreams with others. When I was in the company kitchen getting my morning tea and someone (usually this obnoxious woman named Heather) came in and said, "I had the weirdest dream last night," I could not disappear fast enough. Jana and Cleo loved sharing their dreams—describing them, analyzing them. I never understood the allure. Dreams are not reality. They are completely nonsensical.

That said, I do think the dream I had last night must have some inherent meaning. I would probably need to consult The Therapist to decipher it, which is not something I am interested in doing. I figure maybe I can interpret it myself by writing it out, assessing it as I would a math problem.

In the dream, the scene was exactly as it had been the night Edie came to the house. Edie, Cleo, and I were in the kitchen. I was cutting the cake, placing the slices on three individual plates. When I took Edie's and Cleo's plates to the table, Edie turned around to thank me and I saw it wasn't Edie at all. It was Mirai. With her long dark hair and the beaded bracelets on her wrist. She was smiling at me.

That's it. Then I woke up.

I try not to think much about Mirai. *You need to work on containing your anxieties.* The Therapist said that to me once. After Jana died, I imagined taking a little ball with the word MIRAI on it and placing that ball in a container, then screwing the lid on nice and tight. In my mind, the container is glass, like the Mason jars Jana used to buy to hold flour and sugar. There are other balls in it, balls marked with SUPERVOLCANO and GLOBAL WARMING.

Sometimes, though, I can't help but think about Mirai, about how things would be different if she'd never come into our lives.

Jana met Mirai at work. So many problems seemed to originate at Jana's work. After all, it was at work that Jana learned about Asperger's (via that coworker with the son who was diagnosed). What if I had been a husband who demanded that his wife focus solely on homemaking and childrearing? If that had been the case, Jana would still be here (unless, of course, some other tragedy ended up befalling us).

I never had any desire to limit Jana's life, though. A part of me understood that she needed people and things beyond me to feel fulfilled. If you had asked me if I wanted to be her everything, I would have said yes. Once, The Therapist asked me, "Do you ever get jealous when you witness Jana interacting with her friends?" And I admitted that I did. The depth of their conversation, their connection—it baffled me. I understood that to be everything to her, I would have to offer this depth, and I knew I could not. I was not even interested in it, if I'm honest. I knew all of this before I was given The Label. "You are like a restaurant with a limited menu," The

Therapist explained, "and your wife has varied tastes." That was fair. That summed it up.

Mirai came into our lives in the summer of 2017. I remember this so precisely because the first time she came over, it was ninety-something degrees outside (which was unusually hot for the beachside community where we lived then) and our air conditioning was not working. It was a Saturday. I had been tinkering with the damn AC unit in the side yard all day, while Cleo (fourteen years old at the time) complained incessantly about her boredom before resorting to collapsing on the couch and watching a show about sharks. Jana had said she was going to lunch and a movie with a friend from work, which was something she did somewhat regularly. What she did not do regularly was bring the friend back to our house. Most of the time, Jana's friends existed in another world, separate from me. She probably knew I preferred it this way.

I heard the two of them—Jana and her friend—come into the kitchen because I had all the windows open while I worked outside.

"Cleo, this is my friend Mirai," I heard Jana say.

I could feel the subtle increase in my blood pressure as I contemplated the necessity of my interaction with this Mirai person.

"Oh, hi," Cleo said. "Nice to meet you."

"Nice to meet you too," Mirai said. Her voice was sing-songy. "I've heard so much about you."

"Mirai and I work together," Jana said. "She does accounting."

"Your mom says you're a math whiz," Mirai said.

Cleo gave a little laugh. "I don't know . . . "

"You're better at math than I'll ever be," Jana said.

Which was true.

"Mom, most people are better at math than you'll ever be," Cleo said.

I smiled as I listened to the three of them laugh.

"Do you want anything to drink? I brewed some iced tea yesterday," Jana said.

"That would be wonderful," Mirai said.

"Clee, where's Dad?" Jana asked.

Part of me hoped Cleo would lie, say that I was out, at the store or something. After all, Cleo was well aware of my proclivities and anxieties—all my -ies.

"He's trying to fix the AC," she said with a sigh.

I was disappointed in her failure to save me. I had this nasty habit of forgetting that she was just a kid.

At that, the sliding door in the kitchen opened and the two women stepped into the side yard. I looked up and feigned surprise.

"Oh, hello!" I said, with too much enthusiasm. Sometimes I overcompensate.

"Babe, this is my friend Mirai," Jana said as they walked over to me.

I was surprised to find a woman who appeared to be Indian. When I'd overheard her talking inside, I hadn't detected even the slightest accent. I stuck out my hand and she took it. Her handshake was very gentle, her hand almost limp. Weak handshakes are a pet peeve of mine, but her smile compensated for this. She seemed a bit shy, which was a relief to me. I'm deeply discomfited by highly sociable people.

"Dave?" she said. "I've heard so much about you."

She was pretty in an exotic kind of way. I do not know if that's a politically correct term—exotic. That's just the word that came to mind when I first saw her. She had long black hair that she had tied in a ponytail that hung over one shoulder. Her eyes were too big for her face, like the eyes of a baby.

(Fun fact: At birth, a baby's eye is about 75 percent the size of an adult eye. It's these kinds of facts that torment me on a regular basis. They are always on the tip of my tongue, and I must exercise great restraint to avoid sharing them at inappropriate times.)

I knew I was expected to tell Mirai that I had heard a lot about her too, but I had not. Or if Jana had mentioned her, I did not remember. There were many times when I was guilty of zoning out while Jana shared with me the details of her day. I had learned—effusive thanks to The Therapist (note: sarcasm)—that it was important for me to actively listen as Jana shared about her day. Most of the time, I admit that much of my listening was not *active*. It was rather lazy.

"It's nice to meet you," I told her.

Cleo leaned out the sliding glass door, her body nearly parallel to the ground while her hands gripped the door handle. I had told her many times not to do this.

"What movie did you guys see?" she asked Jana.

Mirai and Jana both turned toward Cleo.

"*The Big Sick*," Jana said.

"Oh, my god, I want to see that one," Cleo said.

Mirai said, "It was cute," and Jana said "I'll take you, Clee."

And there I was, on the outskirts of a conversation, per usual.

That night at dinner after Mirai had gone, I'd learn that Mirai was not actually Indian. Or, rather, her ancestors were but her family was from Guyana.

"I guess a lot of Indian people came to Guyana as contract laborers in the 1800s," Jana said. "Isn't it weird that there's so much history we have no idea about?"

"Well, we are not from India," I said. "Or Guyana."

Jana ignored my comment and continued right on: "I didn't even know where Guyana was," Jana said. She looked to Cleo: "Did you?"

Cleo shook her head.

"I know where it is," I said. Geography has always been one of my peculiar strengths. I had an obsession with maps (and bus schedules and calendars) as a kid. "It's between Venezuela and Suriname."

"*Suriname*?" Jana said. "You made that up."

"I did not."

Cleo laughed.

According to Jana, Mirai's Guyanese background was problematic when she sought to marry a traditional Indian man in the United States.

"Apparently, Indian families can be very particular about heritage," Jana said.

She went on to explain that Mirai and her family had sought the help of a matchmaker to arrange an appropriate marriage. Then she explained the concept of an arranged marriage to Cleo.

"I didn't even know people had arranged marriages here," Jana said. She looked at me. "Did you?"

I had never really thought about it. It sounded like a reasonable idea to me. Why *didn't* people have arranged marriages? It seemed way more logical to supply a matchmaker with information about oneself and then have that person find someone with compatible information.

"I suppose Match.com arranges marriages here," I said.

Jana laughed. "Not that successfully."

She went on: "Anyway, Mirai didn't like any of the matches and it was causing problems between her and her parents. Then she was at a grocery store and met Sean in the checkout line, of all things."

"Sean?" I asked, confused by this new character.

"Her husband," Jana said.

"That's so sweet," Cleo said. "Like in a movie."

"And he's Indian?" I asked, still confused.

"No, he's white as can be. Sean McCann. Irish, I'd guess. But Mirai's parents approve and all that. When it's not an arranged marriage, they call it a 'love marriage.' Which I think sounds better anyway."

"A happy ending," Cleo said, clearly interested in the story of this Indo-Guyanese woman's love life.

Cleo leaned back in her chair so far that the front legs came off the ground. *You're going to hurt yourself.* I have made that foreboding prediction hundreds of times in my fledgling parenting career, and I have been less accurate than a county-fair palm reader. Cleo has always been a cautious kid, with only two injuries of note in her life—she cut her finger with an X-Acto knife when doing an ambitious art project in sixth grade, which required several stitches; and she broke her wrist when she was eight years old when catching her fall from a horse (she had a brief interest in horseback riding, an interest that ended with a fiberglass cast).

"I wouldn't mind if you guys arranged my marriage," Cleo said.

Just as I was thinking that this was an excellent idea, that I'd love to select Cleo's husband (at the appropriate time, of course), Jana said, "Oh, honey, that's sweet, but we completely trust you to find yourself and then find the person who makes you happy."

I did not agree with this, but I knew better than to contradict Jana. She was usually right in matters of the heart. Except that she chose *me* as the person to make her happy, which is something that perplexes me to this day. And, upon overhearing her conversations with Mirai, conversations that I was definitely not meant to overhear, I came to understand that her choice often perplexed her too.

CHAPTER 12

Cleo

I am waiting for Edie to pick me up for our Ghost Walk date. Yes, I'm choosing to think of it as a date, even if Edie is not. There's no way Dad is thinking of it as a date. He seems to have no clue that I'm interested in Edie in *that way* (which is fine by me—fewer questions to answer). I'm still shocked that he's letting me go at all, especially because he doesn't know Edie's driving record (unless that type of thing is publicly available, in which case Dad probably *does* know Edie's driving record). He is letting me go in spite of his fears, and that's a big deal for Dad (and me).

Last night, when I was lying in bed, staring at the ceiling, I thanked Mom. Not out loud, but in my head. I feel like she had something to do with Dad allowing me to go. He might not even know she had something to do with it. She may have visited him when he was fast asleep and whispered something in his ear that he did not remember, but that influenced him in a subliminal way. Dad doesn't believe Mom visits us, but I do. Because I want to. I also believe she would want me to go on this date with Edie. She would be excited for me. She would help me curl my hair—because I can never get the desired "beach waves" I'm going for on my own. She would have a strong opinion on which outfit I should wear. She would be sitting on my bed, waiting to chat, when I came home. *Tell me everything*, she'd say, patting my comforter with one hand while holding a mug of chamomile tea in the other. And I would tell her everything, because we never had the type of parent-child relationship with limits to what can be shared. Because I never feared her judgment. Because I trusted her, and she trusted me.

Without her guidance, I resort to texting Carter photos of myself wearing two outfits.

Which one?

He texts back immediately.

Not the black dress. Ur already going to a freaking ghost walk. U don't need to look more goth

The other outfit is a blue romper that I bought on a whim at the mall with Carter over holiday break. I know Mom would have steered me away from it if I'd been shopping with her. *That thing is going to be a pain if you have to pee.* It is a pain. I wore it once and quickly realized that I had to take the whole thing off to use the bathroom. But it's cute. Carter thinks "cute" is worthy of all kinds of sacrifices.

Dad is sitting on the living-room couch with Poppy watching *Storage Wars,* which is a show about people who buy abandoned storage units with the hope that they contain treasures worth thousands of dollars. I don't know why Dad likes this show, but it's right up there with *The Office* for him.

"You look nice," he says.

"Do I?" I say, doing a twirl.

"You do."

I want to ask him if the necklace—a turquoise one that Mom described as "chunky"—is too much, but I know he won't know the answer to this question. I've decided that I don't care if it is too much. It was a gift from Mom, one of the last ones, and I never get to wear it because I never go anywhere besides school. School is not the place for chunky necklaces.

"So, just to review the plan," I say, sitting next to Poppy on the couch, "Edie will be here any minute, and she's going to drive me to the Ghost Walk. It starts at seven and they said it's only an hour. We might get some food after, but I'll be home by nine."

We have already reviewed this plan twice before, but I know the repetition is comforting to Dad.

"Okay, sounds good," he says.

His face does not imply that it sounds good, but I've learned over the years that I cannot trust his face. And I cannot trust his tone. I can only trust the words themselves.

As if on cue, Edie's car comes up the dirt road.

"I'm just going to meet her outside," I say. "Love you." I'm out the door before he can respond.

Edie is opening her car door when she sees me.

"Well, look at you," she says. "I like the necklace."

I can't tell if this is just a friend-to-friend compliment, or flirting. I choose to think the latter, but maybe I'm totally wrong and setting myself up for major disappointment.

I finger the necklace. "Thanks. My mom gave it to me."

I get in the passenger seat, and we go on our way. For the entire drive to the Mission, I rub one of the necklace's turquoise stones between my thumb and index finger as if it's a rosary bead.

The leader of the Ghost Walk is not difficult to spot. He is tall and wearing a black top hat that makes him even taller. He is dressed in all black except for a blue satin-y vest that has big brown buttons. A chain travels between one of the buttons and a pocket of the vest where, I'm assuming, a pocket watch sits. If his goal is to look like someone from the nineteenth century, he has succeeded.

"Welcome, all," he says in a big booming voice that causes several passersby to crane their necks. "My name is Samuel and I shall be your leader."

Downtown San Juan Capistrano is busy—tourists looking for dinner after visiting the Mission, couples out for dinner at one of the new restaurants by the train tracks, teenagers swarming the movie theater. Our fearless Ghost Walk leader does not seem aware of these crowds. In his mind, maybe they are not there. In his mind, maybe we are in the 1800s and the dirt streets are quiet because the horse-drawn carriages have gone home for the night.

"This guy is not creepy at all," Edie whispers in my ear, her breath hot on my cheek.

"He totally is not a serial killer in his spare time."

"Totally not."

Samuel starts our tour across the train tracks in the Los Rios District, which is the oldest neighborhood in California. I know that before he even says it, because Mom told me. We went to the tea house here every so often—a big Victorian house that serves English-style tea (and crumpets). Mom loved the little shops on Los Rios. She never mentioned the supposed ghosts.

"That's crazy, isn't it?" Edie whispers.

This is when I realize I haven't been paying attention.

When I do pay attention, I learn that people have seen a dark-haired woman dressed in white, right here on Los Rios Street, often under the giant pepper tree where we stand now. She's known for tossing her mane of long, black hair, beckoning people to follow her. Then there is *La Llorona*, "the Wailing Woman," who drowned her children and mourns their deaths for eternity. Sometimes people see her wandering Los Rios; sometimes people hear her along Trabuco Creek. Supposedly.

At the O'Neill Museum, formerly called the Pryor House, the ghost of Albert Pryor is sometimes seen wearing a gray sweater, rocking in a chair on the front porch. The Rios Adobe has ghostly footsteps, sometimes heard by members of the family when doors were locked and everyone was asleep. The Ramos House—now a restaurant that Mom said is ridiculously over-priced—was once known for its poltergeist activity. Across the street at the Montanez Adobe, people have heard chanting and seen strange lights.

Everyone in our group—about ten of us—"oohs" and "aahs" at these stories. I'm not sure what I think. I don't like the idea of ghosts, like *La Llorona*, tormented for all eternity. I want to think that Mom is still with me, but not like that. I don't want her to be angst-ridden, wandering Los Rios Street. I can almost hear her laughing at me for having that thought.

Samuel leads us around the corner to El Adobe Restaurant, which Mom, Dad, and I have been to several times. They have good tacos. Samuel says it was originally built in 1797 as the home of Miguel Yorba and also served as the town's court and jail in the early 1800s. He says the jail is now the restaurant's wine cellar and is considered haunted. Over the years, several employees have reported a strange presence. Samuel says some of them have quit because of it. There are reports of a friar haunting the premises. Some say he is wielding an ax used for beheadings; others say that he himself is headless.

As we walk away from El Adobe, Edie touches my forearm. At first, I think it's because she wants to get my attention, whisper something in my ear; but when I look at her, she just smiles. Her hand continues to travel down to my hand, which I realize is her intended destination. She links her fingers with mine and there we are, holding hands. I tell myself not to get too excited; sometimes friends hold hands. Carter holds my hand sometimes. But this feels different. Or at least I think it does. Is my hope brainwashing me? I must be smiling like a freaking idiot, because Samuel looks at me and says, "I am glad to see you are enjoying yourself so thoroughly."

With his old-timey way of talking, it's impossible to tell if he's being sarcastic, so I just nod.

"I'm having a great time," I say, squeezing Edie's hand.

We walk to the Mission and learn about the legendary ghosts there—a faceless monk who roams the back corridors at night, a headless soldier who stands guard near one of the buildings. Samuel says sometimes the bells at the Mission ring of their own accord in the middle of the night. Sometimes there is a smell of tobacco when nobody is around.

"And then there is the ghost of Magdalena," Samuel says, his eyes big and wide. "Magdalena was about fifteen or sixteen years old, young and beautiful."

He looks right at me as he says this, and Edie squeezes my hand.

"She fell in love with a young man named Teofilo, a promising artist who painted the wall frescos inside the Great Stone Church. Magdalena's father was a soldier who forbid her to see Teofilo, but Magdalena still managed to meet Teofilo secretly."

I whisper in Edie's ear: "Why is he staring at me?"

Edie whispers back: "I've decided that Samuel is a ghost."

I pull my lips into my mouth to prevent laughter and turn my attention back to Samuel.

"One day they were caught by Magdalena's father, and he demanded that she confess to the priest. As part of her punishment, she was to walk in front of the congregation, holding a penitent's candle. This was on December 8, 1812. At the early-morning mass, she went inside the Great Stone Church and lit her candle. As she carried the candle up the aisle, the ground began to shake. The bell tower swayed and fell on top of the church. Forty people were buried alive under the rubble. Over months, the rubble was cleared, and Magdalena's body was found, the candle still in her hand."

There was a rumbling of whispers among the group. This was, by far, the best story we'd heard on our little tour.

"It is said that on the night of a half-moon, one can see Magdalena's face in the remaining window of the Great Stone Church, still doing penance for her forbidden love."

He points toward the remaining window, and I watch everyone's faces tilt in that direction as if they are expecting to see her there, winking at us. I am the only one looking at Samuel instead of the Church. I am hoping to catch a glimpse of the real Samuel, not this person-from-the-past he is playing. He does not relax a single facial muscle, though, as far as I can tell.

He tugs on his pocket-watch chain and then removes the watch, staring at its face.

"My friends, that brings us to the end of our tour," he says, a Cheshire-cat-type grin on his face. "You may now go forth, at your own risk, and explore these haunted streets. It has been my pleasure to share with you my ghostly knowledge."

A couple of people start clapping—a slow, tentative clap. A couple more join in, and then we are all clapping. Samuel ducks his head and presses his hands together in prayer as he bows to us. Edie jerks my hand.

"I'm sufficiently creeped out. Let's go."

We separate ourselves from the group and walk the dark street back to the main drag of downtown, where the lights of restaurants assure us that Samuel has not, in fact, taken us to another era.

"Well, that was odd," Edie says.

"I thought it was cool."

"Cool, yes. And odd," she says. Her strides are long. I walk quickly at her side to keep up. "You hungry?" she asks.

"Starving."

We get a table on the patio at the Mexican restaurant next to the train station. We're across from each other, at too awkward a distance to hold hands, and I wonder if I have imagined the whole hand-holding thing. Is my mind that powerful? Dad would say yes.

We make small talk about the Ghost Walk and order a plate of nachos. When the waiter brings them, we make small talk about nachos, about how the cheese is so stretchy and delicious in a way it never is when attempting homemade nachos.

"Thank you, by the way. This is literally the best birthday present I've ever received."

Except for the turquoise necklace.

"Well, I owe you for letting me infiltrate your life."

"Infiltrate? You sound like my dad," I say, checking my phone for the time. "Speaking of which, we have a whole half hour before I turn into a pumpkin."

"Is that what happens?"

I cringe. "I've been trying to find a way to tell you—"

"Your dad's on the spectrum and you turn into a pumpkin. Got it. Any more secrets?"

I figure this is my chance.

"Actually, yeah, kind of."

I put down the chip that's currently in my hand. I've lost all desire to eat. Edie's brows furrow with worry, which in turn worries me.

"So," I begin. "I feel bad if this comes as a surprise . . . and I don't have any idea how you feel . . . and I'm fine with being friends. . . . I mean, I'm *great* with being friends. But you should probably know that I'm not really . . .straight."

Her brows unfurrow. "Oh, that's it?"

She says it like it's no big deal, which relaxes me, though I still wonder whether it's no big deal because she's open-minded and doesn't care about my sexual orientation, or if it's no big deal because she's also "not really straight."

"Okay," I say. "Is it obvious?" I've never thought it was obvious. If it were obvious, I assume I'd be teased incessantly at school about it.

She shrugs. "I guess I picked up on a vibe. I feel like lesbians can spot each other."

I take in this information. She is a lesbian. She likes girls. She possibly likes me.

"Oh, I didn't know . . . I mean, that's awesome."

She laughs. "I tend to agree."

I feel the need to clarify one thing, in the name of honesty: "Just so you know, I'm not really, like, a lesbian. I like girls *and* guys."

She looks surprised, but not disapproving. "You're bi?"

"I guess so."

She brings the straw from her Coke to her lips, takes a sip. "Well, that just means I have more competition."

There it is—she likes me.

"If it makes you feel better, nobody else is really in the running right now," I tell her.

She smiles. "That does make me feel better."

"Do your parents know?" I ask her.

"My mom knew before I did. I told her when I was thirteen, and she said, 'I've been waiting for you to tell me.' Which was kind of annoying, you know? For me, it was this big announcement, and she sort of acted like it was yesterday's news or whatever."

While I understand her annoyance, I also think it's pretty cool that her mom knew all along. Isn't that what all kids really want—to be seen for who they are? Maybe that's what all humans want, no matter the age.

"Anyway, she's supportive, so I'm lucky. If she had it her way, we'd have a rainbow flag permanently installed in front of our house."

I laugh. "That's cool."

"It is. My dad is not nearly as cool. He knows but just, like, avoids the subject entirely."

"My dad avoids subjects entirely all the time," I say.

I tell her about Carter, about how his parents split up in some part because he came out. Edie says that's lame, and I agree.

"Does he know about you?" Edie asks.

"Carter? Oh yeah—"

"No, your dad," she says.

"I don't know. Like I said, he avoids the subject entirely."

"Do you think he'd care?"

I've asked myself this same question. Dad is not a very emotionally charged person, so I can't see him being upset about it. He would think about it in practical terms only. He might even be relieved to know I like girls. *They can't get you pregnant.* I can see him saying that.

"Probably not. I just don't feel like telling him, I guess. What good is that going to do? He doesn't really know anything about my inner life anyway."

Mom had.

"Maybe if you tell him, he'll want to know more."

"Maybe."

We hold hands for the entire walk back to Edie's car and my head is spinning with the reality that this is actually happening. The question lingering in the air—well, in my air—is whether she'll kiss me. I've never kissed a girl. I've kissed a few boys in very unoriginal settings—the playground in sixth grade, during a spin-the-bottle game at a party in eighth grade, and in a closet during a party at Julia's house the year Mom died (that was Justin, my last boy crush). I don't know if kissing a girl is different. All I can do is hope my lack of experience isn't obvious.

"You thinking about something?" Edie asks as we approach her car.

She follows me to the passenger side.

"Huh?" I say.

"Never mind," she says with a laugh.

We stand at the passenger-side door and it occurs to me that this is when it will happen. Right now. She can't do it when she drops me off at home because of Dad. She knows that. She has thought ahead. What is about to happen is completely premeditated.

"Would it be all right if I kissed you?" she asks.

I cannot speak. I just nod.

Then it happens. I close my eyes, not because that's the romantic thing to do, but because I'm scared. I close my eyes the way I close my eyes on roller coasters, because I'm not sure I can handle the sensory stimulation I would receive if my eyes were open. Her lips are so soft, softer than all of the boys' lips that came before her. Before I can analyze it more, it's over. Done. More than a peck, but less than *making out*. If I keep closing my eyes, I can hear Mom cheering for me, like she's in the stands of a sporting event.

"You okay?" Edie asks.

That's when I open my eyes and feel embarrassed that I don't know how long they were closed, how long she's been standing here staring at me with my closed eyes.

"Yeah, good, yeah," I say, unable to hide how flustered I am.

She seems amused by this, which I guess is better than her looking at me like I'm a total freak. The fact that she is not at all flustered makes me think she has kissed many girls before—twenty, thirty, a thousand. I'm afraid to ask.

"Okay," she says. "Good."

She opens the car door for me, and I get inside. My heart is still hammering in my chest. Before she gets in the car, I quickly touch my lips, as if I expect to find something different there. They feel the same. Or, I think they do. When was the last time I touched my lips? When did I ever notice my lips before? How can I ever *not* notice them, now that I see their potential?

She gets in the car, and we pull out of the parking lot and start the drive back to my house. I have no idea what to say, so I don't say anything.

"I hope I didn't play my cards too soon," she says after a few minutes. She laughs, but it's an insecure, uncertain laugh, a laugh that's asking for reassurance.

"No," I say. "They are good cards. Great cards. You should play them again."

She laughs again, less uneasily this time.

"Good to know," she says.

There is more silence, and we are now just a few minutes from my house, right on time. I expect Dad will be waiting up and I'll have to act like nothing of interest has happened so that I'm not interrogated. I'm sure I'm blushing. My cheeks feel flaming red. They will give me away.

"I kind of have to tell you something," Edie says.

It's not a flirtatious "I kind of have to tell you something." She is not about to say "I have a crush on you." It is a foreboding "I kind of have to tell you something." My brain, flooded with joyful hormones, cannot make sense of this tone.

"You might hate me," she says.

My heart drops. Like, I literally feel something inside me drop. She's going to say she regrets the kiss. She's going to say she has a girlfriend back in San Diego. She's going to say I have bad breath.

"I've been kind of curious about your mom. You never really talk about her," she says.

This is not the same kind of bad as "you have bad breath," but I still feel like I'm going to throw up.

"When I was at your house for your birthday, I saw pictures of her, which I thought was weird if your parents aren't still together. So, then I wondered if something, like, *happened* to her. And I know I probably should have just asked you, but I knew you didn't want to talk about it, so I did some googling. . . . I know that's basically the same thing as spying on you. . . ."

She stops there. She doesn't have to say anything else. Just googling my name would bring up all kinds of news articles. She knows what happened.

"Oh," I say. It's all I can manage.

"I should have just waited for you to tell me," she says. "I'm sorry."

We turn onto the dirt road that leads to my house. We are running out of time to say anything meaningful. Even if we had all the time in the world, I'm not sure there would be anything meaningful to say.

"It's awful, what happened," she says. "I can't even imagine. . . ."

"Don't do that," I say.

This was my fear. The Pity Face.

"What?"

"Don't look at me all different, okay?"

I can feel the tears come in their abrupt and unwelcome way. I curse them silently, tell them to please just wait five minutes. They do not obey. They never do.

"I don't look at you any differently. I mean, I do, but not, like, in a bad way," she says.

"God. Did you kiss me because you feel sorry for me?"

We are in front of the house now. I can see the silhouette of Dad sitting on the couch.

"What? No way, Cleo. Not at all," she says.

But I find it hard to believe her. How could I possibly believe her?

I get out of the car in a hurry because the tears are threatening, and I can tell there are a lot of them, accumulated after several days—a couple weeks, maybe—of damming.

"Cleo, just hang a second," she calls after me.

I can't. She will go home thinking I'm furious with her, and I'm fine with that misunderstanding right now. Because I can't let her see the tears, the force of them. She says she doesn't see me differently, but if she sees the tears she surely will. She will see the sheer brokenness of me and, despite any and all attempts, she will not be able to unsee that.

CHAPTER 13

Dave

If you had the ability to see gamma rays, you would see a bright flash appear in the sky about once a day, briefly outshining everything else before vanishing. Because we cannot see them, we don't know that they happen. But they do.

These gamma-ray bursts originate in distant galaxies and are powerful in a way that is difficult to fathom. For reference, one quadrillion is 1,000,000,000,000,000, and a gamma-ray burst is 10 quadrillion times as energetic as the sun. *Ten quadrillion.* Astrophysicists think the bursts are likely the result of two collapsed stars merging together. When this happens, there is no advance warning. If such a double star was in our galaxy, we would have no idea. But if a burst were to happen, there would be no missing its force. At a distance of 1,000 light-years, which is farther than most of the stars you can see on a clear night, it would appear about as bright as the sun.

Why is this dangerous? Well, Earth's atmosphere would initially protect us from most of the rays, but there would be aftereffects. The powerful radiation would cook the atmosphere, creating nitrogen oxides that would obliterate the ozone layer. Without the ozone layer, ultraviolet rays from the sun would be able to reach the Earth's surface at nearly full force, causing skin cancer. More seriously, tiny photosynthetic plankton in the ocean would die off, and that's significant because those plankton provide oxygen to the atmosphere and bolster the bottom of the food chain.

Scientists are the first to admit that they understand little about these explosions. So far, all observed gamma-ray bursts have been extremely far away. But it would be foolish to assume that such a thing couldn't happen in our galaxy. As I say about most things, it's just a matter of time.

I have always been a collector. When I was a kid, it was maps and coins and baseball cards (even though I never played baseball and had no interest in sports, categorically). As a teenager, I collected cassette tapes, not because I was a music aficionado (I'm not), but because I liked the plastic cases, the different covers (which I organized by color). I got into model cars in college—specifically 1:18 scale diecasts made in the 1960s—and spent most of my twenties and thirties focused on that hobby. Left to my own devices, I was known to spend hours in online forums or on eBay stalking potential purchases. Since I've become interested in disaster preparedness, my interest in model cars has waned, but I do keep my collection in boxes in the bunker (along with boxes of my maps, coins, cards, and tapes). I suppose I am still a collector, but now I am a collector of survival supplies.

Cleo likes to make fun of my bunker, but I suspect she will regret her jokes if something ever happens that necessitates its use. I come down here a few times a week, usually when Cleo is at school and I have a break between work meetings. It's quiet down here, cool, like a cave. The previous owner relied on a single overhead lightbulb to illuminate the entire space, and I have yet to upgrade to a more robust light source. I like that it's dim. But I know that if Cleo and I ever have to stay down here, we will want more light.

That's my next step—creating a small living space for Cleo and myself. Obviously, the bunker cannot protect us from every disaster that may come. For example, the sea level is expected to rise more than 260 feet in Cleo's lifetime, according to the U.S. Geological Survey, and a bunker won't do a damn thing for us then. I'm already researching areas inland. It's unlikely that I'll be able to save enough on my salary to purchase a second home farther from the ocean, but that's a long-term goal.

The bunker will come in handy in the event of a nuclear attack, radiation, war, or pandemic. I'm pleased with the stockpile of supplies that I have created. Sometimes I come down here just to stare at the full shelves in all their organized glory. Looking at them is my version of Xanax. I have purposefully left an empty area in the back, meant for two twin-size beds, a toilet, and a sink. It will cost a substantial amount of money to plumb the bunker, but I think it's a worthwhile investment. I have been saving in a Bunker Fund, but only after I meet my monthly contribution requirements for Cleo's College Fund. It is difficult for me to believe that she will be going to college in a little more than a year. I have communicated to her my preference that she attend a local university—Cal State Fullerton or University of California in Irvine, for instance—so that she could continue to live at home (with access to the bunker). She said, "Dad, college is a ways off," which leaves me to assume that she is delaying the conversation because she knows her wishes will conflict with mine. *You're thinking ten million steps ahead again.* That's what Jana would say. I cannot help but think ahead, but perhaps ten million steps is excessive.

On one of the back shelves, next to a stack of mylar blankets, in a box with hundreds of batteries, is something that Cleo does not know exists. Nobody but Jana was supposed to know it exists. It would pain her to know I've discovered its existence. Sometimes I wonder what would have happened if I'd found it when she was alive, if I'd confronted her with it. I can see her face turning white, red blotches blooming on her neck, her tell-tale sign of distress. *It's just a journal, Dave. I exaggerate things.*

I think of that line from that movie again: *The great thing about people with Asperger's is that it's very difficult to hurt their feelings.* I agree with it, on the whole, but that journal managed to hurt my feelings. That journal still accomplishes that feat, even though I've read it hundreds of times by now. Each of those journal entries is its own gamma burst.

The content of the journal should not have been a shock. I knew Jana wasn't entirely happy with our marriage, because I'd heard her conversations with Mirai. When Jana had first introduced me to Mirai, I hadn't expected I'd see her again. I certainly hadn't expected that she would become a regular visitor; but that's what happened. Jana and Mirai developed a Thursday evening routine, involving yoga class after work, followed by dinner and a "nightcap" at our house.

On Thursday mornings, Jana would leave for work with her rolled-up yoga mat in a bag made specifically to transport rolled-up yoga mats. She would say, "Remember, it's yoga night," and Cleo and I would nod obediently. Mirai didn't introduce Jana to yoga. Jana had dabbled in it before. But Mirai was the reason Jana began referring to herself as a *yogi*. I am not one to judge someone else's hobbies, but I did think it was strange that a group of people would gather in a room together to stretch and breathe. It was the breathing thing that perplexed me most. Jana took to performing "breathing exercises" every night before bed and every morning. She'd sit cross-legged with her eyes closed, her index fingers touching her thumbs, creating little circles. I did not understand (and still don't) how a person can make an *exercise* of something managed by the autonomic nervous system, something that happens on its own, without conscious effort. It seems as ridiculous to me as "heartbeat exercises."

After yoga, they went to a vegetarian restaurant next to the yoga studio. Mirai is to blame for Jana's conversion to vegetarianism, which ultimately motivated Cleo's conversion to vegetarianism too (which is something I presume will be lifelong, as it is now part of her mother's legacy). By the time they came back to the house, it was around nine o'clock. I enjoyed these nights because they gave me permission to order pizza for Cleo and me, then go to bed early, which is always my preference. I'd usually be asleep by the time they came home, then awakened briefly by the sound of Jana's key in the door, their voices low but audible. I don't know if Cleo was awake or asleep on these nights. She'd usually go to her room when I went to mine, and she'd begun closing her door, something Jana said was an appropriate adolescent assertion of her right to privacy. I never heard her open her door, so if she was awake, she stayed in her room.

I usually have no difficulty going back to sleep if I'm awakened, but, for some reason, I found myself alert on one of the nights Mirai and Jana came back to the house. It was a few months into their "yoga nights." I heard Jana ask Mirai if she wanted wine, and Mirai said, "Oh, sure." I heard giggling that was reminiscent of Cleo and her girlfriends on the dreaded weekends it was our turn to host a sleepover.

"I can top your story," Jana said. I did not hear whatever story she was trying to top; it must have been something Mirai had relayed in the car or earlier in their evening.

"Years ago, when Dave and I first started therapy, the therapist wanted us to do this exercise of writing down what we considered to be important parts of an ideal marriage. You know what Dave's number one thing—"

"Sex," Mirai interjected.

I was relieved that this was not the case, that I was not like the stereotypical man. I'm sure I have the physical sensations of a stereotypical man, but I take pride in my ability to override my physical sensations with logic. I have sufficient control of my base instincts.

"Nope," Jana said. "Time to himself. That's what he said. In his ideal *partnership*, he wants *time to himself* for his *hobbies*."

They laughed, and a strange tingly feeling spread throughout my body. Jana's laugh sounded different than normal. Was this her real laugh? If it was, what was the one she used with me? Did she think my model cars were stupid? There was a time she thought they were charming.

"Well, I mean, I guess that makes sense with the Asperger's," Mirai said.

The tingly feeling intensified. The way Mirai said it so casually—*the Asperger's*—made it sound like they had discussed this on numerous occasions. They had discussed *me* on numerous occasions.

"That damn Asperger's," Jana said.

And they laughed again.

"Sean's number one thing would definitely be sex," Mirai said.

"So unoriginal."

"There are nights I'm changing into my pajamas and I can just feel his eyes on me and I'm like, 'God, no, not tonight.'"

"I will say Dave never bugs me about sex," Jana said. "Sometimes I wish he would, but he's not ever going to have that kind of . . . urgency, you know? Desire is a spontaneous thing. Or it should be, right? He is the farthest thing from spontaneous. We have sex once a week, on Saturdays. It's not officially scheduled, but it may as well be."

"Do you two still go to therapy together?"

"Not so much anymore. We went a lot before he was diagnosed and right after, but then it became apparent that there's nothing to really *do* about it. He is who he is. There are certain things he's just not capable of. It's more about me figuring out if a marriage without deep emotional connection is enough for me, you know?"

"And is it?"

She sighed heavily.

"I don't know. Sometimes I think it's okay. Cleo loves him. He's such a reliable, loyal guy. His heart is good. But sometimes I want more. I want someone who *gets* me," she said.

She had presented this to me as a problem before: "I feel like you don't *get* me." I interpreted it very literally at first: "I don't get you what?" She seemed exhausted by the notion of having to explain to me what she meant. Finally, she said, "I feel like you don't *understand* who I am, like at my core." I had no idea what to say to that. This concept of her "core" was as foreign to me as yoga.

"It's something I talk about with my therapist all the time," she told Mirai.

This was news to me, that Jana saw a therapist on her own.

"Your therapist sounds amazing," Mirai said.

Clearly, this was something else they had discussed before.

"She really is."

"Maybe I need a therapist," Mirai said.

"You aren't happy?"

It was Mirai's turn to sigh.

"With Sean?" Jana asked.

Mirai must have nodded, because Jana said, "I had no idea. You never talk much about him."

"What is there to say? He's just . . . not who I thought he was when I married him," she said. "He was so sweet and kind in the beginning. It's like the minute the marriage became official, he started to change."

"Change how?"

"Maybe 'change' is the wrong word. Maybe he always was who he was, but he hid that person when I first met him. He seemed like this progressive guy, like he'd be supportive of me having my own life. Then we got married and he got so . . . controlling."

"Like . . . how?"

"He's just very particular. And so traditional, like he's from the 1950s. He expects meals made. He expects a clean house. He says it's fine if I work, but I have to keep up the house and all that. He doesn't like me to have friends. When I see you, I tell him I'm working extra hours. At least Kyra is old enough to look after herself now, because he'd never let me leave the house when she was younger."

I'd learn later that Kyra was Mirai and Sean's daughter, in the same grade as Cleo.

"He doesn't know about our yoga nights?"

"I tell him we have big projects that require late nights on Thursdays. He doesn't really care, as long as I leave dinner for him to heat up."

"Would he go to therapy?"

Mirai laughed. "You're cute," she said. "Would a man in the 1950s go to therapy?"

"Does he know you're unhappy?"

"I don't think my happiness has ever crossed the man's mind," she said.

There was a moment of silence before Mirai asked, "Does Dave know you're unhappy?"

Jana sighed again. "I wouldn't say I'm unhappy. Some days, maybe. It's more like I'm restless. And it makes me sad that Dave doesn't notice."

"Sean doesn't notice either," Mirai said.

I resented this implied commonality. I wasn't Sean. Sean sounded like a complete asshole.

"Dave is never mean, though," Jana said, and I felt momentarily vindicated. "A little clueless, a lot aloof, but never mean."

"Sean is mean," Mirai said. "I hear him on business calls, and he transforms into the charismatic man I first met. It's the strangest thing."

"Dr. Jekyll and Mr. Hyde," Jana said.

"Speaking of which, I better get home and find out which one I'm going to get."

"He'll still be awake?"

"Depends. Dr. Jekyll stays up late. Mr. Hyde goes to bed early."

The next morning, I didn't ask Jana anything about what I'd overheard. I hoped she would tell me, but all she said was that she'd mastered the crow pose in their yoga class. I looked for signs that she was unhappy with me, with us, but didn't see any. *Be curious, Dave.* That's what The Therapist had always told me. That was, supposedly, the key to connecting with my wife, despite my Asperger's brain.

"Is the crow pose a hard one?" I asked.

She looked at me like I'd just asked her if the sky was blue. "It's a hard one for me," she said.

"Did you two have a nice dinner after?"

Her brows furrowed in true concern. "Why are you asking all these questions?"

"Why not?"

"You never ask," she said.

She said it with a smile, but I supposed this was what was behind her unhappiness—my failure to ask, my failure to be curious, on a regular basis.

The following Thursday, I stayed awake in bed for the express purpose of listening in on their conversation when they returned from dinner. I suppose that's wrong, to eavesdrop, but I could not resist this ongoing investigation into my wife's true feelings. That's what it felt like—an investigation. I was amassing data, creating a hypothesis, testing this theory that, unbeknownst to me, she'd come to see our marriage as something she was *stuck in.*

They engaged in the same routine—opening wine, sitting on the couch.

"So, wait, how much did you find?" Jana asked. Again, she seemed to be continuing a conversation that had started earlier.

"A lot," Mirai said.

"What kind? Oh god, do I want to know? There are no animals involved, right?"

They laughed. "No animals. Just threesomes. A lot of threesomes."

Jana made a sound like she was dry-heaving.

"Has he always been a porn guy?"

"No idea. This is the first I'm finding it," Mirai said. "Maybe he left his computer unlocked so I would find it, as a way to let me know how dissatisfied he is with our sex life."

"Is he that . . . conniving?"

"I'm telling you he is."

"God, Mirai, that's terrible."

There were a couple seconds of silence before Mirai asked, in more of a hushed voice, "Does Dave watch porn?"

I knew Jana must be shaking her head.

"Not *at all?*" Mirai asked.

"No. I asked him when we were dating what kind of porn he likes, because I *assumed* all men like porn, and he said he never really watched it."

"And you believed him?"

"Not at first," she said. "But then when I found out about the ASD, it kind of clicked. People on the spectrum can have a hard time imagining people and feelings. They prefer facts over fiction. Porn is all fiction."

"Well, that's something for the 'pros' list," Mirai said.

I thought that was just a figure of speech. Little did I know that Jana had created an actual list, in the journal that I would find after she died.

"It is," Jana said. "There are a handful of pros."

"I'm not sure what Sean's pros are at this point."

"He makes good money, I'm guessing."

"Yes, but who cares? I make enough money for Kyra and me to rent a small apartment. That's all I need."

"He's Kyra's father," Jana said. "That's a big one for me. Dave is Cleo's dad. They love each other."

"Yeah, that's true. Sean's nicer to Kyra than he is to me. But, still, Kyra sees his dark side. I worry for her, mostly. That she'll think this type of man is normal."

"So no pros, then?"

"I can't think of any," Mirai said. "But there is this one huge con. If I were to leave him, he would make my life hell. I stay because the current hell is familiar. The one he would create for me would be far worse."

"That's not a reason to stay."

"Isn't it, though?"

"So you really wouldn't consider leaving him?" Jana asked.

"Of course I *consider* it," Mirai said. "I just don't see it happening."

There was more silence.

"Do you think anyone really has a happy marriage?" Jana asked.

I thought *I* did. I still think I did. The best years of my life had been with Jana, and I anticipate that will be true fifty years from now.

"Hard to say. We all applaud the couples who stay together for fifty years, but maybe they shouldn't have stayed together."

"I've thought the same thing," Jana said.

"Have you ever thought about leaving Dave?"

I thought Jana would respond quickly with *No, never.*

Instead, she said "Of course."

I felt the need to leap out of bed and run into the other room to restrain her, as if she was planning to leave right then.

"Why do you stay?" Mirai asked.

"Because of the pros. And because of Cleo. I've read the psychology books. . . . Divorce is so hard on kids."

She'd read psychology books on divorce?

"I thought about it a lot when Cleo was young. Being the active parent, the one tuned in with her all the time, was hard on me. I resented Dave a lot. But I didn't feel right about splitting up the family. I kind of just put it out of my head. Cleo's older now. She understands about Dave's ASD. So I've been thinking about it more again. Dave would be crushed, though. Our marriage is great for him. He would be totally blindsided."

She was right. I would. I *was.* I am.

"Sean probably thinks I don't have the courage to leave him," Mirai said.

"Do you?"

"I guess that's the question."

I heard the ding of the wine bottle against the glass. Jana must have been pouring more wine.

"I have to ask you something," Jana said.

"What?"

"Does he hurt you?" Jana's voice was quiet and tentative.

There have been many times I have wished she hadn't asked Mirai this question. The answer to it would change our lives forever.

"He doesn't hurt me in the way you're thinking," Mirai said. "He sometimes puts his hands on my shoulders and shakes me. Or pushes me against a wall if he's angry. But there are no marks."

"Mirai. . . ."

"You see me at work every day. Do I come with bruises? Black eyes?"

"No," Jana said. "Not yet. But men like this, they just don't improve. They don't get better."

"It's been *fifteen years* like this. This is my normal."

"It might be familiar, but it's not *normal*."

"Maybe you should be a therapist," Mirai said.

"Would you tell me if it got worse?"

"You are my one friend. If I were to tell someone, it would be you."

The next morning, while eating breakfast at the kitchen island, I thought about saying, "I heard you and Mirai talking last night," but Cleo was there, and who was I kidding? I didn't really want to have that conversation. I wanted to go on thinking everything was fine.

Jana didn't say a thing about the previous night. I was certain she would tell me about Mirai's potentially abusive husband. Jana has always liked discussing other people's lives—something else that I'd never understood, but assumed was commonplace among neurotypicals. She didn't mention anything about Sean, though. She seemed to be her normal self—which was concerning for me, as I'd become aware of the fact that she'd been harboring resentments and fantasies of leaving me.

I made a pact with myself to be a better husband. I allotted myself only two hours a day to focus on my model cars (a drastic reduction). I dedicated myself to cleaning the house more obsessively than normal—running the dishwasher at least once a day, doing a load of laundry any time the hamper became halfway full, sweeping the wood floors and vacuuming the carpets and rugs daily, and dusting during any downtime (I placed a feather duster in both the kitchen and living room for this purpose). I also focused on maintaining the yard to exceptional standards, putting an inordinate amount of energy into selecting drought-friendly plants to optimize our landscaping and then watering and trimming the plants regularly. I scheduled a Costco trip once per week, even if there was nothing on Jana's list. I liked going, purchasing things, feeling purposeful and needed. The tasks themselves were a validation of my role as Jana's husband, Cleo's father. Completing them gave me the assurance I needed.

I figured this task mastery would compensate for whatever emotional connection Jana professed to be lacking in our marriage, and I assumed this compensation was satisfactory until she died and I found the journal.

I wasn't looking for a journal, because I didn't think one existed. I was looking for the necklace that Jana always wore because I had been given the worst task of my life when the funeral home asked for jewelry she might want to be buried with. They made a point of telling me that she was already wearing her engagement ring and wedding band. I have never been someone who cries, but my eyes welled up when I heard that.

The necklace was silver—three interlocking loops that Jana said represented her, me, and Cleo. When I didn't see the necklace in the bathroom drawer, I checked her nightstand drawer. I didn't find the necklace there either (I later found it hanging on a hook in the closet meant for belts), but I did find the journal. I flipped to the middle of it and saw her handwriting, then sat on the bed and started from the beginning. I don't know how long it took me to read the whole thing—an hour, two hours. By the time I finished, the sun had gone down and Cleo came to check on me: "You've been in here a while. You okay?"

I didn't tell Cleo about the journal.

I don't know why I didn't burn the thing that very day. I don't know why I kept it when we moved out of the old house and into this one. I don't know why I put it here in the bunker with all the supplies that are meant to save us during catastrophe. Its contents are the farthest thing from lifesaving.

The first entry:

So, here it is. My journal. I haven't kept a journal since I was 12. And then I called it a diary. Is there a difference?

This was Amber's idea. She wants me to get more in touch with my feelings. She says she thinks I'm repressing a lot . . . about Dave mostly. Sadness at not having the marriage I want. Resentment that he isn't able to be who I need all the time. Guilt for having my needs. I'm keeping this journal in my nightstand drawer because I know Dave would never look here. He wouldn't snoop, because he doesn't think there's anything to snoop about, and he has so little curiosity about my feelings anyway. Isn't that sad? I know it's not his fault. He's wired differently, that's all. Hence the guilt. Anyway . . . we'll see how this journal thing goes.

(It became obvious to me, after reading the journal, that Amber was the therapist she saw.)

Another entry:

Dave doesn't hit me. He never would. That's something. That's a BIG something. Mirai has to leave Sean. I don't see how she can stay. Here I am, wondering if I can stay in a marriage with a GOOD man while she is in this clearly abusive relationship. The thing is, though, do I stay with Dave just because of all the things he doesn't do? He doesn't hit me. He doesn't berate me. He doesn't yell at me. He doesn't cheat on me. He doesn't gamble. He doesn't spend our money frivolously. He doesn't drink. He doesn't do drugs. It seems like if you stay with someone because of what he doesn't do, your life is being dictated by fear.

Another:

I talked to Amber today about how I ended up with Dave. She says every-thing ties back to childhood, so then we talked about my childhood. I told her about how Dad was the quintessential military guy with the stiff upper lip. I told her how Mom deferred to him on everything. They were "good parents" in that they provided me with a roof over my head, food, education—the basics. Amber said it sounds like I experienced emotional neglect, which I didn't know was a thing. It fits. I was this sensitive kid with big feelings, and they treated that like a freaking disability. We never talked about feelings in my family—did any families talk about feelings back then? As Amber said, "You're used to emotional deprivation." I guess I am. I asked her why I would choose Dave, though. Wouldn't I want to choose someone who was the opposite of my parents? Why would I choose MORE deprivation? She laughed and said that's not how it works. Appar-ently, we gravitate toward the familiar, even if the familiar is not ideal for us. She said there is something physiological that happens when we meet someone who replicates something from our childhood—the sense of a key fitting into a lock, that clicking, that oh yes, this feels like something I know. We like things we know. We like things that are predictable. It gives us a sense of control, safety. Familiar. Family. It makes sense.

If I'd grown up with different parents, maybe I wouldn't have been attracted to someone like Dave. Not because he's a bad guy, but he's not going to be the guy who has that deep connection with me (or anyone). I'm sure it doesn't help that Dave's parents were pretty detached too. His dad was an engineer. I only met him once before he died, so I didn't know him well, but I'd venture to say he had ASD. Dave's mom has always been strange—disconnected (too disconnected to notice her kid had Asperger's, apparently). I could ask her about it now, but we don't have that type of relationship. She doesn't have "that type of relationship" with Dave, either. Anyway. . . . It's all kind of sad when I think about it. How did I not see it? What do I do, now that my eyes are open?

There were dozens of entries like this—her dissatisfaction with our marriage, her wondering if this was "it" for her life, her nagging desire for "something more." Had she tried to talk to me about this and I hadn't listened? Had I not understood the seriousness of it? It's possible. It's also possible that she hadn't even tried to talk about it because she'd given up on my ability to understand her years ago. Is this how a marriage ends—with a slow erosion that both people may not even realize is happening?

I do remember her saying that she worried that we weren't compatible. "On an emotional level," she said. I dismissed this immediately, saying, "Not compatible? We've been married sixteen years. That implies a good deal of compatibility." To me, it was that simple. I should have asked her more about her concerns, but I didn't.

Be curious, Dave.

At the end of the journal was the list—two columns, pros alongside cons. It was obvious that she added to the list over time. Some lines were written with different pens, some of the handwriting looked neat, some looked rushed and sloppy.

PROS:
- He's extremely reliable. If he says he'll be somewhere or do something, he will
- He's very predictable, which gives me a lot of security

- He's so loyal. He would never cheat on me
- He's not demanding of sex
- He cleans. A lot
- He's hard working. I never worry about him not having a job or making money
- He's happy being a homebody. I am too, most of the time, so this is a nice compatibility (though I wouldn't mind a little more socializing . . .)
- He's honest. Like, he's incapable of lying (because of difficulty with imagination, I suppose)
- He has a good heart. There is no maliciousness in him

Cons:
- He needs a lot of alone time. He gets overwhelmed easily and needs to retreat
- He doesn't like to cuddle. I've read that people with ASD are highly sensitive to physical sensation, and I'm guessing even holding hands makes him feel like his skin is on fire. He hasn't said as much, but I assume. I'm guessing this is why he leaves our bed to sleep on the couch sometimes
- He doesn't tell me very often that he loves me or is thankful for anything I do. Words seem hard for him. He's more about actions . . . which is great, but words mean more to me
- He takes me for granted
- He is very OCD with cleaning. It adds a certain anxiety to the house when the dishwasher has to be loaded in a precise way
- Communicating with him is like pulling teeth. It's so hard to get him to articulate anything he's feeling
- Sometimes he just "shuts down" like a computer . . . Sensory overload, I guess?
- On a similar note, he's very robotic. Sometimes I think he has a control panel on his back, like Vicki in that show *Small Wonder* I watched as a kid. Sometimes I want a human, someone with emotion, someone who isn't always so logical and rational and practical
- He can be very blunt and insensitive
- He embarrasses me sometimes in social situations
- He's not really interested in my thoughts or feelings or interests
- He has such a hard time with empathy

- Because he's so rigid and regimented, daily life with him can be rather boring. Example: *The Office*
- He can get grumpy if he has a plan in his head that Cleo or I somehow interrupt unknowingly

The last entry was written seven weeks before she died. For whatever reason, there are no entries right before her death. I like to think it's because she'd made up her mind to stay with me, to quiet the "what-ifs" and put to rest the grievances. Did she realize her grievances paled in comparison to Mirai's? People say not to compare yourself to others, but perhaps it's a good thing sometimes.

This was Jana's last entry:

> *Maybe it's selfish to even entertain the idea of leaving him. It's not his fault that he has limitations. And we ALL have limitations. I've lived with his this long. How could I leave him now? I always think of when that actor, Christopher Reeve, was paralyzed after falling off a horse in the '90s. His wife (I even remember her name—Dana) was so dedicated to him. Did she ever consider leaving? Surely all of her needs weren't being met. Maybe that's too much to ask of life—to have a partner who meets all your needs. If Dana Reeve had left Superman, she would have been ostracized.*

> *I love Dave. That much I know. I care for him deeply. I see who he is, in his heart, even if he doesn't see who I am, in my heart. Can that be enough? Maybe it can. Maybe I can get my emotional needs met by friends like Julie, Steph, Mirai. Maybe, maybe, maybe.*

Still, I wonder if she would have left me, if she hadn't died. I wonder if she *should* have left me. I can't say I understand her unhappiness, but it's clear that she was unhappy. And it's clear that I played a part in that unhappiness.

In dark, private moments, I'm thankful that she died instead of leaving me. I know that's a terrible thing to say. Her death has broken me, but her leaving me would have broken me in a possibly more brutal way. What would it be like to know that she was out there, somewhere, just choosing not to spend her life with me? Would Cleo choose to live with her instead of me? She probably would.

The cruel irony is that now Cleo is with me. Every day. All the time. I am without a guide. That's what Jana was to me—a guide. I guess that's not what a spouse, or lover, should have to be, and maybe that was part of the problem, but I'd be lying if I said she wasn't that. Now there is nobody to show me the way, nobody to compensate for what I lack. I must do the impossible—try to lack less.

CHAPTER 14

Cleo

It's Sunday night and I'm lying in bed with Poppy at my side, trying to decide what to text Edie. She's texted me several times since yesterday:

Do you hate me?

Don't hate me. I advise against that.

Are you going to ignore me at school tomorrow? I need advance warning if that's the plan.

Thinking ahead. . . School's out soon. What if I need math tutoring over summer?

OK, here it is. . . I miss you. Already.

Am I sounding pathetic?

Don't answer that.

I'm not mad at her. She thinks I'm mad at her, but I'm not. That's not it at all. In a weird way, I'm flattered that she googled me, that she wanted to know more. I suppose it could just be curiosity, but I choose to see it as care.

I wanted to tell her about Mom and what happened to her. I wanted her to understand that those are two different things—who she was, and this terrible thing that everyone talked about for a month before never mentioning it again. I suppose I was waiting for the right time, though I don't know when that would have been. It's just such a weird, sad, freaky story.

I knew Mom had her Thursday yoga nights with her friend Mirai. Sometimes I'd hear them talking when they came back from dinner. I never heard anything they said, just muffled voices. Now I wonder if I should have opened my door so I could hear better. It would be nice to know all the conversations that took place before what happened.

One Thursday night, just as Dad and I were saying good night to each other, Mom came in the front door looking frantic. Mirai wasn't with her.

"What's wrong?" I asked.

There's that phrase *you look like you've seen a ghost*. Mom looked like she'd seen an army of ghosts. I'd never seen her like that—the color gone from her face, her eyes big and scared. She was in her yoga pants and a tank top, flip-flops on her feet. Her hair was in a bun on the top of her head. Some strands had escaped and were hanging at the sides of her face. She looked like she'd run straight from her class to our house. I could see her car outside, though, so I knew she'd driven.

"Clee, can you go to your room so I can talk to Dad?"

"Okay," I said, though I was hesitant. "Are you okay?"

She attempted a smile that was meant to reassure me but only made her look unhinged.

"I'm fine, sweetie. Everything's fine, okay?"

She came to me and gave me a hug. It was impossible to take comfort in it, because I could feel her hands trembling against me.

I went to my room because she wanted me to. I've never been the disobedient type. But, once in my room, I pressed my ear against the door so I could hear what she was telling Dad.

"What happened?" Dad asked her.

"I'm fine, I'm just a little shaken up."

"Sit, sit," Dad told her.

I pictured them sitting on the couch. I pictured Dad putting his hands on Mom's shoulders to calm her, though that's probably not what he did. He probably just sat there, waiting for her to explain.

"We were in yoga class. Mirai and me. And then this man comes into the room. Like, forcefully opens the door. And he was so angry. One of the women screamed. A group of us huddled in a corner. It was instinct or something."

"A man? What man?"

"I don't know. I mean, I didn't know. It was just obvious he was angry. Like, furious. And then Mirai says 'Sean, Sean' and I realize it's her husband."

Mom was talking fast, in a voice on the verge of crying.

"He started yelling at her in front of everyone. No hesitation. No care for what people thought. Like it was totally normal to him." It sounded like Mom was going to hyperventilate.

"Okay, okay," Dad said.

"I mean, imagine what happens behind closed doors if he's doing that in *public*. At a *yoga* class. I don't even know how he knew she was there. Do you think he put a tracker on her phone? Or her car? Or something? Dave, this guy was terrifying."

"What happened? Did Mirai leave with him?"

"She was totally calm during the whole thing. Embarrassed, maybe, but she wasn't rattled like I was. Like I *am*. She told him to wait in the car and she would be there in a minute. Then she apologized to everyone and she just *left*. I kept saying, 'Mirai, wait,' but she wouldn't even look at me."

"Okay, well, so it sounds like she's okay?"

"Dave!"

Mom sounded completely exasperated.

"Maybe that's just how they are together."

"How they *are* together? Are you kidding me?"

"I don't know. I wasn't there."

"Right, you weren't there. Exactly. You have no idea how dangerous this man seemed. He's going to hurt her. I have to do something."

"Do what?"

"I think I should tell her to come stay here for a while. With Kyra. Her daughter. I guess I have to make sure he doesn't know how to find her again and—"

"Wait, wait, do you even know if that's what Mirai would want? We can't just go throwing ourselves into their lives."

"I'm not *throwing* myself. She's my *friend*. I know you don't know much about friendship, but . . . Jesus, Dave."

I had never heard them talk like this before—heated, emotional. I had heard them bicker. I had seen Mom roll her eyes at Dad. But never this.

"Look, if it's that important to you, then fine. Like you said, she's *your* friend. I don't know much about her."

"Right, okay, yeah," Mom said, calming down.

"I guess they can share the guest bed," Dad said. That's Dad, logistics-focused.

"Mirai has talked about leaving him," Mom said, still making her case. "I just didn't know he was *that* bad. You should have seen his eyes, Dave."

"All right, well. I don't want this guy coming to our house, so make sure it's safe, whatever you decide."

One Christmas, Dad got Mom a dish towel that said HAPPY WIFE, HAPPY LIFE. She'd laughed, which made me think it was a joke gift. But I've come to see that it was really his life philosophy. What happens now that he has no wife?

"I'll talk to her at work tomorrow," Mom said. "I don't want to text her in case he's checking her phone or something. God, what if she doesn't come to work tomorrow? Should I call the police or—"

"Why don't you wait and see, okay?"

"Right, yeah. Wait and see."

She still sounded worked up, but not nearly as bad as she had been.

"I don't know if I can sleep," she said. "I might have a glass of wine and watch a dumb show to calm my nerves. See you in bed later?"

I heard the sound of their bedroom door clicking shut. I heard the sound of the TV on low volume in the living room—it was still on when I happened to wake up at one in the morning. I had a bad feeling in my stomach. I didn't know why. Sometimes it's only in hindsight that you realize the power of intuition.

Mom must have seen Mirai at work the next day and discussed things with her, because that night at dinner, she said "Clee, we want to talk to you about something." We were eating what Mom called "Mexican lasagna"—tortillas layered with refried beans and cheese and whatever veggies Mom could sneak in there without me protesting.

"What is it?" I asked, trying to sound oblivious, though I knew what was coming.

"You know my friend Mirai?"

I nodded. When I looked at Dad, he was staring intensely at his Mexican lasagna, as if he wanted nothing to do with this conversation.

"Well, she and her daughter, Kyra, are going to come stay here for a little while," she said.

"Oh. Um . . . okay."

"She's having some problems with her husband, so this will be temporary, until she can get her own place and all that. Kyra is your age. She goes to that private school off Ortega. Really sweet girl."

Mom made it sound very casual and fun. She still seemed jittery, but most of the angst she'd displayed twenty-four hours earlier was gone.

"They're staying in the guest room?" I asked.

"Yes. They'll share the bed. Like I said, it'll be temporary."

For a minute, there was only the sound of our forks scraping against our plates.

"Is that okay with you?" Mom asked.

It didn't feel like a genuine question. It seemed more like a statement: *That's okay with you, isn't it?* I felt weird about it. Our house was small. We had two bathrooms—the one in Mom and Dad's room, and the one in the hallway that was accepted as "Cleo's bathroom." I didn't want to share mine with these two people who were basically strangers to me. But it seemed important to Mom and, like she said, it was temporary.

"Sure, yeah," I said.

And that was that.

Mirai and Kyra came to the house on Saturday morning. Kyra looked like her mom, just with slightly lighter skin, and hair that was dark brown instead of black. They were like Instagram filter versions of the same person. She was wearing a backpack and carrying a duffel bag in each hand. Her mom had a large rolling suitcase and a bag hanging over each shoulder. They didn't look like people planning on a short stay.

Dad and I sat on the couch, pretending to watch one of his shows—*Pawn Stars,* I think. I gave Mirai and Kyra a small smile and a wave, but I didn't have much interest in showing them to their room or helping at all. I was feeling pretty annoyed by the whole thing, if I'm honest. Kyra gave me a small smile and a wave back. She looked as annoyed as I was, but her annoyance was also tinged with embarrassment.

Mom was cheerful as ever. She told them to follow her down the hall: "Let me show you your room." *Your room.* As if it belonged to them, as if it had been empty all this time in anticipation of their eventual arrival. I heard Mom telling them how she'd just put new sheets on the bed and cleared out the dresser drawers for them. We used those drawers to store seasonal things—bathing suits, mittens, scarves, Halloween costumes. I don't know what Mom did with our stuff. She probably boxed it up and put it in the garage.

"This is weird," I told Dad.

He was staring straight ahead at the TV, seemingly engrossed in the episode. Maybe he hadn't been pretending to watch at all; maybe it was only me who was.

"What?" he said.

"This. Is. Weird." I jerked my head toward the hallway, where our new roommates were settling in.

"Yeah. I know," he said. "It won't be for long."

I sighed. I wished—and still wish—he'd told Mom "No," said, "I don't think it's a good idea to have a second family basically living in our house." He'd become so accommodating to her, like he was desperate to make her happy.

I had been in denial about them actually moving in with us, so I hadn't spent any time picturing what it would be like. When Mom welcomed them to the dinner table with us that night, it occurred to me that our family dinners would no longer be "family dinners"; they would be "dinners with family and these other people." They seemed nice enough. I just hated that I couldn't wear my ratty old pajama pants to the table and burp with reckless abandon (a Garrison family pastime). I hated that we couldn't talk like we usually did—an often-hilarious stream of consciousness that made sense only to the three of us. It was like we were all on our best behavior, sitting up straighter, minding our manners. Mirai and Kyra seemed so formal—maybe because that's how their meals were at home, or maybe because they were trying to be respectful toward us. Whatever the reason, it was super awkward.

"So, Kyra, what do you do for fun?" Mom asked, trying to spark conversation.

Kyra was holding her fork and knife nearly perpendicular to the plate as she cut her baked potato.

"Oh, I like to read and watch TV and . . . I don't know, boring stuff," she said with a self-conscious laugh.

"Sounds familiar," Mom said, giving me a wink.

"You go to Via Sierra, right?" Mirai said to me.

I nodded. "Yep."

After that, it was like nobody could think of anything else to say. We finished the rest of our dinner in the most uncomfortable silence of my life.

Dad cleared the plates and disappeared into the garage, probably to tinker with his model cars or whatever. Mom and Mirai decided to stay at the table and have a glass of wine. I intended to go straight to my room, but I felt bad seeing Kyra just sitting there on the couch, looking sad, tugging on the cuffs of her sweater so they covered her hands.

I sat on the other end of the couch from her and said, "You wanna watch TV?" As it was, she was just looking at the dark screen.

"Oh, sure," she said.

I turned it on, selected a benign home-improvement show. I just needed noise to temper the awkwardness.

"Must have been a crazy day for you, huh?" I said.

The facts, as I knew them, were that she and her mom had packed up their things and left the house they shared with her dad. I tried to imagine what that would be like, if Mom and I packed up our things and left Dad. It would be fun if it was for a spontaneous road trip. It would be crushingly sad if it was for any other reason.

"Yeah, pretty crazy." She raised her eyebrows and sighed.

"Does your dad know you left, or . . . ?"

She looked at her watch, one of those fitness-tracker watches.

"He probably knows now. He usually gets home from work around now."

She seemed scared, so I said, "Is he going to be mad?"

She looked at me like I was crazy. "Um, yeah."

"What if he, like, files a missing person report or something?"

She shook her head. "We left him a note. Well, my mom did. It explains that we're leaving. My mom's going to get a restraining order."

"Oh," I said, "wow."

Part of me wanted nothing to do with this adult drama; and part of me was intrigued. This is the conflict of adolescence, I guess—wanting to remain innocent and wanting to grow up.

"Then she'll file for divorce."

Kyra sounded very matter-of-fact, as if she was reading directions on a recipe.

"Is that a bad thing, or a good thing?"

She shrugged. "Bad for my dad, I guess. Good for my mom."

"What about you?"

She shrugged again. "I don't know. My dad is okay with me, but he's kind of a jerk with my mom, you know?"

I didn't know, but I said "Yeah."

"I'd be happy to be with my mom. And she'd be happier. So, it's good. . . . It's just weird."

"Yeah."

She started biting her fingernails, so I decided to stop asking questions. I didn't want to make her upset.

"I'm kind of worried he'll find us," she said. Even as she expressed this worry, her voice remained eerily even.

"How would he? Does he even know who my mom is?"

She shook her head. "My mom says no. And she checked her car for any trackers. I guess he had one on her car before, but she took it off. And we turned off our phones so there's no signal or whatever."

"That's good. How could he find you then?"

I was asking for myself. I didn't want this supposedly awful man to show up at our house.

"He probably can't. But, I mean, he knows where I go to school. So he could come there. My mom said she's calling the school first thing Monday morning to make sure they know not to let him in."

"It sounds like she's thought of everything."

She sighed again, heavily. "I hope so."

"Well, look at you girls," Mom said, coming up behind the couch. "Learning how to renovate houses?"

Mirai was standing next to her, the two of them holding glasses of wine. Mirai had the same look of subdued fear as Kyra. I was sure neither of them would sleep that night. I didn't know if I would, either.

"I always love these shows," Mirai said. "They show you that you can take a beat-up place and make something beautiful."

Mom laughed, and the laugh irritated me. This didn't seem to be a time for laughs.

"Cheers to that," she said, and the two of them clinked glasses.

I text Edie:

Hey dork.

She responds immediately.

Does that mean you forgive me?

The hugeness of the smile on my face embarrasses me, even though I'm just lying in bed by myself.

I was never really mad, weirdo. Talk tomorrow?

In response, I get the party hat emoji.

CHAPTER 15

Dave

Every few hundred thousand years or so, the Earth's magnetic field diminishes to almost nothing for about a century, then gradually reappears with the north and south poles flipped. The last such reversal was 800,000 years ago; so, as I've said with other disastrous phenomena, we may be overdue. In the past hundred years, the strength of our magnetic field has decreased about five percent, which is foreboding.

The magnetic field is important for a few reasons. Many living creatures navigate by magnetic reckoning. A flipping of the poles could cause serious ecological issues. But that's not my biggest worry.

The magnetic field's most essential job is to deflect particle storms and cosmic rays from the sun, in addition to even-more-energetic subatomic particles from deep space. Without magnetic protection, these particles would enter our atmosphere and erode the long-suffering ozone layer.

Or worse.

Solar flares are huge magnetic outbursts of the sun that bombard the Earth with high-speed subatomic particles. As it is now, Earth's atmosphere and magnetic field negate the possibly lethal effects of these flares. (As a side note, solar flares are a good thing, generally. Without them, the resulting dimming effect would cool the Earth and send us into another Ice Age.)

But, with no magnetic field, solar flares could be dangerous. Superflares, which are millions of times more powerful than regular solar flares, could be deadly. With a weak magnetic field, a superflare on the sun could fry the Earth, and everyone on it, within minutes.

The day Jana died, the poles flipped and I was struck by a superflare that, for some reason, did not kill me. I am still trying to make sense of this—her death, and my survival of it.

It was the Monday after the weekend Mirai and Kyra came to stay with us. That morning, Jana, Mirai, and Kyra left in Jana's car. The plan was to drop off Kyra at school, then go to work. The three of them left a few minutes before Cleo and I did. I dropped Cleo off at school, then drove in to the office in Irvine. Aside from the fact that the usual morning routine was disrupted by the presence of Mirai and Kyra at the house, it was a typical Monday. I settled in at my desk and put on my headphones, not to listen to music (or anything, for that matter), but to deter others from talking to me.

I was working on an FDA submission for a blood-pressure medication when my cell phone rang. I didn't recognize the number, so I ignored it. I detest telemarketers. Then it rang a second time, from the same number. I wondered if it was Cleo's school (a number I did not have programmed into my phone). I assumed that's what it would be. She wasn't feeling well. Or she'd forgotten something at home. Something like that. I removed a headphone from one ear and put my phone there.

"Hello?"

"Is this Dave?"

It was a woman's voice, and that voice sounded shaky and upset.

"Uh, yes. Who is this?"

"I'm Rhonda. I work with Jana," she said.

Her voice went from shaking to cracking.

"What is it?" I pressed. I wasn't thinking ahead to the possibilities, to what could have been wrong. In some cases, the "trouble with imagination" associated with Asperger's is a blessing.

"There was an incident," the woman, Rhonda, said. "At work."

"Oh," I said. "Okay. Can I talk to her?"

It dawned on me that it was strange that Jana wasn't already on the phone, that this woman had called on her behalf.

"They took her to the hospital."

"The hospital?"

She gave me the address. "You should meet her there." Every word she said sounded strained, as if she was attempting to speak with a throat the size of a drinking straw.

"Is she okay?"

"I don't know," she said, her words turning to sobs.

I stood from my desk and gathered my things—car keys, wallet. As I left the building, I still had the phone pressed to my ear (though Rhonda was no longer there), and the headphone still on the other ear, the cord dangling around my neck like a necklace.

The scene at the hospital was, and is, a blur.

> *She arrived by ambulance a few minutes ago.*
> *Critical condition.*
> *The doctors are working on her.*
> *Someone will come see you soon.*

These were the things told to me by people I didn't know. I paced the waiting area, feeling like a caged lion. I still had no idea what had happened.

I don't know how soon the doctor came out to talk to me. It could have been a few minutes or an hour.

"Are you Mr. Garrison, Jana's husband?" the doctor asked.

She was young, thirty-something, probably a resident. She had dark, heavy bags under her eyes. I once heard that doctors make a point of cleaning off their shoes before going to talk to loved ones, because of the inevitable blood spattering that occurs in the midst of trying to save someone's life. I stared at the doctor's shoes. She had missed a spot.

"I'm Dr. Lopez. Do you want to sit?"

I knew that was bad—the invitation to sit. I wanted to refuse. If sitting meant bad news, I would remain standing in the hope of better news. She pulled a chair away from the wall for me, though, motioned for me to take it. So I did.

"Your wife lost a lot of blood at the scene and in the ambulance," she said.

I stared at the spot on her shoe, marveled at my wife's DNA in this odd location.

"She had no heartbeat when she arrived here. We did what we could to revive her, but I'm sorry to say we weren't able to."

My initial thought was: *So, you're bringing in other people who will be able to?* She had presented it as a failure on the part of the medical team, after all.

She looked at me expectantly, begging me to say something, so I said, "Okay."

"Is there someone here with you? A friend or family member?"

She turned her head one way and then the other, in search of these alleged friends and family members who were meant to comfort me so she could go on her way.

I shook my head.

"I can have a social worker come talk with you if you'd like."

I shook my head again. "Can I see her?" I asked.

I was not sure yet that she was dead. Or, rather, I understood it logically, but I didn't feel it yet. I didn't *want* to see her; but I also didn't want to leave the hospital without seeing for myself what the truth was.

"Give us a little time, okay, Mr. Garrison?" she said, patting my leg with her hand. I stared at the hand on my leg, resenting her closeness, her touch. "Someone will come back for you soon."

Because Jana wasn't fit to be seen. That's what it was. This fact made me feel like I was going to vomit.

I remained sitting there in that chair for a half hour or so before someone came to fetch me, just as the doctor promised. The fetcher, a nurse, was another young woman. Her scrubs looked two sizes too big for her. We took the elevator down, and I followed her through a maze of hallways, feeling like I had a baseball in my throat, unable to swallow it down no matter how hard I tried.

We stopped in front of a room that had a small plaque next to it that said VIEWING ROOM. They had a room dedicated to this. It was a fact I never wanted to know. Across the hall was a door with another plaque next to it: MORGUE.

The fetcher-nurse said, "I'll wait here. Take as much time as you need."

The room was dimly lit and too cold. Jana was lying on a gurney that had a fabric skirt running around the lower half. She was draped with a blanket. Her neck was wrapped in bandages. I still didn't know what had happened to her. I hadn't even thought to ask yet.

I was afraid to get too close. Jana didn't look like herself, and I wasn't sure if I wanted this to be the last image of her imprinted on my brain. Her face was beautiful, not a scratch; but she was so pale, vampirically pale. Her hair was greasy or wet, I couldn't tell which. I didn't want to touch it, in case the wetness was blood. I didn't want to touch any of her, knowing her skin would be waxy and cold. It was obvious that she wasn't *there* anymore. This body of hers was lying here on this gurney, but she was gone. I took odd comfort in that, in knowing she had left this horrible scene.

I didn't stay long. Ten minutes, maybe. When I left, the nurse escorted me through the maze again.

"What happened to her?" I asked.

I didn't realize I'd asked the question out loud until the nurse turned around and said, "I'm sorry, what?"

We were at the elevators, waiting. I decided I might as well repeat the question: "What happened to her?"

She looked confused, unsure how to answer. "Has nobody talked to you yet?"

"They did. I didn't ask. This is the first time I'm asking."

"Oh," she said. She shifted the weight of her body from one hip to the other, looking uncomfortable. "I'm so sorry, sir. She was stabbed."

"Stabbed?"

It seemed like such a violent and barbaric thing. *Stabbed.*

I didn't have to ask where. I remembered the bandages. Who would stab her in the neck? What kind of person would stab any other person in the neck? I wondered if it was an accident of some kind. It had to have been. Something freak, unexpected. Someone coming around a corner too fast holding a pair of scissors. There was no other explanation. Not then, at least.

A pair of police officers—a short woman and a fat man—confronted me when we returned to the ER floor. They said they needed to speak with me, now that the case had become a homicide. *A homicide.* They apologized for my loss, before questioning me about Jana and her relationship with a man named Sean, who was "the perpetrator."

"Relationship?" I said.

At first, I thought perhaps Jana was having an affair, something that had ended in this unbelievable violence. That name was familiar—*Sean.*

"We're told he is the husband of one of the women Jana works with," the fat man said.

The woman flipped through her little spiral notebook. Before she could present the name, I said, "Mirai?"

She looked up at me. "Yes, that's it. You know her?"

So then I had to tell them about Jana's Thursday yoga nights with Mirai, and about Mirai and Kyra coming to stay with us, and about Sean sounding like a total asshole. And then they had to tell me that Sean had shown up at Jana's work, intent on harming Mirai. But Jana had put herself between the two of them and been attacked in the process. Mirai was stabbed in the shoulder and was being treated in the same hospital.

"Mr. Garrison?" the short woman said.

I must have done my mental disappearing act—*alakazam, he's gone*, Jana used to say—because I had no idea what they were asking me.

"What?"

"Do you know the whereabouts of the daughter? Kyra?"

Thinking about Kyra was thinking about another life. It felt like a year had passed between waving good-bye to Jana's car that morning and talking to these police officers. How was I to know where Kyra was?

"You said she was staying with you, right? Did she go to school this morning?"

This morning.

I was so disoriented.

"Yes," I said. "She was in the car with Jana and Mirai. They dropped her off. The private school off Ortega."

The woman jotted down notes, then looked at the fat man.

"We need to get an officer to the school," the man said to the woman.

They started asking me more questions, but I was zoning out again, until the vibration of my phone in my pocket brought me back to reality.

Cleo.

When I answered, she said, "Daaad, did you get lost in a work project again? You're late."

I had no idea what time it was. I had no idea what day it was. Just hearing Cleo's voice was jarring. I know it sounds terrible to say, but I'd forgotten about her. Or, maybe, I'd chosen to forget about her for the time being, fooling myself into thinking that I could compartmentalize this event like I compartmentalized everything else in my life. This terrible thing could have happened to Jana, and Cleo could go on with life as normal. The absurdity of this dawned on me at the same time it dawned on me that it was Monday afternoon and I was supposed to be picking up Cleo at school.

"Hi, yeah, sorry."

The police officers were both looking at me, so I turned around, away from them.

"Dad? You sound weird."

"Weird?"

"Yeah, weird." She laughed when she said it. She had no idea that she was about to enter a phase of life when laughing would be impossible.

"I'll be there soon, okay?"

"Um, okay. You are freaking me out." She laughed again.

She thought I was just being strange (a common occurrence). She had no reason to think anything was seriously wrong. Most kids have no reason to think anything is seriously wrong. That is the blessing of youth.

Before I left the hospital, I was approached by someone who wanted to talk to me about organ donation. I signed the forms as quickly as possible. I didn't want to think about it. Jana was dead. Gone. If her organs could help others, then donation made logical sense. I was more concerned with picking up Cleo than I was with the fate of Jana's body. I don't know what kind of person that makes me.

On the drive to the school, I thought about how to tell Cleo. I had no idea what to say. I wanted so badly to text Jana, to ask her for advice: *How do I tell her you died?*

When I got to the school, Cleo was waiting at the usual pickup location, looking bored and annoyed. She stomped to the car, opened the door, and said, "This might be your worst brain fart yet."

"Sorry," I said.

We started driving, and I could feel her eyes on me. She could tell something was wrong—not by my silence (I am often quiet), but by something else. Intuition, I guess. Something I've never possessed.

"What's wrong?"

We were still ten minutes from home. I didn't want to tell her in the car.

"Wrong?" I said, stalling.

"Something is wrong."

I didn't say anything. I've never been good at lying.

"Dad?"

I kept my eyes on the road, hands gripping the steering wheel.

"Dad," she said, again. "What is it? What happened?"

I was focused on just getting home, on telling her there, in the safety of the walls we both knew so well.

"I'm sorry, something bad did happen," I said. "But let's wait until we get home, okay?"

"Oh my god, Dad, you can't do that to me," she said. "Is it Mirai? Did her husband do something?"

I wasn't sure how to respond—the answer was "no" to the first question, and "yes" to the second.

"Dad, you can't just say that and not tell me," she said. "Is it Kyra?"

"No, sweetie, it's not Kyra."

"*Sweetie?* You never call me 'sweetie.' What's going on?"

She was nearly hysterical. We were just a few turns from home.

"Please just calm down, okay? I'll tell you when we're home."

She commenced chewing on her fingernails, a bad habit she'd gotten from me.

When we pulled into the driveway, Cleo jumped out of the car before I'd even put it in Park. I think she must have been going to the house to find Jana. Jana was not usually home from work until after five, but Cleo may have been thinking that whatever had happened meant Jana had come home early.

"Where's Mom?" she said. "At work?"

"Let's go inside, okay?"

I put one hand on each of her shoulders and guided her inside the house. Cleo and I often came home to an empty house like this. It was my job to pick her up from school and then work the rest of my day from home while Cleo did her homework. But the house felt especially empty right then. My eyes went to the stack of dirty cereal bowls in the sink—two more than usual because of Mirai and Kyra. How could something so terrible happen on a day with dirty cereal bowls in the sink?

Cleo sat on the couch. She looked scared. I'm sure I looked scared too. I hated that I had the job of telling her this news. I hated the way she looked to me as her source of information. I hated that she would look to me for that from now on.

"Talk," Cleo said. "Please."

Her arms were crossed against her chest. It looked like she was hugging herself, bracing.

I sat on the couch next to her, an empty cushion between us.

"There was an incident at Mom's work," I said, relying on the same words that Rhonda had used with me.

"An incident?"

"Mirai's husband showed up there," I said. "He intended to hurt Mirai."

Cleo was completely still. She didn't nod or mumble or anything.

"Mom was trying to protect Mirai, and she got hurt."

I regretted this phrasing immediately, knowing the question that would come next.

"Is she okay?"

I hesitated just long enough for Cleo to draw her own conclusion. She started crying, tears running down her face in rivers.

"Dad, is she okay?" she asked, her voice desperate this time. She already knew the answer.

"I'm sorry, sweetie."

"No," she said.

The rivers began rushing.

As previously noted, I have never liked being in the presence of emotional outbursts. I have no idea how to respond to them. My instinct is to run away, go to another room, avoid the anguish. But in this moment I knew I had to stay, endure.

"No," Cleo said again, this time making the one-syllable word into several syllables, singing it like a song.

I moved closer to her, put my arm around her, and pulled her into my chest. She was sobbing in an uncontrollable way that made my own eyes well up. I could feel my shirt getting wet from her tears, the wet spot spreading wider and wider. Her entire body shook against mine.

She shook and sobbed like that for nearly an hour (I was staring ahead at the clock on the cable box, that's how I knew). Slowly, the intensity of the sobs eventually waned. I don't think she felt any better; I think her body was simply exhausted and could not continue expressing itself in the way it had been.

When she leaned away from my chest, my entire shirt was damp. She wouldn't look at me. She stared down at her lap, rubbing her eyes, still emitting jerky sniffles. Finally she looked at me, her eyes puffy and red. I had never seen her in pain like this. I had never seen anyone in pain like this.

"What did he do to her?" she asked.

When I told her, she collapsed into me again, crying quietly.

"I can't believe this," she said.

"I can't either."

"What happened to Mirai?"

When I told her, she said, "So she'll live?"

I said I assumed she would, that I had no reason to believe otherwise. Cleo just nodded. We were still in the process of absorbing the shock of Jana's death. This absorption process would never be fully complete; but once it was adequately underway, we had the brain space available to develop an acute hatred of Mirai (and Kyra, by association). I still hold this hatred. I know I shouldn't. I know it's not good for me. But forgiving Mirai feels like accepting what happened to Jana, and I do not want to accept it. I cannot accept it.

"Do you want anything to eat?" I asked Cleo.

It was, after all, dinner time, and I was desperate to be helpful in some way.

Cleo looked at me like I was from another planet. "Eat? You could *eat* right now?"

I shrugged. I am one of those people who is capable of eating through most anything. The distresses of my head do not connect to my stomach.

"I feel like I'm gonna barf," Cleo said.

"Okay, then, no food. We can just sit here."

She mumbled agreement, and we just sat there, until we both fell asleep sometime after midnight.

CHAPTER 16

Cleo

When I see Edie before homeroom on Monday morning, she gives me a hug, as if we have not seen each other in months, as if something monumental has occurred in that expansive time apart. It is a long hug, a hug long enough to have a beginning, middle, and end. In the beginning of it, my body is tense because any physical touch with Edie has that effect on me. In the middle of it, I begin to relax into the generosity of this hug. At the end of it, when I feel her hold on me release, I am sad and grateful at the same time.

"Hi," I say.

"Hi," she says. "I'm sorry, again. I should have just *asked* you about your mom."

"Maybe," I say. "But I probably wouldn't have told you anyway. It's good you forced the issue."

We had one minute until we had to be inside.

"Can we talk about it more? At lunch, maybe?"

"I'll meet you at the lawn."

She's already sitting in our spot by the time I get there, cross-legged and slouched as she examines the contents of her brown paper bag. Her mom packs her lunch every day, which I've told her is "cute, bordering on pathetic." I've made my own lunch since middle school.

"What did Mama pack you today?" I call out as I come up behind her.

She turns around. "An extra cookie for you, but I don't like your tone, so two cookies for me."

I laugh with the relief that we are back to normal.

I sit next to her, also cross-legged, my kneecap kissing her kneecap. I make an inane comment about the weather (it's beautiful), and she makes an equally inane comment about her history homework. And then I decide we may as well get to it.

"So," I say. "My mom."

"We don't have to talk about it," she says. "I mean, if you don't want to."

"I never want to; but you're, like, my best friend, so you should probably know."

"I think Carter would be upset with you for saying that," she says.

"He would," I say. "Don't tell him I gave you that title."

"Does he know about what happened to your mom?"

I nod. "That's pretty much why we're friends. Two misfits in this weird world."

"That's why we're friends too, huh?"

"Basically."

She uncrosses her legs and stretches them out in front of her on the grass.

"So, it just happened last year, right?"

I nod. "Yeah, the anniversary was a week before I met you, actually."

The anniversary sucked. The entire first year sucked. My first birthday without her (my fifteenth). My first summer without her. First Fourth of July. First Halloween. First Thanksgiving. First Christmas. First New Year. It all sucked. This second year without her sucks too, but at least all those firsts are behind me.

"You've been a nice distraction," I say to Edie, and she smiles.

"I guess what I don't get is—why does what happened to your mom make you a misfit?"

"You kind of had to be there, I guess."

"Tell me."

I sigh. "I don't know. The whole thing was like this spectacle. What happened was so dramatic and everyone was talking about it. But nobody was talking *to* me. They were, like, talking *around* me. When they did talk to me, it was all these clichés—*she's in a better place, God has a reason for everything*. Nobody was real with me. Even my friends. So, not only did I lose my mom, I felt like I lost everyone."

"God, that sucks."

I keep going: "Something like two hundred people came to her funeral. Two hundred! We had no idea that would happen. Dad would have made it a private thing if he'd known. It's not like Mom was a social butterfly. She wasn't. At all. And there were all these people there, some of them crying like she was their best friend. It pissed me off."

Ms. Murray said they were probably crying because they were contemplating their own mortality and the fragility of life and blah blah blah. It wasn't about Mom as a person. It was about *them*. They made her funeral about *them*. Grief hijackers, that's what I called them.

"And it's not what Mom would have wanted—this sensational thing. Nobody except Ms. Murray asked me about who she was. She was the victim of this tragedy, and she will always be associated with that violence, you know? I can't change that."

"Well, they might always associate her with that, but you won't."

I take a bite of peanut butter sandwich. "I know that. It still bugs me."

"It bugs me on your behalf," she says. "People suck."

"They do. Except for you. And Carter. And my dad, most of the time."

She hands me a cookie. "Here, I have to stay on your good side."

"You know what's weird? I don't even think about how Mom died. Maybe I'm trying to block it out. I'd much rather think about the years I spent with her before what happened. Everyone else just focuses on those few minutes when she was attacked."

"Their loss."

"Yeah."

She takes a bite of her own cookie as I nibble the edges of mine.

"What was she like?" she asks.

It's the question I wished people would ask me in the wake of her death. Instead, I got stupid questions like "How *are* you?" *How the fuck do you think I am, moron?*

"She was funny. She had the best laugh. I mean, she had to have a sense of humor to put up with my dad. She was smart, but not snotty about it. She was loving—like always hugging me, kissing my cheeks. Super expressive—she'd squeal during TV shows and cry during those animal-welfare commercials."

"So, like, the opposite of your dad."

"Or the antidote to him."

"That's deep."

"She always came up with these fun outings for us. Before she died, she took me to the makeup store at the mall and told them she wanted us to look goth."

"Please tell me you have a picture of this."

I reach into the front pocket of my backpack for my phone. I scroll through the photo album I've titled "Mom" to find it. It's one of the last ones, so it's easy to find. There we are, the two of us, our eyes lined heavily in black, our lips almost as dark. The woman at the counter was so irritated with us. Mom kept telling her she would buy something before leaving, to compensate for the time spent. She bought three bottles of face wash.

"You look like her," Edie says.

"I like to think so."

"No, you do. Objectively speaking."

"Thanks." Because it is, and forever will be, the best compliment anyone could give me.

"Can I see more?" she asks.

We spend the remainder of lunch huddled together as I scroll through pictures and videos on my phone. There are selfies of the two of us, so many of those. In some, we are sticking out our tongues. In some, she is kissing my cheek. In some, I am kissing hers.

"Oh, this is her dancing," I say, selecting one of my favorite videos.

"Is that . . . the Dougie?"

I laugh. "Yeah. She used to love the dance tutorials on YouTube."

She was always dancing in the kitchen, twerking in front of Dad because it was so hilarious to watch his response (a blank stare). I used to feign embarrassment and tell her I'd disown her if she ever danced in public. I didn't mean it, though. I loved her dancing, as awkward and ridiculous as it was. I miss it daily. The kitchen is a boring, sad place now.

"You must miss her so much," she says.

"Yeah." I look down because I feel like I'm going to cry. "You know that scene in *The Wizard of Oz* when Dorothy goes from black-and-white Kansas to colorful Oz?"

"I've never seen *The Wizard of Oz*," she says.

"*What?*" My threatening tears have subsided in response to this outrageous revelation.

She shrugs. "I haven't seen *E.T.*, either."

"These are, like, *classics*."

She shrugs again.

"I have the DVDs," I say. "You can come watch them."

"Deal. Now what were you saying?"

I try to explain the scene to her. "Anyway, it feels like I went from Oz back to black-and-white Kansas."

"She was the color," she says.

"She was the color."

Mom used to like those adult coloring books that have become all the rage. She had one of different animals drinking martinis, one of swear words in big bubble letters. She colored them in with the boldest, brightest crayons in the box—orange, red, magenta, yellow. When she died, it's like she took those colors with her.

"You might not know this," Edie says, "but you are the color too."

I roll my eyes. "That might be the cheesiest thing you've ever said to me."

"It might be the cheesiest thing I've ever said, period. But it made you smile."

She's right. It did.

The warning bell dings. Edie stands up and then reaches her hand down to help me stand. She's never done that before.

"Oh," she says. "Before I forget—Mom and I have to go to the new house to meet with a roof guy after school. Can we come say hi? Or . . . you can walk over and say hi to us if you don't want us to come there."

"I'll come to you guys," I say. "Text me."

When Dad comes to pick me up, he says, "You seem happy." My happiness is obvious enough for Dad to notice. I haven't stopped smiling since lunch.

"Edie and her mom are coming to their new house to meet with a roof guy. Can I go see them?"

"A roof guy? Are they at the roof-guy stage?"

He sounds agitated.

"I don't know, Dad. Is the roof-guy stage not acceptable to you?"

"I just didn't know they were that far along."

"Dad, say it with me—we are going to have neighbors."

He doesn't humor me. He just sucks in his breath and stays quiet for the rest of the drive home.

When we pull into our driveway, I can see Edie's car across the way at their house. I jump out before the car has come to a stop.

"I'll be back for dinner, okay?"

I'm already jogging toward Edie's house before I hear Dad mumble "Okay."

Edie's mom is out front, talking to someone who I assume is "the roof guy." When she sees me, she says something that makes the guy give me a small nod before turning his attention to the house and making notes on a pad of paper.

"*Mija*, it's so good to see you."

She reaches her arms out toward me for a hug. I wonder if Edie told her about what happened to Mom. I wonder if the tightness of her hug is a reflection of what she now knows about my sad life.

"It's good to see you too," I tell her.

"I keep telling Edie I miss you and she says I'm not allowed to miss you. 'Mom, she's *my* girlfriend,' she says."

Girlfriend?

I want so much to ask her to confirm that Edie does, in fact, refer to me with this title. But before I can think of a way to do this without sounding like a complete dork, Edie comes out the front door of the house.

"So, what do you think?" she asks, stretching her arms out.

I take it in, the house. While the basic structure hasn't changed—it's still two stories, with the windows and doors in the same spots as before—it looks completely different. The old wood siding that used to be there has been replaced with new wood slabs, painted white. In place of the boarded-up windows are new panes of pristine glass, the manufacturer's sticker still on them. Cement has been laid for a front porch.

"It looks amazing," I say. "I like the porch addition."

"I have visions of a swing there," her mom says, squinting her eyes as if she is conjuring this vision right now.

"And she wants to paint the front door bright yellow, which I think is ridiculous," Edie says.

"It's not ridiculous. Color is good," I say.

Edie winks at me. "I guess that's true. Color is good."

"You want to see inside?" her mom asks.

I nod and she leads me inside, Edie on my heels. The inside is a mess. They've pulled up whatever floor used to be there so that now there is just concrete, barely visible through wood shavings. The dust in the air is palpably thick.

"It's very much . . . *en progreso*," her mom says.

I do my best to suppress a sneeze, but my best is not good enough. They both say "Bless you."

"Mom wanted to take down some walls so that it's more . . . what's the word they always use on HGTV?" Edie says.

"Open concept," her mom and I say in unison. Edie gives me a look that is a mix of impressed and perplexed.

"I like home-improvement shows," I say.

"You'll have to help me make some decisions, then," her mom says.

She grabs my forearm and leads me around the bottom floor, pointing out where everything will go—the kitchen island, the stovetop, their future L-shaped couch, the fireplace, the big-screen TV. She has the eyes of a dreamer—lit up, big, hopeful. I wonder if this is how she ended up with Edie's dad, if she saw in him a project that she could beautify. It must be terrible to be mistaken about such a thing.

"Edie, show her the upstairs. I need to finish talking to Mario."

Mario must be the roof guy.

The staircase does not have a railing yet—just wooden steps waiting to be carpeted or tiled or whatever.

"Don't fall," Edie says.

"Words of wisdom."

At the top of the staircase there is a small open area with a bench seat under a window that looks out across the way to my house. On each side of the open area is a doorway (actual doors not yet installed).

"Mom's room will be over there," Edie says, pointing toward the doorway that's behind me. "And mine is this one."

She walks toward it and I follow, and my heart beats faster because, even though I know there is nothing *in* her bedroom (namely, a bed on which to make out), it's still *her bedroom*.

"Welcome to my humble abode," she says.

The room appears enormous, maybe because there's nothing in it. There is a closet (door removed) and a large window. I imagine her bed will be on the wall opposite the window. I imagine she'll be able to look out at the stars.

"It's going to be awesome," I say.

I go to the window, look out at her view of the mountains. It's the same view I have from my bedroom.

"*Going* to be? It already is."

"Well, yeah. But it'll be *more* awesome when it has, like, floors."

"Sshh," she says. "You're going to hurt the floor's feelings."

She sits on the floor, as if to show her acceptance of the floors in their current state.

"Come sit with me," she says. "Get to know the floor."

I do as she says, sitting cross-legged across from her. She takes my hands in hers and just holds them there in the middle of us.

"Mom says we might be moving in sooner than we thought," she says.

"Really? It's that close to done?"

"Oh, no. Not really. But I guess her settlement funds are dwindling and that stupid hotel is pretty expensive."

"So you would just, like, stay here? In the dust?"

She shrugs. "We could probably get it pretty cleaned up, or at least good enough to be livable. I can help more when school's out."

Finals are next week, then summer break.

"Maybe your girlfriend could help out too," I say.

The word is out of my mouth before I realize. *Girlfriend.* I imagine it floating across the space between us, entering Edie's ear canal. I wait for her reaction.

"Maybe she could," she says with a mischievous smile. "She's cool that way."

She leans forward until our noses touch. Mom used to touch noses with me before bed—"Nose kiss," she'd say.

"You'll have to tell this girlfriend of yours hello for me," I say.

My eyes are still wide open, but hers are closed. Her lips touch mine, and she says:

"Hello."

June 2019

CHAPTER 17

Dave

Last year's wildfire season, 2018, was the deadliest and most destructive wildfire season in California history. It was also the largest on record.

That year, more than 8,500 fires burned nearly two million acres, about 2 percent of California's total land area. It set the record for the largest area of burned acreage recorded in a fire season, ever. A total of 24,000 structures were damaged or destroyed, and 103 people died—85 in the Camp Fire alone, which decimated the ironically named town of Paradise. The estimated economic cost of that year's wildfire season was 400 billion dollars. Global warming, it turns out, is not cheap.

The Carr Fire. The Thomas Fire. The Tubbs Fire. The Woolsey Fire. The Ranch Fire. These are among the most destructive California wildfires of all time, and they all occurred in 2017 and 2018. It is only going to get worse. In 2017, there were two separate news stories about elderly couples taking cover in their backyard pools as their homes were consumed by fire. One of the couples survived, emerging after six hours to see everything they'd known turned to ash. When the other couple emerged, only the husband was alive, carrying his dead wife in his arms. This image stays with me, which says a lot; most images do not stay with me.

Obviously, horrific fires isolated to California would not end the world. But these events are not isolated to California. Over the last five decades, the wildfire season in the western United States has grown by two and a half months. By 2050, destruction from wildfires is expected to double. For every additional degree of global warming, it could quadruple.

And it's not just America under siege. In Greenland, fires in the last couple of years have burned ten times more area than a few years before. Fires in these up-north areas concern scientists because the soot and ash from them can blacken ice sheets, which then absorb more of the sun's rays and melt more quickly. It goes without saying that fires destroy trees, releasing into the atmosphere the centuries-old carbon stored within them. That leads to more warming, and more fires. No matter which way I spin it, it does not look good.

I try to focus on what I can control, my own little world. We are approaching summer, and I'm concerned that this fire season will be worse than the last. Last year, the closest fire to us was the Holy Fire in the Cleveland National Forest. It's only a matter of time before there's one in our hills. I knew this risk when we moved here, and it's one of the reasons I've been so invested in the bunker. In a worst-case scenario, Cleo and I can take shelter there, even while everything above us burns. Then there is the matter of our neighbors. Yes, they have moved in, though their house is still a construction site. I have to worry that, in case of emergency, Cleo will want me to invite Edie and her mother to join us in the bunker. I have not accounted for guests. I have no desire for guests. I did not anticipate Cleo's desire for guests.

Cleo stands before me with too much eye makeup for my liking. I remember that when she was little—two or three years old—she used to hate when Jana wore eye makeup (which was rare; its rarity is probably why it was so unsettling for Cleo). Cleo would look at Jana as if she was seeing a monster instead of her mother and would shout, "Take off your eyes!" Jana would do her best to suppress laughter and console Cleo, sometimes resorting to using a damp tissue to remove the makeup (which I'm guessing she then had to reapply once in the car on the way to wherever she was going). These are the small sacrifices a parent must make every day, the inconveniences accepted.

"You look nice," I say to Cleo, though what I really want to say is *Take off your eyes!*

"Thanks, Dad."

Her smile collapses, and a look of concern comes over her face.

"You really don't have to go to this. I can tell Edie's mom you're sick or—"

"I said I would go."

Edie's mother Camila has invited us to have dinner in their construction-site-of-a-house. I have no interest in the social nature of this invitation, but I am curious to see the state of the house. I have not given up hope that they will become overwhelmed by the project ahead of them and return to the hotel from whence they came.

"Okay . . . you're sure?"

Even someone as obtuse as me can tell that Cleo is not so much worried about my comfort as she is about her own. I do not have a good track record of positive first impressions. I know I will come across as odd. I suspect Cleo has already warned them of this, so I will be walking into an audience that is expecting odd. I will not disappoint.

I look at my watch. We are supposed to be there in five minutes.

"We should get going," I say.

Cleo looks me up and down as I stand from the couch, clearly assessing my attire, to which I have given zero thought. I am wearing my usual working-from-home uniform of jeans and an old T-shirt. This particular old T-shirt says YOSEMITE on it and was purchased when Jana and I were newly married and ventured to the national park. I believe Cleo was conceived in one of the cabins at Tuolumne Meadows.

Cleo walks slightly ahead of me to their house, her pace quick and eager, her toes bouncing off the ground with each step. She is excited for this little get-together. As much as I do not enjoy the idea of these new neighbors, I do appreciate the improvement in Cleo's mood. I suppose that's why I am attending this dinner—to be supportive. I have proven incapable of sparking Cleo's happiness. Edie has proven capable. So, to support Cleo's happiness, I must support her friendship with Edie. It's a simple equation in my mind.

As we approach the house, Cleo turns to me so quickly that I nearly run into her.

"Okay, Dad, just be cool, okay? When in doubt, less words. Be polite. Okay?"

She takes my two hands in her hands, moves them up and down with each command. *Be cool. Less words. Be polite.* I hate that she feels the need for such a pep talk.

"Cleo, I have been to dinner parties before."

She looks at me, confused and maybe relieved. "Have you?"

"Yes," I snap back.

It's probably been years, though. When Jana and I dated, we went to dinner at her friends' houses. Then Cleo came along, and we lacked the energy or resolve to venture into the world in the way we had before. We became less of a couple and more like teammates. Jana still went to friends' houses, but she took Cleo with her so I could have time to myself. On some occasions—too few, in hindsight—I would watch Cleo so Jana could go out. We attempted a few playdate situations, the three of us, but those never went well. I could barely handle the noise level with my own child; incorporating other children into the mix made it impossible for me to "be cool." There were certain events once or twice a year when we got a babysitter and went out together—our respective company holiday parties, her birthday (I never expressed a desire to go out anywhere on my birthday). But we rarely socialized with others. It was one of those things that I thought was a compatibility of ours—we both hated socializing, preferred to be at home. But now I have to wonder if it was a concession on her part.

The entire front yard is still dirt. They haven't started landscaping. Still, they have strung twinkly lights from one end of their front porch (a good addition, I admit) to the other, as if they think their house is worthy of decoration despite its unfinished state. On the porch are a wood saw, cans of paint, a bag of cement, tarps, workmen's boots. It's a mess.

Cleo knocks on the front door and, just a moment after her knuckles hit the wood, the door swings open to reveal the woman who must be Camila. She is short and barefoot, and she appears far too enthusiastic about our presence.

"*Mija*," she says to Cleo, pulling her in for a hug that is alarmingly intimate. Cleo does not react, so I assume this is how they hug on a regular basis. Camila's eyes are squeezed shut tightly, as if she is hugging Cleo with every ounce of strength in her little body.

When she opens her eyes, she meets mine and raises her eyebrows.

"You must be her *papi*," she says, still hugging Cleo.

I do not know if I should extend my hand for a formal shake, or just stand as I am until they are done embracing each other. I choose to stand as I am.

"Yeah, this is my dad," Cleo says as they finally pull apart.

I take this as the cue to extend my hand. "I'm Dave."

She disregards my outstretched hand and moves toward me like she is going to give me a hug, which would be absurd as she has only known me for twenty seconds and—

She hugs me.

I remain still, hoping it will be over soon.

Out of the corner of my eye, I see Cleo covering her mouth with her hand, trying not to laugh.

"Come in, come in," Camila says, finally releasing me from her intimidating grasp.

She goes inside ahead of us. Cleo loops her arm through mine and whispers "Thank you." For submitting to the hug and for not embarrassing her, I guess.

Edie is inside in what appears to be the living room, though it is not arranged for living. The flooring is not yet laid, but the location of the fireplace makes it easy to imagine where the standard furniture pieces will go.

Cleo untethers her arm from mine and goes to Edie.

"Hi, guys," Edie says. "Nice to see you, Mr. Garrison."

"You as well," I say.

A little dog wearing a sweater comes running in from another room, barking at me with fixed intensity. "*Cállate*, Doug," Edie commands, and he stops, then retreats behind her legs.

"As you can see, the house is still a work in progress," Camila says, appearing beside me with a pitcher of what looks like fruit punch and two plastic cups with ice cubes in them. I dread the implication that one of them is for me.

"You have accomplished a lot so far," I say.

She sets the pitcher and cups on a makeshift table—a piece of plywood set across two sets of stacked bricks.

"I made sangria for us," she says to me. "Edie, there's lemonade in the fridge for you and Cleo."

Before I can tell her that I appreciate her gesture, but I would not like any sangria, she is pouring some into a cup for me. I don't know if I've ever had sangria, but I do know that it contains alcohol and I generally do not like alcohol. I enjoy feeling in control of my surroundings and, therefore, see alcohol as nothing but an impediment.

Despite these reservations, I say "Thank you" when she hands me a cup that is full to the brim. Cleo gives me a small nod that encourages me to take a polite sip. Upon taking the sip, I am surprised at how much I enjoy the beverage. It is, in a word, delightful.

"Let's give him the tour," Cleo says.

The four of us (and the dog) walk around the house, which, much to my chagrin, is coming along better than I anticipated. There is still much to be done, but most of the work is cosmetic and just a matter of time. I am impressed with their fortitude, living in such conditions. Each of the bedrooms features just a mattress on the floor and moving boxes—some used as tables, some functioning as drawers with clothes hanging out of them. The bathroom they share is plumbed, but there is no sink. It appears they are brushing their teeth and washing their hands over a large mixing bowl.

The kitchen seems to be where they spend most of their time. The island is not yet finished, but they have placed a tarp over it and are using it as a table and food-preparation station. There are stools positioned around the island. Their fridge is installed, though the space for the oven and stove is still empty. A microwave is on the floor, perched atop a stack of books. I believe Cleo said we would be eating fajitas for dinner, but I do not see how it would be possible to cook fajitas in this kitchen.

As if reading my mind, Camila says, "We've been using the barbecue for almost every meal."

Cleo starts raving about the portobello mushrooms Camila roasted the other night (she's been having dinner with them once or twice a week), and, during this brief reprieve from participating in the conversation, I notice that my head feels funny, like a balloon slowly floating away from my body.

I follow the three of them (and the dog) through a sliding glass door to the backyard, which is less of a yard and more of a dirt lot. There is the aforementioned barbecue, along with a patio dining table, four chairs, and an umbrella.

"So, you liked my sangria?" Camila says.

It takes me a second to realize that she is talking to me and that my sangria cup is empty except for the ice cubes. This explains my balloon-head feeling.

Cleo and Edie sit at the patio table and start looking at something on Edie's phone. I stand there dumbly, not sure what to do. I should probably ask Camila if she needs help with anything, as this would be the well-mannered thing to do, but she seems like the kind of person who would actually give me a task, then demand conversation in the midst of that task. So I do not say anything. I just stand at the barbecue, manning it, as they say (which, now that I think about it, seems like a sexist term).

"More?"

I turn to see Camila behind me with her pitcher. Before I can answer, she is pouring more into my cup. Then she disappears inside again, returning a few moments later with the makings of fajitas. I step out of the way as she turns on the barbecue and arranges chicken and beef on one side of the grill, veggie kabobs on the other.

"I love that Cleo is vegetarian. It's forced me to get more creative," she says.

"I guess that's one way to look at it."

"She's been educating Edie and me about how eating less meat can help the environment. She told me just the other day that making just one beef burger releases enough greenhouse gases to fill sixty balloons. Sixty!"

She says this as she uses tongs to reposition the strips of chicken.

"Yes, she feels very strongly about it," I say. Then I add: "Her mom was vegetarian."

Camila closes the top of the barbecue and looks at me with an expression that I cannot quite decipher. "Oh, was she?"

I nod.

"Well, that explains the passion she has for it."

"I think climate change explains the passion she has for it."

She takes a sip from her own cup of sangria and nods. "Oh, yes, she mentioned that you are . . . what do they call it? A disaster prepper?"

"Doomsday prepper," I say. "But I disagree with the label."

She takes a longer sip from her cup.

"Okay, then. Can I ask why?"

"I'm just preparing for scenarios that may occur."

"Fair enough, it's always good to be prepared," she says. "A Scenario Prepper then."

"Okay."

"You must have been a Boy Scout."

"I'm afraid not."

"Well, then you are a Man Scout now."

She laughs at her own joke, and I give a courtesy laugh to be nice. She nods toward Cleo and Edie at the patio table. They are still looking at something on Edie's phone, their heads bent down, foreheads touching.

"Those two are *inseparable*," she says, letting the word roll off her tongue in Spanish.

"Seems that way."

"Cleo is such a good kid. You have done an amazing job, I must say."

"Have I?"

I did not intend to say this out loud, but there it is.

"Oh yes, she is a very mature girl. I suppose she has to be, after what she's been through."

Camila knows what she's been through. What we've been through. I would prefer she not know, but I have come to understand that Cleo wants to share her feelings with people besides me. She wants a life that is bigger than the two of us. She is willing to take the risk of welcoming others, confiding in them. Somehow, I have to find a way to be okay with this.

The meat on the grill sizzles. Camila goes inside and returns with her pitcher, which is now almost empty. She pours the remaining liquid into each of our cups.

"So, what kinds of things do you *prepare* for?" she asks.

"Right now, my focus is on fire season."

Her eyes go big. "I suppose we have to worry about such things, living here."

We have to worry about many things, living anywhere, I want to say. Instead I just nod and the conversation dies a predictable death.

Thankfully, the food is ready a few minutes later and Camila busies herself with taking it to the patio table. She tells me to take a seat, so I do. Edie and Cleo pull their heads away from the screen of Edie's phone, and Cleo says, "You made me veggie kabobs!"

"*Por supuesto, mija,*" Camila says.

The closeness they share is disconcerting. Cleo reminds me of Jana in the optimistic way she trusts.

The dinner itself is fine. Cleo compliments Camila on the food, so I follow suit and deliver my own compliment. It is good, objectively speaking. I have had too much sangria, so I am hesitant to open my mouth and contribute anything to the conversation. I do not trust my communication skills under normal circumstances; they certainly cannot be trusted when I am under the influence of whatever alcohol is in this deceptive fruit punch.

"Dad, Camila's family, like, founded San Juan Capistrano," Cleo says.

I find this hard to believe, but I just say "Oh."

"Tell him the story," Cleo says to Camila. "You tell it better than I would."

Camila has also had too much sangria, perhaps more than me. Her face is flush, which is how Jana's face used to get when she had too much to drink.

"I don't want to bore your poor father," Camila says. She is clearly just saying that to elicit a pleading response from Cleo, which is exactly what Cleo delivers.

"Please, it's interesting," Cleo says.

"It *is* pretty cool," Edie echoes.

Camila makes a show of complying, and I ready myself to display facial expressions that demonstrate the interest I am expected to show.

"Well," Camila starts, placing her napkin on the table and leaning back in her chair. "Have you heard of Juan Avila?"

I have, in fact, heard of him. I pride myself on knowing quite a bit of history of San Juan Capistrano. I feel it is the duty of every resident to have a healthy respect for their city, and such respect can be cultivated in the understanding of history.

"I know of him," I say.

"What do you know?" Camila asks. She must sense that I see this question as an offensive challenge to my intelligence, because she says, "I just don't want to repeat things you already know."

I clear my throat.

"I know he raised and sold cattle. He was granted rights to thousands of acres of grazing land in this area."

Camila nods and smiles like a grade-school teacher does when the prized pupil delivers the correct answer.

"I am impressed," she says.

"My dad knows way too much about way too many things," Cleo says.

Cleo is not impressed.

"Knowledge is a good thing," Camila says, offering me a wink that I do not know how to respond to.

I also know that Juan Avila was known as *El Rico* because of his success and wealth. I know that during the Gold Rush, he amassed a fortune by taking his cattle herds to San Francisco and capitalizing on the increased demand for beef from all the prospectors flocking to the area. With that fortune, he constructed an adobe on Camino Capistrano. A fire partially destroyed it in the late 1800s, but part of it was restored and is still there today. I've pointed it out to Cleo many times, but it appears she has no recollection.

"So, my great-great-great-great-grandfather, José de Silva, worked for Juan Avila in the 1860s, when there were terrible droughts. Nearly all of Avila's cattle died and he was forced to sell most of his land to another ranchero."

"John Forster," I interject.

She gives me the grade-school-teacher smile again, then turns to Cleo. "You were not kidding, *mija*."

"He's, like, a genius, Mom," Edie says.

Is this how Cleo describes me to people? A genius? I suppose it's better than "weird," which is how I thought she described me.

"You probably already know this," Camila continues, turning back to me, "but there was a smallpox outbreak that lasted for years. Juan Avila's wife died of it."

This mention of smallpox reminds me of my recent research into the risk of a deadly pandemic. I try to resist thinking about this and refocus on what Camila is saying.

"My great-great-great-great-grandfather, José, helped Juan's daughter, Rosa, take care of Juan. Or so the story goes. And Rosa introduced José to his wife, Gardenia. When Juan passed away, he left some land to José and, long story short, that is the land on which we are sitting right now."

"Right now, Dad," Cleo says, more amazed than I am. She puts her hands by her head and makes a gesture like an explosion is going off. Mind blown. I get it.

"Interesting," I say.

What Camila's story does for me is to confirm how she acquired the land, though I do not know why she is just now deciding to reside on it. I assume this has something to do with Edie's father, who is mysteriously absent and has not been mentioned. Camila does not wear a wedding ring. A divorce is most likely. Very few families are separated in the precise and catastrophic way mine was.

"Now we just have to hope it doesn't all turn to ash," Camila says with a levity that can only be interpreted as making fun of me.

"Oh, god, did Dad talk to you about his apocalypse obsession?"

I shift in my seat. "It's not an obsession," I say.

"Okay, his apocalypse interest," Cleo says.

Which, I suppose, is fair.

"He just told me he was concerned about fire season," Camila says.

"As he should be. Global warming is real, Mom," Edie says.

Edie is earning favor with me.

"I know it's real," Camila says with a hearty eye roll. "I suppose I just try to stay positive."

She sounds like Jana. *A life lived in fear is not a life lived.* Jana had a fridge magnet that said that. In hindsight, she might still be alive if she'd lived her life in fear.

"In any case," Camila goes on, "did you know 'apocalypse' is a Greek word that means revelation?"

"Why do you even know that?" Edie asks.

"I know lots of things too. Maybe not as much as Mr. Dave here, but a lot," she says.

I force a smile.

"My point is," she says, "that the apocalypse doesn't have to be this big, scary thing. It may reveal a whole new beginning. So, you know, bring it on."

She claps her hands together as if preparing for a game. The apocalypse, for her, is a game.

"I think you've had too much sangria," Edie says.

Camila instructs Edie to clean up the table and do the dishes, and Cleo goes along with her, the two of them *inseparable*, as Camila said.

"What a beautiful night, eh?" Camila says. Her neck is craned up at the sky.

"It is," I say.

"Maybe I should get a telescope. There are so many stars here," she says, neck still craned. "There weren't so many stars where we used to live."

I want to tell her that this is incorrect. The number of stars does not change depending on location; all that changes is one's ability to see them. In general, I find that people are so limited by their own perspective. It is one of the many reasons they annoy me.

"The stars are very visible here because there are no lights from buildings and whatnot," I say, just to ensure that she's educated.

"Mm-hm," is all she says.

She finally looks down, a relaxed smile on her face. Her eyes look glassy, from the sangria, probably. I wonder if my eyes look that way. They feel as if they might.

"Anyway," she says. "Thank you for coming. I wanted to let you know that we will be good neighbors. I don't want you to worry."

Cleo must have told them I'm worried. She must tell these people everything.

"Cleo and I will be good neighbors as well."

She laughs. "Oh, I have no doubt about that."

There is silence, and I wonder if I should stand and begin my departure from her property. I am prematurely relieved at the notion of this social event coming to an end.

But then she says, "I'm sorry if you thought I was poking fun at you about the apocalypse stuff."

I find this apology strange and unnecessary. Her opinion of me matters very little, and I do not plan to have frequent interaction with her in the future. Apologies are only necessary when there is a relationship at stake. I have no relationship to Camila. Perhaps my acceptance of this dinner invitation implied otherwise.

"There is no reason to apologize," I say, plainly.

"Well, then, okay."

She meets my eyes with hers, so I shift my gaze to avoid whatever interaction she is trying to manifest.

"You know your apocalypse already happened, right?" she says.

I don't understand what she's talking about. I have no choice but to shift my eyes back to her to try to decipher the meaning of what she's just said.

"Excuse me?"

It might be that she is referring to the previous mass extinctions that have occurred. This knowledge would impress me. Maybe I misjudged her. Given her optimism, I expect her to say that life, on a macro level, will go on, despite the extinction to come. I find myself eager to engage in this conversation.

"Your apocalypse. It already happened."

I don't know why she's phrasing it this way—*your* apocalypse. It is all of our apocalypse. It is humanity's apocalypse.

"*My* apocalypse?"

"Yes, your world already ended once, no?" She cocks her head to the side, inquisitive.

I'm still not sure what she means. "*My* world?"

"Yes, your world. It already ended once," she says. "And you survived."

Her glossy eyes twinkle.

"Okay," I say, chalking this up to the sangria.

Cleo and Edie come outside, announcing that they have finished cleaning the dishes.

"Is my mom being weird?" Edie asks me.

I want to tell her that her mother is, in fact, being weird, but I just force another smile and assure myself that this will all be over soon. In a matter of minutes, I will be home, on the couch, watching *The Office,* and all will be right with the world.

"Oh, Eden, be nice to your *mami*," Camila says, swatting at Edie's hand.

"You ready, Dad?" Cleo says.

I am, of course, very ready.

I stand, mildly surprised to find that I am unsteady on my feet. Cleo links her arm with mine, as if she thinks I need assistance. I do my best to hide my unsteadiness.

There are various pleasantries exchanged before Cleo and I are truly free, on our way back to our house.

"That wasn't so bad, was it?" she asks.

Honesty, I've found, is not always the best policy.

"It was fine."

"Such enthusiasm, Dad!" she says, with mock enthusiasm.

The dry dirt crunches under our shoes as we walk.

"What did you think of Camila?" Cleo asks.

Like most people, Cleo does not like silences. She strives to fill them. Jana was the same way, always seeking out conversation, connection. It's still hard for me to accept that this is just part of being human for most people, that I am the abnormal one.

"She seemed nice," I say.

More dirt-crunching.

"Dad, you're giving me, like, nothing."

"What do you want me to say?"

"Did you enjoy talking with her?"

Not really.

"It was fine."

"You've already used that line."

"The part about her family history was interesting," I try.

"She's an interesting person. She has lots of stories."

"Where's the dad?" I ask.

"The dad?"

"Edie's dad," I say.

"Oh," she says. "They're divorced."

As I predicted.

"And they know about Mom," I say.

She nods. "Is that okay?"

"It's fine."

We get to the house.

"Dad," she says. "You need to come up with other words besides 'fine.'"

She sounds like Jana, so much like Jana.

Cleo walks inside ahead of me. She goes to the kitchen for a glass of water and then says, "See you in the morning" and disappears to her room, closing the door.

I proceed to make my earlier vision a reality: I sit on the couch and turn on the TV. It's the "Sexual Harassment" episode, the one where Todd Packer shows up to offend everyone in the office right as Dunder Mifflin orders a company-wide review of its harassment policy. I watch it and laugh even though I've seen it at least ten times before. My eyelids are heavy by the time the theme music comes on for the next episode. I start to fall asleep right there on the couch.

Your apocalypse. It already happened.

I startle awake as Camila's strange words come back to me. In my head, it's Jana's voice saying them. And it's only then that I understand what Camila meant.

CHAPTER 18

Cleo

I lie in bed, Poppy curled into my side, and stare at the ceiling, trying to summon the energy to greet the day. It's one of those California days that does not meet expectations. Wasn't that a rating on my report cards in elementary school? *Does not meet expectations.* Except I never got that rating, because I've always been a good student.

Most people who don't live in California probably picture our summer days as bright and sunny, with people flocking to beaches wearing sunglasses and slathering on sunscreen. There would be no sunglasses or sunscreen needed today, though. May Gray has turned to June Gloom, the mornings socked in with a thick marine layer that sometimes vanishes in the late afternoon and sometimes stays around all day.

I'm not sure if the weather is solely to blame for my lethargy. Ever since summer break started, I've felt a little . . . off. It's something about being in the house with Dad, the two of us, without the structure and distraction of school. It brings me back to last summer break, which was the worst summer break of my life. Mom died in April of last year. I came back to school in time to feel horribly awkward and take my finals, and then summer break started. Carter and I hadn't befriended each other yet. I had no interest in friends from my before-Mom-died life. Dad was working from home, holing up in the guest room that he'd converted into his office. Work was his coping mechanism, until the bunker and his apocalypse obsession became his coping mechanism. I spent entire days, literally, just lying in bed, thinking about Mom or trying *not* to think about Mom. I was grateful for June Gloom then. It seemed like the sky was as sad as I was, like the universe was commiserating with me, like maybe I wasn't as alone as I felt.

Objectively speaking, life is awesome at the moment. I have a girlfriend who lives within walking distance from me. The John Green storyline is in full swing. Hanging out with Edie is what will make this summer break different from last summer break. My plan is to spend as much time with her as possible, helping her with the house. On the days her mom works, it's just the two of us, free to kiss and touch each other. Edie is clearly more experienced than me—she had a girlfriend at her old high school—but she seems to like that I have no idea what I'm doing. If only Dad knew. . . . This is why I'm fine with him assuming I'm straight. It's working in my favor.

I finally drag myself out of bed at nine. I can hear Dad in the kitchen, going through his usual motions of preparing his tea and breakfast. He eats the same breakfast every day—a bowl of Cheerios (plain, never honey nut) with almond milk. Then he doesn't eat again until dinnertime because he says the act of eating interrupts his "rhythm" for the day.

"Morning," he says when I walk into the kitchen, the throw blanket from my bed wrapped around me like a skirt.

When Mom was alive, I used to love summer break. I'd eat breakfast with her and Dad. Mom would linger after Dad left for work. She had an understanding with her boss that she'd come to work later in the morning during summer. We didn't do anything in particular during our mornings—Mom had an extra cup of coffee, and we chatted about all the little things people chat about and never remember. It's only now that I think about all I've forgotten, all the little moments.

When I was a kid, Mom would take me to day camp (god, I hated day camp), or a babysitter would come to the house (I hated those too). But the summer before she died, she let me stay home by myself. She'd text me throughout the day, just to check in. Some days, if she could get away from work, she'd come home with lunch from the fish taco place. In the evening, she was always home right at five (another understanding she must have had with her boss). That last summer together, we went on walks to the beach most days. Then we came home and made dinner so it would be ready when Dad came home. It was a sweet routine.

"I hate this weather," I say as I make myself a cup of tea and sit at the table with Dad.

"Ah, yes, June Gloom," he says.

I wait expectantly for him to share some fact about June Gloom.

"Did you know that May and June are the cloudiest months of the year in southern California?"

There it is.

"San Francisco's probably worse. Carter's there with his mom, and he said it's sixty-five degrees and he has seasonal affective disorder."

"Really?" Dad says.

"No, Dad. Probably not really."

I put two pieces of cinnamon-raisin bread in the toaster and lean against the kitchen counter.

"Are you going over to Edie's house again today?" Dad asks.

He's been asking this every day since break started, and every day I've been saying yes.

"I am. Are you working from home again today?"

I'm poking fun at him, but he takes me seriously and says, "I am."

"Do you ever want to go back to the office?"

It can't be good for him, staying at home like this all the time. He has no interaction with other humans. Besides me. I know I'm not supposed to worry about him. *Remember, Cleo, you're the kid.* Ms. Murray continues to say that to me. We had our first summer break phone check-in a few days ago. She said we can do them weekly, like last summer.

"I can do all my job functions from home," he says.

"I know. I just thought it might be good to get out of the house more."

"It makes much more sense to be at home. I can avoid the commute and the unnecessary dangers of driving on the freeway."

I wait for him to share a statistic about the number of freeway deaths a year, but he just says, "And I can be closer to your school in case I'm needed. Or, during summer, I can be right here."

I want so badly to roll my eyes, but I know he means well, so I will myself to just nod.

"I know, Dad, I know."

Predictably, at precisely 9:25 a.m., he goes to the sink with his dishes, rinses them and places them in the dishwasher, then disappears into his office. He must have a rule (self- or company-imposed, I don't know) about being online for work by 9:30 a.m. He does not leave his office except for two bathroom breaks—one around 10:30 a.m., one around 3 p.m. I don't *try* to notice these things about him; it's just impossible for me *not* to notice. I guess it's a skill I've honed all my life. When you're an only child, your parents are everything. You study them because there's not much else to do.

I finish my breakfast of cinnamon-raisin toast, spend ten minutes making myself look like I did not just roll out of bed, and then jog across to Edie's house.

Edie's car is alone in the driveway; her mom is at work today. Usually there are contractors, but nobody appears to be on site today. They might be taking a break; they just finished putting the flooring in yesterday.

I open the front door to find Edie standing in the will-be living room with a mop. Doug the dog barks once, tail wagging in recognition of me.

"Hey," Edie says. "I was hoping you'd come."

It dawns on me that I didn't even text her: I just came right over. I feel both embarrassed at the assumption I've made about our comfortability with each other, and excited by it.

She comes to me, mop still in hand, and gives me a kiss. These kisses of ours have become frequent, but they still make my heart all fluttery.

"The floors look awesome," I say.

They've chosen a dark wood throughout the house. On the home-improvement shows, they would call it "sleek" and "classic."

"Just trying to get them clean so we can move in the furniture."

"Is it furniture time?"

We have been talking about "furniture time" for a while now. We are focused on this because it would be far more comfortable to make out on a couch than it is to make out on a throw blanket on the floor.

"Mom said we can move stuff in starting tomorrow," she says. "Might have to put you to work."

They have had all their things in a storage unit since moving here.

"I'm in!"

She leans the mop against the wall and comes to me, wraps her arms around me, pulls me close to her. She rests her chin on the top of my head. I love that she's taller than me. It's such a silly, superficial thing to love, but I do.

"I've been cleaning all morning. You want to take a beach break with me?"

Instinctively, I pull away and look out the window, toward my house, back toward Dad.

"Would he care?" Edie says.

I shrug. "I don't think so, but let's just go. He won't even know."

"You sure?"

"He just sits in his office all day," I say. "Trust me."

We get in Edie's car, which is crammed with boxes of possessions that Edie deemed too essential to lock away in the storage unit, and not essential enough to be transported to the house. I don't even know what's in the boxes; they're all taped shut, proving that they weren't as essential as she thought they were.

I've never been to the beach with Edie. She goes a lot—to surf, usually in the early mornings. She says she doesn't want to surf today. It's too late in the morning for that, apparently. The waves are "closing out" (I don't know what this means).

"I have a spot I love," she says. "I've been wanting to take you."

I wonder if I should text Dad. I could tell a white lie (my specialty) and say I went to the grocery store with Edie. But what if he said, "I'd prefer you didn't" and then I'd already left, and he'd look out the window and see Edie's car gone, and it would become this whole thing. If I don't say anything, he'll likely just stay sitting in front of his computer, experiencing the bliss of ignorance.

Edie and I drive south on the 5 and when we pass through San Clemente, I say, "Wait, are we going to Mexico?" She laughs and says, *"Hablas español?"*

"Un poco."

Dad would *not* be okay with Mexico.

We get off the freeway at the final exit before the long stretch of highway through Camp Pendleton. I assume we're going to Trestles, the famous surf spot, but we pass that and keep heading south.

"Are we going to the nuclear power plant?" I ask.

Dad has told me all about the San Onofre nuclear power plant. It's in the process of being decommissioned, but the facility is still there, famous for its twin buildings that some of the boys at school refer to as "The Giant Tits" (they do look like boobs). According to Dad, the buildings were designed to contain any unexpected releases of radioactive material from the power generators. The whole plant was shut down a few years ago because of some equipment failure that Dad says posed a danger to anyone living within fifty miles of the plant. I don't know if he was exaggerating. This was before Mom died, when he was less prone to thinking we were all doomed.

"Yes, my plan is to break into the plant and get arrested because I think your dad would love that," Edie says.

"Ha ha, not funny."

We pass The Giant Tits and come to the entrance of the state park. I've seen the parking lots and campgrounds from the freeway, but I've never been here myself.

Edie shows her pass to the woman in the booth, and we drive inside.

"You've been here, right?" she says.

"Nope."

"Oh, wow. Okay, pick one: Trail one, or trail seven?"

"Seven," I say.

She nods. "Good choice."

We drive through the parking lot, past surfers carrying boards on their heads. Near the end of the lot, we park. It's just our car and a yellow VW van.

"You ready?" she asks.

I give her an enthusiastic "Yep!"

"We can take the boring way around to the beach, or the fun way," she says.

"I feel like this is a test for you to see what kind of person I am."

"It is," she says, deadpan.

"Okay, well, I'll consent to the fun way, but you should know that in life, I am much more likely to choose the boring way," I say. "I am my father's daughter."

"You're not boring."

"I'm kind of boring."

"Well, I'm not bored of you."

"Yet."

We hold hands until we get to the part of the trail that is skinny and slightly treacherous. Well, treacherous in my estimation. Like I said, I am my father's daughter.

Edie seems to have no problem navigating the terrain. I, on the other hand, am walking in a crouched position so if (or when) I fall, I am close to the ground.

"People do this trail with surfboards on their heads?" I ask.

"Sure do."

"That's ridiculous."

We make it to the bottom, and the ocean appears before us. Even though I've grown up near the beach and have seen the ocean hundreds of times, it never ceases to overwhelm me—not in a bad way: in the very best way. It's impossible to feel like my problems are that big of a deal in the presence of the ocean. Witnessing its expansiveness is like a dose of instant perspective.

I can see one surfer out in the water. Otherwise, the beach is empty, except for the lifeguard tower and whatever people it contains.

"I can see why you love it here," I say.

"Yeah, it's never crowded. People don't want to pay the state park fee, and even if they do, they park in the first lot and go down to the beach there. They don't even know this one is here."

We chuff through the soft sand until it turns dark and solid near the water. Edie kicks off her sandals, and I do the same.

"Close your eyes," she says.

I'm wary, but I comply. She takes my hand and pulls me toward the waves.

"Edie, if you get me soaking wet, I'm going to kill you."

"It's a trust game," she says.

The water laps at my feet and then recedes. I feel the tingle of goosebumps forming up my legs. Edie tugs on my wrist: "Come on."

I take tentative steps. It feels like we're going out too far, like the next wave is going to come and crash into us, knock us backward. When I hear the rumble of the incoming tide, I squeeze Edie's hand. Water splashes into my calves. I shriek, which makes Edie laugh.

"Seriously, I'm going to kill you if I get soaking wet," I say.

"You're not," she says. "It's like Lake Mission Viejo out here today."

"Lake Mission Viejo?"

"It just means the waves suck."

We keep walking out, the lower half of my legs now submerged in water. I hold my breath when I feel the water recede because I know it will come back with renewed force.

"Uh-oh," she says.

I open my eyes. "What?"

Before I know it, she's pushing me back toward the shore, but it's too late. The wave crashes into us—well, Edie, mostly. The water recedes and we run faster, the two of us laughing like giddy children at an amusement park.

"Shit," she says, out of breath.

"Lake Mission Viejo, huh?"

We survey the damage. I am mostly dry, but Edie's backside is drenched.

She runs her fingers through her hair, wetting it. "That wave came out of nowhere," she says.

"Right."

We sit on the sand.

"I seriously did not intend for that to happen."

"If that was a trust exercise, then I do not trust you."

She laughs. "Fair enough."

She lies on her stomach in the sand, forehead resting on her hands. I lie next to her, my neck turned, cheek to sand, staring at her closed eyes. She reaches over and takes my hand in hers.

"We'll dry off soon," she says. "The sun has superpowers."

Neither of us says anything. We just lie there. I can hear Dad's voice in my head, telling me to wear sunscreen: *Just one bad sunburn as a kid can double your chance of getting skin cancer later.* I'm not saying he isn't right; he probably is. But all that knowledge means he can never enjoy a spontaneous sunbathing. Actually, knowing Dad, anything spontaneous is unlikely. And even if he was caught in unexpected sunshine, he probably has sunscreen in his car for just-in-case scenarios.

"I could take a nap right here," Edie says.

"Go ahead," I tell her, though I'm a little worried we'll be here too long and Dad will notice I'm gone.

"Did I tell you I have to go see my dad this weekend?" she asks.

Since I've known her, Edie hasn't gone to visit her dad, even though she's supposed to. She says her dad hasn't asked about it, which is just . . . sad.

"It's been a while, hasn't it?"

She grunts agreeance. "It's his birthday. I feel obligated. I wish you could come with me."

"I could," I say. If I lied to Dad again.

"I don't know. My dad is an asshole. I don't want to subject you to that."

"I've subjected you to *my* dad," I say.

She opens her eyes, squints at me. "Your dad isn't an asshole. You know that, right?"

I feel embarrassed for the way I've criticized Dad, for the subtle ingratitude I've shown by complaining about him to Edie when Edie's dad clearly sucks.

"I know he's not," I say. It sounds more defensive than I intend.

"I mean, he *is* a weirdo. I'll give you that."

We both laugh, the tension broken. Edie closes her eyes again.

"Hey," she says, eyes still closed. "I've been thinking about something."

"That's never good."

"It's about what happened to your mom, so we don't have to talk about it if you don't want to."

"Oh," I say. I sit up, hug my knees to my chest. "Well, what is it? Then I'll tell you if I want to talk about it."

She sits up too, crosses her legs with her hands on her knees, like she's about to meditate. She looks at me, but her eyes are just little slits in the bright light.

"So, like, I've read the articles about the whole thing, and I know the basic answer to this question . . . but what happened to Mirai and Kyra McCann?"

I sigh. I'm sort of annoyed by the question. Why has she been dedicating brain space to wondering about *them*? Mom died because of them, basically. Even though they survived the whole thing, they are dead in my eyes. Gone.

"I don't know," I say.

"You don't want to talk about it."

"Not really."

She uncrosses her legs and lies on her back.

"I shouldn't have brought it up. Sorry," she says.

I lie on my back. "No, it's okay."

I close my eyes and hear nothing but the waves. The predictable rhythm of them is soothing. I can see why people buy machines that emit this sound when they're trying to sleep at night.

The last time I saw Mirai and Kyra was the day before Mom's funeral. They came to the house, unannounced. Or, as far as I know, they were unannounced. Mirai may have attempted to contact Dad, but when they showed up at the door, he seemed as bewildered as I was to see them there.

Mirai's arm was in a giant sling and her face had lost all its color. I could barely see Kyra's face because her chin was seemingly glued to her chest.

"What are you doing here?" Dad asked them. He sounded angry, which, for once, didn't embarrass me. I was angry too.

"We just wanted to pay our respects," Mirai said, the words strained.

They were both just standing there, on the straw mat that said WELCOME, the mat that lied.

"Consider them paid," Dad said.

He started to close the door when Mirai said, her voice stronger, "Wait."

Dad exhaled an annoyed breath and said, "What? What could you possibly say?"

"I'm just so sorry," Mirai said. She started to weep, her face crumpling. "I had no idea Sean would be capable of something like this."

"You had *no idea*?" Dad said. "I think you had a perfectly good idea."

He started to shut the door again.

"Cleo," Mirai said from behind the nearly closed door. "Cleo, I'm so sorry."

I didn't know what to say. Normally when someone says they are sorry, I say "It's okay," but in this case it *wasn't* okay. Her apology meant nothing to me.

"Mom, what about our stuff?"

That was Kyra's voice, barely audible.

Dad and I looked at each other. The day after Mom died, Dad had gone into the guest room, collected all of Mirai's and Kyra's things, and put them in a giant trash bag meant for yard waste. The garbage man came the next day, and that was that.

Mirai shushed Kyra and said, "Let's go, sweetie."

In retrospect, it was cruel of Mirai to bring Kyra with her, to have her witness this scene. Hadn't the girl been through enough? Couldn't Mirai have had her wait in the car?

Since that day, I've tried not to give much thought to Mirai and Kyra. Sean was sentenced to life in prison. As they say, justice doesn't bring back the dead. But it does help. I didn't attend the trial—Dad wouldn't let me. *You have school*, he said. As if that was the only reason why it wouldn't be appropriate for me to attend. At the time, I wanted to go, but I'm glad I didn't. It would have been too hard. Dad didn't tell me much about it, except that it was a short trial. There was never any question of what Sean had done. Everyone expected him to plead insanity, but he didn't. I think he was too proud to present himself as crazy.

I've assumed that Mirai and Kyra have gone about their lives, taking solace in each other. I resent that they have each other, that their mother-daughter relationship continues while mine was brought to an abrupt end. In a way, the two of them got exactly what they wanted—a life without Sean. While I'm sure they carry the burden of guilt, and while I'm sure that weight is heavy, it can't be heavier than the weight of my grief, and Dad's grief. It can't be.

"You think we should head back?" Edie asks.

Her voice startles me. For a few moments there, I was so far away from the beach, in a place I haven't visited much lately.

"Yeah, probably," I say.

She stands, then takes my hands to help me stand. I brush the sand from my clothes, and we start the trek back to the trail.

Going up the trail is less daunting than going down. It's like climbing a poorly constructed staircase.

"I probably have more adrenaline going through my body today than I ever have," I say. I fact-check the statement in the confines of my mind, remember the surge of adrenaline when Dad told me Mom had died. That was a different kind of adrenaline, the not-happy kind. This kind with Edie is more like the roller-coaster kind.

"Is that a good thing?"

"Definitely," I say.

She's about six feet in front of me, hopping around like a mountain goat.

"You make this look way too easy."

"I've been on this trail, like, a hundred times," she says.

"I guess that makes me feel better."

"You're doing great," she says.

And right as she says that, my foot slips off the trail and catches in a crevice. For a brief moment, all I feel is embarrassment. But that is soon trumped by overwhelming pain.

I emit some kind of animal sound and Edie turns around.

"Oh my god," she says. "Are you okay?"

I sit on the dirt, pull my knee toward my chest to get a better look at my ankle. It's already swelling.

I find it impossible to construct a sentence. I just grunt.

"You rolled it?" Edie says.

She is next to me now, crouched. She reaches out to touch my ankle and I push her away, instinctively.

"Okay, okay, let's just chill a sec. Take some deep breaths."

I attempt some regular breaths because deep ones do not seem realistic. It does help. After a couple minutes, I feel much better. My ankle is still killing me, but the panic is starting to subside.

"Do you think I broke it?" I say.

She shakes her head. "No, no, probably just a sprain."

I nod, comforted, though I know Edie has absolutely no idea what she's talking about.

"Did you hear a pop or anything?"

"I don't know. It happened really fast. I *felt* a pop."

"Okay, okay," she says.

"What do we do?"

"Do you want to try to stand?"

Standing does not seem like a good idea, but staying on the ground also does not seem like a good idea.

"Okay," I say.

She takes my hands, pulls me up. "Don't put weight on it right away."

I stand like a flamingo, my ankle throbbing. It feels huge, like someone inflated it four times its size.

"Okay, good," Edie says.

"Now what?"

"Do you want to try putting any weight on it?"

I shake my head. I am quite certain I do not want to do that.

I lean into Edie's shoulder for balance.

"I'll carry you, then," she says.

"Then you'll break *your* ankle."

"I won't. And your ankle isn't broken."

"The denial is strong with you."

"I'll take it as a good sign that you're joking."

"I'm not joking."

She tells me to put most of my weight into her side, and we hobble along the remaining part of the trail, each step careful. Neither of us says anything until we make it to the top. Then she says, "For the record, this is way too much adrenaline. I don't recommend we replicate this experience."

"Noted."

By the time we get to her car, she is sweating profusely, beads of it collecting on her forehead and then traveling down her face.

"You're welcome for the workout," I say.

"Yeah," she says, out of breath, "thanks for that."

She opens the passenger-side door and helps me into the seat. I lift my leg to rest my ankle on top of the glove compartment. She goes around the front of the car and sits in the driver's seat.

"Why do they call it a glove compartment?" I ask. "I mean, who keeps gloves in there?"

"Cold people. Or old-timey people," Edie says. "And, again, I'm taking it as a good sign that you have the ability to ponder such a thing right now. Is it feeling any better?"

"No. I'm just adjusting to the horrific pain."

"You're not going to like me for saying this, but I think we need to call your dad."

She's right—I do not like her for saying this.

"No," I say.

This whole situation is going to trigger Dad in several ways. First, the injury itself, which will reinforce his belief that I am fragile and in need of protection. Second, the occurrence of this injury in the presence of Edie, which will reinforce his belief that I am safer at home (or, better yet, in the bunker), away from perils and forces of evil.

"I think this is beyond just getting some bandages at the drug store," she says. "You need to see a doctor. And they're not going to see you without your dad's consent."

I know all this. I just don't want to accept it.

I groan. "He is going to freak out."

"Probably," Edie says.

I groan again and rest my head against the back of the seat, staring up. "This sucks."

"It does," she agrees.

Reluctantly, and with excessive trepidation, I text Dad.

Hey. I'm a clumsy idiot and I rolled my ankle. Edie is taking me to urgent care. Can you meet us there?

Perhaps he will choose to ignore the details of how this happened and turn his immediate focus to addressing the injury. That's the hope.

He texts back immediately.

What happened?

So much for hope.

A few text exchanges later, he is in possession of the facts of the situation. It is hard to determine how angry he is via text. His texts always come across angry, because he uses periods at the end of every sentence. Hostile punctuation, Carter calls it. In any case, Dad has agreed to meet us at urgent care.

When we pull into the parking lot, Dad's car is already there. He's sitting in the front seat. Waiting.

"If this is the last time I see you, then it's been fun," I say to Edie as we unbuckle our seat belts.

"Your dad isn't going to actually kill you," Edie says.

We each open our car doors, and I say, "I know that. I'm worried about you."

CHAPTER 19

Dave

We all know that layers of rock hold records of our past. What some don't know is that ice works that way too. Layers of Arctic ice represent millions of years of history. And trapped in that ice are diseases that have not circulated for all those millions of years. Meaning, if they were released, our body would have no idea how to fight them.

Until somewhat recently, there was no concern about their release. But now we have global warming, and all bets are off.

In labs, scientists have started bringing microbes back to life—"reanimating," they call it. A Russian scientist brought back a 3.5-million-year-old bug and self-injected it to see how his body would respond. He survived.

In Alaska, scientists have discovered remnants of the 1918 flu that infected as many as 500 million people, killing between 50 and 100 million. They suspect that smallpox and the bubonic plague are trapped in Siberian ice.

Many frozen organisms won't survive the thaw, but some will. In 2016, a boy was killed and twenty others infected by anthrax that was released when the retreating permafrost exposed the frozen carcass of a reindeer killed by the bacteria at least seventy-five years earlier. More than 2,000 present-day reindeer died.

My concerns about disease go beyond thawing ice. With global warming, tropical climates are gradually creeping northward, bringing mosquitoes with them. That means more mosquito-borne illnesses. Zika. Yellow fever. Malaria. The World Bank estimates that by 2030, 3.6 billion people will be reckoning with malaria.

Global warming aside, the very nature of today's world is a threat. In past times, a virus could wipe out a community, but in most cases it couldn't travel much farther than its victims. It was contained. Now, with the world so connected and people traveling between countries more than ever before, diseases will travel too.

Some theorize that the sudden wave of mammal extinctions that swept through the Americas about 12,000 years ago was caused by an extremely virulent disease, which humans helped transport as they migrated into the New World. That was when migration was slow. Imagine an extremely virulent disease in today's world.

We are due for a pandemic. Mark my words. My guess is it will be a catastrophic flu, something we do not have a vaccine for. Millions of people could die in a matter of months. I'm not the only one who thinks this—Bill Gates did a TED talk about this in 2015. If it were up to me, I would home-school Cleo, to limit her exposure to viruses. Schools are cesspools. If it were up to me, we (as a society) would stop shaking hands. We would replace this disgusting custom with a bow, like the Japanese. We would wear face masks as standard daily protection. I have stockpiled one thousand medical-grade masks in the bunker, just in case.

The reality is that Cleo would not comply with wearing a mask, and she would not comply with my wearing a mask when in her vicinity in a public place. As Jana once told me, parenting involves relentless compromise. I have settled on deploying hand sanitizer in every room of the house, as well as in the cup holder in the car. I also encourage Cleo to wash her hands frequently throughout the school day. I have no idea if she does, but I like to think so. We get our flu shots, and we take daily echinacea and zinc. Cleo takes the pills reluctantly. She says, quoting her mother, "Dad, this is all an illusion of control." I don't care. I like the illusion.

I hate going to medical facilities. You never know what germs are lurking. But my concerns about germs are secondary to my concerns about Cleo and whatever has happened to her ankle.

There's a tap at my car window and I see Edie's face there. Cleo's face is next to hers, Cleo's body leaning against Edie's. She gives me a smile that looks pained.

The two of them back up as I open the door, Cleo hopping around on one foot. I put one arm around her, try to pull her close to me (and away from Edie).

"Edie, thank you for getting Cleo to safety, but I can take it from here," I say.

Edie looks from my face to Cleo's and says, "Oh, uh, okay. You sure?"

Cleo won't look at either of us. Her gaze is now fixed on the ground.

I nod at Edie, and she slowly transfers the weight of Cleo to me.

"I'm sorry, Mr. Garrison," she says once the weight is transferred. She jams her hands in the pockets of her shorts.

"Dad, it was my fault," Cleo says, looking up at me now. She looks so young, more like a six-year-old than a sixteen-year-old.

"It doesn't matter," I say. Because it doesn't.

I start walking toward the entrance of the urgent care center, my gait awkward as I support Cleo alongside me. When we get to the glass front door, I can see Edie in the reflection, still standing where we left her, hands still in her pockets.

"Dad, seriously, it wasn't Edie's fault," Cleo says.

I don't respond because I have already responded to this particular comment. I open the door, and we make our clumsy way inside. I lower Cleo into a chair, then help lift her foot onto an adjacent chair. There are three other people sitting in the waiting room—a woman with a toddler, and an older gentleman. I fish into my pocket for my face mask and put it on.

"Dad, are you for real?" Cleo whisper-shouts at me.

The woman with the toddler looks over at us.

"Here's yours," I say, handing Cleo the mask I've brought for her.

Her eyes are big, incredulous. "Dad!"

The woman with the toddler is still looking at us.

"Cleo, I don't think you should be giving me a hard time right now."

She swipes the mask from my hand and makes a show of putting it on, pulling the elastic straps as far as they will go before letting them snap against her ears. Then I go to the front desk to sign in.

After three hours at urgent care, we are finally on our way home. Cleo has, in fact, broken her ankle—a small lateral malleolus fracture, the doctor said. I broke my ankle once in a fall from my bike when I was maybe ten or eleven years old. I had to wear a bulky white plaster cast that seemed to weigh twenty pounds. Cleo is spared this encumbrance and given a sleek-looking walking boot.

Cleo stuffs her face mask in the glove compartment box and leans back against her seat. They gave her a high dose of Ibuprofen, but that's it. Nothing to make her loopy.

"Thanks, Dad," she says, with zero enthusiasm.

"I'm sure you know I have a few questions."

She sighs.

"Go on, ask away."

She is offering nothing.

"Well, where did this ankle-breaking incident happen, exactly?"

She sighs again. "At the beach. I stepped into this crack thing in the dirt and rolled it."

"The beach," I say.

"Yes, Dad, the place with sand and ocean. Do you remember it?"

Sarcasm.

"I do remember it," I say, noting that she's correct—it's been a while, more than a year.

"That's where it happened."

"Okay. Why were you at the beach?"

"I went to Edie's house like normal and she wanted to go, so we just . . . went."

"Without notifying me."

"Dad, if I had *notified* you, you would have *notified* me that I couldn't go."

This is very true.

"I thought we would just go for an hour or so and you wouldn't know so you wouldn't have to worry. I didn't think I was going to, like, break a bone. Obviously."

"Obviously," I say.

"I mean, that's true, right? You wouldn't have let me go?"

I cannot lie: "Probably. Yes."

"Sometimes I just want to be a sixteen-year-old kid, Dad. I want to do stuff. It's not like we snuck out at midnight, stole a six-pack, and went to graffiti a wall or something."

It's weird to hear Cleo say "six-pack." I like to think that she doesn't even know what a six-pack is. I might be delusional.

"I understand that, but you are still a child living under my roof and you know the rules."

"Oh my god, Dad," Cleo says with a humored snort, "you sound like every dad character on every sitcom ever made."

"Cleo," I say, my tone condemning her humored snort.

"Dad, I get it. Okay. I broke a rule. I should have told you. Let's just get it over with. Am I grounded, like every kid on every sitcom ever made?"

That had been my idea, to ground her. But now she's made it seem stupid.

"I think you should take a break from spending time with Edie for a while," I say.

I want to add that I believe Edie's a bad influence, but I'm aware that that supports her argument that I sound like "every dad character on every sitcom ever made."

"You *think* I should? Is that, like, an expression of your opinion, or—?"

"You can't see Edie for a while," I say, making it clear.

"Stupid," Cleo mutters under her breath, loud enough, of course, for me to hear.

After a couple minutes, she asks, "How long?"

I hadn't thought of specifics yet. As Jana said once, so much of parenting is building the plane as you fly it.

"Two weeks," I say.

"*Two weeks?*" Her reaction would imply that she has mistakenly heard me say "Two years."

"Yes," I say.

"That's ridiculous."

"You are allowed to think so."

She crosses her arms over her chest, and we don't speak for the rest of the drive home.

When we get to the house, I go around to the passenger side to open Cleo's door and help her out. I offer my hand, and she swats it away.

"I can do it myself," she says.

I remember when she was a toddler and made that declaration at least ten times a day. I remember when she was three and Jana called her a "threenager." I can see now what she meant.

Cleo proves that she can, in fact, do it herself, getting out of the car and then hobbling toward the house, putting as little weight on her booted foot as possible. It would be much easier if she just allowed me to assist her, but she is stubborn. Like Jana. Like me.

I follow her inside and say, "Can I get you a snack?"

She must be starving. The wait at urgent care had taken us right past lunchtime and into the afternoon.

"No," she says, hobbling down the hall toward her bedroom.

I let her be, figuring it's the least I can do.

I expect Cleo to come out of her room before dinner, for food if nothing else. But her door remains closed. I make a pot of spaghetti and empty a jar of sauce on it—a lazy version of cooking that is representative of my general approach to meal preparation. Then I go to Cleo's room and knock on the door.

She doesn't answer at first: doesn't even say "Go away," which makes me wonder if she's managed to escape through a window, the ultimate teenage stereotype. But when we moved in, I replaced her sliding window with one that doesn't open. It wasn't because I feared her getting out, but because I feared someone else getting in. I debated it at the time, because a sliding window would be best for a fast escape in the event of a fire. To compensate, I placed a fire extinguisher under Cleo's desk and explained to her how to use it. I've also told her she can throw it through the window as a last resort. It should go without saying that this would only be the case if I wasn't available to save her myself.

"Cleo, I made spaghetti. I'd like you to come eat," I say.

There's no response.

"Cleo, you're giving me no choice but to think something has happened to you in there."

I hear her groan, and then she comes to the door, opening it with dramatic flair.

"Nothing has *happened* to me, Dad," she says. "I'm not hungry."

"You must be hungry."

"I said I'm not. Sometimes, when people are upset, they aren't hungry."

Her tone is condescending, like she's teaching me the alphabet.

"I understand that, but the body still requires energy."

She rolls her eyes. "Not all our bodies are machines like yours."

She starts to close the door.

I remember the words of The Therapist all those years ago: *Be curious, Dave.*

"Can we talk about why you're upset?"

Saying these words feels dreadfully uncomfortable, as I have no intrinsic desire to talk about why she's upset. But I know other people, neurotypicals, desire this type of conversation. To put it simply, I'm trying.

She reopens the door, just a crack.

"You want to *talk* to me?" She still sounds irritated, but also intrigued, which is a good thing.

"Yes."

She swings the door open so I can come in, then goes to sit on her bed, arms crossed over her chest. I stand near the doorway, not sure whether I should join her on the bed or not. The crossed arms deter me.

"I mean, you must know why I'm upset," she says. "Right?"

"You're upset because I don't want you to see your best friend for a while." She nods once.

"Okay, but you understand why *I* am upset, right?" I say. "You need to tell me where you're going, Cleo."

"There's no way you would have let me go. The way you live your life . . . it gives me no room to just be a kid." If I'm not mistaken, her eyes look glassy, watery. My heart rate accelerates as I mentally prepare for the dreaded tears. "I felt like I *had* to lie, Dad. It was either lie or never do anything fun ever. Don't you think that's sad?"

She's definitely crying now. I watch one tear—the leader of a pack that is likely lying in wait—roll down her cheek. I debate whether or not I should go sit with her. I take one step forward.

"Well?" she says.

"Well what?" I ask.

"I asked you a question. Don't you think that's sad?"

"I thought it was a rhetorical question."

She grunts frustration and throws her body backward on her bed so she's looking at the ceiling.

"Oh my god, Dad, it is so hard to get through to you."

I take the risk of moving closer and sit at the end of her bed.

She sits up.

"I get that you're afraid of stuff," she says, finally. "I just need you to get that I'm a teenager who wants to do normal teenage things."

"Is breaking your ankle a normal teenage thing?"

She leans forward and puts her head in her hands.

"Dad, seriously, you are too much."

Thankfully, when she lifts her head, she's smiling.

"I know I can be . . . intense," I say.

Own your part, Dave. Jana said that. Or maybe it was The Therapist.

"Understatement of the year," Cleo says.

She sighs and then looks at me with her still-glassy eyes.

"How about from now on I am honest with you, no matter what," she asks.

I open my mouth to tell her I agree with this approach, but she holds up a finger at me, telling me to wait.

"But when I'm honest with you, you need to be willing to allow some things that may make you uncomfortable."

I close my mouth, because I do not know what to say to this. It does not sound good to me.

"You have to trust me, Dad," she says. "At least a little."

This does not sound good to me either.

Trust has led to awful things before.

"Dad?" Cleo says after a moment of silence.

"Hmm?"

"Are you good with that?"

I am not, I am not, I am not. "Okay," I say.

This is me trying.

"Okay."

"Am I still forbidden from seeing Edie?"

"*Forbidden* is a strong word," I say.

"Well, that's basically what you said before."

"I still think you should be punished for lying to me," I say.

"I didn't lie to you."

"Withholding information is a kind of lie."

She sighs.

"That said, two weeks may have been excessive," I concede. "One week. Okay?"

I should probably not be presenting this as up for negotiation, as if I'm seeking her approval. But, really, I am seeking her approval. She is the only person who can tell me if I'm doing this right.

She slumps, but says, "Fine. Whatever."

I stand from her bed. "Do you need more Ibuprofen?" I ask.

She nods and pushes herself up off the bed.

"You can stay. I'll get it for you," I say.

"No, I'm coming with you," she says. "I'm starving."

CHAPTER 20

Cleo

The only thing that makes this not-seeing-Edie thing more acceptable is that she's visiting her dad in San Diego for two days anyway. So, essentially, I'm only missing out on five days when we could have been hanging out. That's what makes me sad—the could-have-been. A day not spending time with her feels like a day wasted. Dramatic, I know.

I asked Dad if Carter could come over because I'm bored out of my mind, and he said, "I guess that would be okay." We're not on great terms, Dad and I, but we're fine. I can't honestly be that mad at him. I snuck off to the beach without telling him. I knew it was wrong when I did it. I'm just mad that I got caught. And I'm mad I broke my stupid ankle.

Carter hasn't been over in a few months, since before Edie came into the picture. I feel bad that Edie's presence in my life has equated to Carter's absence, but Carter's been cool about it.

"Oh, my god, stranger," he says when I open the front door.

He hugs me so tight that my feet—ankle boot and all—lift off the ground. It feels good to be hugged like this. Mom used to hug like this, as if each hug was the last hug she'd ever give me. Dad is not a hugger. I saw this segment on a news program a while back about how scientists are comparing the brain scans of people with autism to people without it. When normal people see the word "hug" on a screen, the parts of their brain that light up are associated with relationships and human connection. For people on the autism spectrum, those parts don't light up. What lights up is the part of the brain that is used to understand concepts—meaning, they are not thinking about the act of hugging someone, or the feelings that

that would create; they are thinking of the plain and simple meaning of the word "hug." It's sad. But I guess it's not sad for Dad. He only knows what he knows.

"It's so good to see you," I tell Carter.

"You too, my adorable little gimp."

"Hello, Carter," Dad's voice says from behind me.

"Mr. Garrison! Hi!"

Carter moves toward him like he's going to give him a hug, but he must see the look of terror in Dad's eyes because he stops a few feet away from Dad and just gives him a wave.

"Dad, we're just going to hang in my room, okay?"

"I suppose that would be fine," he says.

When I first befriended Carter, I made sure to tell Dad he was gay, because I knew there was no way he'd allow me to have a boy over otherwise. I could have said "I'm not exactly straight either," but I didn't want to pry open that particular can of worms (and still don't).

Carter and I go to my room, and I close the door. He dives onto my bed and kicks off his shoes. Then he rolls onto his back and pushes himself up on his elbows.

"So, tell me everything," he says.

I sit next to him on the bed.

"You first," I say. "I want to hear about San Francisco."

"You mean my future place of residence?"

"I knew you'd love it."

"It's my idea of heaven, Clee."

I miss hearing someone call me Clee. That's what Mom used to call me, and Carter does sometimes too.

"I'm totally going to apply to San Francisco State," he says.

It's weird that I'm at this stage of life when I have to think about college, when I have to consider *my future*. Unlike Carter, I have exactly zero plans yet.

"Then I could come visit you," I say.

"Or you could go there with me," he says. "We could be roomies."

"I don't think colleges allow guys and girls to room together."

"It's San Francisco. The rules might be different," he says. "But, besides, you're going to go wherever Edie goes, am I right?"

I can feel myself blushing.

"You are *so* smitten," Carter says. "No wonder I never see you."

"I'm sorry about that," I say, reaching over to take his hand in mine.

"Oh, please. If I was smitten with someone, you'd never see me either."

"What about that guy you met at the skate park?" I ask.

"Derek? I'm pretty sure he doesn't know he's gay."

"Lame," I say.

"Totally."

Carter starts tapping his fingers on my arm as if it's a piano.

"So, your Dad's not letting you see Edie, huh?"

"No. Just for a few more days, though."

"Lame," he says.

"Totally."

"It's kind of hot, though," he says. "Very Romeo and Juliet."

"Um, yeah, well, they die, so let's hope it's not like that."

He rolls his eyes. "Fine. Pre-death Romeo and Juliet."

He keeps tapping my arm and then stops suddenly, as if something important has just occurred to him.

"Are you two . . . *doing it*?" he asks. "No, right? You would have told me. You *better* tell me!"

"Oh my god, weirdo, stop. We're not *doing it.*"

A few weeks before I told Mom I liked both girls and guys, she had The Talk with me. I was in my room, and she came to my doorway and said "You have a sec?" I knew, just by the look on her face, what she wanted to talk about, and I said, "Oh god, Mom, we don't have to do this." But she insisted. She didn't say what I expected her to say, she didn't tell me to save myself for marriage or whatever. All she said was that she trusted me and that she wanted me to know that I could come to her with any-thing—"birth control, advice, anything. But definitely birth control." She told me to take my time having sex, because it changes everything. She said she lost her virginity in high school and it was too soon. "Your body is going to want certain things before you're ready. Just remember, Clee, you'll only have one first time." Now she's not here and I can't tell her about Edie . . . and all the things my body wants to do.

"Wait, I don't really know what *doing it* even means in my case," I say.

"I think there has to be genital-on-genital contact."

I punch him in the arm. "Ew, Carter. I've only known her for, like, two months."

"That's like *a year* in teenager time."

I shake my head at him.

"Do you love her?" he asks, the question bursting from him with force.

"Like I just said, I've only known her for, like, two months."

"This fact is irrelevant to my question."

"I'm barely comfortable calling her my girlfriend."

"Also irrelevant."

I sigh.

"Have you ever loved someone?" I ask.

I know the answer is no. Carter routinely laments the fact that he hasn't even kissed a boy yet.

"I think I love Colton Haynes."

At first I'm caught off guard by this confession of a relationship I know nothing about, but then the name settles in my brain and I say, "The actor?"

"And model."

I punch him in the arm again.

"Hey, a guy can dream," he says.

He lies flat on his back and I do the same.

"I can't believe you still have a cottage cheese ceiling," he says. "Don't those things have chemicals in them that kill you?"

"If that were true, my dad would be all over it."

"Good point."

He waits a few seconds before saying, "So are you going to tell me anything?"

"About?"

"You and Edie."

"What do you want to know?"

"You *know* what I want to know," he says. "Throw me a bone. Or a boner. Throw me a boner."

I laugh so hard, I snort.

"She's a good kisser," I say.

"Bor-ing. Has she gotten into your pants yet? In any way, shape, or form?"

I hesitate to answer, because I don't want to trigger another onslaught of questions.

"Oh my god, she *has*," he says. "Go on."

I laugh again. "Just with her hands," I say.

"Well, I would hope not with her feet."

"I mean, she hasn't been there with her . . . mouth."

"Oh, well, yeah, that's more intimate than actual sex, if you ask me."

"I think it *is* actual sex," I say. "Technically."

"According to who? Monica Lewinski?"

"Nice reference."

"I have a weird affinity for nineties pop culture."

"Very weird."

There's silence again, and I debate asking him about what's been nagging me for a few days now.

"Edie said something kind of out of the blue the other day," I say.

We're still lying flat on the bed. Carter turns his head to look at me. I remain staring at the ceiling. He waits for me to say more.

"It was the day we went to the beach, when this whole ankle thing happened," I say, gesturing toward my boot. "She asked if I knew what happened to Mirai and Kyra."

Carter doesn't respond right away, and I wonder if he remembers who Mirai and Kyra are. I'm prematurely mad at him for not remembering, for not noting their names for all eternity, for not realizing that this is a requirement of our friendship.

"I'm sorry, but I still hate those people," he says.

He remembers.

"Me too," I tell him.

"What did you say to her?"

"That I didn't really want to talk about it."

"I don't blame you."

We lie still, in silence, again.

"But now I'm wondering," I say.

It feels good to say it, to admit it, out loud.

"About what happened to them?"

"Yeah."

He sighs heavily. "God, Clee, I don't know if you want to know. Do you?"

"Probably not," I say. "They're probably going about life, la-di-fucking-da."

"I mean, I doubt it's la-di-fucking-da," he says.

I sit up. "You think?"

He sits up too. "If it's la-di-fucking-da, then they are in major denial, or they're sociopaths. There's no way that shit couldn't have been totally traumatic for them."

I nod.

"Not that I feel *bad* for them," he clarifies. "I still hate them."

I nod again.

"What are you thinking?" he asks.

I shrug. "I guess I never thought about them or how it was for them."

"Rightfully so."

"Why do you think Edie wanted to know?"

"Curiosity," he says. "But I'm sort of irritated she shared her curiosity with you. She should've kept that to herself."

"Maybe she wanted to, you know, be honest about her thoughts."

"That's a terrible idea. Who does that?"

"You are ridiculous," I tell him.

He pushes himself up and off the bed.

"Where's your cat? I love that damn cat."

"Probably on the couch."

"And can we go scavenge for food in your pantry? I. Am. Starving."

"Sure, yeah," I say.

I push myself off the bed, and he takes my hand.

"Do you still have those imitation goldfish crackers from Trader Joe's?"

"They're not goldfish. They're cheddar rockets."

"I'm sure that's what the Trader Joe's lawyer told the goldfish lawyer."

And with that, we go to get cheddar rockets and interrupt Poppy's afternoon coma.

Dad tells Carter he can stay for dinner, but Carter says his mom is taking him out for Italian. We say our goodbyes, and then Dad and I sit down to a boring dinner of burgers cooked on the stovetop (beef for him, veggie for me) and oven-baked french fries that are soggy and flavorless. Dad has a very utilitarian view of food. He sees it as necessary for sustenance and does not seem to value taking any pleasure in it. Every meal makes me miss Mom. She was the flavor, the spice.

"You two have fun catching up?" Dad asks.

"Uh-huh," I say, dragging a trio of fries through the ketchup. Without the ketchup, they are thoroughly depressing.

I know the rest of dinner will be silent without my intervention, so I decide to attempt a conversation. I brace myself for disappointment, knowing Dad probably won't be as forthcoming as I want him to be, but figure I have to at least try.

"Dad, do you know what happened to Mirai and Kyra?" I ask.

He looks up at me, startled. For a few seconds, he stutters, struggling to find words. Then he blurts, "Why are you thinking about them?"

I know better than to tell him that Edie made me think about them. Edie is in enough trouble with Dad.

"I don't know, it just crossed my mind."

He looks down at his plate, resumes eating, taking a giant bite of his burger.

"We never really talked about them," I say. "I know Sean went to prison. I have no idea what happened to Mirai and Kyra."

"He killed himself," Dad says, still chewing on his giant bite of burger.

"What?"

"Sean," he says. "He killed himself."

"He did?"

Dad nods as he finishes chewing. He swallows and looks up at me. "In prison."

I assume that some people in my position would be happy at this news—at the very least, relieved; at most, vindicated. For them, Sean dying might equate to some kind of justice. He took Mom's life, then his own. The evil threat has been neutralized. Or something. I don't feel happy at all. I feel kind of like I want to throw up.

"God," I say.

The first feeling I'm able to adequately identify is anger at Dad.

"When did this happen? Why didn't you tell me?"

"It happened in March," he says, his attention fixed on his plate again as he eats one fry at a time, in a procedural way that I'm sure makes all kinds of sense to him.

I repeat my question: "Why didn't you tell me?"

"I didn't think it was something you needed to know."

It must have been in the news. I'm surprised I didn't hear something at school, didn't notice kids whispering around me all over again.

I can't tell how Dad feels about it, Sean's suicide. He seems very matter-of-fact, which is how he seems about nearly everything.

"Are you . . . happy? I mean, that he's dead?" I dare to ask.

He has finished his fries. He looks up at me again.

"I'm not *un*happy about it," he says.

I nod. Like I said, I know most people in my position would feel that way. Am I supposed to feel that way? Would Mom want me to feel that way? The truth is I'm sad—sad to realize that Sean evidently had some remorse for what he'd done. In a way, it was easier to think of him as a remorseless monster.

"Did he leave a note or anything? Like, why did he do it?"

Dad shakes his head. "No note. Or not that I know of. He probably just didn't want to spend the rest of his life in prison."

And maybe that's true. Maybe remorse had nothing to do with it. But nobody but Sean could know for sure. Or Mirai and Kyra, maybe. If they were visiting with him and talking with him.

"I wonder if Mirai and Kyra still live around here," I say.

It's possible they do. It's not like we live in a tiny town where I would run into them.

"No idea," Dad says.

He stands from the table, plate in his hand, announcing with this action that he has no further interest in talking about this with me.

I remain seated, even though I'm done with my food, until Dad washes his dish and goes into the living room. Then I tap the screen of my phone, unlock it, and go to my Google app. In the search bar, I type SEAN MCCANN, and the first two results that auto-populate are SEAN MCCANN MURDER and SEAN MCCANN SUICIDE. I click on the second.

The article is about the high rate of prisoner suicides in California, with Sean's death being the central focus. Like Dad said, he died in March. The article says he hanged himself with a bedsheet. There are no other details— nothing about his thoughts or feelings or motivations, nothing about his wife and daughter. I click through more articles, but they all say the same thing, which is not much.

I do the only thing I can think of—I text Edie.

Hey, I wish you were here

I texted her earlier today, before Carter came over, to see how things were going in San Diego with her dad, and she said she missed me and couldn't wait to come home. She drives back tomorrow.

I would say the same, but I really don't wish you were here. I wish I was there

I send her the link to the first article about Sean's suicide.

My dad just told me about this

There is no reply as I imagine her reading it. Then I see the three dots and shortly after:

Holy shit.

It occurs to me that Edie could have googled this information herself. Maybe her shock is fake. Maybe I'm the only one who is shocked.

So you didn't know?

She responds immediately:

No. Wow. Wait . . . this happened in March? He just now told you?

Me: I know.

Her: U ok about it?

Me: I don't know. Not really sure what to think. I feel kind of weird about it

Her: Yeah, I bet. Man. Wow.

Me: Anyway, I just wanted to talk to someone who would have a normal human reaction

Her: Haha. U can always count on me for human reactions . . . not sure if they're normal

Me: Haha. I miss u

Her: Same. I gotta have dinner with my dad. Text u later?

Me: Kk

"I think I'm going to head to bed," Dad says.

He usually goes to bed early—*retires*, I like to think, like in the Victorian-era books they make us read at school—but this is particularly early. It's only 7 p.m.

"Oh, okay," I say.

He seems melancholy, and it's probably my fault. For mentioning Mirai and Kyra. For breaking unspoken rules.

I hear the door to his bedroom close and then it's just me, in the too-quiet house. I go to the living room, curl up at the far end of the couch, and pick up the remote control with the intention of finding something mindless on TV, something to distract my brain from what it really wants to think about.

What happened to Mirai and Kyra?

It's a question that nags at me, even when I start watching old episodes of *Gilmore Girls* on Netflix, which is my TV comfort food.

What happened to Mirai and Kyra?

I tap the screen of my phone, and it lights up.

I go to my Facebook app.

I have a few notifications, so I look at those. This is when I usually go down the social media rabbit hole and forget why I got on my phone to begin with. But this time I don't forget.

I type KYRA MCCANN into the Facebook search bar.

There are two results.

The first has a sunset as the profile picture.

The second is the face of a girl with big brown eyes, dark hair in a bun on top of her head, and a tiny, unsmiling mouth. It is, without a doubt, Kyra.

CHAPTER 21

Dave

Though I have lived near the ocean all my life, I cannot say that I have appreciated it sufficiently. I am not referring to its alleged beauty, as I do not place significant value on such things, but its functional role for our planet. If I was the type of person to have a bumper sticker on my car (I am not), I would have one that says SAVE THE REEFS. Because without them, we are, for lack of a better word, toast.

Reefs support as much as a quarter of all marine life and supply food and income for half a billion people around the world. As oceans absorb more and more carbon dioxide from the atmosphere, ocean oxygen levels decrease, changing the entire ecosystem. If the Earth warms by "only" two degrees, ninety-nine percent of the coral reefs would die off. Many species of marine life rely on these reefs for spawning and feeding grounds. Some also rely on the reefs for protection and cover. Gradually, that marine life will die too. It's no wonder scientists call these "dead zones." People living near these "dead zones" must then find other sources of food and livelihood. Or move. Our future is going to be one in which millions of people are competing to inhabit fewer and fewer inhabitable areas of Earth.

Dead zones are already starting to happen. They are quite advanced in the Gulf of Mexico and off the coast of Namibia, where hydrogen sulfide is bubbling out of the sea along a thousand-mile stretch of land appropriately named the Skeleton Coast. Hydrogen sulfide is toxic, so toxic that evolution has trained us to recognize even the smallest traces of it, which is why we are so adept at smelling farts.

Scientists suspect that hydrogen sulfide was a key player in the End-Permian Extinction, also known as "the Great Dying." During this "Great Dying," up to 96 percent of all marine species and 70 percent of terrestrial vertebrate species became extinct. I believe we are on the cusp of another Great Dying. I believe it may already be too late to stop it.

———————

It's Sunday morning, and Cleo is on her phone at the kitchen table, her thumbs tap-dancing across her phone screen. Guessing by the smile on her face, she is either texting Edie or a new love interest. Does Cleo have a love interest? Her demeanor as of late is very happy-go-lucky, which suggests that she might. I don't know where she would acquire a love interest, since she is at home or at Edie's house most of the time. I remind myself that kids these days acquire most everything online, including significant others. Of course I know how social media works, though I do not participate in it myself (being that the word "social" is right there in the name and I have no interest in the particulars of others' lives). It would not surprise me if Cleo is flirting on Facebook with someone, a soon-to-be boyfriend. It would not surprise me if she was keeping this boy a secret. It's easy to keep secrets from me. I miss so many signals.

I clear my throat, figuring I might as well just ask, instead of torturing myself with wondering.

"Can I talk to you for a second?" I say.

I'm not sure whether I should sit with her at the table or remain standing. Standing feels more authoritative, and I'd like to feel more authoritative right now. So I don't move.

She looks up from her phone.

"Yeah?" she says, eyebrows raised.

She probably thinks I want to talk about last night, when she asked me, out of nowhere, what had happened to Mirai and Kyra McCann. I was disturbed by the inquiry, had hoped she had blocked out everything about them, forgotten their names. After all, that's what I've been trying to do. I had assumed it was a shared goal.

"I was just thinking that I probably owe it to you to have a conversation," I say.

She looks at me expectantly.

"Not about Mirai and Kyra McCann," I clarify.

Her shoulders slump. "What is it?"

"Well, it's occurred to me that you are likely to have a love interest one of these days, and I just want you to be prepared in case you feel certain . . . desires."

I immediately regret my choice of word.

Cleo winces, and her face turns pink in an instant. She puts up both hands, the universal gesture for STOP.

"Oh my god, Dad. No," she says.

She keeps her hands up.

"Cleo, I feel it's my duty, as your father, to—"

"Dad, seriously, check it off your mental list. Mom already talked to me about this."

The way she says it, so casually—*Mom already talked to me about this*—makes me think, for a split-second, that Jana is just in the other room, overhearing this awkward attempt at conversation and laughing that high-pitched laugh of hers.

"Oh," I say. Then: "She did?"

When did Jana talk to her? How long ago? How long has Cleo been a girl (or woman?) in need of this talk?

"You're off the hook, Dad. Mom had this one covered."

Why hadn't Jana told me she'd had The Talk with Cleo? Did she think I wouldn't have cared? *Would* I have cared? Probably not, come to think of it. I left all the child-raising decisions to Jana. In the very beginning, when Cleo was a baby, she may have consulted me—not so much because she thought I had any knowledge she didn't have, but because she wanted validation in the choices she was making. Breast milk or formula? Preschool or nanny? It's impossible not to have doubt when you're newly responsible for a small human being. Over time, I guess she gained enough confidence in her own decision-making to bypass me. If I'd been disappointed in this development, I could have inserted myself. But, quite honestly, I was relieved to be spared the burdens of parenting. Which is ironic now that I must bear all of them, alone.

"Do you happen to have a boyfriend?" I ask, trying to sound casual and accepting.

She looks like she's going to laugh. "No, Dad. You can rest easy."

"Well, if you acquire one, I know how the male mind works, so if you need me for anything, you can—"

Cleo stands from the table, her hands still in their STOP position.

"Oh my god, Dad, seriously, no."

"Okay, then," I say.

She stands at the island. I can see her phone lighting up with texts. She looks at me with a smirk on her face that, if I'm not mistaken, mocks me.

"Did you seriously think a random Sunday morning was the best time for that convo?" she asks.

Frankly, it seemed as good a time as any.

I've never been good with timing. Jana used to say I'm like a bull in a china shop when I have a task in mind. I just enter a scene and impose my will upon it. When Cleo was a toddler and refusing to get dressed, I'd interrupt whatever playtime she was engaged in to force her clothes on her. This would lead to a crying fit, and then Jana would get upset with me. *She's in the middle of something, Dave. She's not ready to get dressed. Can't you tell?* I couldn't tell, though. All I knew was that she needed to get dressed. Her emotional state was beyond me. *Read the room, Dave.* Jana said that to me once. It was when Cleo was in middle school, crying because a boy had made fun of her, and I walked in and started talking about the new sprinkler system I wanted to install in the yard. *Read the room.* That's a very tricky command for someone with The Label.

Cleo rests her elbows on the island and resumes texting. She's probably telling Carter all about this embarrassing interaction of ours. Or Edie. Or the love interest she may or may not have.

Cleo spends the majority of that day in the backyard, in her bathing suit, lying on an old chaise longue chair that I'd forgotten we had. She and Jana used to sunbathe at our old house. I've never seen Cleo do it here. It's a good day for it—sunny, but not too hot. It takes everything in me not to ask Cleo if she's applied sunscreen. I must trust that she has. Or I must trust that she will be okay if she has not. Every day demands such things of me.

I go down to the bunker, which is where I spend most of my weekends. I enjoy having projects, tasks. I've never understood the concept of *relaxing*. Sitting around, doing nothing, sounds extremely anxiety-provoking to me. I prefer to be in motion. Stillness, to me, is not peace, but a kind of death.

I don't have any particular project in mind today, so I decide to take an inventory, checking and double-checking my supplies, even though I just did this two weeks ago. It makes me feel good. I don't know how else to describe it. I assume it's a form of OCD, separate from, or related to, The

Label. ASD, OCD—all my idiosyncrasies may be explained by a few simple acronyms and initialisms.

I go to the plastic bin on the back shelf and open the lid, just to be sure that the contents of the bin have remained in place. If I'm honest with myself (which I rarely choose to be), this plastic bin is my task for today. Ever since Cleo mentioned Mirai and Kyra McCann, I've been thinking about it, wondering if she's found the bin and the shoebox it contains.

The shoebox is there, inside. I open the lid and the letters are there, in their neat stack, ordered (by me) from first to last. They appear undisturbed, so I do not think Cleo has found them. I would have been surprised if she had; she never comes down to the bunker, says it gives her the creeps.

Mirai persisted in writing for months after Jana died. Even when we moved, the letters were forwarded to our new house. I suppose this was the only way she had to contact us. She didn't have my phone number, no ability to call or text. For all I know, she still attempts to write, but the Post Office has stopped the forwarding service. Anything she attempts to mail now will come back to her, stamped RETURN TO SENDER. Maybe she doesn't care, though; maybe just the act of writing is what she wants. Maybe she just has to know she tried so she can sleep at night. I'd prefer she didn't sleep at night ever again.

There are twelve letters in the stack. I don't know why I kept them, why I continue to keep them. It's not as if I ever re-read them. I suppose I like knowing they exist. The desperate apologies they contain do not change my feelings about what happened, but it is nice to have the confessions of guilt on paper. Not that Sean's guilt was ever in question. But Mirai's was. The letters make it clear that she feels responsible for what happened. As she should.

I take the first envelope from the stack and remove the letter within. I unfold the paper—it's just one page—and read.

Dear Dave,

I know you do not want to hear from me. I realize that writing this letter is, ultimately, a selfish act. I am not writing for absolution, as I know I should never be granted that. But I am writing to at least express my remorse. I feel this need to do so. Again, I know this is a selfish act. I know you care nothing about my needs, and I would not expect you to.

That said, I am so dreadfully sorry for what has happened. I must tell you that I never, ever would have thought Sean would be capable of something like this. I wonder if you think I knew he had this in him. You must think so, since Kyra and I came to stay with you. You must think I knew he was violent, dangerous. I did know he had anger, and I did know he could hurt me, but he has always been a private and law-abiding man. What he did that day, coming to our workplace, it's just not something I ever would have predicted. Obviously, if I had thought it was a possibility, I would not have gone to work that day. I was his target. Not Jana. This fact will always haunt me.

In so many ways, I wish I'd never befriended Jana. I wish I'd spared her from the truths of my life. But then I think of all I would have missed. Your wife was such a beautiful person, as you know. We had many long talks, and she was caring in a way that I'd never experienced before. She spoke fondly of you and she loved Cleo so much. I am so sorry that you two must go on together, without her. There will not be a day that goes by when I do not think of you both.

If you have read this far, thank you. I would love an opportunity to speak with you—on your terms, of course. I am including my contact information below. I hope to hear from you but, if I don't, I will understand.

With care,
Mirai

When I first received this letter, it didn't have much of an effect on me. I expected her to apologize, out of a need to make herself feel better about the whole thing. I was pleased that she was racked with guilt. I was pleased with her admission of responsibility, as I had thought of her as partially responsible since the day Jana died. Yes, Sean committed the heinous crime, but Mirai was behind the chain of events that led to that crime. According to my logic, she also deserved to be in prison for the rest of her life, but I knew the justice system wouldn't see it that way. And, besides, I didn't want Kyra to be an orphan. I am not completely heartless.

Now, reading this letter again, I feel more aggravated than I did upon the first reading. My brain is catching on a few words that I must have skipped over before.

She spoke fondly of you.

Having overheard some of their conversations, I know this to be false. I know that Jana complained to Mirai about me, that she expressed a mysterious desire for something more, something different from what our marriage offered her.

I'm overcome with a sudden and overwhelming fury. My hands start to shake, the letter shaking along with them. *You are a liar.* I want to stand before Mirai and say these words to her. I want to spit them at her. I hate her. For lying to me. For knowing more about Jana's feelings toward me than I did, or ever will.

I stuff the letter back in its envelope forcefully and close the shoebox, a Pandora's box if there ever was one. I have no desire to read the other letters. I cannot say I even remember what they say. It's possible they contain more lies about Jana's undying love and affection for me. I simply do not remember. When they arrived, I skimmed them in search of relevant information, and then stored them away. I don't know what I considered "relevant information." For months after Jana died, it was like I was waiting for some bombshell, something that would make sense of her death. Maybe she was having an affair with Sean. Maybe she had threatened to kill him. My mind was wild with theories. Mirai's letters just confirmed the senselessness of reality: Sean came to Jana's office with the intention of hurting Mirai (I don't think he intended to kill her, just scare her); Jana intercepted him; and Jana became the recipient of all his rage. In some of my worst moments, I am angry at Jana—for being so kind, for caring so much, for having this ongoing allegiance to doing the right thing. If I had been in her situation, I do not think I would have approached Sean. I would have stood back, with the rest of the coworkers, and watched the scene unfold.

"Dad?"

I wheel around to find Cleo leaning in the doorway of the bunker, sunglasses perched atop her head, towel tied around her waist, booted foot kicked out to the side.

I close the lid of the bin quickly and clumsily, and Cleo looks at me with understandable suspicion.

"Is that where you hide your porn?" she asks.

I try to laugh in a casual way that does not elicit concern; but by the look on Cleo's face, I fail miserably.

"Oh god, Dad, you don't really have porn in there, do you?"

I have never been interested in porn, as Jana correctly relayed to Mirai during one of the conversations I overheard. I am still raging inside with the memory of all that Mirai knew, all that Jana made her privy to.

In middle school, my few friends in the neighborhood were fixated on finding their fathers' stashes of *Playboy* magazines. When they succeeded, they retrieved one magazine from the stash (usually the bottom one, as they figured it would not be missed) and shared it with the rest of us. While I could appreciate the female form and was quite sure I was attracted to women, I could not manage to create a fantasy about the women in the magazines. They were paid models trying to appeal to my base instincts. I could not overcome this fact.

I wait way too long to say "It's not porn."

Cleo looks at me skeptically.

"Okay, good," she says. "Because nobody has magazines anymore. People just go on the internet, Dad."

"Cleo, I don't engage in that—"

She puts up her STOP hands again.

"I really don't want to know," she says. "And I probably also don't want to know whatever illegal arsenal of weapons you have in that bin."

"I don't have weap—"

She still has the STOP hands.

"Dad, really, I don't want to know. Your bunker, your secrets," she says.

I sigh.

"An-y-way," she says, "I was just wondering if I could take the car to the grocery store. We are all out of those microwave burritos that I am currently living off of."

"You are not driving with a broken ankle," I say.

"It's not my driving foot."

"Cleo."

"Dad."

"No," I say, irritated that we are even having this conversation. The teenage lack of logic is incredibly frustrating for me.

She rolls her eyes. "Okay, can *you* go to the grocery store, then? Or would you prefer I starve to death?"

"You are being dramatic."

I restrain myself from reminding her that the freezer in the garage is packed with frozen dinners in the event that we are ever unable to go to the grocery store. We are unlikely to starve to death, unless one of my more dramatic world endings becomes reality. When I've mentioned those stocked dinners before, she's said, "Dad, those are gross." But I know she'll be thankful if we ever need to use them for sustenance.

"We can go together," I tell her, even though today is not my usual day for going to the grocery store. I figure this is a sign of personal growth for me.

"Fine," she says. "Meet you at the car."

My usual grocery-store day is Tuesday. I've found that to be the least-crowded day. Crowds introduce more risk for various calamities, so I prefer to minimize encounters with them as much as I can. Sunday, today, is the very worst day to go to the grocery store. Sundays are everyone's errand day, a day to prepare for the week ahead after a dose of fun activities on Saturday. It is just before noon, which is peak errand time. Everyone's morning routines have been completed—church services attended, exercise goals accomplished, brunches consumed—and they are coming to Trader Joe's, Walmart, and Costco in relentless droves.

Trader Joe's is the store that sells the burritos that Cleo is currently fixated on procuring, and Trader Joe's is the store that gives me the most anxiety. The ceilings are too low, the aisles are too narrow, people are aggressively chit-chatty, and the parking lot is a nightmare where I am assuming several fender-benders occur on a weekly basis. When I do visit Trader Joe's, on Tuesdays, I go alone, when Cleo is in school. Even on Tuesdays, the place gives me anxiety, and I do not like Cleo to see me in that state. Now here we are, together, on a Sunday, approaching the parking lot of horrors. I attempt a deep breath that is supposed to be calming, but find I cannot take a deep breath, which gives me even more anxiety.

"Dad, are you okay?" Cleo says.

I'm already failing at hiding my angst. I don't know what, specifically, is making it obvious—the whiteness of my knuckles as I grip the steering wheel? The beads of sweat forming along my hairline? The speedy departure of color from my face?

"I'm fine," I lie.

"God, I hate this parking lot," Cleo says.

It relieves me to know that I am not alone in this.

I maneuver the car slowly, watching for cars backing out suddenly with no regard for who might be behind them. Luckily, a spot right near the front of the store opens and I pull in, feeling a surge of relief upon accomplishing the first step of this journey.

The store is bustling, which is not how I ever want to see a store. I over-hear someone saying to one of the employees: "Wow, you guys are so busy today!" It's like she's mocking me.

Cleo takes one of the baskets by the entrance, then hobbles straight to the frozen-food aisle. I follow, not knowing what else to do. Most people would probably *browse* at this point in time, peruse the aisles for something that piques their interest. But, like I said, this is not my usual grocery day. We do not need anything. The food inventory at the house is very carefully calculated (though I have apparently neglected to purchase enough of the frozen burritos that Cleo claims to need for survival).

Cleo puts four of the burrito packages in her basket and now appears to be browsing. She takes a container of chocolate-covered pretzels from the shelf above the freezer and inspects it.

"Dad, can you go wander or something?"

"I thought you just needed the burritos."

"I did, but now that we're here, can I, like, look around?"

Because Cleo never comes to the store with me, she's like a kid in a candy shop, enthralled with the options. Admittedly, I stick to the basics when I shop for us. I do not come home with chocolate-covered things.

I respect her request and "wander." I consider what items I might want to buy, even though there is nothing we need. Like Cleo said, we're here. May as well maximize the outing.

I go to the produce section because, if I'm remembering correctly, we could stand to get another bunch of bananas. Cleo has started making smoothies that require the use of a banana. They are going faster than usual.

As I approach the bananas, I stop dead in my tracks—a phrase that I have never actually used before, but that fits this moment exactly. There, over by the bags of lettuce and spinach, is a bizarre sight. There, over by the bags of lettuce and spinach, is Mirai McCann.

Her hair is in a bun on the top of her head, like I remember it. She looks thinner. She's wearing a pair of black pants—yoga pants, I believe they're called—and a zip-up hooded sweatshirt. Kyra is not with her, or not that I can see. I panic at the thought of Cleo running into Kyra. I turn back toward the frozen food aisle, where Cleo is, wondering if I should check on her, or usher her out of the store quickly. Then I turn back toward Mirai, wondering if I should say something. But what? What is there to say?

It irritates me that she is here, shopping, doing this normal thing that people do. In yoga pants, no less. I have always feared running into her—

the area we live in is quite populated, but not so populated that it's unheard of to run into someone you know. It hasn't happened thus far. Granted, I do not go out much. But, that aside, I've liked to assume that she is holed up at home, getting groceries delivered, afraid to show her face in public ever again. Not that anyone would recognize her. She was never in the papers. Even if she was, people forget, move on. There are new tragedies every day to distract them, to satisfy their morbid curiosities, to make them grateful for their own good fortune.

I did not realize how much I'd comforted myself with the idea of Mirai living the rest of her life as a hermit until right now, as I feel myself getting angrier while watching her paw through the spinach bags to the ones at the back, the ones with the later sell-by dates. The nerve. The entitlement.

It's a baffling coincidence, seeing her here after just re-reading that letter she sent. And I truly think that's all it is—a coincidence. I do not believe in fate. I do not believe in signs. I do not believe that this is an act of Jana's from the great beyond, her way of encouraging me to approach Mirai, to make amends or what-have-you. Yet, I can't help but think of Jana. I wonder what she would want me to do. If she were me, would she approach Mirai, say something? When I think of her shirt that said INTROVERT across it, and of how we joked about our mutual discomfort at parties, I think no. But then I remember how she died, standing between Mirai and a madman, and then I'm not so sure.

I settle on staring, deciding that if Mirai happens to notice my stare and turns to look at me, I will put the onus on her to approach me. I am a statue, as far as I'm concerned.

She puts two bags of spinach in her cart, and then continues meandering through the produce section, looking only at the fruits and vegetables, never at me. She looks so small, so demure. It is hard to imagine that she might have the ability to shatter me. I believe, have always believed, that she possesses the answer to the one question that haunts me. *Was Jana going to leave me anyway?* I feel the question forming in my mouth, like a tropical storm gathering power over the ocean before making landfall as a category 5 hurricane.

I pick up a bag of organic kiwis, just to have something to do. I am staring at the back of her head now, willing her to turn around. I've never known if I want the answer to that question. Will it make me angry? Will it make me sad? Will it forever change my memories of Jana? As an appreciator of facts, I want to know. I want to know all that I clearly did not know when Jana was alive.

She picks up a carton of strawberries and puts them in her cart. She is nearing the end of the produce section. At that point, she will be required to turn her cart. She will see me. I watch, now holding the bag of kiwis in my hand like they're a security blanket.

"I'm ready," a voice says directly behind me.

I jump, startled.

It's Cleo.

"Whoa," she says. "Did I scare you?"

"No," I lie. "I was just. . . ."

She eyes the bag of kiwis in my hand. "Getting fruit?" she says.

I am not known to eat fruit, categorically, so the skepticism on her face is warranted.

"Kiwis are very high in vitamin C."

"Right," she says, still looking at me like I'm insane.

She has the basket hanging from the crook of her elbow. It contains various frozen meals, popcorn, chips, cookies.

"You want me to take that?" It can't be easy to carry that basket while walking with her boot.

"I got it," she says. "Should I meet you at the front, or . . . ?"

"Yeah, yeah, I'll be right there."

I wait until she has rounded the corner at the end of the aisle and then turn my attention back to Mirai. Except she's not there. She's moved on from the produce section.

I go to the next aisle, the one with the pastas and canned goods and baking things. There she is. She is surveying the olive oil options before selecting a bottle from the top shelf. As she puts it in her cart, she starts to look up toward me, as if she is finally feeling the force of my stare.

I stand still, cemented to the floor. A woman with a cart grazes me. "Excuse me," she says before moving on. I remain still.

Mirai looks right at me. She smiles.

It's only then that I realize it's not Mirai at all.

This woman does not even look like Mirai, not really. She has dark hair in a bun on her head. That is where the similarities end. She is not Indian. She is white. She is young—twenty-something. She is not Mirai.

The friendliness of her smile starts to dissipate as I watch her wonder if I'm some kind of creep staring at her.

I force a smile that I'm sure does nothing to dissuade her from thinking I'm a creep, and then I walk past her, toward the cash registers, the damn bag of kiwis still in my hand.

My heart is hammering in my chest when I find Cleo in the line at the end, by the wine section.

It was not Mirai.

I might be losing it.

"So, just the kiwis?" Cleo says with a humored smile.

I hold them up, as if they are a prize. "Yeah."

"Dad, you are acting strange, even for you."

"I know," I say. What else is there to say?

"Are you okay?"

Am I okay? I have been living under the assumption that my grip on reality is strong, firm. Now I am not so sure. Perhaps I can chalk this up to the fact that I revisited the shoebox right before coming here. Mirai was on my mind. It is not that strange that my brain would make this mistake. Is it?

"I'm fine," I tell Cleo.

It's not as if I can tell her about my brain's misfiring. Cleo, much like Jana, would want to analyze the whole thing. *Maybe you* wanted *to see her, Dad. Maybe you* wanted *to ask her questions.* I would dismiss this, but would I be right in doing so? *Do* I want to see Mirai? *Do* I want to ask her questions?

"Uh, okay, if you say so," Cleo says.

It's our turn to check out. Cleo chats with the cashier, a boy who can't be much older than her. He's scrawny and has the speech pattern of a surfer— he makes two-syllable words into three, draws out his vowels. In between scanning items, he runs a hand through his greasy hair. Chatting is effort-less for Cleo, something that astounds and impresses me. I can decipher from their conversation that this boy went to the same high school as Cleo, graduated last year. He asks about her boot and when she tells him what happened, he says, "That blows," and Cleo says, "It does." Cleo helps bag the groceries, which prompts the boy to thank her and say she is "the shit." Then they both stare at me.

"Dad?"

I stare back at Cleo. "Huh?"

"We have to pay."

"Oh," I say. I take out my wallet and insert my card in the little machine.

When the receipt rolls out, the surfer kid hands it to me and tells us to have a "groovy" day.

I take the two bags of groceries and follow Cleo out of the store, glancing at the cash registers to see Not-Mirai in line. I look away, not wanting to further solidify my appearance as a creep. She is so obviously not Mirai. I am embarrassed of myself, as unsure of my own mental state as I've ever been.

We get to the car, and I put the groceries in the back seat.

"Are you sure you're okay?" Cleo asks as we each buckle our seat belts.

I refocus my brain on surviving the exit from the parking lot.

"Yeah," I say, putting the car in reverse and looking over my shoulder to make sure I'm not going to hit someone.

"It's the parking lot, huh?" Cleo says.

"I hate this parking lot," I tell her, stealing her words from earlier.

She looks over her shoulder. "You're good to back out, Dad. I'll watch this side."

"Thanks," I tell her.

And just like that, I let her think she's solved all my problems.

CHAPTER 22

Cleo

While Edie was out of town visiting her dad, her mom hired people to move the furniture into their house. She came home to her room being fully furnished. We are enjoying this new development by lying on her bed.

"I swear you look different," I say.

Our faces are so close together that she appears blurry.

"Cleo, it's only been a week," she says with a laugh.

Then she kisses me, for the hundredth time since I got here.

"I missed you," I say.

"I'm pretty sure I missed you more."

We are gag-inducing, and I love it.

"*Mija*, I'm cutting up a watermelon if you two want some," her mom calls from downstairs.

I cannot believe her mom allowed us to come up to Edie's room, alone, unsupervised. "She trusts me," Edie said when I expressed my disbelief. What a concept. When Dad attempted his little birds-and-the-bees talk with me, I texted Edie immediately, which led to an awkward text conversation about our own sexual history (or lack thereof).

Me: Have you ever . . . ?

Her: Nope . . . u?

I was flattered that she thought it was even a possibility that I'd lost my virginity.

227

Me: That would be a no

Three dots appeared, like she was typing something. Then they disappeared. Then they reappeared. I could guess what she wanted to say, and I understood why she was hesitant. So I just said it for her. For us.

Me: Do you want to?

Her: In general, ya. But I'm not in a rush or anything

I was so relieved to hear this.

Me: Ok, good, same

I didn't tell Edie about Mom's words of wisdom. *Just remember, Clee, you'll only have one first time.* I didn't tell her that I consider this one of the final lessons Mom gave me. I didn't tell her that I feel a need to heed Mom's advice, to wait. It's like a way of honoring her. I'm not sure why I don't tell Edie these things. Maybe a small part of me thinks if I do, she'll be disappointed.

Our lips are like magnets. Without intervention, we could be up here for hours.
  "We should go down," I say, putting my hand on her wrist gently. I feel weird knowing her mom is downstairs.
  She sighs. "Can't we just lie here for another twenty minutes . . . or hours?"
  "Twenty *hours*?"
  She nods.
  "I'm pretty sure my dad would come looking for me."
  She sits up, and I do the same.
  "Okay, fine," she says, "let's go."

Camila is just finishing cutting the watermelon when we appear in the kitchen. She's already given me my welcome hug, but she gives me another for good measure. I can't look her in the eye. I'm sure I look like someone who has been making out for a half hour, and I don't want her to smile at me in a way that confirms that she knows. I put my hand over my mouth, as if trying to hide what my lips have been doing.

"The kitchen looks so good," I tell her as we sit on the stools at the island. I've already told her this but feel the need to repeat myself. The house looks like something in a magazine.

"It does, doesn't it?" she says, proud.

She leans on the island across from us and says, "So, Cleo, what have we missed in your life since we last saw you?"

Edie laughs. "Mom, it's only been a week. You two are so dramatic."

She throws a dish towel at Edie. "A lot can happen in a week. Just look at this house."

"Touché," Edie says.

"How is the ankle?" her mom asks me.

I shrug. "Fine, I guess. It doesn't hurt anymore. Just annoying getting around with this stupid boot."

"You'll be healed before you know it," she says. "How's your father?"

I shrug again. "Hard to say. We went to Trader Joe's yesterday, and he was acting super weird. I've given up on trying to understand him."

"He tried to have a 'birds and the bees' talk with Cleo," Edie interjects.

I give Edie a look. My face gets hot.

"Oh, wow," Camila says. "Wait, he does realize that it should be more of a 'birds and the *birds*' talk with you, right?"

I can feel myself blushing.

"Cleo is open to birds *or* bees, Mom," Edie says. "I told you, remember?"

The blushing intensifies. I shift in my seat, uncomfortable with the idea that Edie and her mom have had conversations about my sexuality.

"I remember, I'm just thinking about you two birds right now," she says.

"He doesn't know," I interject. "My mom knew, but I don't think he has any idea."

Camila raises her eyebrows. "Oh," she says.

She's definitely surprised, but I sense a tinge of disapproval too.

"I'm not, like, ashamed of who I am or anything. I just don't want to tell him," I clarify.

"Can I ask why?" she says, gently.

I shrug. "I just don't think he'd get it."

"You don't think he'd get *you*? His own daughter?"

"Well, yeah, I guess."

"That's sad, *mija*," she says.

Out of the corner of my eye, I see Edie nodding.

"You guys, I'll tell him when I'm ready, okay? He doesn't need to know right now. I'm not, like, getting married any time soon."

"*Verdad*. You take your time," she says. "But if there is even a tiny bit of shame in the reason you're not telling him, you tell me so I can tell that shame, '*Vete!' Bien?*"

"*Bien*," I obey.

She looks at her watch and says, "Oh, shoot, I told Lauren I would call her."

She starts tapping on her phone.

"Lauren is Mom's new friend. From the women's group," Edie says.

Camila has joined some kind of support group for divorced women. Edie thinks it's weird, but I think it's cool. I wish Dad would join some kind of support group, although a group for widowers on the autism spectrum might be a little specific.

When Camila opens the sliding glass door to go outside for her phone call, Doug the dog runs inside. Edie picks him up and puts him in her lap.

"What did I tell you the first time you met my mom?" Edie says. "She's a bit much."

"Are you kidding? Every queer kid should have a mom like yours."

"Well, that's true."

I take a piece of watermelon from the plate.

"We should go back upstairs," Edie says, raising her eyebrows suggestively.

"We're supposed to be eating watermelon."

"Watermelon over making out? I see how it is."

"I don't want your mom to think I'm a floozy."

"*Floozy*? I don't think I've ever heard someone actually use that word."

"You're missing out. It's a great word."

"Floozy," she says, letting the word roll around her mouth.

I'm procrastinating, hesitating to tell her what's really on my mind. I take a bite of watermelon and decide to just come out with it.

"I did something weird while you were gone," I say.

Doug jumps out of Edie's lap and goes to his water dish.

"Weird like you dressed up in a bunny costume and hopped around? Or weird like you ate a steak for breakfast? Or weird like—"

I throw my watermelon rind at her. "Be serious for two seconds."

"Well, now you're scaring me."

"It's nothing bad, it's just—"

"Dude, just tell me."

So I do.

"I looked up Kyra on Facebook."

She takes a minute to respond, likely having to remind herself who Kyra is.

"Oh," she says, finally.

"I guess when you asked me what had happened to her and her mom, I started thinking about it. I was curious. I don't know. It was probably stupid."

"It's not stupid."

"Her account is private, but she had a few posts that were public. Nothing that showed much about her life or anything, but it was still weird to see."

"Yeah, I bet."

I can tell she doesn't know what to say. I'm sure she wants to see the Facebook page, but doesn't want to come out and ask, so I make it easier for her:

"Do you want to see?"

"If you want me to."

I bring up the Facebook app on my phone and go to Kyra's page, a page I've visited at least twenty times since I first searched for her, even though it doesn't show me much of anything.

"There," I say. "That's her."

The profile photo betrays nothing. She looks like an average teenage girl. Pretty, but not gorgeous. I can't see any other photos. There are a few public posts on her page—a plea for people to sign a petition for animal rights, posts from friends wishing her a happy birthday back in April. It occurs to me that her birthday was just a few days after Mom died, right after her father was arrested and her life changed forever. I wonder if she can ever feel happy on her birthday again, if it will always be tainted.

"Huh," is all Edie says.

She probably has no idea what the right thing to say is. I'm not even sure. Part of me wants her to say *Why don't you contact her?* Because that's what I've been thinking about. With just a couple taps on my phone, I could send her a message. I'm not sure why I would, though. I'm not sure what I want to know. Do I want to find out that her life is awful and that she lives with a cloud over her head at all times? My first vindictive thought is *Yes, I want to know that.* Because I also live with a cloud over my head at all times, and her parents are to blame for that. But the thing is, *she* isn't to blame. For all I know, she resents her parents as much as I do. For all I know, we have things in common.

"I keep thinking maybe I should, like, send her a message," I say, sending the idea out there like a raft on a river, seeing if it'll float.

Edie nods. "What would you want to say?"

She's reminding me a lot of Ms. Murray right now, withholding any obvious opinion, responding to what I share with probing questions.

"I don't even know."

"I think you do," she says.

Totally Ms. Murray.

She's right, though. I have written at least a hundred messages to Kyra in my head already. I know what I want to ask, I just don't know how to ask it. What I want to ask is: *Are you as fucked up by what happened as I am?* But then I'm not sure I want to know the answer, even if I could ask that exact question. What if she's not fucked up at all? What if Mom's death had little effect on her? What if she's happy her dad went to prison? What if there's no remorse? That would fuck me up even more.

"What if I just send a starter message?" I ask.

"A starter message?"

"Like, 'Hey, I don't know if you remember me, but. . . .'"

Edie looks alarmed. "Um, Cleo, I think she remembers you."

I shrug. "Well, I don't know. Maybe she, like, blocked out that whole time of her life."

She shakes her head. "If that were possible, you probably would have done it yourself."

She has a point.

"Okay, maybe like 'Hey, I've been wondering how you're doing'?"

Edie considers this. "That's safe."

She seems unsure, though.

"You're hesitating," I say.

She neither confirms nor denies this. She just looks at me.

"What?" I say.

She sighs. "I mean, I thought you *hated* her."

"I thought I did too. Maybe I still do? I don't know."

"And why hasn't *she* messaged *you*? I guess that annoys me."

I've thought of this myself. When I found her on Facebook, so easily, it occurred to me that she must have searched for me too. I'm also easy to find. But she never sent a message, never inquired about my well-being. And it was my well-being that was clearly compromised. I lost my mom. Her father *killed* my mom. If anyone reaches out, it should be her. And it should have been a year ago.

But Ms. Murray always tells me to consider things from the perspective of others. She says that's the way to empathy and that empathy will solve all the world's problems. So I've tried to jam my feet into Kyra's shoes. I've tried to understand.

"Maybe she's ashamed," I say. "Or maybe she's afraid it will upset me."

"Maybe," Edie says. "But still."

"Maybe her mom told her not to."

"Maybe," she says again.

"You don't think I should message her?"

"I just don't want you to get hurt."

She stabs another piece of watermelon with her fork.

"What if she doesn't write back?" she says.

I hadn't thought of this yet. I hadn't thought much beyond the sending of the message.

"I guess that would make it clear that she has no interest in talking about it. . . ."

"And no interest in apologizing," she says.

"I don't know if she needs to apologize," I say. "She didn't have anything to do with it."

"I guess. I still think it'll piss you off if she doesn't write back. And then you have to live with the pissed-off feelings, and that's never any fun."

"I think if I write to her, it has to be for myself, without expecting anything in return."

That's what Ms. Murray would say.

"How very evolved of you."

"You think I'm kidding myself?"

She shrugs. "Maybe not. Maybe you're just way more mature than I am."

"Well, that's a given."

We sit there, eating watermelon, in silence, for a couple minutes.

"I think I'm gonna do it," I say.

"Okay," she says. I can tell she's trying to sound nonjudgmental, but I still hear the apprehension in her voice.

I tap on the "message" icon on Kyra's Facebook page.

"Wait, *right now?*" Edie says.

"No time like the present."

She scoots her stool closer to me and looks over at my screen.

I type:

Hi Kyra. I've thought about contacting you for a while. I hope this is OK. I just wanted to see how you and your mom are doing. I hope you know

I don't blame you for anything. My mom wouldn't want me to hold that kind of grudge. No pressure to respond, but would love to hear from you if you want to write.

—Cleo

"Is that okay?" I ask Edie.

"Like I said, you are clearly way more mature than I am."

"You would hold a grudge?"

She scrunches her nose in disgust—with herself, I guess. "Yeah, probably."

"But she literally had nothing to do with it."

"Guilty by association," she says.

"I guess the more I've thought about it, I don't see it that way."

"Evolved," she says.

I read the message again, contemplating whether to send it or not.

"Do you think my dad would be upset if he knew I'd contacted her?"

Edie doesn't hesitate: "Absolutely."

I don't even know why I asked. Of course Dad would be upset. He would rather I completely forget who Mirai and Kyra are. It's like he stored away the whole event in his bunker and never intends to revisit it again.

"Can't you just lie to me?" I ask.

"Never," Edie says, holding up her right hand as if she's testifying under oath.

Just then, Camila comes back inside and the energy of the room changes. I forget the heaviness of the decision weighing over me.

"Isn't this the *best* watermelon?" she says, taking a piece. As she puts it in her mouth, her eyes roll back in her head in a display of exaggerated pleasure. "You just never know with watermelons. You cut them open, hoping for the best, but you just never know."

"A metaphor for life, Mom," Edie says.

Camila excuses herself from the kitchen, says she's going to throw in a load of laundry. My fingers are still hovering over my phone.

"I think I just need to slice open the stupid watermelon," I say to Edie.

She looks at my phone, understanding.

"Slice away," she says.

And I hit Send.

CHAPTER 23

Dave

Low on my list of apocalypse concerns, but still there, is an attack from another planet. Yes, aliens. I have not mentioned this concern to anyone, and I will not, as I do not want to be institutionalized. If Cleo knew I dedicated any time at all to thinking about aliens, she would be gravely worried. But if she would hear me out, I think she would understand where I'm coming from.

There is a legitimate, reputable institute called the SETI (Search for Extra-Terrestrial Intelligence) Institute in Mountain View, California, dedicated to looking for life on other planets. Their very existence makes me feel like some of my concerns may be valid. According to their website, there may be close to one hundred *billion* potentially habitable planets in our galaxy. They say that Mars and several of Jupiter's and Saturn's moons have environments that could support biology. And beyond our solar system, there are so many planets, it's reasonable to imagine that at least some are populated with intelligent beings.

If there are other intelligent beings out there, somewhere, will they want Earth's resources? Will they want to conquer us? If they make contact with us, even just for the purpose of harmless exploration, will they unknowingly bring deadly diseases with them? In a 1979 interview, the late physicist Gerard O'Neill said, "Advanced Western civilization has had a destructive effect on all primitive civilizations it has come in contact with, even in those cases where every attempt was made to protect and guard the primitive civilization. I don't see any reason why the same thing would not happen to us."

Meaning the aliens would be the advanced civilization. And we would be, essentially, ripe for domination and, ultimately, destruction.

All of this made me curious to look into accounts from people who claim contact with UFOs or extraterrestrial beings. Most of these accounts are easily dismissible with logic. Or they are accounts from a singular person, who could be assumed to have a few screws loose. But there is one account that continues to intrigue me.

On September 1, 1969, multiple people in Berkshire County, Massachusetts, reported seeing or experiencing something having to do with a UFO. The fact that multiple people, in different locations within the county, reported this makes it hard to discount. Many of the people claim to have seen the stereotypical giant flying saucer. One says he was abducted, taken from his lawn and up into the spacecraft. A witness reports that this man was, in fact, gone and then reappeared in a different area *hours* later. One man, who was a child at the time, says he was in a car with his mother (who was driving), his grandmother, and his brother. They took a shortcut over a local bridge and saw a bright white light that then became an orange light. They saw the flying saucer and then went unconscious. When they awoke, a few hours had passed and nothing had changed, except that his grandmother was in the driver's seat and the ignition was off.

Cleo would actually enjoy that story, I think. But, again, I can't even suggest to her that this is where I've let my thoughts wander. She'll think she's lost me. And she's already lost one parent.

I have opened the shoebox again. I am in the bunker, alone. Cleo is at Edie's house again. I have a card table in the bunker, against the back wall, a place where I can organize things before placing them within my system of shelving units. This is where I've placed the shoebox. I have removed the twelve letters and placed them in three rows of four per row. I open them one at a time and read them, in order. Taken as a whole, they are very repetitive, with the same theme of remorse and sorrow. There are no further mentions of Jana speaking fondly of me. Perhaps Mirai could only stomach that lie once. At the bottom of each letter is her phone number and email address. I do not know what she would plan to convey via phone or email that she could not convey in these letters themselves. Her apparent desperation to be in touch with me makes me think there is something beyond these letters, something she has not put on paper. This has awakened a curiosity within me that is like a fly buzzing in my ear—persistent and impossible to ignore.

I remove my phone from my pocket and input the numbers. I stare at the green phone icon. I do not know what I would say to her, beyond stating my name. According to these letters, she should be the one to talk. She is the one with things to say. I am the recipient—of apologies, explanations, whatever else she possesses.

I press the button and the ringing begins. There is a brief panic, an adrenaline shot accompanied with a singular thought—*what have I done?* I immediately regret my impulsiveness, but before I can press the red button and end the call, a woman answers.

"Hello?" she says.

She does not recognize the number because she does not have my number. It's strange that she would pick up at all. I never pick up calls from unknown numbers due to the recent proliferation of robo calls, which I consider a personal assault on my daily life. It occurs to me that she answers every call from this area code because she hopes it will be me. I wonder if this is narcissistic of me, or accurate.

"Hello?" she says again.

If I do not say something soon, I am going to seem like a creep who has called just to breathe in her ear. And if she traces the number back to me, I will suddenly be the bad guy when I should never, ever be the bad guy in relation to Mirai McCann.

"Hi," I blurt.

"Can I help you?" she says. Her voice is soft, tentative. There is none of the annoyance that one would expect in this situation.

"Mirai McCann?"

I don't know why I say her whole name like this, as if I'm calling from a collection agency. I've always thought of her and her daughter with their full names. I've never wanted to think of them on a first-name basis alone.

"Yes, this is she."

"This is David Garrison."

I never refer to myself as David. I am only David to people who don't know me at all.

"Dave?" she says, insisting on familiarity.

"Yes," I say, giving in.

"My god, it's so wonderful to hear from you. Thank you so much for calling."

The gratitude in her voice makes me need to sit. I feel dizzy. I have no chairs in the bunker, so I sit directly on the concrete floor.

"I was . . . I was organizing some things and came across your letters," I say, making it sound as if I had never received the letters myself, as if they had been stored away by someone else and I had just now discovered them, like an archaeologist digging up a dinosaur skeleton.

"Oh," she says. I can hear her confusion, her wondering if I did not read them sooner, back when she originally sent them.

"You sounded eager to speak with me, so I decided to call."

"Oh," she says again. "Yes, well . . . yes."

There is silence, the awkward kind with which I am very familiar. Then there is a sound coming from her side, something like. . . .

"I'm sorry," she says, sniffling.

Yes, she is crying.

"I've just wanted for so long to speak with you," she says.

As I've stated, I am not good with tears. I am thankful that this is over the phone, that I am not expected to provide any kind of physical comfort. The expectation to provide verbal comfort is dreadful enough.

I want to bypass her emotions and get straight to the point. I want to ask if there is any additional information she felt compelled to convey to me. *Jana was going to leave you.* I imagine her saying these words. Would these words be a relief? Would they enable me to see Jana's death differently? It sickens me that I am looking to Mirai to make me feel weirdly grateful that Jana left me in the way she did, instead of the other way. What kind of person am I?

"I don't even know where to begin," Mirai says, still sniffling. "You've caught me a bit off guard."

The subtle accusation in this statement angers me. She destroyed my life, but I've caught *her* off guard? Does she expect me to apologize? I will not.

"I just. . . . Wow," she says. "Thank you for calling."

She has now thanked me twice. I have no idea how to respond to her, so I say nothing. She knows about The Label. And even if she didn't, I don't have anything to explain to her.

"Is there something you wanted to say to me?" I ask her.

I know it comes out blunt, but I don't have the energy to make it come out any other way.

"Oh," she says, again. *Oh.* A purposeless, one-syllable word—the epitome of conversational inefficiency. I stand, start to pace the length of the bunker.

"If there is nothing to say, that's fine," I say. "The letters implied there was."

"There is . . . I mean, there's so much to say, isn't there?"

I don't know whether this is an actual question, or a pondering of hers that she is saying aloud. I wait.

"It would be easier, I think, if. . . . Could we meet?"

I stop pacing, take hold of one of the shelving units, as if to keep myself steady. "Meet?"

I do not want to meet. I never, under any circumstances, want to meet, but especially not now. I shouldn't have called. I shouldn't have instigated this reconnection. I should have known she would suggest this, the same way coworkers suggest a meeting when a two-sentence email would suffice.

"I just think it would be nice to see you," she says.

I don't know why this would be nice for her. I have no interest in seeing her. But I must admit there is this lingering curiosity about what she wants to say to me, this lingering hope that she has something to say beyond "Oh," something worthwhile.

"Well . . . when?" I ask.

It is a stall tactic, this asking of *when*. I figure we can distract ourselves with the logistics of this proposed meeting for a few minutes while my brain attempts to catch up to the realistic possibility of seeing Mirai McCann again. When it's caught up, it will tell me what to do.

"I'm free now," she says, without any of the hesitation I was anticipating.

"*Now?*"

It is five o'clock on a Wednesday. Cleo said she would be having dinner at Edie's house, which is what she's done the past two nights. She will be home by eight, because that is the curfew I have imposed.

"If now's not good—"

"It's fine," I say. "I have a three-hour window."

"A window," she says.

I hear her talking with someone in the background, a female voice. Her daughter, I suppose.

"Where would you like to meet?" she asks.

Nowhere. This is my first thought. What was I thinking, entertaining the idea of meeting her at all? I am not a person who *goes out*. I do not frequent coffee shops. I do not *meet up*.

"I . . . I don't. . . ." I am having difficulty managing words.

"Have you eaten dinner? There's this quiet place near the Mission. I think I'm their only patron." She emits a little laugh that unnerves me. I am not someone around whom she should be emitting laughter.

"I'm not hungry," I tell her. Because I'm not.

"Okay. . . ."

It is now up to me to propose an idea. The ball is in my ill-equipped court.

"I can still meet you there," I say. "I just won't be eating."

"Oh," she says. That word again. "That's fine."

"Okay, then."

I am about to end the call when she says, "You'll need the name of the place, right?"

I sigh in response to my own stupidity and say, "I suppose I do."

She gives me the name, and we agree we will meet each other in a half hour. This is all happening extremely fast.

I leave the bunker and make my way to the kitchen to retrieve my wallet and car keys. Then it occurs to me that I should probably put on more appropriate clothing. I am currently wearing sweatpants that I have cut at the knees to make shorts, and a Hawaiian Tropic T-shirt that I got for free at CVS when I bought a tube of sunscreen. I go to my bedroom and paw through the jeans hanging in the closet (yes, I hang my jeans in the closet). I only own a few pairs, along with a handful of button-up shirts. The rest of the closet, previously dedicated to Jana, is still empty.

I put on a pair of jeans and the blue-gray shirt that Jana said was her favorite, and then I am ready. To set an example of responsibility, I text Cleo:

I will be going out for a couple of hours. Home by 8.

She responds right away:

Out? U don't go out

She knows me alarmingly well.

Me: I won't be gone long.

Her: Where r u going?

I should have known she wouldn't just say Ok, bye.

Me: I forgot to get something at the store.

While it is very difficult for me to lie in person, as my face conveys deception very clearly, it is less difficult to do so via text.

Her: U never forget things. R u ok?

Me: I'm fine. I'll see you in a couple hours.

Her: Ok. Ur being super weird

Me: I thought you expected that from me.

Her: Omg, u made a joke. R u having a stroke?

Me: Cleo, I'm fine. I'll see you soon.

She texts me a thumbs-up emoji and that is that.

As I drive away from our house, I wonder if she's watching from the front window of Edie's house. I wonder what she would think if she knew I was going to meet with Mirai McCann.

CHAPTER 24

Cleo

Edie, her mom, and I sit around the dinner table, bellies full from enchiladas and way too many chips with guacamole. I check my phone to see if Dad's texted again. He hasn't.

"Do you guys think he has a *date*?" I ask them.

At the start of dinner, I'd told them about Dad's highly suspicious and unusual text saying he was "going out." Edie's mom didn't think it was that big of a deal because she is a normal person who goes out for various things all the time. Edie knows better. She said she didn't buy that Dad would forget something at the store and then rush out to get it. "What could be *that* important?" she said. Camila waved us off and we ate dinner, getting into a long conversation about the celebrity moms accused of paying exorbitant sums to get their spoiled kids into college.

"A *date*?" Camila asks, clearly suppressing a laugh.

She is right to laugh. I laugh with her to let her know it's allowed. Dad on a date? It's ridiculous to even consider. I simply cannot imagine Dad on a date. Not just because I persist in thinking of Mom as his life's love, but because I can't picture Dad sitting across from someone at a restaurant or bar or wherever, having an actual conversation. Where would he even meet someone? In one of his doomsday-prepper online forums? I just can't see it.

"Oh, come on, you guys, don't be mean," Edie says.

I stand to start to clear the plates. It's the least I can do.

"Edie. Can you honestly imagine him on a date?" I say.

"It's not unheard of. He's an attractive guy," Edie says.

I have never, ever thought of Dad as *attractive*.

"Are you serious right now?"

Camila interjects: "Objectively speaking, he is nice-looking."

"Most people on dating apps only pay attention to the photo," Edie says.

"You think he's on a *dating app*?"

Camila nods effusively. "Edie is right. I can't tell you how many terrible dates I've been on because I was lured by the photo."

"God, Mom, I don't want to hear about your dates," Edie says.

I busy myself with hand-washing the dishes. Edie comes to help dry.

"In any case, *mija*, your dad snagged your mom and she sounds like she was a great woman," Camila says, sitting at the island behind us.

"That's true," I say. "She was."

I don't realize I'm rinsing and re-rinsing the same dish until Edie takes it from me.

"You okay?" she asks.

I nod, though I suddenly feel sad—about Mom's greatness and the possibility of Dad seeking to find a replacement for it. Of course it would be natural for him to seek companionship with someone else. Science would support it. In chemistry, bonds break all the time. A change in bonding or atomic identity is not just the end of one state but the beginning of another. I know this, but it still makes me sad.

"It's probably not a date, *mija*," Camila says, her voice calm and soothing. She opens a container of chocolates on the island and starts nibbling at them.

I turn off the water and turn around. "You don't think so?"

She shakes her head. "He doesn't strike me as being at all ready for that. He still wears his wedding ring. He is still grieving."

She says this definitively and I want to think she is right, that there is a checklist of requirements for a widow, to be ready to date and he fails to meet the criteria.

I check my phone again. No texts. While I'm at it, I check my Facebook messaging app too, something I've been doing at least once an hour for the past two days. At first, I had been anticipating a response. Now, I just hope to see the little checkmark that means Kyra has seen my message. There has been no checkmark. I've started to wonder if she even uses her Facebook account. Maybe, like most kids, she has abandoned Facebook for Instagram and Snapchat and whatever else. I deleted all those apps after Mom died, when it became too hard to see my friends (or former friends) going about their regular teenage lives. I kept Facebook because I hardly ever went on there anyway, and I'd accumulated so many contacts over the years. I figured it would be good to have in case I needed to get in touch with someone. Which is what I'm doing. I can't say I anticipated this particular use, connecting with the daughter of the man who killed my mother. Or, attempting to connect.

There's no checkmark, no message.

Edie looks at me with raised eyebrows. She knows what I'm doing. I shake my head, and she twists her mouth into a look of disappointment.

"I guess I better get home," I say.

Dad said he'd be home by eight, so I should be too.

Camila gives me one of her tight hugs and Edie walks me to the door, Doug on her heels.

"You sure you're okay?" she asks.

Her eyes scan my face.

"Yeah, I'm just weirded out by this lack of Kyra response. And now this weird thing with my dad."

"I'm sure it's nothing. He probably wanted to get something at the store for his bunker."

I smile, and then smile bigger as I consider how lucky I am to have someone who can cheer me up so easily.

"Like it dawned on him that he didn't have enough Band-Aids and he just *had* to go?"

"Totally," Edie says.

"I can actually see that."

I stand on my tip-toes to give her a kiss. She holds me against her body, the two of us pressed together.

"Text me later," she says, pulling away slowly.

"I will."

"I swear I need your texts now to go to sleep."

I give her a look. "That deserves a barf emoji."

"Okay, sassafras," she says, utilizing a new nickname she's given me (it started as "sassy pants" and then evolved—or devolved).

I walk quickly across the field between our houses, nearly jogging. I don't know why I'm in such a hurry. I don't see Dad's car. I guess I just want to be settled, on the couch, ready to interrogate him when he walks in the door.

The house is eerily quiet when I open the slider. It occurs to me that I don't think I've been in the house alone since Mom died. Dad is always here—for my sake, or his own, or both. I lie flat on the couch and turn on the TV. I don't want to watch anything, I just want noise, the illusion of company. Five seconds later, I'm bored, so I take out my phone, realizing that I am becoming (or have already become) a human being in need of constant distraction. I chastise myself for what I'm about to do—check my Facebook app again, even though I just checked it. I'm becoming obsessive and pathetic.

But, then, there is something—a red notification indicating I have one message waiting for me. I tap to see my inbox, and there it is—a message from Kyra McCann.

Hi Cleo. I'm so sorry. I don't go on Facebook much anymore. How are you? I'm so glad you wrote. To be honest, I've sort of assumed you hated me (and my mom) so I didn't want to reach out and make you more upset. I think about what happened all the time. I hope you're doing ok. You asked how my mom and I are doing… I don't know. Depends on the day, I guess. We moved . . . not far, just to Laguna Niguel. Fresh start or whatever. This might be totally weird, but would you want to meet up? I don't have to tell my mom if you don't want. I have a car and stuff. No worries if you don't want to. I'm just glad to hear from you.

Kyra

I read it again, then a third time. She sounds so . . . normal. There is nothing to dislike about her, based on this message (except for the fact that she has a car, which is very envy-provoking). I don't know if I was hoping for something to dislike, some kind of closure-forcing message like "Please don't contact me again," or no response at all, which would have suggested that she couldn't be bothered with me. What I have instead is confirmation that what I suspected is true—she is like me, attempting to go on in the wake of this horrible thing that happened. We are the innocent bystanders. We are victims of losing one parent while the remaining parent lives but also seems lost.

I text Edie.

She responded

She texts back immediately:

I knew she would. What'd she say?

I take a screenshot of the message, send it to her.

Wow. Do u want to meet up with her?

Do I? Maybe I do. Maybe it would be nice to sit across from someone who is a bit like me, someone who gets it. But what if, in person, she's different? What if it's awkward? What if talking with her makes me feel worse? What if it's a mistake to dredge up the past in the name of healing? What if there's no such thing as healing?

Me: Would u want to if u were me?

Her: I think I would. I'd be too curious not to

Perhaps that's all it is—curiosity. Perhaps that's enough, on its own. No grander purpose required.

Me: I mean, she doesn't sound like a monster, right?

Her: No, doesn't sound like a monster

Me: Ok. I think I'm gonna go for it. Should I wait a while to respond? Or should I respond immediately so she knows I'm not at all cool?

Her: Ha.

Me: U were supposed to say I'm cool

Her: I told you I'd never lie to you

I send her an eye-roll emoji and then switch back to Facebook. I keep it short and simple:

Hi Kyra! It would be nice to meet up. Let me know when and where. I'll be there.

Cleo

It might be tricky, because Dad won't let me drive with my stupid boot, and he's made it pretty clear he's not too excited about Edie driving me places. I'll figure it out, though. If Dad can "forget something at the store," so can I.

CHAPTER 25

Dave

There are a number of people who have predicted the end of the world. In 2017, conspiracy theorist David Meade said the planet Nibiru would collide with Earth and destroy it. When this prediction failed, he then said the rapture would take place and the world would end on April 23, 2018. That date has now come and gone.

Ronald Weinland, founder of the Church of God Preparing for the Kingdom of God (far too long a name, if you ask me), previously predicted the world would end in 2011, 2012, and 2013. Then he said that Jesus would return on June 9, 2019. That date has passed, and CNN did not report any Jesus sightings.

Jeane Dixon, a psychic, predicted that Armageddon would take place in 2020. I imagine some are holding their breath. She previously predicted the world would end on February 4, 1962.

Pastor F. Kenton Beshore says Jesus will return between 2018 and 2028, with the rapture by 2021 at the latest.

The Messiah Foundation International says the world will end in 2026, when an asteroid collides with Earth.

Kent Hovind, a Christian fundamentalist evangelist (and convicted criminal), says 2028 is the most likely date for the rapture.

There are a few predictions further out. Sunni Muslim theologian Said Nursi says doomsday will come in 2129. According to the Talmud in mainstream Orthodox Judaism, the Messiah will come in 2239, with the destruction of the world a thousand years after that. Rashad Khalifa, an Egyptian-American biochemist, says his research on the

Qu'ran has led him to believe the world will end sometime during the year 2280.

Most discussions of the apocalypse are in a religious context, which I find strange. I do not follow religion. I do not believe in God. I am a man of logic, and I see no logical evidence to support the existence of an all-knowing being. I believe the apocalypse is coming, but it will be explained by science, not God. There will be no Jesus or Messiah or rapture. It will just . . . happen. That's the most disturbing thing about life, isn't it? It just . . . happens.

The café across from the Mission is a French place with a difficult-to-pronounce name (it starts with an "H" and I cannot be bothered to dwell on what comes after that). As I approach the entrance, I run through a script in my head: *Mirai, hello. Nice to see you.* I will not extend my hand for her to shake, but if she extends hers, I will take it.

I have arrived five minutes ahead of the agreed-upon time, which is typical of me. I find tardiness both extremely anxiety-provoking and disrespectful. I also prefer to be the one who chooses a table—preferably a table apart from other diners, as the noise of adjacent conversations is often distracting for me.

When I enter the restaurant, an older man dressed in a suit greets me with a menu in his hands. His suit makes me wonder if I have dressed inappropriately, if this is a fancy establishment. I take a quick look around, and it does not appear fancy. It has a cottage-y feel. I would guess that the restaurant was formerly an adobe inhabited by the first settlers of this area, who are probably turning in their graves at the thought of it now being used to make French food.

"Good evening, *monsieur*," the man says with a heavy accent. "Dining alone?"

"No, I'm meeting someone."

That's when I hear a voice: "Dave?"

I turn to see a woman standing from a table in the back, coming toward me. Mirai. She has arrived earlier than me, which is something I was not at all expecting.

"Hello," she says, giving a polite side-eye to the man with the menu, who steps away.

Mirai is wearing a long dress that seems much too large for her. Its function appears to be to hide the shape of her body. She looks smaller than I remember. Thinner, but also shorter. Can people lose height? I know this happens with age, as vertebrae compress and what not, but she is not old—my age, or less. Perhaps she was just taller in my mind's eye, towering over my life for the past year.

She does not extend her hand, and I am grateful for this.

"Shall we?" she says, motioning toward the table at the back.

The table she has selected is the table I would have selected. I am grateful for this too. There are only two other diners, sharing a table toward the front of the restaurant, as far from the table Mirai has selected as possible.

The table has four chairs. She sits in one, and I take the chair across from her. She does not seem to have any problem staring directly at me. I look down, at my folded white napkin, at the menu. When I dare to look up at her, for an obligatory few seconds, I see her brown deer eyes framed by long black lashes on the top and heavy, dark circles underneath.

She sips from a cup of tea, and I wonder how long she has been here. Did she immediately leave her house after our phone conversation? Did she happen to be already wearing this enormous dress, primed and ready for the special occasion of our meeting?

"I know you said you wouldn't be eating; but if you change your mind, the filet here is wonderful. My treat, of course."

Her treat, because her husband killed my wife? Because there is so much she owes me that she can never repay? I feel the need to make clear that even if she did purchase a meal for me—which she will not, because I am not eating—that does not put a tally mark on her side. It earns her nothing.

"I'm not hungry," I reiterate.

I wonder how many times she has been here since Jana died, enjoying the filet. How many delicious forty-dollar entrees has she enjoyed in her alleged mourning period?

"Something to drink?" she asks me, her eyes begging me to order something. I would like some tea and I hate that this will please her.

"Just tea," I say.

She raises a tentative hand to flag down the waiter, something I wish she wouldn't do. I am a man, after all, indoctrinated to believe that such a responsibility should be mine.

The waiter comes, and I tell him I'd like a chamomile tea. This close to bedtime, I cannot have caffeine. He returns a moment later with a teacup on a saucer and a small white teapot. He opens a wooden box containing a multitude of tea bags, which is annoyingly unnecessary as I already told him I wanted the chamomile. I find the desired tea bag, open it, and place it in the hot water. I am happy to have this mini-project. I think this is why I like tea—each cup is a mini-project.

"So," Mirai says.

I look at her because social manners dictate that I do so. I command my lower facial muscles to activate and create a small smile.

"So," I say.

"Are you as nervous as I am right now?" she asks with the same little laugh she had on the phone. She looks down at her teacup, which means I can also look down.

"I suppose this is an awkward meeting," I say.

"Thank you, again, for calling. I just . . . I think about you and Cleo every single day."

I nod. I am not willing to admit that I think about her and her daughter too, despite many heroic attempts not to.

"How is she?" she asks.

"Cleo?" I respond.

She nods.

I shrug. "She is doing as well as can be expected." I say this because that's what I hear other people say. I have no idea if it's true. I have no idea how well Cleo is doing. The emotional state of others is often a mystery to me (as is the emotional state of myself). I also don't know what is expected of a teenager in this situation. What would be signs of trouble?

"I'm glad to hear that," she says. "Kyra has had a hard time."

I don't know how to respond to this. I would be lying if I said I wasn't interested to know what a "hard time" involves. I would like to know if Cleo meets any of the criteria for having a "hard time."

"How so?" I ask, curiosity getting the best of me.

"Oh, well, usual things, I guess. Smoking pot. Blowing off school. Her lack of creativity with rebelling is almost more disappointing than the actual rebelling." She adds another little laugh.

I don't think Cleo is smoking pot, and I know she does well in school. It surprises me to hear these things of Mirai's daughter. When I met her, she seemed so meek and innocent. I had her pegged as a harmless nerd, a class of teenager with which I am very familiar. I have no idea what to say to

Mirai. I can't, in good conscience, reassure her, as I would be very concerned if Cleo was ingesting drugs and failing classes.

"She used to be such a good kid," Mirai says. "What happened . . . it just took a toll. And, admittedly, I haven't been there for her as much as I should be. All those parenting books talk about being present, but how can I be present when I'm dealing with my own things, you know?"

I nod, though I don't know. She lost me at "being present." She assumes that as parents of teenagers, we have things in common. We are both people whose spouses have died and now have to raise teenagers. But I refuse to see us as anything alike.

The waiter returns and asks if we are ready to order. Despite singing the praises of the filet, Mirai orders French onion soup. It's an odd choice, since it's 90-something degrees outside and she must be hot in that tent of a dress.

The waiter walks away, and Mirai takes a sip of her tea. I take a sip of mine too.

"I am really glad to hear Cleo seems to be doing okay," she says. "Does she have a boyfriend or—"

"No."

"—or a girlfriend?"

"A girlfriend?" I ask.

"You know, kids these days are all over the spectrum."

"The spectrum? Cleo's not on the—"

Her face goes red. "Oh, that's not what I meant."

She takes another sip of tea and then sets down her cup.

"I think Kyra might have a boyfriend, but I don't know for sure. She doesn't tell me much," Mirai says. "I know I should keep a better eye on her. Sean was the strict one. He was the bad cop, I was the good cop. I don't know how to play his role, you know?"

Again, I don't know. Why do people always end sentences with this assumptive question?

"Did you tell Cleo you were coming?" she asks me.

I shake my head. "No. Did you tell your daughter?"

She shakes her head. "I wasn't sure how she'd feel about it. And I wanted to see how things went first. . . ." She looks down and then up again. "Honestly, I thought you might just want to scream at me because that's what I would probably want to do if I were you."

"I'm not much of a screamer," I say.

She smiles. "That's a relief." Then: "But, really, you must hate me, right?"

I'm not sure how to answer this question. For fourteen months, I *have* hated her, but sitting in front of her now, that word does not seem appropriate. She's just a small woman who seems sad.

"I hate what happened." That is a fact I am comfortable confessing.

"I hate what happened too."

Something else we have in common.

The waiter returns with the bowl of soup. Mirai thanks him and then proceeds to jab the cheesy top of the soup with her spoon, steam rising in response.

"I love French onion soup," she says.

This we do not have in common.

She leans back in her chair, arms crossed against her middle, waiting for the soup to cool enough to be edible. She stares right at me with an unnerving intensity and says, "There must be things you want to say."

Was she going to leave me anyway?

The question lingers in the back of my mind, requesting to be brought forward, out into the light. It is not time yet.

"I don't have a particular agenda," I lie.

"You just felt it was time to meet?"

I shrug. "Yes, I guess so."

She nods. "Well, I'm glad."

She takes a small, tentative bite of her soup. It appears to be to her liking, because she then takes a bigger bite.

"Sean was remorseful, at the end," she says. "He didn't leave a note, but I had seen him the week before he killed himself, and he expressed remorse over what he'd done."

This has no effect on me. If she thinks I give a damn about what that monster felt upon his death, she is mistaken.

"I don't know if that matters at all. Probably not," she says, as if reading my mind. "I just wanted you to know that. He didn't kill himself because he hated the idea of being locked up for life. I mean, I'm sure he did hate that idea. But I think he could live with prison . . . but he couldn't live with what he'd done."

I want her to stop talking about him, to stop these foolish attempts at making him sound like anything but a complete psychopath.

"It probably doesn't matter," she says, as if reading my mind again. "He wasn't a good person. He just . . . wasn't."

I nod, communicating my agreement with this.

"So, you visited him, then? In prison?"

If he was, as she admits, not a good person, I don't know why she would do this.

"Kyra wanted to, so yes."

She looks down at her soup, takes another tiny bite.

"How was that?" I ask.

I want the details of his prison attire, his shackled feet, his gaunt face. I want to know his suffering.

"It was dreadful. Prison is a dreadful place. Just so depressing. As it should be, I guess. It was important to Kyra, though. She needed to see him. He was sweet to her when we came."

I cannot imagine Sean McCann as sweet. I change the subject: "How's the soup?"

I couldn't care less how the soup is, but I need to steer the conversation elsewhere.

"It's okay. I'm not that hungry either."

She gently pushes the bowl away from her.

"You know," she says, "I've tried to make sense of it. Him showing up like he did, with a knife. It still seems so absurd. I just want you to know that . . . I'd never seen him with a *weapon* like that. I'd never seen him *that* angry."

I feel heat rising within me. I shift in my seat.

She continues. "I still can't believe it. I relive the whole thing every single day, going over and over it in my head. My therapist says I have PTSD and—"

I can't take it anymore.

"Can you stop?" I say. "I am not here to help you make sense of your husband's heinous actions."

The adrenaline shoots through me. I am both excited by my outspokenness and embarrassed of it.

"Oh," she says. "Right. I'm sorry."

I drink my tea as a stalling tactic, not knowing what to do, now that we have arrived at this conversational dead end.

"You two were close," I try.

Was she going to leave me anyway?

She looks surprised. "Sean and me? I wouldn't say—"

"You and Jana."

I fiddle with the string on the chamomile tea bag.

"Oh," she says.

She fiddles with the string on her tea bag.

"Yes, I think so. We became close," she says.

For the first time since my arrival, she will not meet my eyes.

"I never paid much attention to Jana's friendships. I probably should have," I say. "I don't really know how close the two of you were, how often you talked or went to lunch or whatever else."

A strand of hair falls in front of her face, and she uses a finger to put it back in its place.

"Well, we weren't that close at first. We didn't really talk at all, my first few months at Brighten. Then it was someone's birthday—I can't remember whose—and we were all in the employee kitchen and I happened to be standing next to her, and she said 'I hate these things,' and I laughed."

She smiles at the memory, and I can't help but smile too. That's definitely something Jana would have said. She hated those company events, the necessity of putting on a fake smile and pretending to give a shit about an acquaintance getting another year older. I could share my own stories of Jana saying similar things, but I feel possessive of my stories, my memories. Sharing them feels like handing over control, which is not something I want to do in general, and definitely not something I want to do with Mirai McCann.

"Anyway, it kind of just went from there. We had lunch a few times, got to talking. She found out I loved yoga, and I told her I could take her to a class. . . ."

She trails off with a shrug.

"And you confided in her about your husband? She encouraged you to leave him?"

"Not right away. She put pieces together over time that I was in an abusive relationship. I knew it wasn't a *good* relationship, but I'd been sort of in denial about how bad it was, you know?"

No, I do not know. Stop asking if I know.

"Do you think you would still be with him if you hadn't met Jana?"

Her eyes widen as she considers this hypothetical. I don't know why I'm presenting this alternate reality, why I'm torturing myself with it. Of course Mirai would still be with Sean if Jana hadn't come along and shown her the proverbial light. Mirai would be in her terrible marriage and Jana would be alive—in a marriage she may or may not have considered terrible.

"Jana gave me the confidence I needed to leave him," she says finally.

Her last gift, given to someone other than Cleo and me.

"So, yes, I'd probably still be with Sean if I hadn't met Jana," she says with a confirmatory nod. "And I suppose that would have been bad, but not nearly as bad as this reality we have."

I resent the "we."

"What did you two talk about?" I ask, edging closer to the truth I'm tentatively seeking.

"Marriage, mostly."

So general, so vague.

"Marriage," I repeat.

"It's such an odd institution, isn't it? We join with these people and have this monumental task of making a life together. We make promises despite having no idea what our wants or needs will be weeks or years or decades from now."

She shakes her head at the absurdity of it. I don't disagree with her assessment. I think most of humanity is absurd—relationships, certainly. I married Jana because that's what people do. I learned as a child that this was a means of survival—imitating the behaviors and customs of others, no matter how strange they seemed to me. I learned early on that everything seemed strange to me, and that made me, effectively, strange.

It occurs to me that we have been here for a while, that I have not been paying attention to the time. I look at my watch. It is twenty minutes until eight o'clock.

"I have to get going," I say.

I could text Cleo and tell her I will be later than previously stated. I could stay here with Mirai and force the question from my mouth: *Was she going to leave me anyway?* I'm anxious to leave, though. Maybe it's because, as I've said, I hate tardiness. Or maybe it's because I just don't want to ask my question, for fear of its answer.

"Oh, right," she says. "We're near the end of your 'window.'"

The way she says it, I can't tell if she's making fun of me or not.

I stand from the table, and she does the same. I reach into my wallet to give her five dollars for my tea. Predictably, she puts up both hands and says, "No, please." I could insist, but I sense that will make my departure even more awkward than it's already destined to be.

"I have to get home. To Cleo."

I wonder if she has to get home to her child, or if her child is out smoking pot and blowing off school.

"Okay," she says.

The waiter comes and drops the check at the table. Seeing us both stand-ing, he must be afraid we're going to dine-and-dash—two forty-somethings acting like teenagers.

"Thank you for meeting," she says.

The same strand of hair falls in front of her face, and she uses a finger to put it back again.

"Would you mind if we did this again?" she asks.

I'm not sure if I mind. It will take my brain at least twenty-four hours to process what has just occurred.

"Sure, that's fine," I say.

I push my chair in, trying to signal that I am in a hurry. I don't want to have to set up our next meeting now.

"Okay," she says, calling after me as I walk toward the front of the restau-rant, "thanks again."

On the drive home, I go over what Mirai has told me again and again, looking for answers to my unasked question. They talked about "marriage." She made it seem like they talked about it as a concept, not about their individual marriages. I'm quite sure she was sparing me, tip-toeing around the truth. This might mean I have to see her again, once I have sufficient time to ponder and prepare.

When I open the front door to the house, I'm not expecting to see Cleo there, which is stupid of me. Where else would she be? I told her to be home by eight, so here she is. She does not possess the same rebellious streak as Kyra McCann apparently does.

"Uh, hi," Cleo says. "Did I scare you?"

I feel like she can see on my face that I've just seen the wife of the man who killed her mother.

"No, why?" I say, quickly.

"You look like you forgot I lived here."

I try to smile good-naturedly, but judging by Cleo's furrowed brows, the expression comes across as peculiar.

"Are you okay?" she asks me.

"I'm fine."

I just want to get to my bedroom, where I can be free to pace around in circles as I review the conversation with Mirai McCann in my head and chastise myself for all the things I said (or didn't say).

"Where did you go?" Cleo asks. She's not going to let me off easy. She is her mother's daughter.

"I forgot something at the store," I say, repeating the lie from earlier.

She looks at my hands, and it dawns on me that I have no bags, no evidence of a trip to the store.

"What did you forget?"

I should have known to expect this interrogation. My face is getting warm. I can almost feel the sweat beads forming. I cannot let Cleo see my sweat beads.

"Uh, batteries."

I immediately regret this lie, not because it is deceptive, but because it is so unbelievable. Cleo knows I have hundreds of packs of batteries in the bunker.

"For the flashlight . . . that I keep in the car."

She looks at me like she thinks I am both hilarious and pitiful, which is never how you want your teenage child to look at you. I consider this look my punishment for not thinking through this whole lying scenario.

"I'm going to head to bed," I say, making no effort to hide my desire for escape.

As I start to make my way down the hall, Cleo says, "Wait."

I stop, every muscle in my body tightening in anticipation of what she will say next.

"I might need to borrow the car sometime in the next couple days."

I exhale. That's it? She's already moved on from my forgot-something-at-the-store lie?

"This girl at school borrowed a book from me a long time ago and I want to get it back from her."

"Oh," I say. "Okay."

"Okay?"

I remember her ankle. "Well, I can drive you."

"It might be during your workday. Can Edie just drive me? I'll only be gone a couple hours. Like you were."

I see what she's doing, and I'm impressed with her cleverness.

"Can we talk about this tomorrow?"

I do not have the mental fortitude to uphold my typical authoritarian parenting style.

"Sure," she says. "Good night."

Once in my room, I pace in circles, which is what usually calms me when I'm inordinately stressed or agitated. Meeting with Mirai McCann has definitely overstimulated my nervous system. I do not anticipate being able to sleep.

I play back my mental recorder:

We join with these people and have this monumental task of making a life together. We make promises despite having no idea what our wants or needs will be weeks or years or decades from now.

Did she say this as a teaser for harder truths to come? I take it that way. She has conceded that she and Jana discussed marriage, seemingly in cynical and disillusioned terms. She is not going to come out and tell me the painful details of Jana's inner life; she will not want to hurt me in that way. I will have to request the details, ask to be hurt.

I strip down to my boxers and get into bed, staring at the ceiling. I have to wonder if this quest for truth is its own kind of apocalypse. It's like Edie's mother said—apocalypse means revelation.

CHAPTER 26

Cleo

I wake up the next morning after a night spent tossing and turning (and checking Facebook). Kyra finally messages me as I'm eating a bowl of frosted flakes and granola at the kitchen table. She suggests we meet today— *today!*—at a coffee shop she likes in San Clemente.

"Dad?" I say.

His back is to me. He's at the sink, rinsing his morning dishes. When he turns around, there are bags under his eyes, suggesting he had a sleepless night too. After seeing him come home last night, I don't think he was on a date, but who knows? He seemed spent, like whatever he went to do sapped him of all energy. I suppose a date could do that, but there was a certain melancholy to him. If it was a date, it wasn't a good one.

"Yeah?"

"Do you think I can take the car . . . or have Edie drive me . . . today?"

He shrugs. I've never seen him this tired, not even after Mom died. He was strangely energized then, cleaning the house, arranging the funeral service. Maybe he was that way for my sake. Maybe he wanted me to see that we could go on, just the two of us.

"I guess that would be fine," he says.

Something is wrong with him. Clearly.

"Oh, okay, cool. Yeah, it should only be a couple hours, like I said."

"That's fine," he says. He seems defeated—by fatigue or something more sinister, I don't know.

He traipses off to his home office to start his workday, and I go to take a shower and make myself look like . . . like what? What do I want to look like in front of Kyra? I guess I want to look like someone who made a bit of an effort, like someone whose mother's death didn't lead her to give up on everything.

I decide on a sundress and a cardigan sweater that used to belong to Mom. Some of her things fit me—a little big, but good enough. I know wearing her sweater doesn't mean she's actually with me, but I'm not above being comforted by objects.

It's been so long since I've worn earrings that I basically have to re-pierce my ears as I jam in the silver hoops I used to love. I run a tube of ChapStick over my lips—I've never been into lipstick, it makes me feel like a clown—and brush my cheeks with just a hint of blush. Mom didn't wear much makeup. We never had one of those mother-daughter tutorial sessions. Still, I watched her when she put it on. I took note that she spent no more than five minutes on it. If she couldn't be bothered to spend longer, then I can't either.

I call "bye" to Dad and then go across the way to Edie's house. Kyra wants to meet at eleven, which is a couple hours away. Edie can help me prepare. I don't know exactly what to prepare, but just the idea of "preparing" feels right—something to quell the anxiety or whatever.

"Wow, you look nice," Edie says when she opens the door.

She has gotten used to me not trying much to impress her, and she still likes me, which might be my definition of love.

"Thanks," I say. "You surfed today?"

She's wearing board shorts and a black T-shirt—her hair is wet, either from the ocean or the shower.

"Just got back," she says.

"I don't know how you get up so early."

Her mom is not here; it's one of her workdays. She leans in, kisses me.

"Can I take you upstairs?" she asks.

She kisses my neck, which she knows is a very vulnerable tickle spot for me. I laugh.

"Yes, but I can't go to meet Kyra looking like I just got ravished by my girlfriend."

She pulls back. "You're going to meet her *today?*"

"She just messaged me."

"And here I am thinking you put on that pretty dress for me."

"No way," I say. "Also, you're driving me."

"Your dad is cool with that?"

"Weirdly, yes."

She runs a hand through her wet hair. "Okay. Wow. Are you nervous?"

"I'm jittery, yeah."

"Should we, like, rehearse?" she asks.

She goes to the kitchen and I follow her. She takes a bottle of Kombucha from the fridge and offers me one. I shake my head.

"I don't know if I need to *rehearse*. I think I just need a pep talk."

She sits at the island, twists off the top of the bottle. "That's easy," she says. "You're going to be great. You are the kindest, most open-hearted person I know. I have no idea what Kyra is like, but if she's an asshole I'll be waiting in the car, ready to take you to get burritos at Lupe's."

I smile. "That helped, actually."

"Okay, cool, let's go make out."

I use the mirror in Edie's car to check that I still look decent. My hair is a little mussed. My lips look a little . . . used.

"We're gonna be early," she says as we exit the freeway in San Clemente.

"Early is good. We can scout it out."

"It's a small place."

"You've been there?"

"A couple times," she says. "Good post-surf coffee."

The coffee shop is in the same center as a Ralph's market, next to a taco place. There's a wood bench out front, nobody sitting on it. It's difficult to see the inside through the window. I can't tell if Kyra is already there, early, like me.

Edie parks the car in a decent spying location and turns off the ignition.

"Let's just wait here and see her walk in," I say. "Assuming she's not already in there."

Edie sits back in her seat. She seems so relaxed, which annoys me. I feel like someone let loose a hummingbird in my chest.

I check my Facebook messages, preparing myself for the possibility that Kyra wants to bail: *I'm so sorry, I can't make it.* There's no message, though. The last one in our chain is me agreeing to the time and place of our meetup.

A few minutes later, a white Honda Accord pulls into the lot and the driver looks like it could be Kyra. The car parks right in front of the coffee shop, suggesting that Kyra has no plan to spy from a distance. This makes me feel silly.

"I think that's her," I say.

Edie looks.

It's definitely her. She has the same striking face I remember, dark hair piled on top of her head in a sloppy bun. Her clothes are not what I'd pictured—black tunic, bright magenta leggings, black combat boots. She wasn't a magenta-leggings, combat-boot person last year.

She closes the door of her car, a messenger bag swinging from her shoulder. She walks up the steps to the coffee shop, opens the door, no apparent hesitation. I can see her inside, going to the counter to order something. Then I can't see her anymore.

"She probably got a table in the back," Edie says.

"Are you sure this is a good idea?"

I'm desperate for her to say yes, but she says, "Nope. But even if it's a terrible idea, just remember I'm right here. Think of the burritos."

"Burritos," I say.

"Burritos."

Once I walk up the steps, I get a better view inside the shop. Edie was right—Kyra has chosen a table at the back. When I open the door, she doesn't look up. If I were her, I'd be looking up at every person coming in. She's clearly not as anxious about this as I am.

As I approach the table, I see she has earbuds in, her head bobbing to whatever music she's listening to. The person behind the counter calls her name—her order is ready. Kyra keeps bobbing her head, not hearing her page, not noticing that I'm six feet away. I go to the counter, take her order for her—some kind of hot drink and a muffin. I return to the table with my offering and when I'm a foot away, I finally catch her eye and she looks up. She takes out the earbuds and says, "Oh, hi."

As if we just saw each other yesterday. *Oh, hi.* As if we see each other every day.

"Hi," I say, holding out the drink and muffin to her.

She takes them. "Did they call my name? I didn't even hear."

"They did."

"Thanks."

She nods toward the chair across from her and says, "Is this table okay?"

"Sure, yeah, thanks."

I sit. While she busies herself with her drink—taking off the top, putting in a packet of sugar, stirring it with a tiny wooden stick—I take the opportunity to look her over. She has a series of piercings all along the cartilage of her left upper ear. I don't remember her having piercings before. She's wearing more makeup than I am—heavy eyeliner, lots of mascara. I don't remember her wearing makeup before. I can't imagine her father would have allowed piercings or makeup. But he's gone. In a way, her very appearance is a reminder of the tragedy we have in common.

"What happened to your foot?" she asks, looking at my boot.

"I broke my ankle," I say.

"That sucks."

"It's not bad. I can walk . . . obviously."

"Well, that's good, I guess."

She peels the wrapper off her muffin and takes an unself-conscious bite.

"So . . . ," she says.

"So."

She puts down her muffin and starts adjusting the hair on top of her head. This is the only sign I have that she's nervous.

"It was cool of you to reach out," she says. "I've wanted to . . . like I said. I just didn't know. . . ."

"I get it," I say.

"I seriously don't know how you don't hate me." She shakes her head in disbelief.

"I mean, none of what happened was *your* fault," I say.

"I'm half his DNA. And he's not here. May as well blame me," she says.

"I kind of felt like that before," I say, "but I guess I don't see it like that now."

"How do you see it?" she asks.

She gives up on whatever she had planned for her hair and lets it fall from the top of her head. It is long and bouncy and shiny, like hair in a shampoo commercial. She leans forward, elbows on the table, awaiting my reply.

"I guess I see it like it is. Your father did this terrible thing. My mom was the victim of that terrible thing. . . ."

"And you," she says.

"Huh?"

"You were the victim too. And your dad."

"Well, yeah," I say.

"He ruined your lives. You can say it."

I sit back in my chair. This doesn't feel right to me. I refuse to see my life as ruined.

"That sounds kind of hopeless." I force a tension-breaking laugh, which is what I do whenever I'm in an awkward situation. It's like Carter always says: "When in doubt, add an LOL."

"Well, if you don't think he ruined your life, tell me your secret to thinking that way, because I sure as hell think he ruined mine."

She takes another bite of her muffin.

"I guess I just mean . . . if he ruined my life, then he wins, you know? I have to go on. I can't let him ruin everything. My mom would be so upset if I let him do that."

She nods. "You sound like you've had a lot of therapy." She doesn't say it meanly. She says it with a smile.

"I have a cool guidance counselor."

"That's not therapy. Therapy is at some snooty doctor's office and your parent pays, like, two hundred dollars for it and it does nothing."

"Speaking from experience?"

"We go to the same clinic, my mom and me. She goes in one door, I go in another. Quite the mother–daughter outing."

"It's kind of cute."

She makes a face like she just smelled something rancid.

"Not cute," she says.

She resumes eating, and I search my mind for something to say. There are so many questions floating around. I pluck one from the mix.

"You must miss him, right? I mean, no matter what he did."

She looks up at me and pauses chewing. She looks stunned. She swallows. "You are, like, the first person who has said anything like that to me."

"That you must miss him?"

She nods.

"Serious?"

"Totally serious."

"Well, that's lame."

"It is lame. Like, he was still my dad," she says. She looks down, starts fidgeting with her muffin wrapper. When she looks up again, there are tears primed on the ridge of her eyes.

"I get that," I say, even though I cannot picture Sean McCann as a loving father.

"Oh my god, I'm so sorry," she says, pulling a napkin from the dispenser on the table and dabbing at her eyes. "My father killed your mom and you're comforting me? This is wrong."

"I'm not, like, comforting you," I say. "I just said 'I get that.'"

"That's the most comforting thing I've heard since everything happened."

"Like I said . . . that's lame."

The tears crest the ridge of her eyes, roll down her cheeks. She pulls another napkin from the dispenser.

"I hate him every day for what he did. And I hate myself for still loving him. It's all fucked up," she says.

She takes a deep breath and sits back in her chair. The mascara is now smudged under her eyes.

"The whole thing is fucked up," I say.

"I know you probably don't care to hear this, but he wasn't, like, always this awful person. He was kind of a dick to my mom. And he was really strict with me. But he loved me."

"I believe it."

"I just can't believe what he did. He must have, like, snapped."

"Did you visit him? In prison?"

She nods.

"Did you ever ask him?"

"Why he did it? No. It's weird: when I visited him, we talked about random things, but never what happened. Talk about a giant elephant in the prison room, right?"

She laughs a little, so I laugh a little too.

"Then he killed himself. Three days after I'd visited him. Didn't hint that he was going to or anything, just did it. No good-bye, nothing."

She shakes her head, as if shaking off a bug stuck in her hair.

"Anyway," she says. "This really shouldn't be about me."

"I didn't expect it to be only about me."

She ignores me and says, "How's your father?"

I shrug. "I don't know. He's not the easiest to read."

"He seemed nice. You know, when we came to stay with you guys."

"He did?"

"Yeah. Why do you look so surprised?"

"I don't think he comes across as 'nice' to most people."

"How does he come across?"

"Weird," I say.

She laughs. "Okay, maybe he seemed a tad weird. But, like, nice-weird."

"Nice-weird."

"Yeah. I can tell when a guy has the potential to lose his temper. It's like a superpower I developed, living with my father. And your father doesn't have that."

"I guess you're right about that."

She takes a sip of her drink. "Do I seem strange right now? I took a gummy, like, an hour ago. It's stronger than I thought it would be."

I have no idea what she's talking about. "A gummy?"

"A weed gummy," she says.

"Oh," I say. I've heard of them, of course. They were starting to become all the rage at school. I just never had any interest. I smoked weed once with Carter—in the parking lot, on his birthday—and it just made me paranoid.

She reaches into her pocket and displays what looks like a Sour Patch Kid.

"You want one?" she asks.

"Oh, no thanks."

"Please don't tell me you survived this whole ordeal without the assistance of narcotics."

I shrug.

"Serious?"

"I'm really boring," I tell her.

"I used to be really boring."

She starts bouncing her leg up and down. It makes the table shake.

"Do you have a boyfriend?" she asks.

"No," I say. And then I think I want to surprise her, assure her that I'm not *all* boring. "I have a girlfriend."

She stops bouncing her leg and sits up straighter. "Oh," she says, nodding approval. "I'm intrigued."

I don't know what to say, so I just smile like a dork.

"Does your father know?" she asks.

"No," I say.

She leans forward, elbows on the table. "You are getting more interesting by the second."

I laugh. "It's not like this salacious thing. He just doesn't need to know."

She smiles. "That's what I tell myself about my boyfriend."

"So you have a boyfriend?"

She nods. "Blake."

"And your mom doesn't know?"

"Hell, no. She would freak. Actually, I don't know if she would freak. She's so unpredictable these days. She'd ask me like a million questions, though, and I don't have time for that."

"My dad would just be confused."

"He'd probably be relieved you can't get pregnant."

"Actually, that's what I thought too."

We both laugh.

"My mom would be all up in my business about that. She doesn't even know that I'm already on birth control."

I blush at the idea that she's having sex, that someone my age is having sex. I know it happens (duh), but it still seems so . . . *adult*.

"If my dad were alive, he would kill me," she says.

She realizes the gravity of her choice of words a moment after they leave her mouth, then looks down at the table.

"So, I can't stay long, but did you want to, like, do this again?" I ask.

She looks up. "Get together?"

I nod.

She shrugs. "It's cool with me."

"Okay, yeah, it's cool with me too."

"But if you're weirded out, we don't have—"

"I'm not weirded out," I say.

"Maybe it makes you feel better to see that I'm so fucked up."

She laughs, but it's half-hearted.

"You're not fucked up," I say.

She uses her thumb and index finger to spin one of the studs in her ear. "Come on, I'm a little fucked up."

"I think we're both a little fucked up."

She sighs and stops spinning the stud. "Fair."

"We should exchange numbers so we don't have to use Facebook," I say.

She agrees, and we do the exchange.

"It was nice to see you," I say, meaning it.

"Yeah, you too. I didn't think it would be, if I'm honest. Hence, the gummy."

"I told Edie there was a fifty-fifty chance I'd hate you all over again."

"Fair," she says again. "Edie's your girl?"

I like how she puts it: *Your girl.*

"Yeah," I say. "She's waiting out in her car, actually."

"That's so cute."

"I think so."

I look at the clock on the wall, calculate the drive time back home, say, "I really have to get going."

"Oh, yeah, right."

We both stand. She follows me out and sits on the still-unoccupied bench out front. I feel self-conscious as I walk away, knowing her eyes are on me.

When I open the car door, Edie says, "So?" before I can even sit in my seat.

"I need a burrito."

She groans. "That bad?"

"No, I'm just starving," I say.

"Really?"

"Yeah, it was great."

She starts the car and we head for the exit.

"Should we wave?" Edie asks as we pass the coffee shop.

"We should," I say.

We hold up our hands in unison, wearing matching smiles on our faces. Kyra lifts her hand back at us. A moment later, my phone buzzes with a text message. It's Kyra.

Edie's cute

I smile and write back.

I know

July 2019

CHAPTER 27

Dave

If I was interested in connecting with other like-minded individuals (which I am not), I would join the American Preppers Network. According to their website, the mission of the APN is to help every American family become self-reliant so they can better weather disasters, catastrophes, and hardships. Contrary to popular belief, preppers are not only concerned with the apocalypse; they are concerned with preparing for any and all events that would have a major impact on a family's life. In other words, it's not just The End of the World they care about; it's The End of the World As We Know It. They use an acronym for that because it comes up so often in their online forums—TEOTWAWKI. It's the most ridiculous acronym I've ever seen, but I understand the concept. It's like what Edie's mother said to me: *You know your apocalypse already happened, right?* My world already ended once. It's no wonder I've been scrambling to prepare for the ways it could end again. I know this scrambling isn't what The Therapist would call "healthy," but I'm not sure how to stop it.

"You ready, Dad? I told them we'd be there ten minutes ago."

It's the fourth of July, and Cleo has asked me to accompany her to a BBQ party at Edie's house. I have agreed in an attempt to be a "good sport." I owe it to Cleo. Just like I probably owe her a new (well, used) car before the beginning of the school year. She is an objectively good kid. I should be grateful she has not responded to the upheaval of our lives in the way Kyra

273

McCann has. It's been a week since my meeting with Mirai, and I have not been able to stop thinking about her and her daughter—an aggravating circumstance. My brain is not content with where we left things, with the unresolved nature of it all.

As we approach the house, it becomes apparent that this dinner party is not like the last one. This one involves more people. There are five cars parked out front. A woman gets out of one of them and heads for the front door. We follow behind her. When we get to the porch, Cleo stops and turns around.

"Sorry, Dad, I didn't realize she was inviting so many people. You okay?"

"It's fine," I say, an embarrassingly obvious lie.

"They're probably just people from her women's group," Cleo says. "Try to make conversation. Maybe you'll like someone."

She raises her eyebrows with that last part.

"'Like someone'?"

"I mean, I don't know, maybe you want to start dating," she says. "I wouldn't, like, judge you."

Date? I am appalled that she would even consider such a thing.

"I don't want to start dating," I tell her.

She shrugs. "Okay, just putting it out there."

Before I can argue with her *putting it out there*, she knocks on the front door and Edie's mother, Camila, answers with her intimidating level of enthusiasm, the little dog yapping at her feet. She gives Cleo a hug and then ushers me in with grand arm gestures, saying, "*Pasa, pasa.*"

When we get inside, Cleo greets Edie and then abandons me, the two of them going through the sliding door in the kitchen to the backyard. I am left standing in the entry area—like an idiot—with Camila, who says, "Let me introduce you to everyone," which is exactly the thing I do not want her to say.

Against my will, I am introduced to a circle of women with typical Gen X names—Lauren, Tracy, Melissa, Candace, and Jen. They inform me that they are in a group for divorced women, which just makes me fear them more.

"What's your story, Dave?" one of them asks me. It's either Candace or Jen. I've already forgotten who's who.

"My story?"

She's eyeing my wedding ring. I put my hands in my pockets.

"Don't bother *mi amigo*," Camila says before grabbing my forearm and pulling me into the kitchen.

"Sorry," she says. "They are vultures."

I resist the urge to tell her that vultures are known for consuming dead animals and, last I checked, I am living. She is still holding my forearm. I can see the circle of Gen X names staring at us.

"You want a margarita?"

"No, thank you."

She finally releases my arm.

"Okay. Well, let me know if you need anything. I'll be back in a few."

With that, she is sucked back into the female energy and I am in the kitchen not drinking a margarita.

I take my phone from my pocket and consider texting Cleo to tell her I'm going home. Just as I'm about to compose my text, a message appears on my phone. Cleo is the only person who texts me. Whenever my phone vibrates, a part of my psyche still persists in believing it could be Jana. It's one of the terrible tricks grief plays.

It's not Cleo, though.

It's Mirai McCann.

> Hi Dave. Happy 4th! I hope you're doing something fun. Let me know if you want to meet up again soon. No pressure if you don't.

I read it once, twice, three times. I hate that she can tell I've read it. That means a timer starts on how long I'm spending on my reply.

One of the Gen X women laughs, and the sheer volume of it sends me to the backyard. The moment I'm outdoors I breathe a sigh of relief. It's hot outside, but refreshing nonetheless.

I go to sit at the patio table when I hear the unmistakable sound of Cleo laughing. It's coming from around the corner, on the side of the house. I peek, not wanting to interrupt whatever is making her laugh this way.

There she is, leaning up against the side of the house, her booted foot crossed over her other. Her face is tilted up to meet another face. That face is attached to a body that is now pressing against hers, with enough force that Cleo has to steady herself by placing her palms on the wall behind her. They are, as the kids say, *making out*.

My eyes move from Cleo to this other face, this other body. It takes me a few moments to realize who it belongs to.

Edie.

I move quickly away from their view and then hurry back inside. Camila is there in the kitchen, cutting limes.

"Everything okay?" she asks.

I must appear not okay.

"Fine," I say. I command my mouth to smile.

"I'm doing burgers on the grill for dinner—beef, turkey, and veggie," she says. "You can take your pick."

I am still wearing my smile.

"You sure you don't want a margarita?"

I wonder if she knows about Cleo and Edie. I wonder if I am the only one in the dark.

"No, thank you," I say. "I think I'm going to head home, actually."

Her brows furrow as she displays her obligatory concern. "Oh, really? That's too bad."

"Could you let Cleo know?"

"Of course." Her brows are still furrowed.

"Okay, then," I say.

I give a wave and then make my way to the front door, careful to avoid eye contact with the circle of women. As I open the door, I hear one of them say "You leaving?" I close the door quickly, hoping the poor woman just thinks I didn't hear her.

I walk with long, fast strides back home, my brain attempting to catch up to what my eyes have seen. Cleo and Edie. Cleo is gay? I know for a fact that she's had passing interests in boys before. Is this a new thing? Is this her "acting out"? Do I not know her at all?

You know, kids these days are all over the spectrum.

Those words from Mirai.

Mirai!

I remember the text message. I need to respond soon. I suppose I will see her again, with my own selfish motives this time. After all, I have no other sources for parental advice, nobody else to talk to about this new (or new-to-me) development with Cleo.

I open the slider to our house and go inside. I take out my phone and tap a message to Mirai:

Hello. I'd be amenable to meeting up again. Please let me know the time and location. Thank you.

Within seconds, there are three dots implying she is in the midst of a response.

> Great. How about tomorrow? 3pm? There's a park Jana used to love . . . near the yoga studio we went to. I thought it would be nice. Shall I send you the address?

I rack my brain for an objection to this proposal and find nothing.

> Sure. I'll be there.

CHAPTER 28

Cleo

"I have to run some errands this afternoon," Dad says.

We are sitting at the breakfast table and I might be hung over, because Edie and I snuck some from the margarita pitcher and now my head is pounding.

"Okay," I say. "I'm just going to hang at Edie's anyway."

Dad running errands actually works out perfectly. Kyra is coming to Edie's house today. I figured that was the easiest way for Kyra and me to hang out. It's not like she can come to *my* house—I can only imagine Dad's face—and having to lie to meet at a coffee shop is too complicated. Kyra was fine with it. I think she's curious to see where Dad and I live, and I think she's curious to meet Edie.

"You and Edie . . . you spend a lot of time together," Dad says.

He has a strange look on his face. I can't quite figure it out.

"We do."

"I'm glad you have that friendship."

I still can't figure out the strange look.

"Me too," I say.

He nods once, as if we have just made a deal about something of which I am unaware. Then he goes to his home office because his company expects him to work on the day after the Fourth of July. I assume most of his coworkers are calling in sick or taking a vacation day, but not Dad. For Dad, yesterday was the stressful one; going back to work today is a relief.

Kyra is coming to Edie's house around 2 p.m. She doesn't have to come up with elaborate plans to leave her house. She has a car and her mom lets her

278

use it—a truly fascinating arrangement. Edie says there are leftover veggie burgers, so I head over around noon.

Camila is working today, so her car's not in the driveway. Edie is still in her pajamas when she opens the door.

"We didn't drink that much, did we?" she says, squinting at me in the brightness of the sun.

I shake my head. "We must be lightweights."

"My head is killing me."

"Same."

It wasn't my first time trying alcohol. Mom let me have a sip of her wine a couple times. She encouraged me to try beer once, probably because she knew I would hate it. *Don't tell Dad*, she'd said. *Duh*, I'd said.

I sit on the couch and Edie lies next to me, her head in my lap, eyes closed. I pet her hair.

"My mom must use a lot of tequila in her margaritas."

"Obviously."

"She was significantly less chipper than usual this morning."

"I don't think I've ever seen your mom significantly less chipper than usual."

"It's rare."

Edie opens her eyes. "How are you feeling about seeing Kyra again?"

I shrug. "Fine, I guess. I don't know what we're going to talk about. I'm glad you'll be here with me."

She sits up. "Speaking of which, I need to down some coffee and eat some food so I'm at peak performance."

"You don't have to perform. She's cool."

Edie stands and goes to the kitchen. I stay on the couch. A few minutes later, she returns with a mug of coffee and two veggie burgers on a plate.

"Here," she says. "Sustenance."

She sits next to me, our thighs touching. She takes a bite of her burger, and I do the same.

"I was thinking," I say.

"Uh-oh."

"When we go back to school, are we going to, like, tell people about . . . us?"

We don't go back to school for another six weeks, and asking about this *now*, making the presumption that we will be together in six weeks, will probably jinx everything, but I can't help it. I haven't been able to stop daydreaming about having a real relationship. I confided in Ms. Murray about this a couple days ago on the phone, and she said a relationship isn't "real" just because other people acknowledge it, but I sort of disagree.

"I'm not going to *not* tell people," Edie says. "Unless. . . . Do you want it to be a secret, or—"

"No," I say. "Of course not."

"Okay, because sometimes I wonder. . . ."

"You do?"

"You haven't even told your Dad," she says. She gives me the worst look she's ever given me—it's one of disappointment, sadness maybe.

"I will."

"I understand why you haven't, but . . . if the whole school knows, he probably should too."

I sigh.

"Maybe you don't want to tell him because it was a secret you had with your mom," Edie says.

I consider this. It sounds like something Ms. Murray would say.

"Maybe."

"It's like your mom knew certain things about you. She *saw* you. You liked that she was the only one. In a way, maybe telling your dad is betraying a bond you had with your mom."

"Deep," I say.

I attempt to laugh, but it comes out strange.

"Or maybe it's just that you know he won't respond like your mom did, and you're trying to avoid being let down. Like, he'll never compare to her."

"Well, I already know that."

"I know. But if you tell him this big thing about who you are and he doesn't respond how you want . . . I don't know . . . it'll make you miss her more."

That's it. That's exactly it.

I feel tears coming and I swallow hard.

I put my burger on the plate and lie with my head in Edie's lap this time. She strokes my head like I did hers. I close my eyes, but that doesn't prevent a tear from escaping. She uses her thumb to wipe it away.

"Maybe he'll surprise you," she says. "When you tell him."

When.

"Maybe."

Eventually, I sit up and finish my burger. Edie goes upstairs to shower. And then it's 2 p.m. and the doorbell rings.

"Hey," Kyra says, with a casualness that slightly reduces my anxiety.

She's wearing her combat boots again, this time with a baggy David Bowie T-shirt and jean shorts so short that the white pockets are visible past the fringe.

Edie steps out from behind me and offers her hand: "Hi, I'm Edie."

"I know, I stalked you online," she says.

Edie, unlike me, is on all the usual social media sites. She never posts photos of me or the two of us together. When our relationship is "real," maybe she will.

Kyra walks past us into the living room, looking around and nodding approvingly.

"Nice house," she says.

She removes the messenger bag from her shoulder and sets it on the couch. Then she goes to the window and looks out.

"So that's seriously your house over there?" she says to me, pointing.

"Yep, we moved there after . . . what happened."

"It's kind of cute. You two being neighbors out here in the middle of nowhere."

Edie and I look at each other, smile.

"We think so," Edie says.

Edie asks Kyra if she can get her anything, and Kyra says no. She sits on the couch, next to her messenger bag, and lets out a breath. Edie and I remain standing, observing her as if she's an exotic animal in a zoo.

"So," Kyra says.

She crosses one leg over the other. "I wanted to meet up because I have an idea," she says, clasping her hands together like a mad scientist.

Edie sits on the adjacent side of the "L" couch and I sit next to her.

"I'm afraid to ask," I say.

Her eyes seem brighter today. She must have bypassed the gummy.

"I actually think it's a great idea," she says, "but you might think it's stupid."

"Tell me," I say.

"Okay, well, when everything happened, my mom kept saying how she wanted to get in touch with your father. It was, like, really important to her. I think she wrote him letters, but—"

"She wrote him letters?" I ask.

I am not aware of any letters. I would have liked to read her letters.

"Yeah, I'm pretty sure."

"And he didn't respond?" Edie asks.

Kyra shakes her head. "No. It upset her. Not that she had a right to be upset about that. I mean, he didn't *owe* her a response or anything, but I think she just felt this need to talk to him."

"Understandable," Edie says.

I nod in agreement. I know where this is going, and it makes my heart beat faster.

Kyra continues: "I'm guessing he doesn't want to see her or hear from her or whatever. But what if we just, like, arranged a meeting?"

Yes, this is where I thought it was going.

Kyra doesn't understand how Dad is. She doesn't know he hates surprises, in general, and a surprise featuring the wife of the man who killed Mom would be the worst surprise imaginable.

Edie looks at me with raised eyebrows, as if she's intrigued by the idea, which makes me annoyed with her because she knows how Dad is.

"I don't think it would work," I say.

Kyra twists her face to the side in disappointment.

"He hates her that much, huh?" Kyra says.

"It's not like that," I say, though I presume it is exactly like that. Dad won't even say Mirai's name.

"Cleo's dad's . . . different."

"Different?" Kyra says.

"He's on the autism spectrum," I say.

May as well come out with it. It's better if Kyra thinks Dad didn't respond to her mom because of his ASD.

"Oh," says Kyra, surprised. "I didn't know."

"I don't know if he could handle seeing your mom, ya know?" I say.

Immediately, I hate myself a little for painting Dad this way, for making him fragile and weak and incapable. For disabling him, basically.

"Yeah, okay, I get it," Kyra says, looking down at her lap.

"I mean, he could *handle* it," I say. "I just don't know. . . ."

"What's the worst that could happen?" Kyra asks, a desperation to her tone that makes me uncomfortable. "It might help both of them. Closure, or whatever."

I look to Edie to rescue me with an irrefutable excuse, but she's biting her lip, pensive.

"What if he says something mean?" I say. "He says mean things, like, all the time, without even trying."

Kyra shrugs. "I doubt he could say something meaner than what my mom says to herself. She thinks everything is her fault. I've told her she's harder on herself than anyone else would be, but she doesn't believe me. Maybe if she saw your dad, it would convince her."

"Or maybe it wouldn't," I say.

Edie has progressed from chewing on her lip to chewing on her thumbnail. Finally, she speaks:

"It might not be a terrible idea."

I look at her, my eyes as open and wide as I can make them.

"What?" she says to me. "It might actually help your dad too."

I try to imagine the two of them meeting—Mirai and Dad. I imagine Dad's eye twitching, the way it does when he's really nervous. I imagine the color leaving his face. I imagine him realizing he's been set up, looking at me as if I've betrayed him.

"I don't know," I say.

"What do you think your mom would want?" Edie asks.

At first, I hate her for asking this, for bringing Mom into it. But then I close my eyes and I think of Mom. She always wanted to expand Dad's horizons, encourage him to open his mind and his heart to more of life. I have no doubt Mom would have forgiven Mirai, so it stands to reason she would want Dad to forgive Mirai too. And Dad clearly hasn't. Is it my responsibility to force it upon him?

I think of Ms. Murray's words: *Remember, Cleo, you're the kid.* But what if, as the kid, I know more than Dad about certain things? What if I know that this would help him even if he doesn't know it? What if helping him ultimately helps me? If he could forgive Mirai, if he could move on from constantly preparing for our world to come crashing down again, maybe I could actually be the kid, finally. Maybe he would let me breathe.

"Okay," I say.

Kyra and Edie both look at me, shocked.

"Okay?" Edie says.

"Okay," I repeat.

Kyra smiles wide. Then she is coming to me, taking my hands in hers, squeezing. "Oh my god, thank you. This is going to be good, I promise."

In the midst of already regretting my agreement to this ridiculous plot, I don't know what to say, so I fall back on my same reply: "Okay."

CHAPTER 29

Dave

According to a recent Gallup poll, 4.5 percent of the population identifies as lesbian, gay, bisexual, or transgender. That's a higher percentage than I thought. If I apply that percentage to the population of Cleo's high school, there are approximately one hundred kids who identify as LGBT. At least she is not alone.

I am aware of the newer acronym—LGBTQ+—though I had no idea what it meant. Per usual, Google came to the rescue to enlighten me. The "Q" means questioning or queer. "Questioning" refers to people who may be unsure of their sexual orientation or gender identity. "Queer" is an umbrella term for anyone who is not heterosexual or non-cisgender (but finds the terms "gay," "lesbian," or "bisexual" too limiting). I didn't know what cisgender meant, so Google had to explain that one too. A person who is cisgender feels that their personal identity and gender align with their sex at birth.

The "+" is meant to encompass all the other gender identities and orientations that are not specifically covered by the other five initials. Intersex, asexual, pansexual, agender, genderqueer—there are so many terms I had never heard of before. I am a heterosexual, cisgender male. Google says this makes me highly privileged.

My ignorance of various issues related to sexuality and gender identity should not be mistaken for distaste. I am rather neutral on the subject, frankly. I couldn't really care less who someone is attracted to, even if that someone is my daughter. It's a well-known fact that homosexual and bisexual behavior are present in every major animal group in every major geographic region of the world. Interestingly, about 10 percent of rams (males) refuse to mate with ewes (females), but do readily mate with other rams. Among mating giraffes, nine out of ten pairings occur between males. Among penguins, some males mate for life, despite female penguins being available. Giraffes, lions, bottlenose dolphins, monkeys, elephants, bats—they've all been observed to have same-sex pairings. One scientist documented same-sex behavior in over 450 species of animals worldwide. So anyone who says that homosexuality or bisexuality isn't "natural" is, plainly, wrong.

I know those people exist, the "It's not natural" people, and I suppose my only concern is that Cleo will be harassed by those people. It's inevitable. The acceptance of LGBTQ+ people requires some level of critical thinking, and I have found that many human beings lack this. It is one of my lifetime laments. I suppose all I can do is to be an oppositional force to the idiots.

If Cleo chooses to confide in me (which is a big *if*, given my track record of offering support via conversation), I want to be ready. Thankfully, Google has led me to a wealth of guidance on what to say and not say in this exact situation. I have started making a list of do's and don't's:

Do not say "Are you sure?"
Do not say "Maybe it's a phase."
Do not say "You do not seem like that type."
Do say "Thank you for sharing this with me."
Do say "What can I do to support you?"
Do say "I am always here for you."

I will continue to scour the internet for information, but I already feel more prepared. That feeling of being prepared—it is the dragon I continue to chase.

———————

The park Mirai says Jana "used to love" is not one I've ever been to. In fact, I didn't even know it existed. I am annoyed with Mirai for suggesting it, for flaunting her knowledge of my wife's likes and dislikes. Likes: this park. Dislikes: me.

I have arrived twenty minutes early, determined to beat Mirai and familiarize myself with my surroundings before having to engage with her. The park is small, tucked behind a neighborhood built before cookie-cutter homes took over the area. There is a horse trail alongside the park, imprints of hooves dried in the dirt.

I sit on a bench next to one of those little free library boxes. I open the door, curious what books people leave here. There are a few board books meant for small children, a Bible, a worn copy of *Fahrenheit 451*, and a pamphlet from the Church of Jesus Christ of Latter-Day Saints. I begin to flip through the Mormon pamphlet when a voice says "Dave?"

I look up to see Mirai standing there. She is not wearing an enormous dress this time. She is wearing jeans and a shirt Jana used to refer to as a tunic (if memory serves).

"Oh, hello," I say. She is ten minutes early, likely planning to be the first to arrive. I feel as if I have won already.

"May I?" she asks, motioning toward the bench.

It is a long bench, with ample space for the two of us, so I nod. She sits at the opposite end but angles her body toward mine.

"Doing some light reading?" she asks.

I look down to see that I am still holding the Mormon propaganda.

"Oh, well, not really," I say, opening the door of the little library box and putting the pamphlet back.

"I wouldn't blame you if you were. We all need answers, don't we?"

I am not sure what she means.

"I used to be a pretty spiritual person," she goes on. "Not so much anymore."

I just nod. I have never been a spiritual person and have no plans to become one.

"So, how are things?" she asks.

"Fine."

"Did you have a nice Fourth of July?"

I saw my daughter kissing a girl.

The impulse to say this is alarmingly strong.

"It was fine," I say.

"Probably better than mine," she says. "Kyra snuck out to see her boyfriend. I caught her trying to sneak back in the house at six in the morning today."

"Oh," I say.

I resist the urge to suggest that she install an alarm system to keep better track of her daughter.

"Her boyfriend's not a terrible kid, so I should be grateful for that. He's the one who's pushing her to apply to college."

College. A topic I have been carefully avoiding with Cleo.

"Where does she want to go?" I ask.

"Somewhere local. Her boyfriend is set on going to UCLA, but it's so hard to get in there these days. Maybe UC Irvine or San Diego."

I nod. I know nothing about college programs. I assume Cleo does. I assume she is already planning where she would like to apply. I have forced this independence on her by not being supportive of exploring the idea.

"What about Cleo?" Mirai asks.

I clear my throat. "It's something I need to discuss with her."

In addition to her sexual orientation.

"I remember Jana saying she was really smart. Good at math, right?"

I'm impressed with her memory of this. "Yes, that's right," I say. "Math and science." The surge I feel through my body must be pride.

"I can't believe we are at this stage. . . . College!"

We. There she goes again, joining us.

"Well, there is still another year of high school," I say.

"It will go fast, like everything."

I feel the impulse again and before I can question it, I am talking:

"I saw Cleo kissing a girl."

Mirai looks surprised—at what I've shared, or the way I've shared it, I can't tell.

"Oh," she says. "Well, I didn't see that coming."

"Neither did I."

"When was this?" she asks.

"Yesterday. At the Fourth of July party we attended."

She switches the cross of her legs and says, "I'm going to sound like my daughter and ask if this was a hookup . . . or was it something more serious?"

"It was her best friend. Or, the girl I thought was her best friend. Perhaps her girlfriend."

Mirai nods. "Interesting."

"She's also our neighbor."

"Very interesting."

I don't say anything, because I'm not sure what to say. Finally, she says, "How do you feel about this?"

"I don't disapprove, if that's what you're asking."

She tilts her head, as if contemplating something. "But do you *approve*?"

I consider this. If I'm honest, I don't wholeheartedly approve of Cleo becoming involved with anyone, because of the risks involved. But I also know this is unrealistic and I need to adjust to the reality of letting her grow into an adult.

"I don't disapprove," I repeat.

Mirai smiles. "Okay, then."

"So you didn't know?" I ask.

She looks confused. "Why would I know?"

"I thought Jana might have told you."

"Oh," she says. "Well, no. She didn't mention it."

Maybe Jana didn't know. Maybe Cleo didn't want to tell either of us. This makes me feel better. But then I dare to do the thing that has always been hard for me and put myself in Cleo's shoes. If I were her, I would want my mother to know. I would want to have confided in her at least. Maybe Cleo did tell her and Jana considered the confession sacred, something to be kept safe, protected—even from me.

"She didn't share many personal things about Cleo," Mirai adds. "I respected that."

"But she shared personal things about me."

She re-crosses her legs again.

"I shared so much about my difficulties with Sean. I think she was just trying to contribute to the conversation."

I think of my original question: *Was she going to leave me anyway?*

Now would be the time to ask it, but I find my throat constricted, unwilling.

"Are you going to talk to Cleo?" Mirai asks, changing the subject.

"She doesn't know I saw what I saw. Everything I've read online suggests I wait for her to tell me in her own way."

"That's smart," she says. "I'm always way too nosy with Kyra. I suppose it sends the message that I don't trust her."

I state the obvious: "Well, you don't."

She laughs. "I suppose that's the crux of it, isn't it?"

We sit in silence for a moment, and I begin to question the purpose of this meeting. She proposed it, but she appears to have no agenda. I accepted her invitation with the expectation of an agenda. I also thought she could provide parental advice in relation to my situation with Cleo, but it has become evident that she is in no position to dole out parental advice to anyone.

"Did you tell Cleo about us meeting?" she asks.

"No," I say.

"I didn't tell Kyra either."

"Would she be upset?"

"I don't know. She's known I've wanted to talk with you. She's accused me of being obsessive about it . . . which I guess I was. Anyway, she'll think it's strange. She already thinks I'm a nutcase."

"Cleo thinks the same of me. I assume it's a common phenomenon among young people."

She laughs again. "Perhaps."

There is more silence before she says, "I do like talking with you, though. It's healing, in a way. For me, at least. I hope for you too."

That is not the word I would choose—*healing*. But I suppose these two visits have not had any negative consequences. I remember asking The Therapist why it was so important to be officially diagnosed with The Label, and she'd said, "It's good to have things out in the open, where you can see them." I guess meeting with Mirai McCann puts her out in the open, where I can see her. Before, she was somewhat of a bogeyman in the confines of my mind.

"We could make it a monthly thing, if you wanted," she says.

I bring myself back to the present moment. "Sorry, what?"

"We could meet up once a month. If you wanted. We don't have—"

"That's fine," I say.

She smiles. "Great."

I look at my watch. "I have to get back to work. I informed my coworkers that I would be taking a late lunch break, and my hour is almost up."

"Oh, right," she says. "Of course."

I stand, and she does the same.

"Have a good weekend, then," she says.

"You too."

She gives me a wave and I do the same in return. This is how I've spent the majority of my life—emulating others, playing along.

I'm several feet away from her when I hear her say, "Thank you, Dave."

I turn around and smile, having no idea what she's thanking me for.

CHAPTER 30

Cleo

It's Saturday. Tomorrow is the day we are forcing Dad and Mirai to meet. I am having all kinds of second thoughts. Dad's going to freak. But maybe Kyra and Edie are right. Maybe it'll be good for him.

The plan is to persuade him to take me to the harbor tomorrow morning. He knows I love the bagel sandwiches at Coffee Importers, so my asking shouldn't be too suspicious. Kyra says her mom loves to watch the seals on the docks, so it shouldn't be hard to convince her either. Plan A is to let them "run into" each other and act like it's a complete coincidence, a fateful surprise. If that doesn't seem possible, Plan B comes into play. Plan B involves me telling Dad that I want him to talk with someone and then leading him to Mirai and Kyra. Plan B terrifies me.

Dad is out in the front yard, digging holes for plants he's just bought. It's about time he started beautifying the place.

"Hey, Dad," I say, trying too hard to sound casual and without ulterior motives.

He looks up. "Oh, hey. Good timing. I wanted to ask you—I was thinking of putting these two here, and these two over here, but I'm not sure about these two."

He points to the four holes he's already dug and the plants he wants to occupy them, then the two plants that do not yet have a home.

I survey the area, hands on hips, and say, "What about over here?"

He scratches his chin.

"Okay, yeah, that could work."

"Maybe I have a future as a landscape architect."

He looks at me like he can't tell if I'm joking or not.

"I'm joking. I have a black thumb."

His face breaks into a smile. "That's what I thought."

"What's inspired this landscaping effort of yours?" I ask.

At our old house, Dad spent so much time on the yard. It was something of a pride and joy. When we moved and he showed no interest in tending to the yard of our new house, I was left to assume that all of his efforts had been for Mom.

He shrugs. "Figured it was time to spruce it up."

Another reason this is odd is that he usually spends the majority of his weekends in the bunker. Come to think of it, he hasn't been down there in several days. Not that I've noticed, at least. Maybe he did meet someone. Maybe that's who the plants are for.

"Cool. Well, I was wondering if we could go to the harbor tomorrow. I've been craving a bagel sandwich."

"The Elvis?" he asks.

That's the name of the sandwich. It has peanut butter, banana slices, and honey. The three of us—Mom, Dad, and I—used to get it most Sundays.

"Yeah," I say.

I haven't had The Elvis since Mom died.

"Okay," he says. "I can drive you."

"Cool, thanks."

I start to turn back toward the house when he says, "Cleo, I was thinking . . . you'll have that boot off in no time and then you'll be back to driving."

I prepare myself for him to say that he thinks I shouldn't drive again until my ankle is at "optimum strength" or whatever.

"Yeah?" I say.

"I've been looking into cars for you."

"What?"

"Cars. I've been looking into purchasing one for you."

Something is wrong with him. Something is very wrong.

"You *are?*"

He's kneeling, digging. I stand over him, casting a shadow. He looks up at me. "Yes, you want a car, right?"

"Well, yes, but I didn't think you—"

"A used one. I can't afford a new one. Teenagers shouldn't be allowed to own new cars anyway."

There's the Dad I know. I smile.

"Dad, that's awesome of you. I can get a job, I can pay you back—"

"No, that's not necessary."

He stands, brushes off the dirt on his pants.

"I have my eye on a 2016 Prius," he says. "I figured you and I both appreciate the environmental benefits of a Prius. It's done well in crash tests and—"

"It's great, Dad. Seriously."

I cannot wait to tell Edie about this.

"All right, then," he says.

Which, in Dad language, means this conversation is now over.

That night, I don't sleep much. Judging by the speed at which Edie responds to my middle-of-the-night texts, she does not either. I'm nervous, and she's nervous on my behalf. The whole car thing is making me feel guilty about putting Dad in this situation. Here he is offering me a car, and I'm putting him face-to-face with the wife of the man who killed Mom.

Edie: If u really don't want to do it, we just text Kyra and say it's off

Me: I just don't know

Edie: I really think it'll be fine

Me: Ugh

Edie: Try to sleep, k? See how u feel in the a.m.

Me: Ugh

In the morning I'm still a nervous wreck. I consider texting Kyra, telling her I want to wait, do this another time (if at all). But then I remember the desperation in her voice, the way her eyes were pleading with me to make this happen. I don't owe her anything. I know that. But I also don't want to let her down. I just don't know if what we're doing is smart. We aren't, like, psychologists. What if this is traumatic for both of them? What if it does more harm than good?

I crack open a can of cat food for Poppy, my hands shaking as I do so. I'm *that* nervous.

"You still want to go to the harbor?" Dad asks, coming into the kitchen.

He's already dressed to go, wearing jeans and a short-sleeved button-down shirt. This fact alone makes my decision for me.

"Yep."

CHAPTER 31

Dave

I've looked into the best colleges for math and science in California. Stanford is number one. Cleo's grades are good, but she does not have the extracurricular activities or other boastful feats necessary to get into Stanford. Of course, I'll still encourage her to try. Cal Tech in Pasadena is also well-known for its STEM programs, as are UCLA, Pomona College, and Berkeley. I would prefer she not go as far as northern California, but I also know this is supposed to be about what's best for her, not me. I have made a list of ten colleges that should suit her needs, assuming she wants to pursue her interest in math or science. It's obvious that I do not know her as well as I should. Maybe she's lost interest in math and science. That would be disappointing but, again, this isn't about me.

I figure I can instigate the college conversation while we are eating our bagel sandwiches. I will offer to create an applications calendar for her, as I think this would be a good use of my organizational skills while also benefiting her. She will need to complete her applications before the end of the year. Her future is sneaking up on me.

It's just before nine when we pull into the harbor parking lot. It's already starting to fill up, which is typical for summer. I find a spot toward the back.

"Maybe we should go somewhere else," Cleo says when I put the car in Park.

I keep my hand on the keys, which are still in the ignition. "Is that what you want to do?"

"I don't know."

She looks worried. Maybe this place is reminding her of Jana. It reminds *me* of Jana.

"Let's just go here," I say. "I haven't had The Elvis in a long time."

She lets out a breath and opens her car door. "Okay."

As we walk through the parking lot, I notice Cleo is moving at a very slow pace. I am aware that my natural pace is unusually fast, but she keeps up with me most of the time. I turn around.

"You okay?" I ask.

I wonder if it's her ankle bothering her, though she hasn't complained about it much at all. It should be close to healed by now.

"Yeah."

She doesn't look fine, though.

She catches up to me, and we walk down the steps toward Coffee Importers, the bagel sandwich place. Predictably, there is a line. I go to the end of it, Cleo on my heels.

"Do you want anything to drink?" I ask.

She used to get hot chocolate. Jana would get a coffee and I'd get tea.

Cleo shakes her head.

It takes about ten minutes for us to get to the front of the line. I order our sandwiches, and a tea for me. They give me one of those circular devices that vibrates when your order is ready, and I turn my attention to the task of finding a table, which tends to be difficult during the tourist season. I spot an open table bordering the walkway and hurry to claim it. I sit, and Cleo sits across from me. She's looking over my shoulder, eyes darting. It's like she's trying to spot someone. I turn around, in the direction of her eyes. Upon seeing nothing of interest, I turn back. She smiles nervously.

"So," she says.

"So," I say. Then, upon remembering my mission for this excursion: "I was looking into colleges that have good STEM programs."

"Huh?"

She seems confused, or taken aback, which then confuses me.

"Colleges. I know I've been avoiding the subject and I'm aware it's time for you to start considering applications. I mean, if you are still interested in attending. You had said you were. . . ."

"Oh, yeah, right. I am," she says. "Sorry, I just didn't know we were going to talk about that."

"We don't have to. Maybe you've already started looking into it."

"No, that's cool. I definitely need help with all that," she says.

"But you don't want to discuss it now?"

She offers a laugh that sounds strange. "Yeah, maybe later, okay?"

The circular device buzzes and I tell her I'll be right back. I go to the pickup window and retrieve two plastic baskets containing our bagels, along with my tea, steam exiting the little hole in the lid. I'm walking back to the table, staring at the steam, allowing myself to be mesmerized by it, when I hear Cleo's voice:

"Dad, look who I ran into," she says.

She's at our table, but she's standing from her seat. Next to her are Mirai McCann and a girl who must be Kyra, though she looks much different than I remember Kyra McCann looking.

It's in moments like these when I wish I could pause the scene and give my brain time to process the situation. In the absence of my ability to do this, I stand there dumbly, the sandwiches balanced on my forearm, steaming cup of tea in my opposite hand. Cleo does not know I've met with Mirai. She thinks this is the first time I'm seeing Mirai since Jana died. In a matter of several seconds, I determine that I must act as if I am surprised.

"Oh," I say. "Hello."

It is not difficult for me to act confused, because I so often am. It is something of a baseline for me in social situations.

When I look at Kyra's face, I see she is looking at Cleo. When I look at Cleo, she is looking at Kyra. My last stop is Mirai's face. She gives me a small nod and a Mona Lisa–type smile that I do not know how to interpret.

"Dave Garrison?" she says, putting one hand to her heart, an overly dramatic gesture if I ever saw one.

"Mirai McCann?" I say, following her lead.

She winks at me, so I think I am doing what I am supposed to do.

"Wow, what are the chances?" Cleo says.

Her voice sounds as strange as her earlier laugh did.

"Um, Cleo, I was just going to pick up a pint of ice cream," Kyra says, jutting her chin toward the ice cream shop next door. "Do you want to come with me?"

"Sure," Cleo says. "Dad, is that okay? Maybe you and Mirai can talk?"

I look at Mirai, who now appears to be suppressing a laugh.

"Sure," I say.

Cleo and Kyra walk toward the ice cream shop, with an ease between them that baffles me. Once they are a fair distance away, Mirai releases her laugh.

"I don't get it," I say.

I set the sandwiches on the table and take the lid off my tea.

"I think they arranged this," Mirai says.

My brain is still struggling to catch up. "What?"

"Kyra and Cleo. They must have been in touch and arranged for us to meet here."

Cleo has been in touch with Kyra?

"You think so?"

"Well, I don't think this is a coincidence."

I sit. Mirai looks toward the empty chair meant for Cleo, and says, "May I?"

"Oh, sure," I say.

She sits.

"Here we were worried they would be upset about us meeting, and they were plotting to get us to talk."

"How did they. . . . Why would they . . . ?"

I'm still not caught up.

"Facebook, Instagram, one of those things. Who knows how long they've been talking." She shakes her head in disbelief, but she's smiling, bemused. "I'm sure it was Kyra's idea. Like I told you, she knew I wanted to talk with you."

"Cleo was acting strangely when we got here."

Mirai is still smiling. "Looks like she was keeping one more secret from you."

The truth of this is disconcerting.

"Are we supposed to tell them we already met?" I ask. I need to understand the rules of this particular game.

"I don't think so. Why ruin their fun? They're probably pretty proud of themselves for orchestrating this. *I'm* pretty proud of them too, honestly."

I don't feel proud. I feel silly.

"Kyra's mood has been better the past couple weeks. Now I know why," Mirai says.

I'm hard-pressed to note any difference in Cleo's mood. She has seemed generally fine, which I've attributed primarily to inborn resilience and secondarily to her friendship—or whatever it is—with Edie.

"So we're just supposed to be talking right now?"

I turn back toward the ice cream shop. I can see the two of them inside, standing at the window, watching us. When they see me look, they turn away.

"I'm sure they're very nervous about how this is going for us," she says.

"How long do we have to sit here?" .

She shrugs. "An hour, maybe."

My phone buzzes in my pocket. I take it out—a text from Cleo.

"She says you can have her bagel sandwich if you want," I tell Mirai.

Mirai looks at the food in front of her, considering. "That's okay. But you go ahead, eat."

I appreciate the permission and take a bite of my bagel, the flavors bombarding me with memories of Jana, of sitting with her at a table just like this, of staring out at the boats together.

I put the bagel down, swallow.

"There's a reason why I first contacted you," I say.

Mirai's eyebrows are raised expectantly. "Oh?"

"I wanted to know something. About Jana."

Her eyebrows are still raised.

I force the words from my mouth: "Was she going to leave me anyway?"

Her eyebrows fall and then pull toward each other, crashing in the middle. She sighs. "Oh, Dave."

"You can tell me," I say.

She shakes her head and I realize that my autonomic nervous system has temporarily suspended operations, because I am not breathing.

Finally, as I am on the verge of self-suffocation, she says, "I honestly don't know."

I inhale breath. I inhale truth, or lack thereof.

"She didn't tell you?"

Mirai sighs again. When she sits back in her chair, her face crosses a ray of sun so she appears illuminated. She squints.

"She wondered what it would be like to be on her own. She wondered if she was missing something. But I think anyone married for any length of time wonders that. Don't you think?"

"I've never wondered that."

She leans forward, out of the light. "Well, Jana always said you were one of a kind."

"So she didn't have any actual . . . plans?"

"To leave you?"

I nod.

Mirai shakes her head. "No. Nothing she told me. And I think she would have told me, since we'd talked so much about me leaving Sean."

This information buoys me.

Mirai leans even farther forward, her elbows resting on the table, her hands clasped mere inches from my bagel sandwich. I sit back in my chair.

"You know she loved you, right?" she says.

I blink. "My ASD was hard on her."

Mirai tilts her head side to side, considering.

"One time, she told me that it was good for her to have a partner like you, someone logical and rational, someone to temper the intensity of her emotions. We all seek that balance, you know?"

"I don't know."

"And maybe you chose her because you knew you needed someone to show you the emotional side of life. Subconsciously, I mean. Opposites attract, right?"

This is true in relation to the north and south poles of magnets, but maybe it's a mistake to extrapolate its meaning to relationships.

"Or opposites get tired of . . . opposing," I say.

"Dave, you're being hard on yourself."

"I think she was tired of me."

"Maybe she was. That has nothing to do with love."

"Doesn't it?"

"Dave, we all get tired of the people we love. We take them for granted. We imagine other scenarios, other people. Maybe you don't, because of the way your mind works, but most of us do. Most of us get caught up in emotion. Most of us take out our frustrations on the people we love the most. Most of us wrestle with the meaning of life and marriage. Most of us wonder if we're happy. Most of us ruminate. We hem, we haw. Most of us aren't sure if we're doing it all right."

"That sounds exhausting."

She laughs a big, generous laugh. "It *is*."

I take another bite of my bagel.

"If Jana had told me she wanted to leave you, I would have told her she was crazy," Mirai says. "For what it's worth."

It shouldn't be worth much, this opinion of the woman married to the man who killed Jana. But it is.

"Thank you," I say.

"At some point, you'll have to stop torturing yourself."

I take a sip of my tea and prematurely congratulate myself for the witty response I have:

"Touché."

After an hour, the majority of which we spend talking about where we want our daughters to go to college, Mirai texts Kyra and says that we have concluded our chat. With that, Cleo and Kyra return to the table looking sheepish and prepared for punishment.

Mirai stands from the table and says to Kyra, "You ready to get going?"

Kyra looks from her mother to me. "Wait, you guys aren't pissed?"

Cleo gives me her puppy-dog eyes.

"No, we appreciate this opportunity to talk. Don't we, Dave?"

I nod.

Cleo says, "Seriously?"

Mirai answers for me. "Seriously. In fact, we may get together again."

Kyra and Cleo look at each other with amazement.

Mirai puts her arm around Kyra and pulls her into her side. I would do the same to Cleo, except we don't have that kind of touchy relationship. Instead, I say, "I saved your bagel for you."

Cleo smiles, says, "Thanks, Dad. I'm starving."

CHAPTER 32

Cleo

Edie and I lie next to each other in her bed, staring at the ceiling. She holds my hand, rubbing her thumb up and down the length of mine. It's Monday, the day after one of the weirdest days of my life. Weird in a good way, but still incredibly weird. I've just given Edie the play-by-play of the Mirai meeting. I texted her (and Carter) immediately after it happened, but I felt compelled to go over it again. I just can't believe Dad was so cool about the whole thing. I keep waiting for him to have a delayed reaction, but it hasn't happened . . . yet.

"You know, I told you it would be okay," Edie says.

"Yeah, well, I didn't actually *believe* you."

"Nice, glad to know I'm having an impact."

She lets go of my hand and crosses her arms over her chest in mock anger.

"I'm kind of thinking of telling him about us," I say.

She uncrosses her arms and turns onto her hip, facing me. "Really?"

"I mean, if he could handle Mirai, he can handle anything, right?"

"You talk like you're about to tell him you're moving to Brazil. I really don't think he's going to flip out."

"Yeah. . . ."

"He doesn't have it in him," she says.

"Inability to get emotional—an occasional pro of ASD."

"Something like that."

"So why am I so nervous?"

She gives me a knowing smile.

"What?" I ask.

"Do you really want to know what I think?"

"Oh god, do I?"

She laughs.

"I think you know that telling your dad will make it, like, *official*. He's very black-and-white, you know? When you tell him this, there's no going back. You will be cemented in his mind as his daughter who is queer."

I nod, considering this.

"Maybe," I say.

She rolls onto her stomach so she's right next to me. Then she arches her neck up and purses her lips for a kiss. I oblige.

I go home just before 3 p.m. so I can catch Dad when he takes his freakishly predictable afternoon bathroom break. I figure it's better to have a rip-the-Band-Aid-off conversation and then he can go back to his office to process the information, or whatever. It might be stupid to do this today, after what happened yesterday, but they say to strike while the iron is hot. Or whatever.

"Hey, Dad," I say when I hear the familiar creak of his office chair as he stands.

"Cleo?"

He walks down the hallway and then meets me in the kitchen. He's clearly surprised to see me. Usually I'm at Edie's all day and come home for dinner, or after dinner if Camila cooks.

"Hi," I say. "I'm home early."

I take the chocolate milk out of the fridge, pour a glass for me and one for him. A peace offering. We both love chocolate milk.

"How's work?" I ask.

I slide his glass across the island.

"Fine," he says, taking a sip. I take a sip too.

"I wanted to talk to you about something."

"Oh?" he says. "Right now?"

"Or after your bathroom break. If you have time."

"Now is fine," he says. He seems concerned or confused. Or both.

"So, I was, like, really impressed with how you handled things with Mirai, and I guess it made me think you could handle this other thing I've been wanting to tell you."

He takes another sip, this one so long that three-quarters of the chocolate milk is gone.

"Okay, then, what is it?"

I feel dizzy. My palms are sweaty. I have all the telltale signs of panic.

"It's about Edie . . . and me. Or just me, I guess. Yeah. It's about me."

He sets his glass on the counter, dares to make eye contact with me.

"I guess what I'm trying to say is that I'm not . . . straight."

He nods, but there is zero emotion on his face. Per usual.

"You're not straight."

"Right. I'm not straight. Edie and I . . .we're . . . together."

I expect this won't make sense to him. He knows we're "together" in that we are friends who spend a lot of time "together." I decide I must clarify:

"She's my girlfriend."

The moment the word leaves my mouth, I feel simultaneously elated and scared, the way a bird must feel leaving its nest for the first time. Will these wings hold me up? Will I fall? Should I turn back?

He just looks at me for what feels like a freaking hour, then he nods and says:

"I know."

I blink.

"You know?"

"I know," he says.

"What do you mean, you know?"

"I know that you're not straight and that Edie is your girlfriend. I just don't know what letter you are exactly."

"What *letter*?"

"In the acronym. L, G, B, T, Q, or the plus sign, which is still unclear to me."

I don't know what to say, so I burst out laughing.

"Oh my god, Dad. The *acronym*? Seriously?"

He doesn't even break a smile.

"I assume you're an 'L,'" he says. "Or a 'B,' I suppose, though that one seems more complicated."

I know Dad isn't a huggy type person, but I go to him and put my arms around him anyway. It's like hugging a tree trunk, but I don't care. He's my Dad.

"I'm not sure I know my letter yet, Dad."

"I believe that qualifies as a 'Q.'"

I pull back from my hug and say, "Okay, Dad. We can call it a 'Q.'"

The feeling rushing through me is something similar to when I drank that margarita at Edie's house. I am light, floaty, tingly.

"Thank you for sharing this with me," Dad says in his typical robotic way. "Is there anything I can do to support you?"

I am fairly certain someone told him to say this, but I don't care. My vision gets blurry as my eyes fill with tears—the happy kind, not the sad ones.

"What's wrong?" he asks, looking completely confused.

I shake my head. "Nothing," I say. "I'm just. . . . Thanks, Dad."

He nods once, takes the final sip of his chocolate milk, and puts his glass in the sink. My hands are too shaky to even hold my glass.

I assume he'll go to the bathroom, and then back to his office for the remainder of his workday now. Before he leaves the kitchen, though, he turns around.

"Cleo," he says, "I am always here for you."

He does his single-nod thing again.

"Thanks, Dad."

My vision is still blurry.

When he disappears down the hallway, I take out my phone to text Edie. She's already texted me:

So?

I start to text back when Dad calls for me again.

"How about pizza tonight?" he says.

Fridays are usually pizza nights. It's Monday.

"Sure," I call back.

"If you want, you can invite Edie," he says. "And her mother. I guess."

I laugh and wipe my eyes.

"Okay, Dad."

Then I text Edie:

My Dad just did the thing I thought he'd never do.

Edie: Oh god, what?

Me: He surprised me.

Seven months later

February 2020

CHAPTER 33

Dave

On New Year's Eve, the government in Wuhan, China, confirmed that health authorities were treating dozens of cases of pneumonia of unknown cause. Days later, researchers identified the cause—a novel virus.

On January 11, Chinese state media reported the first known death from an illness caused by the virus—a 61-year-old man who was a regular customer at the Wuhan market. The report of his death came right before the Spring Festival Golden Week, when millions of people travel across the country.

Predictably, reports of cases outside mainland China started coming in. According to the World Health Organization's first situation report, the first of these cases were in Japan, South Korea, and Thailand. At this point, I knew the United States would be close behind.

The first known case in the United States was a man in his thirties in Washington State who developed symptoms after returning from a trip to the region around Wuhan. The city of Wuhan was cut off completely by Chinese authorities, with all buses, subways, and ferries suspended. A week later, the World Health Organization declared a global health emergency. Then the president suspended entry into the United States by any foreign nationals who had traveled to China in the past fourteen days.

That brings us to today. This morning's headlines reported the first coronavirus death outside of China—a 44-year-old man in the Philippines. Nearly 400 people have died now, with thousands infected.

This, I fear, is just the beginning.

I am meeting Mirai at a new café in Dana Point for our monthly lunch. It's been approximately seven months since our first reunion, and our meeting has now been incorporated into my routine. It is an expected event, so I do not dread its occurrence any more than I dread, say, the monthly cleaning of my rain gutters. It is simply something to do, a task to be completed. Cleo asks me if I enjoy seeing Mirai, and I don't know how to answer that question. Social interactions are not what I would consider enjoyable, but Mirai is fine. She doesn't unnerve me in the way most humans do. I suppose she is a friend, by most people's definition.

The café is small, with just a few tables inside. We order at the counter, and Mirai chooses one of the outdoor tables as our final destination, even though it's February and cold.

"I have news," she says when we sit.

Judging by her smile and large eyes, it is good news.

"Kyra got into San Diego State, early decision," she says.

She claps her hands together in a way that embarrasses me on her behalf, then returns to clutching her mug of tea.

"That's great," I say.

"Wouldn't that be something if both our girls ended up in San Diego?"

I've already told her that Cleo was accepted into the University of California in San Diego. She has her heart set on Berkeley, though, probably because both Edie and Carter have their hearts set on San Francisco State. They talk about visiting each other using BART. The idea of Cleo using public transportation is nothing short of horrifying, but I am trying not to worry . . . yet.

According to Google, the average length of a high school relationship is four to six months, so I am a bit surprised that Cleo and Edie are, as they say, "going strong." Google has also informed me that only two percent of marriages are from a high school relationship, so the odds are that Cleo and Edie will part ways eventually. I don't share these thoughts with Cleo, of course. Mirai told me, "Sometimes, as a parent, the most important thing is to just listen." So I do that. When Cleo tells me she loves Edie, I listen.

"We could drive together to visit them," Mirai says. "Or take the train!"

She claps her hands together again.

I am not supportive of this idea of sharing transportation to San Diego with Mirai, but I figure I can take issue with that later, when it becomes a reality. I'm learning to take things as they come, instead of attempting to prepare all the time.

A waitress brings our order to the table—a salad for Mirai and soup for me. Mirai arranges her napkin on her lap and says, "I have other news too."

I slurp a spoonful of soup. I know it's considered rude in America, but in Asian cultures, slurping demonstrates enjoyment of the food. In Saudi Arabia, diners burp after eating to compliment the cook. At least I don't do that.

"I met someone," she says.

She looks more excited than I will ever be about meeting someone.

"Who?"

She sighs. "A man, Dave. I met a man. A guy. On an app."

"On an app?"

"A dating app," she says. "Do you live under a rock?"

No, but I'd like to.

"Oh," I say.

"It's early. We've only been on a few dates, but I really enjoy his company. Of course, I won't tell Kyra about him until we're practically married." She laughs again. "Look at me, getting ahead of myself."

There is probably something I'm supposed to say here, but I really don't have any interest in hearing about her love interest.

"His name is Devesh. He's Indian. The irony, right? He's divorced, no kids. I haven't told him about . . . what happened. When do you think I should?"

This may be the first time in my life I have been solicited for relationship advice. Asking me for such a thing is like asking a fish how to fly.

"It's probably best to introduce all the facts in the beginning stages," I say.

She nods and sighs. "I knew you would say that. And I know you are right. That's going to be a fun conversation: 'So, I'm a widow because my husband hanged himself after killing my good friend. What's your story?'"

"Perhaps you don't have to say it exactly like that."

She gives me a look that reminds me of the looks Jana used to give me. "Of course I'm not going to say it exactly like that."

She resumes eating her salad.

"What's new with you?" she asks.

The only thing that is relatively "new with me" is that my interest in model cars has returned. I have taken up photographing them in different settings, at a scale that makes them appear life-size. Objectively, it's a trivial hobby, but that seems to be my forte. Just yesterday, I found a collector in Long Beach who is selling a limited edition 1:18 scale 1964 Mercury Marauder, which has been in the "wish list" column of my spreadsheet for years. It includes a 390 V-8 engine, bucket seats that tilt, full instrumentation, and a 4-speed stick—a total of more than 140 individual parts. We have exchanged emails.

"Not much," I say. I don't expect Mirai would care to hear about model cars.

"How's Cleo?"

"She's doing well, as far as I can tell."

"I still can't believe they're graduating from high school in a few months." She shakes her head as an expression of her disbelief.

"What are you going to do when she leaves for school?" she asks.

It's a strange question. I presume I will go about my life as usual, just without school dropoffs and pickups, and more meat-based meals.

"I don't foresee much changing."

She looks at me like I'm crazy. "You're going to miss her. You know that, right?"

I suppose I'm aware of the concept. I miss Jana, but that's because Jana is completely gone. Cleo is still here, alive and well, and that fact is the best companion of all.

"The house will be quiet," I concede. "I have Apophis."

Mirai scrunches her face. "A—what?"

"The cat. Cleo calls him Poppy for short."

Her face is still scrunched. "I'm not sure a cat is enough for most people."

"I'm not most people."

She un-scrunches and shrugs one shoulder. "Fair enough." Then: "I still think you'll be surprised at how much you miss her."

"Well, we'll see."

Given that the world is in the midst of a waiting-to-be-declared pandemic, I'm not certain that Cleo will even go to college in the fall. She doesn't know that yet, though. Neither does Mirai. Neither do any of these people sitting at tables next to us. I know, though. I take some comfort in the supplies I have accumulated in the bunker, but I also know that no amount of supplies can prepare or protect Cleo and me from everything. What will happen with this virus, or with life in general, remains to be seen. The letting-go is as liberating as it is terrifying.

"Have you thought about dating?"

She asks the question while staring at her plate, and I appreciate the lack of eye contact.

"No."

She looks up. "Really? Not at all?"

The truth: I don't think I could do better than Jana. I'd rather avoid the inevitable disappointment.

"Not at all," I say.

"I think you'll change your mind."

"You are welcome to think that."

"You know you have a lot to offer, right?" she asks.

I have not considered my offerings.

"You're an honest, loyal, smart, reliable man. Many women would love a man like that," she says.

I don't want many women, though. I eat my last spoons of soup.

"Jana would want you to be happy," she says. "Sorry, that's probably overstepping, but I really do believe that."

"I believe it too."

The thing is, I am happy. Cleo seems to be thriving. I am satisfied with my work. I am reinvigorated by my model cars. I am enjoying tinkering around the house like I used to, tending to the yard and what not. And I have the cat.

Cleo is on the couch when I get home, watching the news of all things. They are talking about the coronavirus.

"Hey, Dad," she says. "How was Mirai?"

"Fine.

"Have you heard about this?" she asks, nodding toward the TV.

I sit on the couch with her. "I have."

She smiles. "Of course you have. Stupid question."

An infectious-disease expert is on the screen. He says he is "concerned."

"This is a big deal, huh?" Cleo says.

I don't want to scare her. "It's . . . concerning."

"But not so concerning that we're going to live in the bunker, right?" She's joking.

"Not yet," I say.

She laughs. She thinks I'm joking with the "yet." I don't have the heart to tell her I'm not.

I push myself off the couch. I should get back to my office.

"Dad," Cleo says as I start down the hallway.

I turn.

"It wouldn't be the worst thing in the world to be in the bunker with you," she says.

I do something rare—I chuckle.

"I mean, it would be pretty awful," she says, "but not the worst thing."

We've already been through the worst thing together.

These words come to me with surprising alacrity. I keep them to myself, though. They are too serious for the moment, too solemn.

"It wouldn't be the worst thing to be with you, either," I say.

I hear her change the channel of the TV, something with a laugh track. I go to my office, look at the emails that have accumulated in my inbox.

In a way, Cleo and I have been trapped in a bunker together ever since Jana died. Slowly, we've emerged—limping, emaciated, tired, squinting in the daylight.

We are, the two of us, survivors.

CHAPTER 34

Cleo

"Well, this is it," Ms. Murray says.

By "it," she means the last of our "Tuesdays with Tina" sessions. It's not that I've evolved beyond needing Ms. Murray in my life—I'm not that over-confident. It's that Ms. Murray is taking a job in Los Angeles County so she can be close to "someone special" in her life. She has carefully avoided telling me who this "someone special" is (I don't even know if it's a "he" or a "she"), but she gets this girlish smile on her face whenever she mentions the person. It's nice to see an adult with a girlish smile. Maybe it's supposed to bother me, seeing my elder so vulnerable to the pursuit of joy, but it doesn't. It gives me hope.

"Do you know who's replacing you? Is that person going to be okay with me showing up at lunchtime every Tuesday?"

She laughs.

"His name is Mr. Leong and I'm sure he'll be very welcoming."

I make a face. "I already don't like him."

"Oh, come on, why? Because he's a man?"

"No. Because he's not you."

She lets her shoulders slump as she gives me a smile of concession.

"I'll miss you too, Cleo."

We've been over this already—the missing each other. She's said I can call or text any time. I have her personal number. And her email address. She said I'm the only student in possession of this information, and I'm embarrassed to admit how special that makes me feel.

"Anything new this week?" she asks.

I sit back in my chair. "I see how it is. We're just going to pretend like this is any other week?"

She shrugs. "May as well make the most of it."

"Denial can be a comfort. You said that to me once."

She laughs again. "Good memory."

I take my sandwich out of my paper bag, playing along with the idea of this being any other Tuesday. It's hard, though, because Ms. Murray's desk is cleared of all its usual photo frames and knickknacks, and she's surrounded by taped-shut cardboard boxes.

"Nothing too exciting this week. Edie and I are good. We finally planted that garden we've been talking about."

"That's exciting. What did you plant?"

"Spinach, tomatoes, zucchini, strawberries. I know it's not the ideal time to plant all of those, but we figured we'd just give it a go."

"How very domestic of you two."

I feel myself blush and promptly change the subject.

"Carter has a boyfriend now—did I tell you?"

She shakes her head.

"He doesn't go here. He goes to Dana Hills. He wants to double-date," I say, scrunching my nose.

"Doesn't sound fun to you?"

"I'm always nervous around new people. I get so awkward. I think I have a little of my dad in me."

"Most people are nervous around new people," she says.

"I guess."

"How is your dad lately?" she asks. "You haven't mentioned him in a while."

I haven't mentioned him because he's seemed . . . good. He hasn't been hiding in his bunker all the time. He has his monthly meetings with Mirai.

"He's back into model cars," I say.

She furrows her brows. "You say this like it's a good thing."

"It is, I promise."

Dad has always loved model cars. He doesn't care about cars in the typical male way. Meaning, he doesn't covet the life-size versions or anything. I think he just likes the organization of it—tracking the models and makes. There's a very detailed spreadsheet involved. He's showed me. When Mom died, his model-car hobby died too. It was like he thought he wasn't allowed to have fun anymore. That's when he became consumed with the apocalypse.

I used to think his model-car hobby was so dorky and lame. And I guess it *is* dorky and lame, but it's got to be better than preparing for the end of the world. "It makes him happy," Mom told me once when I asked why he was so obsessed with the cars. She said it with this casual shrug of acceptance, like she didn't have it in her to question or criticize whatever gave him joy. I've decided that every relationship needs casual shrugs of acceptance.

"He's acting more like who he used to be before my mom died," I say.

She nods. "And how is that?"

"Like a weirdo, but a happier weirdo."

She smiles. "I'm sure that's a relief for you."

"It is."

"So he's still . . . abstaining . . . from the doomsday prepping?"

"I mean, he still has his bunker with the stuff in it. He didn't get rid of it or anything. But I haven't heard him talk about it much. And he doesn't go down there much anymore. I think I'm more worried about this coronavirus thing than he is."

She nods. "You and me both."

"I told him we might need his bunker after all."

"Well, let's hope it doesn't come to that."

I shrug. "I don't really fear things so much anymore, you know?"

"I do know. That's one of the side effects of tragedy for a lot of people. You've been through this terrible thing, and it gives you confidence in your own resilience. It gives you courage."

"Yeah," I say, mystified, as always, by her ability to articulate my feelings so perfectly.

"They call it posttraumatic growth."

"It's a thing?"

"It's a thing."

"I bet Mr. Leong doesn't know anything about post-traumatic growth," I say.

She rolls her eyes. "You should give him a chance."

"Nah. I'll just text you until you tell me I'm annoying."

"You've come a long way," she says. "You know that, right?"

I look down. I'm not good with compliments of any kind.

She puts her hand to her chest, and I swear I see tears starting to fill her eyes. "It's been my absolute pleasure to witness it."

I guess she's right. When she first came into my life, I was such a different person. Dad and I were both different people. We haven't returned to who we were before Mom died. That isn't possible. Not completely, anyway. There's this theorem called the Fixed Point Theorem. It says that if you have a photo and make a copy of it, then do whatever you want to the copy (make it bigger, smaller, rotate it, crumple it, whatever), if you put the copy overtop the original, there will be at least one point on the copy that is exactly overtop the same point on the original. Similarly, if you take a spoon and stir up a glass of water, there will be at least one water molecule that is in the exact same place as it was before stirring. To me, this means that no matter the upheaval, no matter the disarray, something stays constant. Seeing Dad with his model cars gives me faith in this constancy. Seeing myself smile again does too.

I'll never be who I was before. But there are fixed points of me and Dad that remain, that prove that life goes on. And, honestly, though I'd give anything to have Mom back, I'd be lying if I said I didn't like who I am now. I hope Dad can say the same for himself.

"I don't know if I would be here if it wasn't for you," I tell her.

There is no mistaking her tears now. One rolls down her cheek and plummets onto the calendar desk pad below her.

"I look forward to your annoying texts, Cleo Garrison," she says. "But if you don't text, for whatever reason, just remember one thing: You are a survivor."

I am, I think. Dad is too.

We are, the two of us, survivors.

THE END

ACKNOWLEDGMENTS

First and foremost, thank you to Turner for publishing this book. You have been such a great supporter of my work and I'm endlessly grateful.

Stephanie, I heart you. Carey, I heart you too.

I did quite a bit of research on world-ending happenings in order to write this book (and, somehow, my mental health is intact . . . mostly). Thank you to several sources of information, including (but not limited to): David Wallace-Wells, author of *The Uninhabitable Earth: Life After Warming*; Corey S. Powell and Diane Martindale, authors of "20 Ways the World Could End" (Discover Magazine); Abigail Higgins, author of "10 Ways the World is Most Likely to End, Explained By Scientists" (Vox.com); Kathryn Schulz, author of "The Really Big One" (*the New Yorker*), which remains one of the most fascinating articles I have ever read. All of you enlightened and terrified me (and Dave).

I also did quite a bit of research on Autism Spectrum Disorder, which I prefer to call Autism Spectrum Difference (ASD). Thank you to Steve Silberman for your amazing book, *Neurotribes: The Legacy of Autism and the Future of Neurodiversity*. I've sprinkled in some facts I learned from you. Thank you also to Camilla Pang and your enlightening book, *An Outsider's Guide to Humans: What Science Taught Me About What We Do and Who We Are*. I've sprinkled in facts I learned from you too.

One of the best books I read about ASD was not even a book explicitly about ASD. *The Silicon Syndrome: How to Survive a High-Tech Relationship* gave me so much insight into the dynamics of a couple when one person is on the spectrum (or has "Silicon Syndrome") and one is not. The author, Jean Hollands, passed away in 2016. I wish I'd had the chance to thank her.

Thank you to Huong for being the first reader of this book and giving all your insight, as a bookworm, a psychologist, and a friend.

ACKNOWLEDGMENTS

Thank you to Chris for being an involuntary muse. I wrote this to understand you better. This book exists because of you.

Last, thank you to Mya for inspiring me daily. I think this book will be something special to you one day when you're old enough to read it. I love you forever.

ABOUT THE AUTHOR

Ways the World Could End is Kim Hooper's sixth novel. Her previous works include *No Hiding in Boise* (2021), *All the Acorns on the Forest Floor* (2020), *Tiny* (2019), *Cherry Blossoms* (2018), and *People Who Knew Me* (2016). She is also a co-author of *All the Love: Healing Your Heart and Finding Meaning After Pregnancy Loss*. Kim lives in Southern California with her husband, daughter, and a collection of pets.